International Relations
THROUGH SCIENCE FICTION

Edited by Joseph D. Olander and Martin Harry Greenberg

CRIMINAL JUSTICE THROUGH SCIENCE FICTION

International Relations
THROUGH
SCIENCE FICTION

Edited by
Martin Harry Greenberg
Joseph D. Olander

New Viewpoints
A DIVISION OF FRANKLIN WATTS
New York | London | 1978

New Viewpoints
A Division of Franklin Watts
730 Fifth Avenue
New York, New York 10019

Library of Congress Cataloging in Publication Data

Main entry under title:

International relations through science fiction.

Bibliography: p.
CONTENTS: Nationalism: Williams, J. Gifts of the
gods.—The concept of national power: Clarke, A. C.
Superiority.—Balance of power: Herbert, F. Committee
of the whole. [etc.]
    1. Science fiction, American. 2. International
relations—Fiction. I. Greenberg, Martin Harry.
II. Olander, Joseph D.
PZ1.I596   813'.0876   77–15486
ISBN 0–531–05401–2
ISBN 0–531–05611–2 pbk.

Acknowledgments

COMMITTEE OF THE WHOLE by Frank Herbert. Copyright © 1965 by Universal Publishing and Distributing Corporation. Reprinted by permission of Lurton Blassingame, the author's agent.

UNLIMITED WARFARE by Hayford Peirce. Copyright © 1974 by the Conde Nast Publications, Inc. First published in *Analog Science Fiction/Science Fact,* November 1974. Reprinted by permission of the author.

THE AMPHIBIOUS CAVALRY GAP by J. J. Trembly, as told to James E. Thompson. Copyright © 1974 by the Conde Nast Publications, Inc. Reprinted by permission of the author.

MEN OF GOOD WILL by Ben Bova and Myron R. Lewis. Copyright © 1964 by Galaxy Publishing Corporation. Reprinted by permission of the author.

A ROSE BY OTHER NAME . . . by Christopher Anvil. Copyright © 1960 by Street and Smith Publications, Inc. Reprinted by permission of the author and his agents, the Scott Meredith Literary Agency, Inc., 845 Third Ave., New York, N.Y. 10022.

TO END ALL WARS by Gordon Eklund. Copyright © 1971 by Ultimate Publishing Co., Inc. Reprinted by permission of the author.

THE NEGOTIATORS by Keith Laumer. Copyright © 1975 by the Conde Nast Publications, Inc. Reprinted by permission of the author and his agent, Robert P. Mills.

TRIAGE by William Walling. Copyright © 1976 by the Conde Nast Publications, Inc. Reprinted by permission of the author and his agent, Kirby MacCauley.

I TELL YOU, IT'S TRUE by Poul Anderson. Copyright © 1972 by Harry Harrison. Reprinted by permission of the author and his agent, the Scott Meredith Literary Agency, Inc., 845 Third Ave., New York, N.Y. 10022.

THE CAVE OF NIGHT by James E. Gunn. Copyright © 1955 by Galaxy Publishing Corporation. Reprinted by permission of the author and his agent, Robert P. Mills.

SUPERIORITY by Arthur C. Clarke. Copyright © 1951 by Fantasy House, Inc. Reprinted by permission of the author and his agent, the Scott Meredith Literary Agency, Inc., 845 Third Ave., New York, N.Y. 10022.

REDUCTION IN ARMS by Tom Purdom. Copyright © 1967 by Mercury Press, Inc. Reprinted by permission of the author and his agent, the Scott Meredith Literary Agency, Inc., 845 Third Ave. New York, N.Y. 10022.

FIGHTING DIVISION by Randall Garrett. Copyright © 1965 by Conde Nast Publications, Inc. Reprinted by permission of the author and his agent, the Scott Meredith Literary Agency, Inc., 845 Third Ave., New York, N.Y. 10022.

PSI ASSASSIN by Mack Reynolds. Copyright © 1968 by Conde Nast Publications, Inc. Reprinted by permission of the author and his agent, the Scott Meredith Literary Agency, Inc., 845 Third Ave., New York, N.Y. 10022.

GIFTS OF THE GODS by Jay Williams. Copyright © 1962 by Mercury Press, Inc. From the magazine of *Fantasy and Science Fiction*. Reprinted by permission of the author and his agent, Russell & Volkening, Inc.

Contents

Introduction

Without getting into a chicken-and-egg argument concerning
the origin of ideas and the motivation behind human behavior,
it is important to realize that ideas can have a vast impact
on the future behavior of states and the role of intergovernmental
organizations.[1]

As a literature of ideas, science fiction has much to offer the
serious student of international relations. In fact, we would argue
that the authors of speculative fiction have already played a
significant role through the visions of possible international
futures they have provided us. Science fiction (sf) has contributed
to the international relations socialization process through which
all of us pass as we grow older. This has been particularly
important in regard to visions of nuclear devastation and the
effects of bacteriological and chemical warfare. Both elite and
mass visions of the effects of a thermonuclear exchange have
been colored to a large extent by the depiction of these events in
science fiction novels and films. Indeed, Soviet visions have also
been affected by their own sf on the subject, as have the attitudes
of movie goers and book readers all over the globe. Partly
because of science fiction there now exists a shared world view
of the consequences of the use of weapons of mass destruction,
one that reinforces the balance of terror system and helps to
ensure that the real thing will never happen.

    The study of international relations has never been an easy
task. Rather, those interested in examining international behavior
have been bedeviled with numerous problems. First, it has proved
difficult to effectively test theories in this area because of the
impossibility of creating laboratory situations that can control

the many variables affecting international politics. Second, the element of secrecy and the need to protect the national interest have resulted in less than full information for the international theorist. Third, and perhaps most important, the study of international relations (like all areas of the social sciences) involves the study of human beings, those most unpredictable creatures of the animal kingdom. We need to constantly guard against a "ratomorphic" view of human beings and to treat concepts like the territorial imperative with great care. In addition, one can never be certain that inflated egos, a sense of one's place in history, and similar factors will not distort the statements and memoirs of those who played key roles on the international stage.

These problems are magnified for those concerned with the future shape of the international system, although this has not prevented the development of important efforts in this area. For example, scholars of international politics are constantly engaging in the extrapolation of current trends in an effort to see what their consequences may be. This is crucial for the purposes of this book because such work involves the methodology (if not the form) of science fiction, which constantly poses the questions of "if this goes on" and "what if." The potential role of science fiction for the study of international relations has already been recognized by a few. "Although largely ignored by the social sciences, science-fiction literature also presents a wealth of thought-provoking scenarios of the future." [2] This view is becoming more widespread.

Science fiction can be viewed as a literary form of simulation gaming and scenario construction through which the scholar and student can bring a dimension of imagination to the study of alternative international futures. Sf is very much a literature of consequences and since the stakes involved in the "game of nations" include survival itself we can expect greater attention to this valuable tool.

Methodologically, one of the important techniques in the study of international relations is the case study, where intensive analysis of previous events takes place in an effort to understand the processes involved. One notable example of this approach is Graham Allison's *Essence of Decision: Explaining the Cuban Missile Crisis*.[3] Once again, science fiction can enrich this technique by providing opportunities for case studies of future events and crises. Indeed, the contingency planning that constantly occurs in the State Department and the Department of Defense is itself a form of science fiction with its emphasis on alternative strategies. We need to remember that the mother of political science (of which international relations is a subfield) is political philosophy which, viewed from one perspective, is a form of science fiction. We do not normally think of men like Plato and Karl Marx as science fiction writers, but anyone who writes about utopias, whether they are called communism or something else, is using the forms of sf. Much of what Marx wrote about a science of history and the future of government can be read as science fiction without dialogue.

II.

Science fiction can contribute to the predictive, evaluative, and normative study of international relations. By extrapolating present trends and tendencies to their logical and illogical conclusions, sf provides us with an opportunity to explore alternatives that are not presently being considered. Further, the conduct of the international process (including the foreign policy decision-making process) itself reduces the likelihood of the consideration of imaginative alternatives; so much of it is crisis-centered that little time remains for thought to be given to alternatives that are drastically different from choices made in the past. There is a strong tendency for policy makers to grasp at the familiar during times of stress, and conservatism is built in when a statesman must protect the interests of his nation. Science fiction can show us radical alternatives and possibilities with no risk and can therefore expand the range of choice. We can never move in the direction of positive change unless we have some vision of what a new world order would look like.

Science fiction can provide the following services to the student of international relations:

First, sf can point out predisposing factors in the present that may lead to problems in the future. These can range from the effect of diminishing fuel supplies on the military balance to the role of alienated individuals in world politics.

Second, sf can help us overcome the impersonal aspects of the study of international relations. The macropolitics approach, while certainly valid, results in the reduction of intensely human problems to statistics, which decreases student interest and the relevance of IR for them. Science fiction, however, captures the discreteness of life, placing men and women at the center of the action and reminding us that a process consists of numerous individual actions, and translates abstractions into particular situations.

Third, in assessing the consequences of decisions, science fiction can enrich the present by drawing attention to those elements whose importance may not be noticed now, but which will be important in the future. In addition, sf can show us how international "presents" might be altered by changing history. The very interesting sub-genre called alternative history has produced several notable works, including *The Man in the High Castle* by Philip K. Dick, wherein Germany and Japan win the Second World War and occupy the United States; *Bring the Jubilee* by Ward Moore, where the South wins the Civil War, with interesting consequences for the world; and *Pavane* by Keith Roberts, in which the Spanish Armada defeats the English fleet and converts England to Catholicism. In addition to being entertaining intellectually, these novels remind us of the importance of specific events and the roles of individuals in history.

Fourth, science fiction permits the creation of ideal types, something that cannot be done as effectively through the use of models.

Finally, science fiction provides an excellent opportunity for the discussion of the ethical issues that are a constant feature of international life. Questions of values, ethics, and justice are woven throughout science fiction, and are usually treated more effectively than in "cold" textbook fashion.

III.

Although science fiction writers have accurately forecast numerous technological developments and social movements, sf does not deserve all the credit for prophecy often attributed to it. This is because sf has predicted so much in its history that it has had a shotgun effect, with some of its predictions eventually occurring while others were far off the mark.

Nevertheless, science fiction has treated almost all the major areas within the field of international relations and has projected numerous international futures. In general, sf writers have, with many exceptions, retained the nation-state as the primary actor in international affairs. The world order systems described in science fiction tend to favor examples from the past and present such as the Roman Empire (the model for Isaac Asimov's famous *Foundation Trilogy*), feudal Europe, and the Cold War of the Fifties and early Sixties.[4] In the majority of these stories the general population plays little or no role in the international process except as its victim; science fiction exhibits a profound distrust of the masses, who are easily led and manipulated. This is not surprising since sf writers emphasize the role of the talented and resourceful individual who can survive in any system and defeat any odds. The "Great-Man Theory of History" would certainly find many supporters in science fiction. At the same time the genre depicts futures where power has passed to those possessing technical expertise, a trend we can identify at work today in all areas of public life. Experts and planners (especially social planners) of all types are suspect in sf and must be controlled to prevent mankind from becoming dehumanized and machine-like.

Among the alternative international futures examined in science fiction, the following are most frequently encountered:

(1) *The world subjected to physical and biological dangers* which in turn affect the international system. This is evident in novels with overpopulated futures like *Stand on Zanzibar* by John Brunner and *A Torrent of Faces* by James Blish and Norman Knight; stories in which the danger is disease, as in John Christopher's *No Blade of Grass;* and those where world-wide pollution threatens mankind as in John Brunner's *The Sheep Look Up.*

(2) *The military dimension of international politics.* See near-future novels like Peter George's *Red Alert* (later developed into the film *Dr. Strangelove*) and *Fail-Safe* by Eugene Burdick and Harvey Wheeler. The interaction between civilian authority and military leadership is frequently stressed in these works and they provide vivid scenarios of what nuclear confrontation at "the brink" might be like. Stories like "Superiority" by Arthur C. Clarke

(contained in this volume) treat the theme of military capability and its limits. A number of these works are explicit criticisms of American intervention in Vietnam—an issue that split science fiction in the same way it divided American society.

(3) *The possibility of accidental nuclear war.* Crazed generals, like crazed scientists, can be found in science fiction and so can the outbreak of a nuclear holocaust against the wishes of the governments involved. "Triggerman" by Jesse Bone, in which a military officer saves humanity with the correct hunch that an incoming missile aimed at Washington is not what it appears, is an outstanding example in this category. Science fiction has also dealt with what Herman Kahn calls cataclysmic war, the initiation of conflict by a third party in the hope that others will destroy themselves and leave the world at their mercy.

(4) *Scenarios involving widespread nuclear proliferation.* This is one of the most dangerous possibilities facing the world today and in sf this development often takes the form of the simultaneous possession of powerful new weapons by virtually everyone. For a superb example, see Frank Herbert's "Cease Fire" in this volume. Science fiction can also show us how nuclear threats and extortion may develop and how they might be counteracted. It would be interesting to compare science fictional treatments of this problem with the contingency plans of the major powers. The diminishing distinction between small and large powers is rapidly becoming a reality, one that sf accurately predicted.

(5) *Meaningful central authority that controls the international system.* All international relations textbooks point out the fact that attempts to manage conflict on a world scale have been frustrated by the absence of an international body with real enforcement capabilities. Science fiction can show us how these bodies might function (or misfunction) in both enforcing international law and regulating the economy of the world. These works range from extrapolation of regional groupings like the Common Market to an ultimate World State. It can also demonstrate the potential effects of unilateral disarmament, with and without an international police force to maintain order.

(6) *The growing power of multinational corporations.* We are just now beginning to realize the tremendous power and influence of the multinationals, many of which have greater resources than small countries have. Science fiction has long given us a wide

variety of dominant non-nation state actors, including societies whose foreign policy mechanisms are controlled by the advertising industry as in Frederick Pohl and C. M. Kornbluth's *The Space Merchants;* organized crime, in *The Syndic* by Kornbluth; and insurance companies, in *Preferred Risk* by "Edson McCann" (Pohl and Lester del Rey).

(7) *Third World politics.* Here themes range from race war scenarios like *Darkening Island* by Christopher Priest and *The Jagged Orbit* by John Brunner, to the inevitability of resource wars and rich-poor struggles over the diminishing resources of the planet. The entire history of colonialism has also been thoroughly worked over in science fiction including the use of aliens as surrogates for oppressed natives. Even the so-called Fourth World of very poor countries has found a place in sf. "Triage" in this book is only one example.

(8) *The dominance of the international system by selected countries or combinations of countries.* These can be divided into the following categories, without attempting an exhaustive list: [5]

a. Dominance by the United States and the Soviet Union. This simplistic extension and interpretation of the present (or recent past) was typical of Cold War science fiction, especially in the early Fifties.

b. The United States and the Soviet Union combining to oppose a powerful and threatening People's Republic of China.

c. China alone dominating the world. The outstanding example in this category is the powerful *White Lotus* by John Hersey, in which a defeated United States is occupied and enslaved by the Chinese. Hersey is one of a large number of writers (including Kurt Vonnegut, Jr., and Vladimir Nabokov) who have used science fiction in their work without being associated with the genre. One of the common definitions of science fiction is that whatever is marketed as sf *is* sf. However, a large percentage of the best science fiction has come from the literary mainstream.

(9) *The imposition of One World* through the activities of actors outside of the international system. Typically, this takes the form of either the imposition of a new international system by superior beings who act in the best interests of earth's population, or more commonly, an earth that unites in the face of an alien threat from another planet.

(10) *The destruction of the international system and most of*

mankind through natural disaster or war. An incredible number of novels and stories take place in the aftermath of a nuclear exchange and these constitute one of the most important categories of modern science fiction. A selected list of the finest efforts would have to include *A Canticle for Leibowitz* by Walter M. Miller, Jr.; *The Long Tomorrow* by Leigh Brackett; and Nevil Shute's *On the Beach.* Post-holocaust novels are important because they provide anthropological case studies of the creation (actually re-creations) of societies, economies, and international systems.

We are by no means arguing that the rich literature of science fiction can supply answers to the problems that plague our world. We are suggesting that it can provide a valuable tool for those interested in the probable outlines of our international future. Sf has come a long way since Buck Rogers and Flash Gordon. The stories you are about to read are but a small sample of the available literature, and you are strongly urged to explore further.

Footnotes

[1] William D. Coplin, *Introduction to International Politics: A Theoretical Overview.* Second Edition (Chicago: Rand McNally Publishing Company, Inc., 1974) p. 213.

[2] David J. Finlay and Thomas Hovet, Jr., *7304: International Relations on the Planet Earth* (New York: Harper & Row, Publishers, 1975) p. 41.

[3] Boston: Little, Brown and Company, 1972.

[4] Dennis Livingston, "Science Fiction Models of Future World Order Systems," *International Organization,* Spring, 1972, pp. 254–270.

[5] For a more complete list, see Finlay and Hovet, *op. cit.,* pp. 52–56.

Nationalism

The need to identify with others is as old as the human race itself. Since time immemorial, men and women have divided themselves into tribes, clans, ethnic groups, racial groups, linguistic groups, and nation-states. Much later, as political ideologies developed, those who believed in internationalism (and many who did not) felt that history was on their side, that the forces that divided people into nation-states were weaker than their common values, and that the world was moving inexorably in the direction of the dissolution of boundaries and toward the promised land of one world. Today, world events give little indication that this will take place. Instead, the international system gives every sign of wanting to reduce itself into smaller and smaller units, many of which may not be economically or militarily viable. Even well-established countries like Canada and Belgium are on the verge of crisis because of the power of nationalism—the strongest ideology in the world.

We do not fully understand the basis of nationalism except that human beings have psychological needs that are met by the identification process that is at its heart. In addition, it has been an efficient (not necessarily the most or only efficient) way to organize humanity. But efficiency has its price, and the conflicts that have characterized the age of nationalism have been cruel and destructive.

Nationalism has had a long and varied history: On some occasions, it has taken extremely destructive forms, as in Nazi Germany, where the element of racism was combined with nationalism with disastrous effects. On other occasions, as in the American experience, it has helped to unify a widely diverse group of people. The history of nationalism has been a violent one, from the first attempts to transfer loyalty from the person of a sovereign to the abstract concept of "the nation," to the present attempts by separatist movements to establish their own independent units.

One unfortunate offshoot of nationalism is the tendency to think of one's own group as superior to all others. "Gifts of the Gods" illustrates the difficulty of measuring "superiority" among groups as well as the relative meaning and dangers of such a notion.

GIFTS OF THE GODS

by Jay Williams

The great golden ship hovered over the Atlantic with lightning crackling about its fins. People stood on the rooftops of the city staring, pointing, shading their eyes, some with pearl-handled opera glasses, some with cheap telescopes, and a few inveterate bird- or window-watchers with expensive field glasses. The ship settled slowly into the bay and was lost in a cloud of steam.

The steam cleared. It could be seen that the ship floated, and all about it were hundreds of silvery specks: dead fish bobbing on the dirty water. A dark square appeared in the golden metal and there was a long, simultaneous "ooh" from the city, like the cry that goes up with a skyrocket. A small craft, curiously-shaped and high-sided, launched from the ship and soundlessly shot towards the Battery throwing up a high fan of white water like a wing.

The five people who stepped ashore looked like people. Their skins were a firm coppery brown, all save one whose color was creamy yellow; aside from this there seemed to be no discernible differences among them. They wore snug, jointed costumes, something like a light armor but of the color of a beetle's carapace, and about their faces were pale blue aureoles barely to be seen in the daylight. They stood calmly looking at the city, at the crowds, and exchanging a few soft words among themselves. One of them bent over, picked up the boat, rapidly folded it into a small packet and thrust it in a pouch that hung at his belt.

Seventeen people died in those few minutes, some being pushed off the crowded rooftops, some trampled in the streets, four or five of heart failure, suffocation, or sheer astonishment. The babblement made the buildings tremble. Slowly, the men from the ship walked up into South Street.

At this point a shrilling of sirens heralded police cars and several large, black limousines. There had been hasty debates over protocol: whether the visitors should be received by the Mayor of New York, or by a representative of the United States government, or by the Secretary-General of the United Nations. In the end all three had come. The Mayor, rowing himself forward with his elbows, held his hat over his chest and tried to bow. The crowd, oblivious of the police, pressed closer to get a good look at the visitors.

The American delegate to the United Nations, who had come as the embodiment of the United States government, held out his hand with a rather fixed smile. "Allow me to welcome you in the name of—" he began.

The Mayor interrupted. "Gentlemen, it gives this great city great pleasure to extend our hand of friendship—" and then stopped, lost in his own syntax.

One of the visitors stepped a little way ahead of his fellows. In a clear, ringing voice, he said, in perfect English, "We thank you for your sentiments and your welcome. It is our desire to go to your—er —Center." He paused, and conferred for an instant with one of the others. "The United Nations Center," he said. "That is where all the governments and peoples of your planet are represented, are they not?"

The Secretary-General, biting down a smile of innocent triumph, said, "It will give me great pleasure to conduct you there. Will you step into my car, please?"

The five visitors nodded. Their leader said, "I will do so. My companions prefer to—um—I do not know how to translate it . . . They will follow us in their own way."

At this, one of them produced the packet into which he had folded their boat. He quickly unfolded it, set it on the pavement, and got into it. The three others joined him. A delicate pink glow appeared and the boat rose to the level of the second-floor windows. One of the Visitors looked over the side with a smile, waved his hand, and called something to the leader.

The leader nodded, and said to the Secretary-General, "We are ready. Shall we go?"

The Secretary-General, a trifle dazed, pulled himself together and bowed the Visitor into the open limousine. As they drove off slowly, with the crowd opening before them, he said, "If you'll pardon the question—why didn't you just float to shore, instead of sailing in?"

The Visitor looked curiously at him. His eyes, it could be seen, had no whites but were round and opaline. "When there is water, why should we not sail," he said.

Then he added, "Floating. Is that what you call floating? I had thought that to float meant to rest on the surface of some material, or to glide along with it. But you see, they are—hm—propelling themselves, while nullifying the attraction of gravity." Then, half-turning in the seat and bending the fixed gaze of his large, iridescent eyes upon the S-G, he said, "Do you mean to say that if you had been in our place, you would have preferred to fly over that lovely water?"

The S-G, utterly confused, was silent.

As they neared Fourteenth Street, the S-G said, "We appreciate your visit. This is a great day for Earth."

"Is it?" said the Visitor politely.

"Well, it's not every day that we have arrivals from another planet," said the S-G with an artificial chuckle, glancing involuntarily back at the Mayor, who sat in his own car, red-faced and annoyed.

"Oh. Yes. I see."

"Yes, another planet . . . Where *do* you come from, by the way?"

"We call it Earth," said the Visitor. "It is quite a long way off. Many parsecs, you would say. It is one of a great many Earths. We are a —well, a United Nations, but of planets." He uttered a quivering, high-pitched sound which the S-G took to be the equivalent of a laugh.

"Yes, this is all very familiar to us," said the S-G. "A Federation of Planets, advanced technology, and so forth. Our science fiction writers have been preparing us for it for years. And now, it is a reality. You have come, I presume, to offer us membership in your Federation?"

The visitor blinked. It was a slow blink, and it came from below the eye rather than above it, a deliberate, unhurried sliding of a kind of nictating membrane. It conveyed wonderment and polite surprise.

"Oh, dear, no," he replied. "Membership? Not at all. Furnishing one's own transportation is one of the first requirements. Your people cannot yet lift an interplanetary vessel, to say nothing of an intergalactic one."

Just then, they arrived at the United Nations building, and the conversation was cut short by the mob of delegates, officials, stenographers, guides, guards, and tourists, who encircled them in one violent hypercenotic outpouring. With some difficulty a space was cleared. The Visitors in the air descended and packed up their vehicle. The S-G led them all into the main building and thence to the General Assembly hall, which was speedily packed with delegates and other gapers. Newsreel and television cameras were focused on the historic moment, and reporters poised pencils over paper.

The S-G, smoothing back his feathery grey hair, said, "We, the assembled representatives of all the nations of Earth, greet you and welcome you, visitors and representatives of another planet."

The Visitors inclined their heads slightly, but said nothing. They had been seated on the dais behind the rostrum, where they could face the hall.

The United States delegate, tapping his fingertips together, said, "I would like to ask that the credentials of the Visitors be presented to this body. A pure formality, of course, but I think we should have some assurance that these gentlemen are—er—what they say they are."

Before the S-G could speak, the delegate from the Soviet Union shot to his feet, and cried, "I also have a question to ask of the—ah—captain, or leader of the Visitors."

That one rose and said, "You may address me as Spokesman, rather than leader. Our captain, as a matter of fact, is still in our vessel."

"Ah. Yes. Well, sir, how is it that you address us in English? I wish to ask this body what assurance we have that this is not simply a hoax on the part of certain Powers?"

Spokesman replied, in impeccable Russian, "I can, as a matter of fact, speak almost all the dialects of your planet. But I cannot address you simultaneously in Turkish, Greek, French, Japanese, Gaelic, Syrian, and so forth. I have chosen to speak English because I am assured by our researchers that it is understood by a majority of your members. It is not difficult to learn a human tongue, of course, provided one knows how. And we have had researchers on your planet for the past twenty years or so, collecting data, accumulating languages, and so on.

"As for our credentials . . ." He paused, surveying the audience solemnly. "Why do you want them?" he said. "We are not 'representatives' to your organization in the sense in which you have used the word. It is of no concern to us whether you believe that we are what we are, or not."

"I'm afraid I don't understand," said the British delegate, recovering first. "Does the gentleman imply that he was not sent by his government to contact us? If so, what does his presence here signify? I was given to understand that his first request was to be taken to the United Nations."

"That is correct," replied Spokesman. "When a planet is sufficiently advanced to have a central governing body, we prefer to act through it for the sake of convenience and efficiency."

The Secretary-General said, rather nervously, "Yes, but, I understood you to say—in the car, you know—that you were not going to offer us membership in your Federation. The question raised by the delegate from the United Kingdom is therefore germane."

"If," began the delegate from Bolivia, knitting his brows, "this is a declaration of war, let it be understood that we are ready—"

Spokesman raised a hand. "No, no," he said. "War? Certainly not. We do not have wars. I will explain.

"You see, sirs, our Federation, as you would call it, has certain laws. One of these is that when a planet reaches a condition we describe as —well, you would say, Federable—and thus meets certain requirements, its space ships are then contacted by members of our organization and it is offered equal membership.

"There are, however, other cases. We continually investigate other inhabited planets, and when we find that a section, or group, or nation can meet certain other requirements—let us call them, pre-Federable requirements—we are then charged to offer that group all the assistance necessary to enable them to come up to Federable level."

"I see," said the S-G. "Assistance. What form does this assistance take?"

"Chiefly, technological improvements," replied Spokesman. "Things the group cannot get or make for itself. In effect, we say, 'Tell us what you want and need and we will give it to you.' But you must understand, sirs, that our law requires us to make this offer, but that acceptance is voluntary."

"Yes, sir, we understand that perfectly," said the United States delegate, with a wide smile. "We understand, and we are proud and humble."

The French delegate put in, "May I ask Monsieur Spokesman to tell us what those requirements are he spoke of—the pre-Federable requirements?"

Spokesman held up a small, glittering object between the fingers of his right hand. From it, a metallic voice spoke:

"A group, or unit, of human beings, shall be said to be in a pre-Federable condition when they have successfully reached the following level of sophistication:

"They must have adapted successfully to their environment without drastically changing the ecology of the region so that it becomes unfit for other living beings.

"They must have developed creative arts which reflect their culture and are an integral part of their social organism, the performance of which arts does not rest on economic or political motivation.

"They must not take other life except for direct protection of their species, or the natural requirements of their own survival.

"They must have developed a social order in which no individual goes hungry or shelterless, and in which the physical well-being of one is the responsibility of all."

The voice ceased, and Spokesman put away his device.

The delegate from the United States broke the stillness. "Well, sir, everything you have said is embodied in the principles by which our great democracy, throughout its history, has attempted to . . ."

He fell silent before the grave, penetrating gaze of the Visitor.

Spokesman said, "We are not speaking of principles, but of practise. Our words are precise and admit of no loose interpretation."

"I protest!" said the delegate from the Soviet Union. "Civilized beings must admit of principle."

"We are not civilized," said Spokesman, placidly.

"But it is not a simple matter to put principles into practise when one is surrounded by hostility," cried the delegate from Pakistan.

"I did not say it was simple," Spokesman returned. "Principles are no more than good intentions. The hungry, the wounded, the dead, are not concerned with good intentions."

The French delegate, who had once visited the prisons in Algeria, cleared his throat several times. The British delegate, too proud to ask whether fox-hunting fell into the third category, shifted uncomfortably in his chair. The delegate from the United States, thinking of the increase in unemployment figures, tapped his teeth with a pencil. The Soviet delegate, considering state edicts on the nature of Art, buttoned and unbuttoned his jacket uneasily. No one spoke.

Then, at last, the Secretary-General said, "If you insist on literal and actual interpretations of your requirements, Mr. Spokesman, I'm afraid you won't find a single nation on earth which can fill your bill."

"Oh, but we have," said Spokesman, brusquely. "That is why we are here. In a place called the Kalahari Desert, in the continent of Africa, dwells a nation of small people whom you call Bushmen. They meet every requirement."

There was a moment of stunned quiet, and then a roar of protest. The S-G, banging furiously with his gavel, finally restored order.

The delegate from Ghana cried, "I protest! These—Bushmen—they are nothing but savages."

Spokesman smiled. He half turned and said something to his friends, several of whom made the odd noises that passed among them for laughter.

Then he said, "Savages? But this implies that they are inferiors, and only a little above brute beasts. As soon as men call other men by such names, they have failed in our third and fourth requirements."

The Canadian delegate, in a cold, nasal voice, said, "I confess I cannot understand how people with the high intellectual and technical attainments of our friends from outer space, can fail to take into account the matter of Progress." As he said it, the shining capital letter could be heard. "What have the Bushmen contributed to human history, or to the good of mankind? They have not progressed in five hundred years."

"I am afraid," said Spokesman, "that you confuse 'progress' with 'change'. It is true that you live in a social community which has changed profoundly in the past hundred years. But have you progressed? Are all your citizens happy, fully alive, intellectually mature?"

"I think I can safely say," put in the delegate from the United States, "that under our system of free enterprise, the vast majority of our people are secure. Yes, sir, I think they are satisfied and contented."

Spokesman's eyes flashed as he turned them on the speaker. "You used the word 'secure'. Do you think that security is essential to a mature being? Security is the least of his needs, for he knows that to be alive is to be insecure.

"As for your other words—do your contented citizens never kill themselves? Do they never take violent action against their employers, or against the state? Are there not Indians in your land whose culture and property has been taken away from them, and who are now living in disease and poverty? Are there not hundreds of thousands of men whose skin color prevents them from earning a proper livelihood, or even from sitting alongside men of another color? Can you tell me that they are satisfied and contented?"

The pale blue halo which surrounded his face had become more pronounced and seemed to give off crisp sparks. One of his companions leaned forward and said something in an earnest tone. Spokesman stood silent for an instant or two while the color faded. Then he went on:

"You equate 'progress' with improved methods for chilling food, with better types of transportation, or with the discovery of cures for disease. Those things are not 'progress'. Progress is what you do with the cured people, and where you go with your improved transportation, and why you go there. Progress is what happens in your heart. Most of you are good people, but you have not progressed an inch in five hundred years, nor even a thousand. Given a chance for personal profit, there is not one of you who would not level the forests, destroy all wild life, kill a thousand other human beings, and turn your backs on the suffering of your fellows."

He seemed to sigh, and his head drooped. Before he could continue, a man in the back of the hall had broken through the police cordon and came running down the side aisle brandishing a pistol.

"Antichrist!" he screamed. "Return to the Devil, your master, ye powers of darkness!"

He was disarmed before he could fire, although there were mutterings of agreement in various parts of the hall.

Spokesman said, "Yes, I had forgotten your religion. I am told that a vast majority of you believe in lovingkindness, forgiveness, charity, and humility. Perhaps we had better not speak of that.

"In any case, we have spoken enough. I call on the representatives of the Bushmen to come forward."

There was a long, awkward pause. Then the S-G, blushing slightly, said, "I am afraid, Mr. Spokesman, that the Bushmen are not represented in this body."

"No? Why not?"

"Well—eh—our principle is that only nations ready for sovereignty may have their delegates seated here. When you come right down to it," he went on, stoutly, "it is very similar to your own laws governing your Federation."

"Similar?" said Spokesman, and again the slow translucent lid rose and fell before his eyes in amazement. "You may consider it similar if you like. I presume that if you saw three big boys bullying a little boy you would consider that similar to the deliberations and decisions of adults."

"But there is also some doubt," said the S-G, "whether the Bushmen can actually be considered a nation."

Spokesman nodded. "I see. What you mean is that they are neither numerous enough, rich enough, nor strategically enough placed. In that case, will you please give the necessary orders to have representatives from their people sent here to meet with us. I know enough about your technology to ask that this be done within, say, forty-eight hours."

"Forty-eight hours?" The Secretary-General turned pale. "But my dear sir, it will take days simply to find the Bushmen."

"It's an outrage." The British delegate rose. "Speaking for Her Majesty's government, we can no longer lend our presence to this travesty—"

Many other delegates sprang to their feet. Spokesman glanced at his companions. The one with the creamy skin got up slowly and with a casual air pointed his finger at the assembly. There was a loud crackling noise and the air was filled with a pungent, yet rather pleasing odor. At once, all the radio and television instruments ceased functioning, the lights dimmed, and every single person in the hall and for a radius of fifty miles around it, was deprived of motion. All traffic froze as engines stopped and people were caught in absolute paralysis, and even airplanes were held motionless in the sky above the spot.

Spokesman said, with no trace of passion in his tone, "I regret that we must employ what appears to be coercion. However, we have learned that our standards do not always apply to primitive peoples. No one will be harmed. But I must warn you that if we are forced to the inconvenience of searching for the Bushmen ourselves, if we are denied the cooperation of this organization, we shall have to keep you all in a state of non-motion until we have concluded our business, simply in order to avoid being interfered with. It may prove to be more inconvenient for you than for us."

In the end, of course, they gave in. To tell the truth, many of the delegates were already contemplating methods of getting control of the Bushmen, while others were simply burning with curiosity to find out what the cosmic goodies would be that the fortunate aborigines were to receive.

As soon, therefore, as they were released from their spell and had agreed to help the Visitors, cabals began to form in various parts of the building.

The Soviet delegate, deep in discussion with Yugoslavia and Hungary, pointed out that it would be necessary to establish the principle of the right of small nations to self-government, and that this would require to be implemented by a strong arm, if necessary, to prevent the encroachment of colonial powers . . .

The American delegate, deep in discussion with Britain and Brazil, made it clear that it would be necessary to establish the principle of the right of small nations to self-government and that this would require to be implemented by a strong arm, if necessary, to prevent the encroachment of colonial powers . . .

The French delegate went about telling everyone that for his part he was only interested in seeing that the right of a small nation to govern itself should be protected, and that France always stood ready to uphold its historic role in preventing the exploitation of the weak and helpless by the powerful and sinister.

The Australian delegate was heard to murmur that a strong case might be made out for the ethnic connection between the Kalahari Bushmen and those of the Australian hinterland. The Egyptian delegate remarked that it was a well known fact that the Bushmen of the Kalahari had originally entered Bechuanaland from the Nile Basin. The Israeli delegate, chuckling, replied that if this were so it ought to be remembered that the whereabouts of several of the Lost Tribes had never been satisfactorily established.

Meanwhile, the Visitors relented in their 48-hour ultimatum, extending the time to one week, and an immense team of researchers set out in hundreds of jet planes supplied by every airline. They were delivered in a matter of hours, along with all their equipment, to Bulawayo, Serowe, and Windhoek, from which clouds of jeeps and trucks were swiftly launched. The world followed with bated breath the news from mobile television and radio stations, as a gigantic net was drawn about two-thirds of the Kalahari Desert, within which the puzzled, frightened, and mild little people were scooped. Eventually, over a thousand Bushmen were cornered at Lake Ngami and the Okavango Swamp. With the help of relays of interpreters they were made to understand that they would not be harmed, but that they must choose representatives to go before the men of another world, who would make them rich gifts.

It took nearly eight hours of steady talking for the Bushmen to realize what was wanted. Once they did, however, they gathered, giggling and whispering, into clans and villages, and then pushed forward their best men—expert hunters, fine singers and musicians, wise old leaders, and gallant young dancers.

These men, drawing together in a crowd and looking shyly at each other out of the corners of their eyes, talked together for a while in their clicking, chirping tongue and then squatted down on the ground. One only, a very old man named Tk'we, remained standing. He had a snub nose, wicked little slanting eyes, and a pot belly, and his skin was the color of ancient, well-weathered ivory.

He said, "Oh Tall Men, we are ready to go."

The Chief of the United Nations Mission dusted his hands together. "Splendid," he said. "How many of you are there, old boy?"

"All that you see here," replied Tk'we. "Except for a very few old women, who prefer to remain behind."

The Chief's mouth dropped open. He began to count without knowing what he was doing. There were, as a matter of fact, one thousand and thirty-eight Bushmen present. Tearing at his curly blond hair, the Chief replied that this was not democratic, and that they must exercise their right to hold a free election by secret ballot, and that they must choose a smaller committee. He was a very conscientious young man, a graduate of the University of Toronto.

Tk'we, leaning on his bow, said that a man didn't get the chance to see the Gods with his own eyes every day in the year, and that consequently they all wanted to go. He said that they did not understand this democracy, and that they didn't want to make any trouble, but that nobody wanted to hurt anyone else's feelings. He said that if he understood this election business properly, it meant that a man would have to say that someone should go and many other someones should remain behind. If that was the case, who was going to be so rude and unfeeling as to deny his neighbors the right to take a ride in an airplane and see the Gods in person, and get presents?

Furthermore, he added, nobody wanted to leave his women and children behind to look out for themselves. "What is more," he said, in his gentle, humorous, clicking voice, "we have never been out in the world, and a few of us would be very frightened. But if we all go together, we will take courage from each other."

He finished by saying that if this arrangement was not satisfactory, the people would be glad to call the whole thing off and return to their peaceful ways in the desert, good-bye, and thank you very much.

The Chief of the Mission thought about Spokesman's level chilling gaze that was all pupil and no whites, and about the pointing finger of Spokesman's companion, and wondered what other disagreeable ways the Visitors might have of showing their displeasure. So one thousand, thirty-eight members of the United Nations Mission had to yield up their places in the planes and were left behind at Windhoek, Serowe, and Bulawayo—because a delegation of three or four small Bushmen had been anticipated—and the Bushmen got into the planes and were taken off into the skies, clinging to each other and silent in delighted terror. It was months before some of the abandoned members of the Mission got home again.

"To scenes of unprecedented pandemonium," in the poetic words of the Associated Press reporter, the Bushmen were disembarked and taken by bus to the United Nations building. At the directions of Spokesman, the General Assembly hall was cleared except for the Secretary-General and his interpreter, a brilliant young Bantu student of African languages. The grumbling delegates were moved to other meeting halls from which they could observe the proceedings by television, and the one thousand, thirty-eight Bushmen, looking with alarm at the incomprehensible murals and other decorations, and at the fixtures and the curving rows of seats, huddled in the aisles and along the walls. Their children, however, wide-eyed and merry, sat or stood on the seats.

Spokesman and his companions faced them from the podium. Piled against the wall were a number of wooden crates and cases which the Visitors had had brought in, that morning. The Secretary-General, repeatedly mopping his forehead with a large handkerchief, settled himself in an armchair, and Spokesman rose and addressed the Bushmen in their own language—or rather, languages, for he had to employ three related but slightly dissimilar dialects.

"My friends," he said, and there was a little stir and then utter quiet, for the Bushmen were not accustomed to being addressed in this way by other people. "We have come from the stars to speak with you. We know how hard your lives are, but we know also how you live, simply and merrily, meeting each day as best you can, going softly among the lions and the wild bees, harming no one, but taking what is fitting. Now the time has come for you to tell us what you want above all else, and that which you ask we will give you."

There was a pause, during which many turned their eyes toward

Tk'we. At last, the old man moved down to the front of the hall and stood under the rostrum. He leaned on a smooth stick, with one foot drawn up so that its sole rested against his other thigh, and although he was less than five feet tall he managed somehow to look very dignified.

"Master," he said, "we are content to have flown in the sky, to have seen this great *werf* with its high tower and shining windows and strange people, and to have beheld you and the other gods with our own eyes. Now, all that we want is to go home again."

Spokesman said, "We can make you richer than all other men. We will teach you how to build *scherms* like this one you stand in, how to wear splendid clothing, how to cure all your ills, how to fly through the air yourselves and speak to other men at a great distance."

Tk'we looked over his shoulder at the others for a long time. He shrugged. "As for me," he said, "I do not want those things. If the Gods will give me some meat, I will not refuse it. Also, some medicines to cure the aches in my bones; that would be very good. But why should I want to fly, or to live in one of these great *scherms*? What I want is to be left alone."

Behind him, hundreds of soft voices murmured discreetly: "Yes, yes, that is so. Meat and some medicines. Do not forget tobacco. Perhaps a little tea, that would be nice."

"I think those are the gifts we expect, Master," said Tk'we, grinning. "If you gave us all the other things, then for a little while perhaps we would seem like great men. But then the Bantus and the white men would come and quarrel with us, and there would be war, as there was in the old days, when many Bushmen were killed and we were driven into the desert.

"It is this way with me," he went on. "I was a good hunter, and I loved hunting. Also, I liked to lie with women. You cannot give me those things again. Nor can you give them to the young men, for they already have them. Now, I like to have a full belly. I enjoy seeing the children play about, and I love to see the young people dance. Sometimes, when my heart is heavy or full of longing, I like to sit apart and play on the *guashi* and sing the songs I have invented. You cannot give me these things, for I already have them.

"What other things are there for men? No one needs more. If he says that he does, he is not yet a man but a child, who, no matter what he has always desires more, and looks from the bag of *tsi* nuts that he has to the bag someone else has. But we are not all children. Therefore, give us the promised gifts and let us go."

Spokesman nodded. He motioned to his companions, and they went and opened the cases. They dragged them down into the audience and began passing out packets of razor blades, pipes, good hunting knives, first-aid kits, small mirrors, boxes of tobacco, soap, tea, lumps of sugar and of salt. They opened other cases and handed round cured hams, flitches of bacon, smoked sausages, and other delicacies. Each Bushman received a small knapsack into which he could stuff his gifts, and even the children were not forgotten. Then, with much hand-waving and smiling and bowing, they filed out of the hall and crowded into the waiting buses.

When they had gone, Spokesman and his companions went out to the plaza before the building and opened their collapsible vehicle. The other four stepped into it, but Spokesman beckoned to the Secretary-General and with an unexpected, kindly gesture put a hand on his shoulder.

"Please give orders," he said, "to clear the area around our ship, for we will be departing for home as soon as we have returned to it. Also, please see to it that the vast numbers of spies from all your member nations are warned to retire. I regret that they were unable to get through the force field we placed about the ship, but I think they would have learned very little in any case. Farewell, and good luck to you. It may be that one day you will all reach the level of the Bushmen—stranger things have happened. In that case, we will return."

The Secretary-General sighed. "You knew they would take noth-ing," he said. "You had the cases ready. Or did you change them, somehow, with some juggling I didn't notice?"

"We knew," said Spokesman.

"But—how?"

"It is what makes them—hmm—pre-Federable."

"But *we* would know what to do with your gifts!" cried the Secre-tary-General. "My God, think of the things we could do—any of us—one of our great nations—"

Spokesman looked at the Secretary-General with compassion, and smiled. When he did so, he looked suddenly and surprisingly like old Tk'we.

"It is a shame, isn't it?" he said.

After all, he was himself no more than human.

The Concept of National Power

There are many definitions of "power," ranging from simply being able to get what you want to more sophisticated attempts centering on convincing others to share your world view. But even if you can reach agreement on what power consists of, you may still be frustrated because you lack the necessary elements to achieve your goals. The sad (some might say fortunate) fact is that all countries are not created equal in spite of the myth of sovereign equality that says they are.

A sizable portion of the study of international relations has consisted of attempts to isolate the factors that contribute to national power, and to rank these factors in importance as well as ranking the countries of the world in this respect. National power capabilities generally focus on the following broad areas:

Military Power: Two factors are particularly important here— quantity and quality. One needs to know as much as possible about one's own abilities and the abilities and weaknesses of one's enemies. Recent technological developments like "spy" satellites (some capable of reading the label off a golf ball from twenty miles up) have made it easier to acquire this information, although surprises are still possible. In recent years, the trend has been toward the acquisition of fewer, more sophisticated weapons, at least in the West. Currently, however, there appears to be growing support for larger numbers of less-complicated weapons and electronics.

Geography, Population, and Economic Strength: The first of these factors is no longer as important as it used to be because the nuclear and missile age we live in has shrunk the world and reduced the previous advantages of easily defensible borders and natural barriers like mountain ranges. Geography can still be important in certain regional situations like the Middle East and can play a role in the economy through its effect upon the agricultural sector. The "fit" between the size of a population and the available food supply is always important. In addition, some countries are just plain lucky to have valuable deposits of natural resources within their borders. Saudia Arabia's oil reserves are an obvious example. Finally, the technological level of a nation's industry and people, its balance of payments, demographic situation, and general productivity all play an important role in its overall power capabilities.

National Morale: A people who identify with, are loyal to, and are willing to fight for national goals are crucial in an assessment of national power. Dissident groups and unhappy minorities may severely reduce the overall strength of a country, but if enough power remains, it may still prevail. The quality of leadership plays an important role in this regard, as it does in general. If the leadership group lacks willpower and skill, all of the other factors may be negated.

Image: The illusion of power can be as important as the actual possession of power as long as power does not have to be actually exercised. Therefore, deception and bluff are engaged in by all countries, including the actually powerful.

"Superiority" provides us with a number of lessons in regard to national power in an *actual* war situation between two civilizations. This story was written in 1951, and used to be required reading at the Massachusetts Institute of Technology. Look for analogies between the story and the American experience in Vietnam, and then think about the predictive qualities of science "fiction."

SUPERIORITY

by Arthur C. Clarke

In making this statement—which I do of my own free will—I wish first to make it perfectly clear that I am not in any way trying to gain sympathy, nor do I expect any mitigation of whatever sentence the Court may pronounce. I am writing this in an attempt to refute some of the lying reports broadcast over the prison radio and published in the papers I have been allowed to see. These have given an entirely false picture of the true cause of our defeat, and as the leader of my race's armed forces at the cessation of hostilities I feel it my duty to protest against such libels upon those who served under me.

I also hope that this statement may explain the reasons for the application I have twice made to the Court, and will now induce it to grant a favor for which I can see no possible grounds of refusal.

The ultimate cause of our failure was a simple one: despite all statements to the contrary, it was not due to lack of bravery on the part of our men, or to any fault of the Fleet's. We were defeated by one thing only—by the inferior science of our enemies. I repeat—by the *inferior* science of our enemies.

When the war opened we had no doubt of our ultimate victory. The combined fleets of our allies greatly exceeded in number and armament those which the enemy could muster against us, and in almost all branches of military science we were their superiors. We were sure that we could maintain this superiority. Our belief proved, alas, to be only too well founded.

At the opening of the war our main weapons were the long-range homing torpedo, dirigible ball-lightning and the various modifications of the Klydon beam. Every unit of the Fleet was equipped with these and though the enemy possessed similar weapons their installations were generally of lesser power. Moreover, we had behind us a far greater military Research Organization, and with this initial advantage we could not possibly lose.

The campaign proceeded according to plan until the Battle of the Five Suns. We won this, of course, but the opposition proved stronger than we had expected. It was realized that victory might be more difficult, and more delayed, than had first been imagined. A conference of supreme commanders was therefore called to discuss our future strategy.

Present for the first time at one of our war conferences was Professor-General Norden, the new Chief of the Research Staff, who had just been appointed to fill the gap left by the death of Malvar, our greatest scientist. Malvar's leadership had been responsible, more than any other single factor, for the efficiency and power of our weapons. His loss was a very serious blow, but no one doubted the brilliance of his successor—though many of us disputed the wisdom of appointing a theoretical scientist to fill a post of such vital importance. But we had been overruled.

I can well remember the impression Norden made at that conference. The military advisers were worried, and as usual turned to the scientists for help. Would it be possible to improve our existing weapons, they asked, so that our present advantage could be increased still further?

Norden's reply was quite unexpected. Malvar had often been asked such a question—and he had always done what we requested.

"Frankly, gentlemen," said Norden, "I doubt it. Our existing weapons have practically reached finality. I don't wish to criticize my predecessor, or the excellent work done by the Research Staff in the last few generations, but do you realize that there has been no basic change in armaments for over a century? It is, I am afraid, the result of a tradition that has become conservative. For too long, the Research Staff has devoted itself to perfecting old weapons instead of developing new ones. It is fortunate for us that our opponents have been no wiser: we cannot assume that this will always be so."

Norden's words left an uncomfortable impression, as he had no doubt intended. He quickly pressed home the attack.

"What we want are *new* weapons—weapons totally different from any that have been employed before. Such weapons can be made: it will take time, of course, but since assuming charge I have replaced some of the older scientists by young men and have directed research into several unexplored fields which show great promise. I believe, in fact, that a revolution in warfare may soon be upon us."

We were skeptical. There was a bombastic tone in Norden's voice that made us suspicious of his claims. We did not know, then, that he never promised anything that he had not already almost perfected in the laboratory. *In the laboratory*—that was the operative phrase.

Norden proved his case less than a month later, when he demonstrated the Sphere of Annihilation, which produced complete disintegration of matter over a radius of several hundred meters. We were intoxicated by the power of the new weapon, and were quite prepared to overlook one fundamental defect—the fact that it *was* a sphere and hence destroyed its rather complicated generating equipment at the instant of formation. This meant, of course, that it could not be used on warships but only on guided missiles, and a great program was started to convert all homing torpedoes to carry the new weapon. For the time being all further offensives were suspended.

We realize now that this was our first mistake. I still think that it was a natural one, for it seemed to us then that all our existing weapons had become obsolete overnight, and we already regarded them as almost primitive survivals. What we did not appreciate was the magnitude of the task we were attempting, and the length of time it would take to get the revolutionary super-weapon into battle. Nothing like this had happened for a hundred years and we had no previous experience to guide us.

The conversion problem proved far more difficult than anticipated. A new class of torpedo had to be designed, as the standard model was too small. This meant in turn that only the larger ships could launch the weapon, but we were prepared to accept this penalty. After six months, the heavy units of the Fleet were being equipped with the Sphere. Training maneuvers and tests had shown that it was operating satisfactorily and we were ready to take it into action. Norden was already being hailed as the architect of victory, and had half promised even more spectacular weapons.

Then two things happened. One of our battleships disappeared completely on a training flight, and an investigation showed that under certain conditions the ship's long-range radar could trigger the Sphere immediately it had been launched. The modification needed to overcome this defect was trivial, but it caused a delay of another month and was the source of much bad feeling between the naval staff and the scientists. We were ready for action again—when Norden announced that the radius of effectiveness of the Sphere had now been increased by ten, thus multiplying by a thousand the chances of destroying an enemy ship.

So the modifications started all over again, but everyone agreed that the delay would be worth it. Meanwhile, however, the enemy had been emboldened by the absence of further attacks and had made an unexpected onslaught. Our ships were short of torpedoes, since none had been coming from the factories, and were forced to retire. So we lost the systems of Kyrane and Floranus, and the planetary fortress of Rhamsandron.

It was an annoying but not a serious blow, for the recaptured systems had been unfriendly, and difficult to administer. We had no doubt that we could restore the position in the near future, as soon as the new weapon became operational.

These hopes were only partially fulfilled. When we renewed our offensive, we had to do so with fewer of the Spheres of Annihilation than had been planned, and this was one reason for our limited success. The other reason was more serious.

While we had been equipping as many of our ships as we could with the irresistible weapon, the enemy had been building feverishly. His ships were of the old pattern with the old weapons—but they now outnumbered ours. When we went into action, we found that the numbers ranged against us were often 100 per cent greater than expected, causing target confusion among the automatic weapons and resulting in higher losses than anticipated. The enemy losses were higher still, for once a Sphere had reached its objective, destruction was certain, but the balance had not swung as far in our favor as we had hoped.

Moreover, while the main fleets had been engaged, the enemy had launched a daring attack on the lightly held systems of Eriston, Duranus, Carmanidora and Pharanidon—recapturing them all. We were thus faced with a threat only fifty light-years from our home planets.

There was much recrimination at the next meeting of the supreme commanders. Most of the complaints were addressed to Norden—Grand Admiral Taxaris in particular maintaining that thanks to our admittedly irresistible weapon we were now considerably worse off than before. We should, he claimed, have continued to build conventional ships, thus preventing the loss of our numerical superiority.

Norden was equally angry and called the naval staff ungrateful bunglers. But I could tell that he was worried—as indeed we all were—by the unexpected turn of events. He hinted that there might be a speedy way of remedying the situation.

We now know that Research had been working on the Battle Analyzer for many years, but at the time it came as a revelation to us and perhaps we were too easily swept off our feet. Norden's argument, also, was seductively convincing. What did it matter, he said, if the enemy had twice as many ships as we—if the efficiency of ours could be doubled or even trebled? For decades the limiting factor in warfare had been not mechanical but biological—it had become more and more difficult for any single mind, or group of minds, to cope with the rapidly changing complexities of battle in three-dimensional space. Norden's mathematicians had analyzed some of the classic engagements of the past, and had shown that even when we had been victorious we had often operated our units at much less than half of their theoretical efficiency.

The Battle Analyzer would change all this by replacing the operations staff with electronic calculators. The idea was not new, in theory, but until now it had been no more than a utopian dream. Many of us found it difficult to believe that it was still anything but a dream: after we had run through several very complex dummy battles, however, we were convinced.

It was decided to install the Analyzer in four of our heaviest ships, so that each of the main fleets could be equipped with one. At this stage, the trouble began—though we did not know it until later.

The Analyzer contained just short of a million vacuum tubes and needed a team of five hundred technicians to maintain and operate it. It was quite impossible to accommodate the extra staff aboard a battleship, so each of the four units had to be accompanied by a converted liner to carry the technicians not on duty. Installation was also a very slow and tedious business, but by gigantic efforts it was completed in six months.

Then, to our dismay, we were confronted by another crisis. Nearly five thousand highly skilled men had been selected to serve the Analyzers and had been given an intensive course at the Technical Training Schools. At the end of seven months, 10 per cent of them had had nervous breakdowns and only 40 per cent had qualified.

Once again, everyone started to blame everyone else. Norden, of course, said that the Research Staff could not be held responsible, and so incurred the enmity of the Personnel and Training Commands. It was finally decided that the only thing to do was to use two instead of four Analyzers and to bring the others into action as soon as men could be trained. There was little time to lose, for the enemy was still on the offensive and his morale was rising.

The first Analyzer fleet was ordered to recapture the system of Eriston. On the way, by one of the hazards of war, the liner carrying the technicians was struck by a roving mine. A warship would have survived, but the liner with its irreplaceable cargo was totally destroyed. So the operation had to be abandoned.

The other expedition was, at first, more successful. There was no doubt at all that the Analyzer fulfilled its designers' claims, and the enemy was heavily defeated in the first engagements. He withdrew, leaving us in possession of Saphran, Leucon and Hexanerax. But his Intelligence Staff must have noted the change in our tactics and the inexplicable presence of a liner in the heart of our battle-fleet. It must have noted, also, that our first fleet had been accompanied by a similar ship—and had withdrawn when it had been destroyed.

In the next engagement, the enemy used his superior numbers to launch an overwhelming attack on the Analyzer ship and its unarmed consort. The attack was made without regard to losses—both ships were, of course, very heavily protected—and it succeeded. The result was the virtual decapitation of the Fleet, since an effectual transfer to the old operational methods proved impossible. We disengaged under heavy fire, and so lost all our gains and also the systems of Lormyia, Ismarnus, Beronis, Alphanidon and Sideneus.

At this stage, Grand Admiral Taxaris expressed his disapproval of Norden by committing suicide, and I assumed supreme command.

The situation was now both serious and infuriating. With stubborn conservatism and complete lack of imagination, the enemy continued to advance with his old-fashioned and inefficient but now vastly more numerous ships. It was galling to realize that if we had only continued building, without seeking new weapons, we would have been in a far more advantageous position. There were many acrimonious conferences at which Norden defended the scientists while everyone else blamed them for all that had happened. The difficulty was that Norden had proved every one of his claims: he had a perfect excuse for all the disasters that had occurred. And we could not now turn back—the search for an irresistible weapon must go on. At first it had been a luxury that would shorten the war. Now it was a necessity if we were to end it victoriously.

We were on the defensive, and so was Norden. He was more than ever determined to re-establish his prestige and that of the Research Staff. But we had been twice disappointed, and would not make the same mistake again. No doubt Norden's twenty thousand scientists would produce many further weapons: we would remain unimpressed.

We were wrong. The final weapon was something so fantastic that even now it seems difficult to believe that it ever existed. Its innocent, noncommittal name—The Exponential Field—gave no hint of its real potentialities. Some of Norden's mathematicians had discovered it during a piece of entirely theoretical research into the properties of space, and to everyone's great surprise their results were found to be physically realizable.

It seems very difficult to explain the operation of the Field to the layman. According to the technical description, it "produces an exponential condition of space, so that a finite distance in normal, linear space may become infinite in pseudo-space." Norden gave an analogy which some of us found useful. It was as if one took a flat disk of rubber—representing a region of normal space—and then pulled its center out to infinity. The circumference of the disk would be unaltered—but its "diameter" would be infinite. That was the sort of thing the generator of the Field did to the space around it.

As an example, suppose that a ship carrying the generator was surrounded by a ring of hostile machines. If it switched on the Field, *each* of the enemy ships would think that it—and the ships on the far side of the circle—had suddenly receded into nothingness. Yet the circumference of the circle would be the same as before: only the journey to the center would be of infinite duration, for as one proceeded, distances would appear to become greater and greater as the "scale" of space altered.

It was a nightmare condition, but a very useful one. Nothing could reach a ship carrying the Field: it might be englobed by an enemy fleet yet would be as inaccessible as if it were at the other side of the Universe. Against this, of course, it could not fight back without switching off the Field, but this still left it at a very great advantage, not only in defense but in offense. For a ship fitted with the Field could approach an enemy fleet undetected and suddenly appear in its midst.

This time there seemed to be no flaws in the new weapon. Needless to say, we looked for all the possible objections before we committed ourselves again. Fortunately the equipment was fairly simple and did not require a large operating staff. After much debate, we decided to rush it into production, for we realized that time was running short and the war was going against us. We had now lost about the whole of our initial gains and enemy forces had made several raids into our own solar system.

We managed to hold off the enemy while the Fleet was reequipped and the new battle techniques were worked out. To use the Field operationally it was necessary to locate an enemy formation, set a course that would intercept it, and then switch on the generator for the calculated period of time. On releasing the Field again—if the calculations had been accurate—one would be in the enemy's midst and could do great damage during the resulting confusion, retreating by the same route when necessary.

The first trial maneuvers proved satisfactory and the equipment seemed quite reliable. Numerous mock attacks were made and the crews became accustomed to the new technique. I was on one of the test flights and can vividly remember my impressions as the Field was switched on. The ships around us seemed to dwindle as if on the surface of an expanding bubble: in an instant they had vanished completely. So had the stars—but presently we could see that the Galaxy was still visible as a faint band of light around the ship. The virtual radius of our pseudo-space was not really infinite, but some hundred thousand light-years, and so the distance to the farthest stars of our system had not been greatly increased—though the nearest had of course totally disappeared.

These training maneuvers, however, had to be cancelled before they were complete owing to a whole flock of minor technical troubles in various pieces of equipment, notably the communications circuits. These were annoying, but not important, though it was thought best to return to Base to clear them up.

At that moment the enemy made what was obviously intended to be a decisive attack against the fortress planet of Iton at the limits of our solar system. The Fleet had to go into battle before repairs could be made.

The enemy must have believed that we had mastered the secret of invisibility—as in a sense we had. Our ships appeared suddenly out of nowhere and inflicted tremendous damage—for a while. And then something quite baffling and inexplicable happened.

I was in command of the flagship *Hircania* when the trouble started. We had been operating as independent units, each against assigned objectives. Our detectors observed an enemy formation at medium range and the navigating officers measured its distance with great accuracy. We set course and switched on the generator.

The Exponential Field was released at the moment when we should have been passing through the center of the enemy group. To our consternation, we emerged into normal space at a distance of many hundred miles—and when we found the enemy, he had already found us. We retreated, and tried again. This time we were so far away from the enemy that he located us first.

Obviously, something was seriously wrong. We broke communicator silence and tried to contact the other ships of the Fleet to see if they had experienced the same trouble. Once again we failed—and this time the failure was beyond all reason, for the communication equipment appeared to be working perfectly. We could only assume, fantastic though it seemed, that the rest of the Fleet had been destroyed.

I do not wish to describe the scenes when the scattered units of the Fleet struggled back to Base. Our casualties had actually been negligible, but the ships were completely demoralized. Almost all had lost touch with one another and had found that their ranging equipment showed inexplicable errors. It was obvious that the Exponential Field was the cause of the troubles, despite the fact that they were only apparent when it was switched off.

The explanation came too late to do us any good, and Norden's final discomfiture was small consolation for the virtual loss of the war. As I have explained, the Field generators produced a radial distortion of space, distances appearing greater and greater as one approached the center of the artificial pseudo-space. When the Field was switched off, conditions returned to normal.

But not quite. It was never possible to restore the initial state *exactly*. Switching the Field on and off was equivalent to an elongation and contraction of the ship carrying the generator, but there was an hysteretic effect, as it were, and the initial condition was never quite reproducible, owing to all the thousands of electrical changes and movements of mass aboard the ship while the Field was on. These asymmetries and distortions were cumulative, and though they seldom amounted to more than a fraction of one per cent, that was quite enough. It meant that the precision ranging equipment and the tuned circuits in the communication apparatus were thrown completely out of adjustment. Any single ship could never detect the change—only when it compared its equipment with that of another vessel, or tried to communicate with it, could it tell what had happened.

It is impossible to describe the resultant chaos. Not a single component of one ship could be expected with certainty to work aboard another. The very nuts and bolts were no longer interchangeable, and the supply position became quite impossible. Given time, we might even have overcome these difficulties, but the enemy ships were already attacking in thousands with weapons which now seemed centuries behind those that we had invented. Our magnificent Fleet, crippled by our own science, fought on as best it could until it was overwhelmed and forced to surrender. The ships fitted with the Field were still invulnerable, but as fighting units they were almost helpless. Every time they switched on their generators to escape from enemy attack, the permanent distortion of their equipment increased. In a month, it was all over.

This is the true story of our defeat, which I give without prejudice to my defense before this Court. I make it, as I have said, to counteract the libels that have been circulating against the men who fought under me, and to show where the true blame for our misfortunes lay.

Finally, my request, which as the Court will now realize, I make in no frivolous manner and which I hope will therefore be granted.

The Court will be aware that the conditions under which we are housed and the constant surveillance to which we are subjected night and day are somewhat distressing. Yet I am not complaining of this: nor do I complain of the fact that shortage of accommodation has made it necessary to house us in pairs.

But I cannot be held responsible for my future actions if I am compelled any longer to share my cell with Professor Norden, late Chief of the Research Staff of my armed forces.

Balance of Power

"If you hit me, I'll hit you back twice as hard" is a phrase that has been heard on more than one school playground. "If you take that car, you will go to jail for it" illustrates the guiding principle of our criminal justice system—the assumption that the threat of punishment will deter the potential criminal from committing antisocial acts.

International politics also operates along the same lines. The great destructive power of nuclear weapons has resulted in a system of mutual *deterrence* wherein all parties know that all sides will suffer grievous losses if war were to break out. In fact, the fear of an all-out nuclear exchange is so great that the present system has been described as a "balance of terror." However, the concept of balance in international politics predates the nuclear era—indeed, it is almost as old as the nation-state itself. During the nineteenth century balance of power politics was a dominant theme as one after another European power grew ambitious and other countries formed alliances to counteract the strength of the challenger. A key country, usually Great Britain, would play the role of the "balancer" in this process, joining one group of countries after another to ensure that the balance was maintained. It was widely felt that if the balance were tipped in one direction or another, the temptation to go to war would be irresistible.

Today, the balance of power concept is being challenged by those who advocate arrangements like the division of the world into spheres of influence and who argue that as nuclear weapons proliferate, balance of power becomes unworkable, if not absurd. Here Frank Herbert, author of the award-winning novel *Dune,* takes the balance of power idea and extrapolates it to its logical (and thought-provoking) conclusion.

COMMITTEE OF THE WHOLE

by Frank Herbert

With an increasing sense of unease, Alan Wallace studied his client as they neared the public hearing room on the second floor of the Old Senate Office Building. The guy was too relaxed.

"Bill, I'm worried about this," Wallace said. "You could damn well lose your grazing rights here in this room today."

They were almost into the gantlet of guards, reporters and TV cameramen before Wallace got his answer.

"Who the hell cares?" Custer asked.

Wallace, who prided himself on being the Washington-type lawyer —above contamination by complaints and briefs, immune to all shock—found himself tongue-tied with surprise.

They were into the ruck then and Wallace had to pull on his bold face, smiling at the press, trying to soften the sharpness of that necessary phrase:

"No comment. Sorry."

"See us after the hearing if you have any questions, gentlemen," Custer said.

The man's voice was level and confident.

He has himself over-controlled, Wallace thought. Maybe he was just joking . . . a graveyard joke.

The marble-walled hearing room blazed with lights. Camera platforms had been raised above the seats at the rear. Some of the smaller UHF stations had their cameramen standing on the window ledges.

The subdued hubbub of the place eased slightly, Wallace noted, then picked up tempo as William R. Custer—"The Baron of Oregon" they called him—entered with his attorney, passed the press tables and crossed to the seats reserved for them in the witness section.

Ahead and to their right, that one empty chair at the long table stood waiting with its aura of complete exposure.

"Who the hell cares?"

That wasn't a Custer-type joke, Wallace reminded himself. For all his cattle-baron pose, Custer held a doctorate in agriculture and degrees in philosophy, math and electronics. His western neighbors called him "The Brain."

It was no accident that the cattlemen had chosen him to represent them here.

Wallace glanced covertly at the man, studying him. The cowboy boots and string tie added to a neat dark business suit would have been affectation on most men. They merely accented Custer's good looks —the sunburned, windblown outdoorsman. He was a little darker of hair and skin than his father had been, still light enough to be called blond, but not as ruddy and without the late father's drink-tumescent veins.

But then young Custer wasn't quite thirty.

Custer turned, met the attorney's eyes. He smiled.

"Those were good patent attorneys you recommended, Al," Custer said. He lifted his briefcase to his lap, patted it. "No mincing around or mealy-mouthed excuses. Already got this thing on the way." Again he tapped the briefcase.

He brought that damn light gadget here with him? Wallace wondered. Why? He glanced at the briefcase. Didn't know it was that small . . . but maybe he's just talking about the plans for it.

"Let's keep our minds on this hearing," Wallace whispered. "This is the only thing that's important."

Into a sudden lull in the room's high noise level, the voice of someone in the press section carried across them: "greatest political show on earth."

"I brought this as an exhibit," Custer said. Again, he tapped the briefcase. It did bulge oddly.

Exhibit? Wallace asked himself.

It was the second time in ten minutes that Custer had shocked him. This was to be a hearing of a subcommittee of the Senate Interior and Insular Affairs Committee. The issue was Taylor grazing lands. What the devil could that . . . gadget have to do with the battle of words and laws to be fought here?

"You're supposed to talk over all strategy with your attorney," Wallace whispered. "What the devil do you . . ."

He broke off as the room fell suddenly silent.

Wallace looked up to see the subcommittee chairman, Senator Haycourt Tiborough, stride through the wide double doors followed by his coterie of investigators and attorneys. The Senator was a tall man who had once been fat. He had dieted with such savage abruptness that his skin had never recovered. His jowls and the flesh on the back of his hands sagged. The top of his head was shiny bald and ringed by a three-quarter tonsure that had purposely been allowed to grow long and straggly so that it fanned back over his ears.

The Senator was followed in close lock step by syndicated columnist Anthony Poxman, who was speaking fiercely into Tiborough's left ear. TV cameras tracked the pair.

If Poxman's covering this one himself instead of sending a flunky, it's going to be bad, Wallace told himself.

Tiborough took his chair at the center of the committee table facing them, glanced left and right to assure himself the other members were present.

Senator Spealance was absent, Wallace noted, but he had party organization difficulties at home and the Senior Senator from Oregon was, significantly, not present. Illness, it was reported.

A sudden attack of caution, that common Washington malady, no doubt. He knew where his campaign money came from . . . but he also knew where the votes were.

They had a quorum, though.

Tiborough cleared his throat, said: "The committee will please come to order."

The Senator's voice and manner gave Wallace a cold chill. We were nuts trying to fight this one in the open, he thought. Why'd I let Custer and his friends talk me into this? You can't butt heads with a United States Senator who's out to get you. The only way's to fight him on the inside.

And now Custer suddenly turning screwball.

Exhibit!

"Gentlemen," said Tiborough, "I think we can . . . that is, today we can dispense with preliminaries . . . unless my colleagues . . . if any of them have objections."

Again, he glanced at the other senators—five of them. Wallace swept his gaze down the line behind that table—Plowers of Nebraska (a horse trader), Johnstone of Ohio (a parliamentarian—devious), Lane of South Carolina (a Republican in Democrat disguise), Emery of Minnesota (new and eager—dangerous because he lacked the old inhibitions) and Meltzer of New York (poker player, fine old family with traditions).

None of them had objections.

They've had a private meeting—both sides of the aisle—and talked over a smooth steamroller procedure, Wallace thought.

It was another ominous sign.

"This is a subcommittee of the United States Senate Committee on Interior and Insular Affairs," Tiborough said, his tone formal. "We are charged with obtaining expert opinion on proposed amendments to the Taylor Grazing Act of 1934. Today's hearing will begin with testimony and . . . ah, questioning of a man whose family has been in the business of raising beef cattle in Oregon for three generations."

Tiborough smiled at the TV cameras.

The son-of-a-bitch is playing to the galleries, Wallace thought. He glanced at Custer. The cattleman sat relaxed against the back of his chair, eyes half lidded, staring at the Senator.

"We call as our first witness today Mr. William R. Custer of Bend, Oregon," Tiborough said. "Will the clerk please swear in Mr. Custer."

Custer moved forward to the "hot seat," placed his briefcase on the table. Wallace pulled a chair up beside his client, noted how the cameras turned as the clerk stepped forward, put the Bible on the table and administered the oath.

Tiborough ruffled through some papers in front of him, waiting for full attention to return to him, said: "This subcommittee . . . we have before us a bill, this is a United States Senate Bill entitled SB-1024 of the current session, an act amending the Taylor Grazing Act of 1934 and, the intent is, as many have noted, that we would broaden the base of the advisory committees to the Act and include a wider public representation."

Custer was fiddling with the clasp of his briefcase.

How the hell could that light gadget be an exhibit here? Wallace asked himself. He glanced at the set of Custer's jaw, noted the nervous working of a muscle. It was the first sign of unease he'd seen in Custer. The sight failed to settle Wallace's own nerves.

"Ah, Mr. Custer," Tiborough said. "Do you—did you bring a preliminary statement? Your counsel . . ."

"I have a statement," Custer said. His big voice rumbled through the room, requiring instant attention and the shift of cameras that had been holding tardily on Tiborough, expecting an addition to the question.

Tiborough smiled, waited, then: "Your attorney—is your statement the one your counsel supplied the committee?"

"With some slight additions of my own," Custer said.

Wallace felt a sudden qualm. They were too willing to accept Custer's statement. He leaned close to his client's ear, whispered: "They know what your stand is. Skip the preliminaries."

Custer ignored him, said: "I intend to speak plainly and simply. I oppose the amendment. Broaden the base and wider public representation are phases of the amendment. Broaden the base and wider public representation are phases of politician double talk. The intent is to pack the committees, to put control of them into the hands of people who don't know the first thing about the cattle business and whose private intent is to destroy the Taylor Grazing Act itself."

"Plain, simple talk," Tiborough said. "This committee . . . we welcome such directness. Strong words. A majority of this committee . . . we have taken the position that the public range lands have been too long subjected to the tender mercies of the stockmen advisors, that the lands . . . stockmen have exploited them to their own advantage."

The gloves are off, Wallace thought. I hope Custer knows what he's doing. He's sure as hell not accepting advice.

Custer pulled a sheaf of papers from his briefcase and Wallace glimpsed shiny metal in the case before the flap was closed.

Christ! That looked like a gun or something!

Then Wallace recognized the papers—the brief he and his staff had labored over—and the preliminary statement. He noted with alarm the penciled markings and marginal notations. How could Custer have done that much to it in just twenty-four hours?

Again, Wallace whispered in Custer's ear: "Take it easy, Bill. The bastard's out for blood."

Custer nodded to show he had heard, glanced at the papers, looked up directly at Tiborough.

A hush settled on the room, broken only by the scraping of a chair somewhere in the rear, and the whirr of cameras.

II

"First, the nature of these lands we're talking about," Custer said. "In my state . . ." He cleared his throat, a mannerism that would have indicated anger in the old man, his father. There was no break in Custer's expression, though, and his voice remained level. ". . . in my state, these were mostly Indian lands. This nation took them by brute force, right of conquest. That's about the oldest right in the world, I guess. I don't want to argue with it at this point."

"Mr. Custer."

It was Nebraska's Senator Plowers, his amiable farmer's face set in a tight grin. "Mr. Custer, I hope . . ."

"Is this a point of order?" Tiborough asked.

"Mr. Chairman," Plowers said, "I merely wished to make sure we weren't going to bring up that old suggestion about giving these lands back to the Indians."

Laughter shot across the hearing room. Tiborough chuckled as he pounded his gavel for order.

"You may continue, Mr. Custer," Tiborough said.

Custer looked at Plowers, said: "No, Senator, I don't want to give these lands back to the Indians. When they had these lands, they only got about three hundred pounds of meat a year off eighty acres. We get five hundred pounds of the highest grade protein—premium beef —from only ten acres."

"No one doubts the efficiency of your factory-like methods," Tiborough said. "You can . . . we know your methods wring the largest amount of meat from a minimum acreage."

Ugh! Wallace thought. That was a low blow—implying Bill's over-grazing and destroying the land value.

"My neighbors, the Warm Springs Indians, use the same methods I do," Custer said. "They are happy to adopt our methods because we use the land while maintaining it and increasing its value. We don't permit the land to fall prey to natural disasters such as fire and erosion. We don't . . ."

"No doubt your methods are meticulously correct," Tiborough said. "But I fail to see where . . ."

"Has Mr. Custer finished his preliminary statement yet?" Senator Plowers cut in.

Wallace shot a startled look at the Nebraskan. That was help from an unexpected quarter.

"Thank you, Senator," Custer said. "I'm quite willing to adapt to the Chairman's methods and explain the meticulous correctness of my operation. Our lowliest cowhands are college men, highly paid. We travel ten times as many jeep miles as we do horse miles. Every outlying division of the ranch—every holding pen and grazing supervisor's cabin is linked to the central ranch by radio. We use the . . ."

"I concede that your methods must be the most modern in the world," Tiborough said. "It's not your methods as much as the results of those methods that are at issue here. We . . ."

He broke off at a disturbance by the door. An Army colonel was talking to the guard there. He wore Special Services fourragere—Pentagon.

Wallace noted with an odd feeling of disquiet that the man was armed—a .45 at the hip. The weapon was out of place on him, as though he had added it suddenly on an overpowering need . . . emergency.

More guards were coming up outside the door now—Marines and Army. They carried rifles.

The colonel said something sharp to the guard, turned away from him and entered the committee room. All the cameras were tracking him now. He ignored them, crossed swiftly to Tiborough, and spoke to him.

The Senator shot a startled glance at Custer, accepted a sheaf of papers the colonel thrust at him. He forced his attention off Custer, studied the papers, leafing through them. Presently, he looked up, stared at Custer.

A hush fell over the room.

"I find myself at a loss, Mr. Custer," Tiborough said. "I have here a copy of a report . . . it's from the Special Services branch of the Army . . . through the Pentagon, you understand. It was just handed to me by, ah . . . the colonel here."

He looked up at the colonel, who was standing, one hand resting lightly on the holstered .45. Tiborough looked back at Custer and it was obvious the Senator was trying to marshal his thoughts.

"It is," Tiborough said, "that is . . . this report supposedly . . . and I have every confidence it is what it is represented to be . . . here in my hands . . . they say that . . . uh, within the last, uh, few days they have, uh, investigated a certain device . . . weapon they call it, that you are attempting to patent. They report . . ." He glanced at the papers, back to Custer, who was staring at him steadily. ". . . this, uh, weapon, is a thing that . . . it is extremely dangerous."

"It is," Custer said.

"I . . . ah, see." Tiborough cleared his throat, glanced up at the colonel, who was staring fixedly at Custer. The Senator brought his attention back to Custer.

"Do you in fact have such a weapon with you, Mr. Custer?" Tiborough asked.

"I have brought it as an exhibit, sir."

"Exhibit?"

"Yes, sir."

Wallace rubbed his lips, found them dry. He wet them with his tongue, wished for the water glass, but it was beyond Custer. Christ! That stupid cowpuncher! He wondered if he dared whisper to Custer. Would the senators and that Pentagon lackey interpret such an action as meaning he was part of Custer's crazy antics?

"Are you threatening this committee with your weapon, Mr. Custer?" Tiborough asked. "If you are, I may say special precautions have been taken . . . extra guards in this room and we . . . that is, we will not allow ourselves to worry too much about any action you may take, but ordinary precautions are in force."

Wallace could no longer sit quietly. He tugged Custer's sleeve, got an abrupt shake of the head. He leaned close, whispered: "We could ask for a recess, Bill. Maybe we . . ."

"Don't interrupt me," Custer said. He looked at Tiborough. "Senator, I would not threaten you or any other man. Threats in the way you mean them are a thing we no longer can indulge in."

"You . . . I believe you said this device is an exhibit," Tiborough said. He cast a worried frown at the report in his hands. "I fail . . . it does not appear germane."

Senator Plowers cleared his throat. "Mr. Chairman," he said.

"The chair recognizes the Senator from Nebraska," Tiborough said, and the relief in his voice was obvious. He wanted time to think.

"Mr. Custer," Plowers said, "I have not seen the report, the report my distinguished colleague alludes to; however, if I may . . . is it your wish to use this committee as some kind of publicity device?"

"By no means, Senator," Custer said. "I don't wish to profit by my presence here . . . not at all."

Tiborough had apparently come to a decision. He leaned back, whispered to the colonel, who nodded and returned to the outer hall.

"You strike me as an eminently reasonable man, Mr. Custer," Tiborough said. "If I may . . ."

"May I," Senator Plowers said. "May I, just permit me to conclude this one point. May we have the Special Services report in the record?"

"Certainly," Tiborough said. "But what I was about to suggest . . ."

"May I," Plowers said. "May I, would you permit me, please, Mr. Chairman, to make this point clear for the record?"

Tiborough scowled, but the heavy dignity of the Senate overcame his irritation. "Please continue, Senator. I had thought you were finished."

"I respect . . . there is no doubt in my mind of Mr. Custer's truthfulness," Plowers said. His face eased into a grin that made him look grandfatherly, a kindly elder statesman. "I would like, therefore, to have him explain how this . . . ah, weapon, can be an exhibit in the matter before our committee."

Wallace glanced at Custer, saw the hard set to the man's jaw, realized the cattleman had gotten to Plowers somehow. This was a set piece.

Tiborough was glancing at the other senators, weighing the advisability of high-handed dismissal . . . perhaps a star chamber session. No . . . they were all too curious about Custer's device, his purpose here.

The thoughts were plain on the Senator's face.

"Very well," Tiborough said. He nodded to Custer. "You may proceed, Mr. Custer."

"During last winter's slack season," Custer said, "two of my men and I worked on a project we've had in the works for three years—to develop a sustained-emission laser device."

Custer opened his briefcase, slid out a fat aluminum tube mounted on a pistol grip with a conventional appearing trigger.

"This is quite harmless," he said. "I didn't bring the power pack."

"That is . . . this is your weapon?" Tiborough asked.

"Calling this a weapon is misleading," Custer said. "The term limits and oversimplifies. This is also a brush-cutter, a substitute for a logger's saw and axe, a diamond cutter, a milling machine . . . and a weapon. It is also a turning point in history."

"Come now, isn't that a bit pretentious?" Tiborough asked.

"We tend to think of history as something old and slow," Custer said. "But history is, as a matter of fact, extremely rapid and immediate. A President is assassinated, a bomb explodes over a city, a dam breaks, a revolutionary device is announced."

"Lasers have been known for quite a few years," Tiborough said. He looked at the papers the Colonel had given him. "The principle dates from 1956 or thereabouts."

"I don't wish it to appear that I'm taking credit for inventing this device," Custer said. "Nor am I claiming sole credit for developing the sustained-emission laser. I was merely one of a team. But I do hold the device here in my hand, gentlemen."

"Exhibit, Mr. Custer," Plowers reminded him. "How is this an exhibit?"

"May I explain first how it works?" Custer asked. "That will make the rest of my statement much easier."

Tiborough looked at Plowers, back to Custer. "If you will tie this all together, Mr. Custer," Tiborough said. "I want to . . . the bearing of this device on our—we are hearing a particular bill in this room."

"Certainly, Senator," Custer said. He looked at his device. "A ninety-volt radio battery drives this particular model. We have some that require less voltage, some that use more. We aimed for a construction with simple parts. Our crystals are common quartz. We shattered them by bringing them to a boil in water and then plunging them into ice water . . . repeatedly. We chose twenty pieces of very close to the same size—about one gram, slightly more than fifteen grains each."

Custer unscrewed the back of the tube, slid out a round length of plastic trailing lengths of red, green, brown, blue and yellow wire.

Wallace noted how the cameras of the TV men centered on the object in Custer's hands. Even the senators were leaning forward, staring.

We're gadget crazy people, Wallace thought.

"The crystals were dipped in thinned household cement and then into iron filings," Custer said. "We made a little jig out of a fly-tying vise and opened a passage in the filings at opposite ends of the crystals. We then made some common celluloid—nitrocellulose, acetic acid, gelatin and alcohol—all very common products, and formed it in a length of garden hose just long enough to take the crystals end to end. The crystals were inserted in the hose, the celluloid poured over them and the whole thing was seated in a magnetic waveguide while the celluloid was cooling. This centered and aligned the crystals. The waveguide was constructed from wire salvaged from an old TV set and built following the directions in the Radio Amateur's Handbook."

Custer re-inserted the length of plastic into the tube, adjusted the wires. There was an unearthly silence in the room with only the cameras whirring. It was as though everyone were holding his breath.

"A laser requires a resonant cavity, but that's complicated," Custer said. "Instead, we wound two layers of fine copper wire around our tube, immersed it in the celluloid solution to coat it and then filed one end flat. This end took a piece of mirror cut to fit. We then pressed a number eight embroidery needle at right angles into the mirror end of the tube until it touched the side of the number one crystal."

Custer cleared his throat.

Two of the senators leaned back. Plowers coughed. Tiborough glanced at the banks of TV cameras and there was a questioning look in his eyes.

"We then determined the master frequency of our crystal series," Custer said. "We used a test signal and oscilloscope, but any radio amateur could do it without the oscilloscope. We constructed an oscillator of that master frequency, attached it at the needle and a bare spot scraped in the opposite edge of the waveguide."

"And this . . . ah . . . worked?" Tiborough asked.

"No." Custer shook his head. "When we fed power through a voltage multiplier into the system we produced an estimated four hundred joules emission and melted half the tube. So we started all over again."

"You are going to tie this in?" Tiborough asked. He frowned at the papers in his hands, glanced toward the door where the colonel had gone.

"I am, sir, believe me," Custer said.

"Very well, then," Tiborough said.

"So we started all over again," Custer said. "But for the second celluloid dip we added bismuth—a saturate solution, actually. It stayed gummy and we had to paint over it with a sealing coat of the straight celluloid. We then coupled this bismuth layer through a pulse circuit so that it was bathed in a counter wave—180 degrees out of phase with the master frequency. We had, in effect, immersed the unit in a thermoelectric cooler that exactly countered the heat production. A thin beam issued from the unmirrored end when we powered it. We have yet to find something that thin beam cannot cut."

"Diamonds?" Tiborough asked.

"Powered by less than two hundred volts, this device could cut our planet in half like a ripe tomato," Custer said. "One man could destroy an aerial armada with it, knock down ICBMs before they touched atmosphere, sink a fleet, pulverize a city. I'm afraid, sir, that I haven't mentally catalogued all the violent implications of this device. The mind tends to boggle at the enormous power focused in . . ."

"Shut down those TV cameras!"

It was Tiborough shouting, leaping to his feet and making a sweeping gesture to include the banks of cameras. The abrupt violence of his voice and gesture fell on the room like an explosion. "Guards!" he called. "You there at the door. Cordon off that door and don't let anyone out who heard this fool!" He whirled back to face Custer. "You irresponsible idiot!"

"I'm afraid, Senator," Custer said, "that you're locking the barn door many weeks too late."

For a long minute of silence Tiborough glared at Custer. Then: "You did this deliberately, eh?"

III

"Senator, if I'd waited any longer, there might have been no hope for us at all."

Tiborough sat back into his chair, still keeping his attention fastened on Custer. Plowers and Johnstone on his right had their heads close together whispering fiercely. The other senators were dividing their attention between Custer and Tiborough, their eyes wide and with no attempt to conceal their astonishment.

Wallace, growing conscious of the implications in what Custer had said, tried to wet his lips with his tongue. Christ! he thought. This stupid cowpoke has sold us all down the river!

Tiborough signaled an aide, spoke briefly with him, beckoned the colonel from the door. There was a buzzing of excited conversation in the room. Several of the press and TV crew were huddled near the windows on Custer's left, arguing. One of their number—a florid-faced man with gray hair and horn-rimmed glasses—started across the room toward Tiborough, was stopped by a committee aide. They began a low-voiced argument with violent gestures.

A loud curse sounded from the door. Poxman, the syndicated columnist, was trying to push past the guards there.

"Poxman!" Tiborough called. The columnist turned. "My orders are that no one leaves," Tiborough said. "You are not an exception." He turned back to face Custer.

The room had fallen into a semblance of quiet, although there still were pockets of muttering and there was the sound of running feet and a hurrying about in the hall outside.

"Two channels went out of here live," Tiborough said. "Nothing much we can do about them, although we will trace down as many of their viewers as we can. Every bit of film in this room and every sound tape will be confiscated, however." His voice rose as protests sounded from the press section. "Our national security is at stake. The President has been notified. Such measures as are necessary will be taken."

The colonel came hurrying into the room, crossed to Tiborough, quietly said something.

"You should've warned me!" Tiborough snapped. "I had no idea that . . ."

The colonel interrupted with a whispered comment.

"These papers . . . your damned report is not clear!" Tiborough said. He looked around at Custer. "I see you're smiling, Mr. Custer. I don't think you'll find much to smile about before long."

"Senator, this is not a happy smile," Custer said. "But I told myself several days ago you'd fail to see the implications of this thing." He tapped the pistol-shaped device he had rested on the table. "I told myself you'd fall back into the old, useless pattern."

"Is that what you told yourself, really?" Tiborough said.

Wallace, hearing the venom in the Senator's voice, moved his chair a few inches farther away from Custer.

Tiborough looked at the laser projector. "Is that thing really disarmed?"

"Yes, sir."

"If I order one of my men to take it from you, you will not resist?"

"Which of your men will you trust with it, Senator?" Custer asked.

In the long silence that followed, someone in the press section emitted a nervous guffaw.

"Virtually every man on my ranch has one of these things," Custer said. "We fell trees with them, cut firewood, make fence posts. Every letter written to me as a result of my patent application has been answered candidly. More than a thousand sets of schematics and instructions on how to build this device have been sent out to varied places in the world."

"You vicious traitor!" Tiborough rasped.

"You're certainly entitled to your opinion, Senator," Custer said. "But I warn you I've had time for considerably more concentrated and considerably more painful thought than you've applied to this problem. In my estimation, I had no choice. Every week I waited to make this thing public, every day, every minute, merely raised the odds that humanity would be destroyed by . . ."

"You said this thing applied to the hearings on the grazing act," Plowers protested, and there was a plaintive note of complaint in his voice.

"Senator, I told you the truth," Custer said. "There's no real reason to change the act, now. We intend to go on operating under it— with the agreement of our neighbors and others concerned. People are still going to need food."

Tiborough glared at him. "You're saying we can't force you to . . ." He broke off at a disturbance in the doorway. A rope barrier had been stretched there and a line of Marines stood with their backs to it, facing the hall. A mob of people was trying to press through. Press cards were being waved.

"Colonel, I told you to clear that hall!" Tiborough barked.

The colonel ran to the barrier. "Use your bayonets if you have to!" he shouted.

The disturbance subsided at the sound of his voice. More uniformed men could be seen moving in along the barrier. Presently, the noise receded.

Tiborough turned back to Custer. "You make Benedict Arnold look like the greatest friend the United States ever had," he said.

"Cursing me isn't going to help you," Custer said. "You are going to have to live with this thing; so you'd better try understanding it."

"That appears to be simple," Tiborough said. "All I have to do is send twenty-five cents to the Patent office for the schematics and then write you a letter."

"The world already was headed toward suicide," Custer said. "Only fools failed to realize . . ."

"So you decided to give us a little push," Tiborough said.

"H. G. Wells warned us," Custer said. "That's how far back it goes, but nobody listened. 'Human history becomes more and more a race between education and catastrophe,' Wells said. But those were just words. Many scientists have remarked the growth curve on the amount of raw energy becoming available to humans—and the diminishing curve on the number of persons required to use that energy. For a long time now, more and more violent power was being made available to fewer and fewer people. It was only a matter of time until total destruction was put into the hands of single individuals."

"And you didn't think you could take your government into your confidence."

"The government already was committed to a political course diametrically opposite the one this device requires," Custer said. "Virtually every man in the government has a vested interest in not reversing that course."

"So you set yourself above the government?"

"I'm probably wasting my time," Custer said, "but I'll try to explain it. Virtually every government in the world is dedicated to manipulating something called the 'mass man.' That's how governments have stayed in power. But there is no such man. When you elevate the nonexistent 'mass man' you degrade the individual. And obviously it was only a matter of time until all of us were at the mercy of the individual holding power."

"You talk like a commie!"

"They'll say I'm a goddamn capitalist pawn," Custer said. "Let me ask you, Senator, to visualize a poor radio technician in a South American country. Brazil, for example. He lives a hand-to-mouth existence, ground down by an overbearing, unimaginative, essentially uncouth ruling oligarchy. What is he going to do when this device comes into his hands?"

"Murder, robbery and anarchy."

"You could be right," Custer said. "But we might reach an understanding out of ultimate necessity—that each of us must cooperate in maintaining the dignity of all."

Tiborough stared at him, began to speak musingly: "We'll have to control the essential materials for constructing this thing . . . and there may be trouble for a while, but . . ."

"You're a vicious fool."

In the cold silence that followed, Custer said: "It was too late to try that ten years ago. I'm telling you this thing can be patchworked out of a wide variety of materials that are already scattered over the earth. It can be made in basements and mud huts, in palaces and shacks. The key item is the crystals, but other crystals will work, too.

That's obvious. A patient man can grow crystals . . . and this world is full of patient men."

"I'm going to place you under arrest," Tiborough said. "You have outraged every rule—"

"You're living in a dream world," Custer said. "I refuse to threaten you, but I'll defend myself from any attempt to oppress or degrade me. If I cannot defend myself, my friends will defend me. No man who understands what this device means will permit his dignity to be taken from him."

Custer allowed a moment for his words to sink in, then: "And don't twist those words to imply a threat. Refusal to threaten a fellow human is an absolute requirement in the day that has just dawned on us."

"You haven't changed a thing!" Tiborough raged. "If one man is powerful with that thing, a hundred are . . ."

"All previous insults aside," Custer said, "I think you are a highly intelligent man, Senator. I ask you to think long and hard about this device. Use of power is no longer the deciding factor because one man is as powerful as a million. Restraint—self-restraint is now the key to survival. Each of us is at the mercy of his neighbor's good will. Each of us, Senator—the man in the palace and the man in the shack. We'd better do all we can to increase that good will—not attempting to buy it, but simply recognizing that individual dignity is the one inalienable right of . . ."

"Don't you preach to me, you commie traitor!" Tiborough rasped. "You're a living example of . . ."

"Senator!"

It was one of the TV cameramen in the left rear of the room.

"Let's stop insulting Mr. Custer and hear him out," the cameraman said.

"Get that man's name," Tiborough told an aide. "If he . . ."

"I'm an expert electronic technician, Senator," the man said. "You can't threaten me now."

Custer smiled, turned to face Tiborough.

"The revolution begins," Custer said. He waved a hand as the Senator started to whirl away. "Sit down, Senator."

Wallace, watching the Senator obey, saw how the balance of control had changed in this room.

"Ideas are in the wind," Custer said. "There comes a time for a thing to develop. It comes into being. The spinning jenny came into being because that was its time. It was based on countless ideas that had preceded it."

"And this is the age of the laser?" Tiborough asked.

"It was bound to come," Custer said. "But the number of people in the world who're filled with hate and frustration and violence has been growing with terrible speed. You add to that the enormous danger that this might fall into the hands of just one group or nation or . . ." Custer shrugged. "This is too much power to be confined to one man or group with the hope they'll administer wisely. I didn't dare delay. That's why I spread this thing now and announced it as broadly as I could."

Tiborough leaned back in his chair, his hands in his lap. His face was pale and beads of perspiration stood out on his forehead.

"We won't make it."

"I hope you're wrong, Senator," Custer said. "But the only thing I know for sure is that we'd have had less chance of making it tomorrow than we have today."

"The Game of Nations":
International Politics as Plaything

War has been described as a game indulged in by "boys" who never grew up. Similarly, international politics often appears to take on the appearance of a game. Indeed, the terminology employed in sports borrows heavily from war and international politics—"the bomb," "blitz," and so on. One of the best books on international politics written from the national-interest point of view is Miles Copeland's *The Game of Nations,* which, while dealing mainly with the Middle East, presents an interesting approach to the study of international relations. Copeland presents a series of "rules" governing behavior in the international arena. For example, "each player wants not so much to win as to avoid loss"—emphasizing the importance of perception and saving face that seems to govern so much behavior in international politics. "All players have no objective except to keep The Game going," because "the alternative to The Game of Nations is war"—highlighting the new conditions of the post–World War II era of nuclear balance and the consequent impossibility of total war as a winning tactic for countries to consider.

This reality constitutes the "board" upon which the game is played, and since the "board" cannot be changed (except by a major technological breakthrough, which is not impossible), one must consider the possibility of "changing the players" through shifts in alliances and intervention in the affairs of others.

In "To End All Wars" Gordon Eklund shows us a possible future where international politics as a game is played a little differently, even though the stakes are very high indeed.

TO END ALL WARS

by Gordon Eklund

"I have to go," Hallmark said. "If I'm not back in time, the ship will leave without me."

"Finish your drink," the girl said. "You can't go yet." She was a redhead with light pale skin and sharp red freckles. Hallmark couldn't remember her name.

"I told you when I met you—I just wanted to talk. You're a nice girl and I like you. But I can't stay. If I don't make that ship, I'll be a deserter."

"Aren't you one now?"

He smiled and shook his head. "I jumped ship. The crew was restricted and I left. I heard there were Terrans in the city and I found you. It's not the first time I've done it. They'll dock my pay and slap my fingers. That's all. But if I don't make it back . . ."

"It doesn't matter," the girl said. "You can't leave. Didn't you notice that everyone left an hour ago?"

Hallmark looked around the barroom. Except for himself and the girl, it was empty. Even the bartender had disappeared.

"I noticed," he said. "But you stayed and I stayed."

"I live upstairs and never go out. Hallmark, didn't anybody tell you about the war?"

"Which war?" He laughed. "There's a dozen raging in this sector right now."

"The Kirkham War," the girl said. "The one that's raging on this planet, the one that's been raging for ten thousand years."

"Wars don't last that long. And, no, I never heard of it. They don't brief you when you're not expected to leave the ship. So there's a war going on? So what? I'm a Terran; you're a Terran. We're neutral. We're always neutral."

She shook her head sadly, red hair swishing across her forehead. "I should have warned you, Hallmark, I should have warned you when I saw you walk through the door. But—you don't know how it is. I haven't seen a Terran in months. I can't talk to the Kirkhamites. They don't think the way we do. I can't—"

"Warn me? Warn me about what?" Hallmark was getting worried. He glanced at his watch. One hour left before departure. He couldn't miss that ship.

"The war—the curfew. Nobody's allowed outside after dark. That's why everyone went home. Why didn't you tell me you had to leave?"

"My ship leaves in an hour. I've got to go."

Finishing his drink, he stood, pulling a spacer's cap over his dark, bristly hair. His thick lips cracked into a grin and he patted the girl lightly on the shoulder.

"If I don't get back," he said, "they'll leave without me. I can't let your local troubles stop me. It's my career—my whole life."

"I understand," the girl said. "It was nice talking to you, Hallmark."

"Good-bye," he said.

"Good luck."

Hallmark went out the door. The street was silent and dark, the dull light of the distant moon providing the sole illumination. The night air was thick and hot and he sweltered inside the tight skin of his spacer's costume.

As he walked along the red-brick sidewalks, the magnetic heels of his boots clicked sharply in the stillness of the night. He stayed close to the squat, square buildings, his eyes probing the darkness, searching for signs of approaching danger.

Three blocks passed, then four. The spaceport loomed ahead, glowing obtrusively in the surrounding blackness. He could see the *Rambler* in its berth, dozens of tiny human figures darting around the ship, preparing it for immediate departure. Hallmark stopped and read his watch. He quickened his pace. Lift-off in twenty-three minutes.

"Halt! Halt or we'll fire!" The voice came from behind and to the left.

Hallmark halted, throwing his hands in the air. A flashlight covered him and two uniformed Kirkhamites approached, their bristly cat-whiskers wagging at him. They held primitive hand-weapons, the barrels aimed at his stomach.

"Who are you?" demanded the tallest of the pair. "What are you doing out here?"

The Kirkhamite spoke Galactic. Hallmark answered in kind: "I'm a member of that ship. The one in port. We're taking off."

"Your name?"

"Hallmark. Engineer Second Class Samuel Baines Hallmark of the *Rambler*. I'm a Terran."

"I can recognize that fact," said the Kirkhamite. "We have many of your species in our city."

The second Kirkhamite spoke softly into a small radio. It hummed at him in reply.

"Are you soldiers?" asked Hallmark.

The taller Kirkhamite acted as if he hadn't heard the question. He walked over to his companion and they conferred quietly in their native tongue. Hallmark kept his hands in the air. His elbows hurt.

The aliens finished purring at each other and turned to face Hallmark. "You are legitimate," said the taller one.

Hallmark lowered his hands tenderly. "May I go?" he asked.

"A question, please," said the Kirkhamite. "Why are you not on your spacecraft? Our leader has requested that all aliens remain outside the limits of our city."

"I had to obtain medicine," Hallmark lied. "Our captain is a very sick man."

"That is indeed a tragedy," said the Kirkhamite. "You must hurry to your craft, Engineer Hallmark. But I would recommend care on your part. Our city is at war."

"So I've heard," Hallmark said. "I will be careful and . . . thank you."

The Kirkhamites turned away and crossed the street. Sighing with relief, Hallmark hurried toward the spaceport. His watch showed a mere fifteen minutes remaining before lift-off.

He'd gone half-a-block when something hard and jagged hit him in the back of the head. He spun on his heel and glared at the night. His vision blurred and a black pool opened at his feet. He threw his arms in the air and fell into it. The black water covered him. He gasped, struggling to breathe. It was useless. He closed his eyes and dreamed of the sun . . .

The ceiling was purple and the walls were orange. Hallmark rolled off the narrow cot and fell to his knees. His head hurt and his body ached. Tiny black dots spun before his eyes.

"Hello!" he yelled. "Anybody home?"

The dots receded and the pain remained. He pushed himself to his feet and sat on the edge of the bed. He looked at the room. It was small, empty, and windowless. He scanned the walls, looking for the outline of a door. The black dots returned and danced across his vision. He raised a hand and pushed them away. He looked at his watch. The figures blurred, then solidified. The hands weren't moving.

I'm lost, he thought. I turned my back and they stunned me. I should never have lied. They knew the medicine story was a fake.

The wall opened and a Kirkhamite walked in. The pale blue fur around his lips crinkled. Hallmark smiled back at him.

"I am Odom," said the Kirkhamite. He stood in front of Hallmark and stuck out a paw. "Would you like to exchange the traditional handshake?"

"I'd rather not," Hallmark said. "I'd like to know where I am. Has my ship left?"

"Your ship?"

"Yes, the *Rambler*. I'm a legitimate crew member. Your soldiers checked me out, then they stunned me. What's this all about?"

"You lied to our soldiers. You had no medicine. Your captain is a healthy man. It was necessary to detain you. We are at war, you know."

"Yes, I know," Hallmark said. "And I'm sick of hearing about it. All right, I admit I lied. Now can I go?"

The Kirkhamite—Odom—smiled again. "Your ship has left our world. You have no place to go."

Hallmark groaned. "I should have known. Look—I want a signed statement from you. I want it explained that I was snatched by your police. I want—"

"You are in no position to make demands. We are aware that you are an impostor."

"I am?"

"You are indeed. You are the Enemy. Normally we dispose of your kind as spies. But fortunately, we have a use for you."

"I'm Samuel Hallmark. I'm a Terran. I'm not your enemy."

"But you are. The Enemy employs many mercenaries. You are not the first Terran we have apprehended. Your disguise was an excellent choice. However, your tale of the medicine was poorly handled—very poorly handled indeed."

"But—" Hallmark rubbed his head and wished the pain would go away. "But I *am* Samuel Hallmark. If I'm not, who is?" He laughed nervously.

"The real Samuel Hallmark has deserted his ship. We are searching for him now. We suspect that he has been captured by the Enemy and executed."

"You have everything neatly arranged," Hallmark said. "I want to see the Terran consul."

Odom wiggled his whiskers. "That will be impossible. We must proceed immediately with the negotiations."

Hallmark stifled an urge to scream. In a calm voice, he asked: "What are you talking about?"

"The peace negotiations, of course. Surely some reports have reached the Enemy. For the past year, we have been talking peace with three of your mercenaries. Unfortunately, two of them just died. Torgans, you know, very fragile creatures. You will have to assume their place at the table."

"I . . . This is getting ridiculous. Look—I can't negotiate peace. I am who I say I am. I know nothing of your war. I don't know who you're fighting or why. I know this war is supposed to have lasted ten thousand years. But that's all I know."

"That's all you need to know. Please—come with me. The discussions are about to commence. And, oh, I did forget to tell you. I am chief delegate for our city."

"Congratulations," Hallmark said.

"Thank you."

The wall opened and Odom passed through it. Hallmark shrugged and followed. Two uniformed guards fell into step behind him. The guards were armed with sophisticated stun-guns.

I have to go along with them, Hallmark thought as he walked rapidly down the narrow corridor. Eventually I can make contact with the Terran consul. He'll get me out of this. I'm lucky they didn't kill me. They must really believe I'm a spy.

Odom passed through a door and gestured at Hallmark to follow. The room was vast and poorly lighted, empty except for two long wooden tables which faced each other in the center of the room. Odom sat down at one of the tables, finding a chair between two native Kirkhamites. Hallmark crossed the room and sat at the other table. Seated next to him was a lanky humanoid creature with dark brown skin.

As the Kirkhamites purred excitedly at one another, Hallmark leaned over and said: "You're not Terran, are you?"

"No, I'm Gouchan." He pointed at two thick horns that protruded from his sloping forehead. "My name is Rejie."

"I'm Hallmark. Tell me—what's this thing all about?"

Rejie chuckled. "Don't try to make sense of it, Hallmark. I gave up months ago. Just lean back and enjoy things. It can be very peaceful in here."

"But, I—"

"Shh, the big man is about to speak."

Hallmark turned in his chair and faced front. Odom was standing behind the opposite table, a long blue scroll clutched in his paws.

"This is the 176th meeting of the Kirkham Peace Proceedings," Odom said, reading from the scroll. "It is now officially in session. At the previous meeting, a proposition was under consideration which would separate our delegation tables by an additional five feet. The arguments of our city in favor of this proposal had been completed and the Enemy was about to make a statement. We will commence negotiations at this point."

Laying the scroll aside, Odom sat down. He glared piercingly at Rejie and waited.

"Our statement died," Rejie said finally. "The Torgans did all our talking. I kept out of things. You know that, Odom."

"Yes, I am aware of your lack of activity. However, with the passing of your comrades, the responsibility has passed into your hands. We regret the demise of the Torgans, but it is essential that the negotiations be carried on. The satisfactory termination of our conflict is necessary for the continued existence of this planet."

"Yes, of course," Rejie said. "I quite agree but . . . what is this table thing all about?"

"Then you agree to our proposal?"

"I didn't say that." Rejie winked at Hallmark. "I'd like a few minutes in which to consult with my colleague."

"That would be allowable," Odom said. "Proceed."

"I need something to write with."

"You will find writing materials in the drawer of your table."

Rejie reached into the drawer and removed a tablet and a lead pencil. Dropping them on the table, he leaned over and whispered in Hallmark's ear: "Let's consult, colleague."

"About what?" Hallmark said, in a low voice. "What's this thing about moving the tables? I don't understand."

"Tables—chairs—pencils and papers—it doesn't mean a damned thing. I've been half-listening to these negotiations for a year. That's all they ever talk about. Hell, they spent six months arguing about the color of paper to use for the minutes. Odom and his friends wanted purple—it's their national color. The Torgans held out for green. As you can see, they eventually compromised at blue. We've been discussing tables now for three months. They've moved them around a dozen times at least."

"But aren't these talks serious? Odom talked like the future of Kirkham rested in our hands. Rejie—are you really a mercenary?"

"No more than you are, Hallmark. I fell down drunk in the street one day and woke up here the next. The Torgans came in a few days later. They fell in love with this whole set-up. Tradition, custom, courtesy—that's what their whole society is based upon. They could beat Odom at his own game. But not me. I just got bored."

"What are we going to do?"

"We're going to put our time to good use, my friend. Watch me." He ripped a sheet of paper from the tablet and drew two vertical straight lines on it. Then, raising the pencil, he crossed the vertical lines with two horizontal ones, creating a neat grid of nine squares. In the upper right hand box, he made a cross.

"I've got the crosses," he said, "and you've got the circles."

"What do I do?"

"It's a game I picked up from another Terran. The first man to get three crosses or three circles in a straight line, any direction, wins. You've got to block your opponent while trying to win yourself."

"I think I see," Hallmark said, rubbing his chin. He picked up the pencil and made a circle in the center square.

"Aha," Rejie said. "That seals your fate." He made a cross in the lower right hand square.

A few minutes later, Rejie clapped his hands and exclaimed: "Got you! Tic-tac-toe!"

The Kirkhamites, deep in consultation, didn't hear. They were playing their own game.

The conference lasted three hours. When it was over, Hallmark was led back to his room. His dinner awaited him and he ate it with pleasure.

Tic-tac-toe, he thought. Is that how they make peace on this planet? It reminded him vaguely of a book he'd once read. In the book, there'd been a croquet game and a queen—the Queen of Hearts —and the queen had made her own rules as she went along.

But even the most nonsensical things had to make sense somehow. An answer was forming in the back of his mind. At the moment, the answer was still incomplete, but what there was of it made sense. It made frighteningly real sense.

The wall slid open and the girl walked through it, her face flushed bright red, matching the color of her hair.

"Hello, again," Hallmark said. "Are these visiting hours?"

"I don't know," she said. "I live here, too."

"Did you tell them that I was the real and original Samuel B. Hallmark? There seems to be some doubt in the matter."

"Are you the real Samuel Hallmark?"

"That's a good question."

"I told them what they wanted to know. They think I'm a spy. Get that, Hallmark. Me—a spy. I've been on this planet three years and suddenly they think I'm a spy."

The girl sat down next to Hallmark. She picked a fat radish off his plate and ate it.

"They feed you good here," she said.

"Have to keep the animals fat and happy. By the way, who is the Enemy?"

"I thought you weren't interested in our petty local disputes."

"I've been made interested. At the present time, myself and a drunken Gouchan are conducting peace negotiations for the Enemy. I'd like to know who I'm representing."

"Your guess is as good as mine." She shrugged. "They're just the Enemy."

"What are you doing here?"

"I guess you were traced to me. I'm living across the hall. They gave me permission to visit you. I join your negotiating team tomorrow." She paused momentarily and sighed. "Hallmark—does any of this make sense to you? If it does, please tell me. So many ridiculous things have happened to me in the last three years that I've gotten used to it. But I still don't like it. When I think about it, it scares me."

"Perhaps it should. Tell me—what are you doing on Kirkham? You're not an immigrant."

"No, I'm not. I came here with my husband. It was a vacation. Richard liked to visit out-of-the-way worlds, like people back on Earth who vacation in Tibet. We didn't live on Earth, so we came to Kirkham."

"Where's your husband now?" Hallmark swallowed his last bite of food and belched.

"I haven't the slightest idea. After we'd been here a week, they slapped a curfew on the city. Richard got caught outside after dark. They put him in the army and sent him to the front—or so they told me. I never heard from him again. I've stayed here since, hoping he might come back. I guess there isn't much chance of that any more."

"You say this war has lasted ten thousand years. I saw a good chunk of the city yesterday. There's no war damage."

"It's fought out in the desert. Most of Kirkham is desert. The armies push each other back and forth, like two big rugby teams. When they clamped the curfew on the city, the Enemy was supposedly only a hundred miles away. But we pushed them back and the curfew stayed."

"Ever seen any wounded—any casualties at all?"

She shook her head. "None—but I've talked to a lot of returning soldiers. You know, trying to get word of Richard."

"Combat troops?"

"I . . . I suppose so. I don't remember. Don't all soldiers fight?"

"What do you know about the negotiations?"

"It's been in the papers for the last year. I really haven't paid very much attention. I mean, this whole war makes me sick. I know that negotiations are being conducted with Enemy mercenaries and that little or no progress is being made. There's never any progress." She laughed sharply. "I never dreamed that I'd become an Enemy mercenary."

"Neither did I. It happens to the best of us."

"How many are there? On our team?"

"Just me and the Gouchan. There used to be two Torgans but they died. The Gouchan claims that he's not a mercenary."

"We're all good guys."

"So it seems."

"Hallmark, I'm tired and I'm going to sleep. I enjoyed our talk and I can hardly wait till tomorrow. And, by the way, my name is Miriam."

"You never did tell me, did you?"

"And you never asked."

After the girl left, Hallmark lay on his cot, his hands folded behind his head. The fragment of an idea formed in his mind and slowly expanded in size and shape. As he watched, the idea became more clear, less formless. It was a good idea, Hallmark decided, the best he'd ever had. *This is the way we win the war.* And he knew that he was right.

Hallmark had been awake for an hour when the guards came to get him. He obediently followed them through the wall and down the corridor. They left him in the negotiating room. The girl—Miriam—was already in place, talking softly to Rejie. Hallmark went over and sat between them.

"Have a nice rest?" he asked Miriam.

"Wonderful—I'm ready to make peace. Rejie was just telling me about tic-tac-toe."

"You two play a few games," Hallmark said. "I'll handle the negotiations."

"Hey," Rejie said. "I thought I was senior man."

"And I thought the whole thing bored you. I've been doing some thinking. I want to put my thoughts into practice."

Rejie shrugged. "Sure, go ahead. Miriam, you take the circles; I've got the crosses."

"No thanks, Rejie. I've got the crosses. I'm not that dumb."

"Hallmark is." Rejie grinned and rubbed his horns. "It took him five games to catch on."

Hallmark ignored the remark, focusing his attention on Odom. The tall Kirkhamite was on his feet, preparing to read from a fresh scroll.

"Is the Enemy ready?" Odom asked.

Hallmark nodded. "Ready."

Odom read: "This is the 177th meeting of the Kirkham Peace Proceedings. It is now officially in session. At the previous meeting, a proposition was under consideration which would . . ."

As the Kirkhamite droned monotonously, Hallmark watched Miriam and Rejie as they played tic-tac-toe. The girl won the first game with a line of crosses diagonally across the board from top left to bottom right.

"A victory for Terra," she said.

"Now it's my turn to win one," Hallmark said. Odom had finished speaking and returned to his chair. Hallmark stood.

"Our side—the Enemy side—would prefer to pass up the argument concerning the positioning of the tables. Instead, we'd like to move into the very heart of the matter—the war itself. We'd like to surrender."

Rejie gasped and Miriam yelped. Odom shook his whiskers and glanced helplessly at his colleagues. The Kirkhamites fastened their eyes firmly to the floor.

"Did you say surrender?" Odom said at last.

"That's what I said."

"But—but you can't surrender."

"Why not?" Hallmark asked.

"Yeah," Rejie added. "Why can't we give up? We're sick of this damned war."

"You—you don't have the responsibility. Your leaders haven't authorized this move. Your generals will continue to fight. This whole thing is absolutely preposterous."

"The hell if it is," Hallmark said. "If we don't have the responsibility to conduct negotiations, what are we doing here? Either accept our surrender or let us go. We relinquish everything. We unconditionally surrender."

"But—but you can't."

"Are you refusing our offer of unconditional surrender? Wait till your press hears of this. I've never heard of such a thing."

"We—we don't refuse," Odom said. "We must confer."

"Go ahead and talk," Hallmark said. "Just make it fast."

Odom turned away and purred nervously at his silent comrades. Hallmark grinned at Miriam and Rejie.

"You shook hell out of them," Rejie said.

Hallmark laughed, "You mean you're not bored any more."

"I want to know what this is all about," Miriam said. "We can't really surrender—can we?"

"I don't know," Hallmark said. "I intend to find out."

"I wish I knew what game you were playing."

"You're not the only one."

The Kirkhamites fell silent and Odom looked at Hallmark. "If we accept your so-called surrender, can you guarantee that your armies will cease fighting?"

"I can," Hallmark said.

Odom twitched. "How can you be so certain?"

"You forget—I'm an Enemy mercenary. Accept my surrender, then go to the war-zone. I bet you won't find a single man under arms."

"I . . ." Odom took a deep breath and said, "This meeting is adjourned."

"No, it isn't," Hallmark said. "We're staying until we get a definite answer. Odom, you're toying with the lives of a hundred thousand men."

"Hallmark, shut up and go to your room. I want to talk privately with you."

"I don't see any need for that. These negotiations are supposed to be open and above-board."

"Hallmark, please."

"Oh, all right." Hallmark chuckled softly. "But anything said to me has to be said to my fellow delegates. After all, we're a team."

Odom sighed and waved a paw. "All three of you go to Hallmark's room and wait. I'll be along shortly."

Grinning, Hallmark climbed to his feet and turned away. Miriam and Rejie followed him. The wall slid open and they passed through it.

They waited in Hallmark's room. Rejie crouched on the floor and lit a cigar.

"I wish I could see the inside of your mind," he said. "You handled Odom like he was a wind-up doll."

"Maybe he is," Hallmark said.

Miriam, lost in her own thoughts, sat silently on the bed. When Odom entered the room, Hallmark tapped her gently on the shoulder.

"The moment of reckoning is here," he said.

"Sorry—I was thinking—about Richard."

"I understand."

Odom carried a chair with him; he planted it in the center of the floor. Glancing uncomfortably at Rejie and Miriam, he sat down. Then he frowned at Hallmark.

"Are you the only one who knows?" he asked.

"The girl has a vague idea."

"How did you find out?"

"It wasn't difficult. You should have stuck with Torgans. They like games. I don't."

"Do you understand our reasons?"

"I don't know what they are. I only have an idea."

"And probably a correct one. Hallmark, this world is almost entirely desert. Ninety-five per cent of the population lives in one city. Do you know why?"

"I haven't studied your history."

"Very few people have. It's a long one. We're an ancient race. Ten thousand years ago, Kirkham was a green, fertile land. Our population was a hundred thousand times what it is now. Then we had a war. The entire planet split into two rival factions. When the war was over, only a handful of people remained alive, the few who'd managed to crawl far enough underground to escape the final decimation bombs.

When the few survivors climbed back to the surface, they were determined that such a war would never happen again."

"So they invented their own war?"

"That's more or less correct. They invented their own enemy, kept him nameless, and fought an endless war with him. As our people struggled back to civilization, the fictitious nature of the war was forgotten. Only a handful of individuals were ever allowed to know the truth. The sands of ten thousand years can cover many secrets."

"And you've been at peace ever since?"

"That's right. We have a small army in the desert which consists entirely of support personnel. Even in an actual war, eighty per cent of an army is non-combatant. I suppose there are certain holes in our scheme. But everyone accepts the war. They always have. There's no reason to disbelieve."

"And these negotiations?"

"It seemed like a good idea at the time. We used alien mercenaries because it never hurts to foment suspicion of outsiders."

Miriam, who had been listening silently, suddenly spoke: "Where is my husband?"

Odom looked at her. "Your husband?"

"Yes, he was drafted into your army. That was three years ago. What have you done with him?"

"Nothing, I hope. He should be out at the front."

"I want him back."

"I'll see what I can do."

"You'll do more than that, Odom," Hallmark said. "We have the upper hand here. You'll do what we say or we'll blab the whole story."

"I doubt that," Odom said. "What prevents us from having you killed?"

"Nothing, but I don't think you will. It isn't necessary. All we ask is that you return the girl's husband."

"And get me off this planet," Rejie said. "After a year, I'm sick of this place."

"I think all of us would rather move on," Hallmark said, "unless you have an objection."

"Certainly not," Odom said, getting to his feet. "I wouldn't have it any other way. I'll try to find the girl's husband. With luck, we should have you on your way before nightfall."

"And I'll need a letter of explanation. Make up your own lies—

you're good at it. I don't want to have to stand trial for desertion."

"I'll take care of it," Odom said.

When they were alone, Rejie turned to Hallmark and asked: "How did you figure that out? It's fantastic. Fight a war to stop a war."

"Sometimes the fantastic is the most logical," Hallmark said.

"And you know, it works," Miriam said. "I've been here three years and I've never seen such a peaceful place. All their energy goes into this war."

"I hope we haven't blown the whole bit," Rejie said.

"I don't think so," Hallmark said. "They'll announce that the peace negotiations have failed and the war effort will have to be re-doubled."

"That's fine with me," Miriam said. "Just as long as I'm far away from it."

"You will be. Rejie—why don't you find a pencil and some paper. I want to play tic-tac-toe."

"I thought you didn't like games, Hallmark."

"I love games—once I figure out how to play them."

The Arms Race

One of the least attractive features of international politics is the seemingly endless competition in armaments. The fear of falling behind the opposition in terms of quality and quantity of weapons is a basic dynamic in foreign and military policy decision-making. This is illustrated by phrases like "peace through strength," which postulates that the resolution of international conflicts can only take place if a country has as much firepower (or more firepower) than its enemies. The balance of power concept is inextricably intertwined with a balance of forces concept.

Moreover, the relative size and capabilities of armed forces are almost always a domestic political issue, especially in the Western democracies. Perhaps the outstanding example of this tendency was the "missile gap" issue in the 1960 election campaign between John F. Kennedy and Richard M. Nixon. In that instance, the "gap" proved to be mostly illusory, but still helped Kennedy to the presidency.

"The Amphibious Cavalry Gap" provides us with important insights into the process by which the arms race develops and accelerates, and does this in only a few hundred words.

THE AMPHIBIOUS CAVALRY GAP

by J. J. Trembly

as told to James E. Thompson

Intelligence reports coming out of Soviet Central Asia and Siberia indicate that the Soviets have undertaken an extensive horse-breeding program.[1] The numbers of horses in the USSR increased fifteen percent[2] or forty-two percent[3] in the period 1968–71. These figures indicate that the Soviet planners have assigned horse-breeding a high priority.

The question now arises: What place does this crash program occupy in Soviet strategic thinking? Here we can only speculate; but, in the light of the Soviet Union's known expansionist aims, it behooves us to consider the possibility that they intend to use those horses against us.

Horses have not been used extensively in warfare since the outbreak of World War Two, when the Polish cavalry proved highly ineffective against German armor.[4] This has led to a consensus of military thought—that is, of Western military thought—that cavalry is obsolete. But can we afford to call cavalry "obsolete" when the enemy has not? The Soviet rulers are not talking about cavalry being "obsolete"; instead, as we have seen, they are breeding more horses.

Someone may object that Soviet cavalry cannot pose a threat to the United States, because the two nations have no common land boundary, but are separated by water; and it has been found that cavalry

---

[1] See DoD Report #BX818RL, "Livestock Populations in Soviet Virgin Lands," Washington, DC, 1971.

[2] Estimate by CIA.

[3] Estimate by US Army Intelligence.

[4] Guderian, Gen. Heinz: "Panzer Leader," trans. C. Fitzgibbon. New York: Dutton & Co., 1952, pp. 65–84.

is effective only on land.[5] Cavalry could, however, be used against the United States by the USSR (or vice versa) if the horses and their riders were transported to the scene of combat by sea or air. If the horses are transported by air, this gives no obvious advantage to one side or the other, as all points on the Earth's surface are equally accessible by air; but if we think in terms of the horses being transported by sea, an ominous conclusion emerges. Let us list the most important cities in the two nations. In our case, this will consist of our national capital plus the four most populous cities; in theirs, of the five most populous, as their capital (Moscow) is also the most populous city: [6]

USSR	USA
Moscow	Washington
Leningrad	New York
Kiev	Chicago
Tashkent	Los Angeles
Kharkov	Philadelphia

When we look at the location of these cities on the map, we find that only one of the key Soviet cities—Leningrad—is located on the sea, while four of the five key American cities are located on the seacoast or very near it—New York, Philadelphia, Washington and Los Angeles. (And even Chicago might be accessible by sea, via the St. Lawrence seaway.) Therefore, we are at least *four times* as vulnerable to amphibious attack as the USSR. When one considers that they also have more horses than we do, the seriousness of the amphibious cavalry gap becomes apparent.

If the horses are to be transported by sea, it must be either by surface ship or by submarine. We can, I think, rule out the use of surface ships, for submarines have the advantage of concealability; if the horses were transported on the decks of surface ships, they could be detected by our sky-spies. So if the Soviets are planning a sneak amphibious cavalry attack on the US, they will almost certainly use submarines, and will be building a larger submarine fleet. This, we find,

[5] See for example, Exodus 14:26–30.
[6] According to population statistics from the 1972 World Almanac.

is precisely what they *are* doing. The Soviet Union now has 401 submarines to only 152 for the United States.[7]

Is there any hope of overcoming the disparity between our military capacity and that of the Soviets caused by our greater vulnerability? In my opinion, there is such a hope; but it can only be achieved by the creation of a greater total striking force proportionate to the enemy's greater invulnerability, that is, four times as many horses, four times as many trained cavalrymen, and four times as many cavalry transport submarines. In the field of submarines alone, this means that, as the Soviets have 401 usable submarines, we need 1,604. Given that our present submarine strength is only 152, we need 1,452 more submarines, to be fitted for cavalry transport, for an adequate defense.

It is urgently necessary that we begin at once to close this gap. The Defense Department should immediately make known the seriousness of the threat, and demand that Congress vote the necessary funds.

Some persons have suggested that a weapons system of the type described poses no real threat; but an experienced submarine commander has assured the author that a cavalry-carrying submarine would be, in his words, "a real *stinker*."

[7] "Jane's Fighting Ships," 1971–72 ed.

Arms Control and Disarmament

Disarmament is one of the most controversial subjects in the field of international relations, and people who advocate the elimination of weapons have been subject to vicious attack. Even the advocacy of arms reduction has brought the patriotism of its defenders into question in the minds of some. This is unfortunate, because the enormous quantity of conventional and nuclear weapons already present in the inventories of the world's armed forces far exceeds the amount necessary to destroy all the major cities in the Soviet Union and the People's Republic of China many *hundreds* of times—the so-called overkill problem.

Advocates of arms control and disarmament also point out that tremendous expenditures on modern weapon systems are very wasteful. The U.S. defense budget of well over $100 billion makes our spending in the social welfare, health, transportation, and energy areas pall in comparison. The new AWACS combat control aircraft may cost as much as $67 million *each.*

Perhaps the most basic question that needs to be answered in the controversy over disarmament (as distinct from arms control) is that of cause and effect. Does the existence of destructive weapons cause antagonisms and fear between countries or is it the other way around—is it fear and distrust that produces the weapons? The majority view is that fear and distrust (which derive from people's suspicion of those different from themselves) produce the dynamics that lead to the acquisition of weapons, and that it is this factor that needs to be overcome before meaningful disarmament is possible. In the final analysis, this may be a task for the anthropologist and psychologist as well as for the international relations expert.

There are also a number of specific technical problems associated with efforts at arms reduction. For example, all weapon systems are not equal. Some aircraft can fly farther, faster, and carry a heavier weapons load than others. Therefore, how many "inferior" planes should one side be allowed to equal a given number of "superior" aircraft? This is called the parity problem and is an issue that has haunted arms control discussions for many decades and is still with us in the current SALT negotiations.

Furthermore, the distrust that produced the weapons in the first place may also be present after an agreement to limit or dispose of armaments. How do we know that the other side is not cheating and hiding its weapons or secretly developing new ones? After all, the *knowledge* to produce weapons will still be present after an agreement. Despite the existence of highly reliable satellites that can tell us a great deal about what is going on in other countries, doubts will remain and we (and the other side) will still have to have some method to physically inspect the territory of the parties to an agreement.

In this exciting story, author Tom Purdom treats us to a vivid example of some of the problems and dangers inherent in the arms control and disarmament process.

REDUCTION IN ARMS

by Tom Purdom

The tip that got us interested in Dr. Lesechko came into Washington from one of our volunteer undercover inspectors, a math teacher from Amarillo, Texas, who was spending a year in the Soviet Union as part of the expanded cultural exchange program. One of our psychologists had planted a file of one thousand names, faces and biographies in her unconscious mind just before she had left the United States in July, and one night in late September she saw Dr. Lesechko and a girl carousing in a restaurant thirty kilometers from the hospital in which Dr. Lesechko was supposed to be a seriously ill mental patient. A name, a picture, and a set of instructions popped into her mind, and she passed the information on to the nearest U.S. consul and gave me the kick in the teeth I had been waiting for ever since I had been appointed Chief of Inspection—the first serious evidence that the Treaty of Peking was the Communist trick all our opponents insisted it had to be.

By itself, of course, the sighting was meaningless. Our undercover inspectors would have been useless without the other secret weapon in our inspection system: a biochemical computer—the biggest in the world at that time—in which we had been filing everything we knew about the Chinese and Soviet blocs and the other nuclear powers. We didn't know something important had happened until a typewriter clattered in an office on the top floor of the computer building, and an intelligence analyst discovered he had a new inconsistency to check. The most promising biochemist in the 1978 graduating class at Leningrad University was not where the official records of the Soviet Ministry of Health said he was supposed to be.

Copies of the analyst's report came into the appropriate offices at the Central Intelligence Agency and the Arms Control and Disarmament Agency marked with a large red URGENT. At ACDA they didn't waste any time bringing it to me.

I read it with my stomach turning over. The strides genetics and biochemistry had taken in the last fifteen years had been one of the main reasons we had insisted that open laboratories had to be part of any treaty to reduce armaments. We were especially worried about a little item the military analysts had dubbed the "ninety-five plus" virus—a disease which could spread so secretly and rapidly the victim nation couldn't possibly develop an immunization (or launch a retaliatory nuclear strike) until ninety-five percent of its population had been killed. Nature and modern medicine had made a virus that lethal a difficult problem—for reasons you will still find in any good textbook on pathology—but at least eight nations had been working on it when we ratified the treaty. Given a brilliant researcher and the new experimental animals Petroyev had just developed at Leningrad University, ACDA's Bureau of Evasion Tactics estimated a secret laboratory could develop a virus in eighteen months or less. The mental hospital in which Lesechko was supposed to be a patient was big enough to house the project on any three floors—and he had been there one year.

My impulse, naturally, was to send a lab inspection team directly to the hospital. I was responsible for the safety of two hundred million people, and I had been working for the Arms Control and Disarmament Agency for fourteen long, frustrating years. If the people I was responsible for were in danger and my life's work was a failure, I wanted to know it right away. If I have to choose between living with an unpleasant truth and living with a question mark, I'd rather live with the unpleasant truth.

If we treated the inspection as if it were something special, however, the Russians would know we were suspicious and would probably destroy anything they might be hiding. I would have to send a team big enough to inspect all twenty-two floors simultaneously. And even that might not be enough. As Evasion had reminded me several times, a determined evader could always blow a site up and make it look like an accident.

I organized a standard lab inspection team instead—one ACDA inspector, one CIA agent, and one biochemist from our per diem consultant list. The Moscow embassy was to issue them a Class A command car—the same kind of hovercar the Army used for a mobile battle group command post—and they were to make a routine, random tour of declared facilities. When they got to the hospital, hopefully, it would look like a routine stop in a journey which hadn't even been planned in advance.

For the ACDA inspector I picked one of the best men on our inspection staff, a young Ph.D. in psychology named Jerry Weinberg. Weinberg spoke Russian fluently—he had been studying it since he was in the first grade—and I had been impressed by his thinking procedures when I interviewed him. He was one of our best human lie detectors, too. According to the tests we gave all our inspectors, he was right ninety percent of the time when he guessed a subject was lying, and seventy percent of the time when he guessed a subject was hiding something. Personnel thought that was phenomenal. Apparently psych training usually dulls the intuition.

Dr. Richard Shamlian of Boston University agreed to fill the scientific slot, and the CIA told us they were sending a veteran agent named Justo Prieto. For eight days I watched the light which represented Weinberg's team creep toward the mental hospital on the big map we used to keep track of our inspectors.

Office hours in the Soviet Union occur during the hours sane people in the United States are home in bed or out enjoying themselves. I had thought about that now and then during the Peking Conference, but I obviously hadn't fully understood what it meant; if I had, I would have been as stubborn as the European and Chinese negotiators put together. When Weinberg called Washington from the mental hospital, it was two p.m. where he was, and I was sitting in a booth in the monitoring room staring at a clock which insisted on reminding me it was only five a.m. on the eastern coast of the United States.

As usual, two cars loaded with Russian secret police had followed the team all the way. Weinberg had made a sudden turn about eighty kilometers from the hospital, however, and he had managed to drive up to the main entrance only an hour after the Russians could have known the hospital was his objective. The team had waited around in the lobby for five or ten minutes after Weinberg had flashed his credentials at the security guard on duty, and then the Assistant Director, Mr. Boris Grechko, had come out of his office and greeted them with great enthusiasm.

They were the first inspection team Grechko had met, it seemed, and he felt the Treaty of Peking was one of the great events in the history of the human race. It was too bad Dr. Rudnev, the Director, had left for the day. Dr. Rudnev had broken into tears the day the treaty had been announced.

Grechko would be happy to show them around, however. He could show them everything but the top eight floors. All the patients on those floors, Dr. Lesechko included, were receiving programmed environment therapy. Rudnev was the only man who could take the inspectors through without wrecking all the progress the patients had made. Dr. Rudnev worked late most nights, poor fellow, and he usually took off one afternoon a week to relax. This just happened to be the afternoon.

I leaned back in my swivel chair and studied the doodles I had been making while Weinberg talked. I had put the picture from the command car on the twenty centimeter screen in the middle of my console, and I could feel the eyes and the brain behind Weinberg's sun glasses evaluating me as I thought. His IQ was about twenty points higher than mine, and I knew he had spent a lot of his spare time studying military history and international politics. I was pretty certain he wasn't going to do research in psychology when he finished his three years with us. He was probably headed for a job with some foundation or non-profit corporation where they would pay him to sit around and think about what the people in the government should be doing. He was the type and the bug had obviously bitten him. Someday he might even find himself on my side of the desk.

"Do you think Grechko's telling the truth?" I asked.

"It feels funny," Weinberg said. "I wouldn't stake my life on it, but I don't feel convinced."

"How can Rudnev take you through without ruining the programmed environments? I thought once you started a programmed environment you couldn't interrupt it for anything."

"It's up to Rudnev. Some psychiatrists won't do it under any circumstances, and some will do it now and then for training purposes. It's a tricky question. Nobody really knows what's right when you've got a technique this new. I asked Grechko if Rudnev had ever taken anybody through before, and he hesitated just a fraction of a second and said "no.""

"Where's Rudnev supposed to be now?"

Weinberg smiled. "Grechko says he doesn't know. He usually goes for a long drive and then takes his wife out in the evening."

I grunted. "Have you asked anybody else in the hospital if Dr. Rudnev does this every week?"

"I asked the security guard in the lobby and Grechko complimented me on my thoroughness."

I grunted again. If they were hiding a clandestine lab in the hospital, somebody had obviously picked up a good tip from the *Congressional Record*. It looked like it was going to be exactly the kind of situation Senator Moro had harassed us about when the Senate had been considering the treaty.

Theoretically every military and scientific installation in the world could be visited by our inspectors at all times. Eight times a year, furthermore, at any time we chose, we could inspect any site which aroused our suspicions. In practice, however, there were bound to be sites which couldn't be inspected under any circumstances. What would we do then?

Our only answer had been the escape clause. Either we would negotiate some satisfactory resolution when such situations occurred or we would abrogate the treaty. To keep the treaty as flexible as possible, we hadn't even included any formal procedure for negotiating. In a world where radical technical change is the norm, we had felt, rigid political procedures are a dangerous mistake.

But that meant we had to feel our way along every time we ran into a problem. We had to keep balancing the military security of the United States against the value of the first inspected arms reduction in the history of the world.

If I told Weinberg to insist on the letter of the treaty and inspect the site at once, and the team discovered Grechko was telling the truth. . . . Even if the Soviet Union didn't withdraw from the treaty in anger, it would be difficult to order an inspection the next time a government made such an objection—and every government in the world would know it.

There was one possibility I had to keep in mind at all times. Instead of a plot to evade the treaty, we might be faced with a plot to wreck it or weaken it. We didn't think the Russians knew about our under-cover inspectors, but things like that have a way of getting out sooner or later; Dr. Lesechko could have been planted in a restaurant to arouse our suspicions—a drugged mentally ill person could probably be manipulated to look like he was drunk and boisterous—and some-one might be hoping I would send our inspectors trooping through the upper floors and wreck the lives of the patients up there for nothing.

Even if the people in charge in the Kremlin wanted the treaty as much as I did, they couldn't exercise absolute control over their sub-ordinates. We were having trouble with people in the CIA and the Pentagon, and they had their hard-liners, too. Sooner or later somebody in the lower echelons was bound to set up a booby trap. If we let them trick us into an inspection which ended in disaster, it would be so easy to put us off that in the future inspection would become a farce, and we would probably have to abrogate the treaty ourselves.

On the other hand, of course, if they did have something hidden in the hospital and I let them stall us, they might use the time to get rid of the evidence. Evasion had calculated it would take five days to move a laboratory big enough to develop a ninety-five plus virus, and at least a day to destroy it without leaving a telltale mess, but that's the kind of calculation wise men forget as soon as they hear it. Whenever some-body on your side proves the enemy can't possibly do something, there's a very good chance the enemy is already developing a way to do it.

"Tell them we want to seal off the hospital until we contact Rudnev," I said. "Anybody can come in but nobody leaves until one of your men searches him. I'll send you six reinforcements right away. You'll be short-handed, but I don't want to put too many people on this yet. They still probably don't know we're especially suspicious. If they are evading, they may think there's still a chance they can talk us into going away."

Weinberg looked thoughtful. I would have given a great deal to know if he approved or disapproved, but I couldn't bring myself to ask. "I'm doing everything I can to make it look like we dropped in on the spur of the moment," he said. "Grechko looked like he really was surprised to see us."

"That's fine," I said. "Don't let anybody leave that place until you're certain they don't have a thing on them—microfilms, samples, anything. If they don't want to be searched, they'll just have to stay there until we get this thing settled. We're taking a risk and I'm counting on you to keep it to a minimum."

"Don't worry," Weinberg said. "If I let anybody slip past me, Justo Prieto will grab them."

"How are you and Mr. Prieto getting along?"

Weinberg shrugged. "He hates the Russians and he probably hates me, too, but so far he's been civil. His Russian is so poor I don't think the Russians know how he feels. He only learned it six months ago, and I think he's got a block against it."

"Keep an eye on him, too," I said. "We still don't know much about him, but he looks like he may be exactly the kind of agent Senator Moro hoped the CIA would send. Let me know right away if you have any trouble."

We signed off and I slumped over the console and went over the whole thing again. Every decision I made had implications which should have paralyzed me. We were moving through unexplored country, and we had to pick our way along step by step.

I called the embassy in Moscow, and the Chief of Inspection for the USSR gave the Soviet Foreign Ministry the good news. The people at the Foreign Ministry who were in charge of relations with arms control inspectors were very polite and understanding, and they assured us they would do everything they could to reach Dr. Rudnev. In the meantime they would telephone the hospital at once and ask the staff to give our inspectors complete cooperation. Semyon Novikov, a diplomat who had been one of our favorite Russians during the Peking Conference, would be on his way to the hospital to help smooth things over as soon as he could get his bags packed.

I put my chief assistant in charge of the monitoring booth and returned to my office and dictated a memo to Ralph Burnham, the Director of the ACDA. Burnham got the tape at a U.N. meeting he was attending in New York and called me while I was eating lunch at my office. He approved of my decision, but he had contacted the White House before he called me, and the President wanted any disturbance at the hospital kept to a minimum. If we entered the site and discovered a violation, we were to keep it a secret and let State take it from there. The President expected to win the election but he was running scared. The continuous deep-probing poll his campaign staff was using indicated twelve percent of the people who were going to vote for him were only mildly committed. They would stampede to the opposition overnight if anything assailed their fears more than Senator Moro was assailing them already. If we discovered a violation before election day and the news got out, the President and the treaty were both dead.

At ten p.m. at the hospital, one p.m. in Washington, the day shift at the hospital went home, and the inspectors searched everyone for hidden records and equipment. It took three hours and there was a lot of grumbling.

At two a.m. at the hospital, five p.m. in Washington, Weinberg and his men settled down to the dreary rhythm of guard duty. The Soviet Foreign Ministry still claimed it was looking for Dr. Rudnev. They had phoned his apartment and sent a man to knock at his door, but no one had answered. In the towns around the hospital the local police were searching the restaurants and theaters.

I called my wife to tell her I wouldn't be home and sprawled on a cot to sleep.

My assistant woke me up at midnight. Dr. Rudnev had returned to the hospital at eight-thirty a.m. hospital time—he claimed he and his wife had spent the night at a lakeside lodge sixty kilometers from the hospital—and Weinberg and Novikov had been talking to him for half an hour. He refused to escort the inspectors through the programmed environment wards. The treaty was important to him, he claimed, but he was a doctor and the welfare of his patients came first. Other psychiatrists might be willing to interrupt a program, but he refused to take the risk. The papers he had read indicated several potentially curable patients had been permanently damaged by psychiatrists who interrupted their programs.

Most of the senior people in my bureau were standing by in their offices. I flashed everybody who might be relevant, and we got together in the conference room and spent an hour and a half looking for a way out. We even considered flying in enough American psychologists to put one American role-player in every programmed environment in the hospital. It would have cost the government thousands, but we all knew the President would get us the money if it would save the treaty.

Unfortunately it was impossible. We always came back to the same problem. If we did anything like that, the Russians would be in control of the inspection. Conceivably they might even move lab equipment from room to room as our inspectors went along with Dr. Rudnev's programs.

We had to think about safety margins, too. To be successful, lab inspections had to take place with the minimum possible notice. They could destroy laboratory equipment and laboratory records, but we couldn't destroy the information in Lesechko's head. I would have insisted on immediate access, in fact, if we hadn't been certain they didn't know we were especially interested. As it was, now that we were there, we couldn't give them more than a few days to study the situation. When your opponent has a static situation to attack, and all the resources of a modern society at his disposal, you have to assume he can knock down any barrier you put up if you give him enough time.

At three a.m. I got on a three-way hookup with Dr. Rudnev and a high ranking assistant to the Soviet Foreign Minster, and we tried some high-level persuasion. I didn't think it would do much good, but I wanted to get a look at the people I was dealing with before I called Burnham and recommended that we use one of our unrestricted inspections.

Dr. Rudnev was a stout, spectacled man who probably looked pleasant and easy going most of the time, but the situation had made him angry and uncomfortable. For a man trained in all the checking, cross-checking and skepticism which are a necessary part of science, he was unreasonable in a very suspicious way. He kept getting angry because I was doubting his word. Nothing I could say could convince him I didn't distrust him any more than a man in my position had to distrust everybody.

"I will not sentence twenty-six human beings to a lifetime of insanity," he kept saying. "If I let your inspectors blunder through those floors wrecking the programs, I'll have destroyed the last hope some of those patients have. We aren't hiding anything. We believe in the treaty as much as you do. Why should I want to wreck a treaty that's given the government enough extra funds that it can add twenty percent to my budget?"

We went round and round the same arguments for at least half an hour before we all got so frustrated and impatient that I decided

I'd better give up before somebody created an international incident. The Russian diplomat apologized to me for the trouble we were having, and I told him it was all right and assured Dr. Rudnev we understood his position.

"I'm certain there's a solution to this," I said. "I'm sorry we've had to bother you, Dr. Rudnev. I'll talk to my superiors, and we'll try to work something out that will satisfy all of us."

Weinberg returned to the command car, and I talked to him over our private, scrambled hookup. He had been watching while I was talking to Dr. Rudnev. "What do you think?" I asked. "Are they telling the truth?"

"There's something wrong with both of them," Weinberg said. "Grechko's too smooth and Rudnev's too excited."

"What about Novikov?"

"He seems all right. I think he's just as worried about the treaty as we are."

I added a few triangles to my doodles. I had already made up my mind, but I still had to hesitate a second.

"I'm going to recommend an unrestricted inspection," I said. "Be ready to go in."

"What if they try to stop us?"

I hesitated again. "Be prepared to force your way in. I don't know if the President will tell you to, but be ready. Don't let anybody you've got there leave the site for anything. If anything does happen, we don't want it to go any further from the hospital than it has to. Nobody you've got there is to talk about this with anybody from outside the site. If Prieto or anybody else disobeys, they're breaking security. Put them under arrest and keep them under guard."

"Anything else?"

"How are you fixed for supplies? Can you eat and sleep there for several more days?"

"Novikov had them put all the facilities of the hospital at our disposal. They may try to poison us, but they won't starve us to death."

I smiled. "Make sure you get served out of the same kettle as everybody else."

I called Burnham's hotel suite in New York, and the President talked to both of us as he flew back to Washington from a campaign speech in Denver. We assumed the Russians would deny us access, and we would have to negotiate with them. Before the negotiations began, we had to let them know we would withdraw from the treaty if they destroyed the lab while we were negotiating and tricked us into inspecting real patients. If they wanted to keep the treaty, they could either prove no lab had ever been hidden in the hospital—let their technical staff and ours figure out how—or they could show us the lab and give us all the information Lesechko had obtained.

Dr. Rudnev turned livid when Weinberg formally demanded access under Article VI. He slammed down an alarm button and hospital security guards scurried to every elevator and passageway in the place.

"We'll guard our patients with our lives," Rudnev yelled. "Go near those floors and we'll shoot to kill."

We notified the Soviet Foreign Ministry at once. "This is the first time any inspector has been threatened," Burnham told the Assistant Foreign Minister in charge of relations with arms control inspectors. "I realize Dr. Rudnev is under exceptional emotional pressure, but this is a challenge to the entire concept of inspection. I have to tell you we consider this the most serious disagreement since the ratification of the treaty."

Phone calls buzzed between Moscow and Dr. Rudnev. Weinberg reported Novikov was doing everything he could to keep everybody calm and make sure nobody got rattled and started shooting. I looked over the plotting board and sent five more inspectors moving toward the hospital.

Burnham arrived in Washington by helicopter just before dawn, and I stood behind him and listened while he and the Assistant Foreign Minister had another talk. The Foreign Ministry now wanted to know why we had to inspect the upper floors. Their talks with Dr. Rudnev, they claimed, had convinced them his objections had some validity.

"In cases such as this," the Assistant Foreign Minister said, "we feel that the inspecting country must offer the host country some reasonable evidence that an illegal facility may be hidden on the disputed site. Why should the welfare of so many patients be endangered by a routine inspection? The Foreign Minister wishes to point out that inspection itself could be used as a weapon to disrupt morale and efficiency."

I went back to my office and took a nap. The White House was in charge now. They would call me if they needed me.

At twelve-thirty a.m. the next evening, hospital time, a car turned off the highway and rolled up the driveway toward the main entrance. The Russian guards at the foot of the hill waved it on after an animated

discussion with the two men inside, and the American inspector halfway up stopped it again and passed the buck to the inspectors posted
in front of the main entrance. The driver claimed they were there to
see a psychiatrist who was an old friend of theirs. They had driven
ninety kilometers out of the way and then discovered that their friend
was on the night shift.

Prieto checked the staff roster and made sure the doctor they were
asking about was actually on duty. An orderly went upstairs to page
him, and an inspector ushered the two men into the lobby and stood
guard while they waited. *"Druzhba i Mir,"* one of the men shouted at
the inspectors standing around the command car. "Friendship and
Peace. Long live the Treaty of Peking."

Prieto waited a minute for some reason and then entered the lobby
and told the inspector to frisk the two men for weapons. Weinberg
was asleep and most of the inspectors present had come to think of
Prieto as the second-in-command. Cooperation with the CIA men assigned to watch us was one of the Ten Commandments I had given our
inspectors. I didn't want the Congress to think the CIA needed more
authority than it already had.

The visitors jerked pistols out of their jackets as the inspector approached them. The inspector dropped to the floor with a bullet in his
chest, and Prieto threw himself behind a chair and started shooting.
One of the Russians went down, but the other Russian ducked behind
some furniture and filled the room with a cloud of gas.

Prieto punched the emergency siren on his gadget belt. He crawled
out of the lobby with a handkerchief over his face just as four hovercars streaked across the snow toward the hospital.

The hovercars came up the hill out of a moonless night. The guards
barely had time to give the alarm. Sirens rang on every inspector's belt.
The men standing in front of the main entrance scattered for cover.
Gas bombs exploded. Bullets raked the driveway and the porch. The
cars halted and men in gas masks jumped out and charged the main
entrance.

Prieto retreated into the lobby. Men plunged toward him through
the gas and he fired at them and crawled under a sofa. The gas was
a sleep-inducer, but somehow he managed to hammer the elevator
controls with bullets while he switched on his mike and told Weinberg
what was happening.

Weinberg had just gone off duty. He was lying in his underwear in
one of the rooms on the second floor which Novikov had made the

hospital provide the inspectors, and he was eating a peanut butter and jelly sandwich—his mother sent him the peanut butter and jelly from Vermont—and putting himself to sleep with a history of the Crimean War. The alarm jolted him out of his stupor, and he switched on his intercom unit and grabbed his pants.

Shots and confused shouts prodded him as he dressed and ran out in the hall. He heard Prieto calling him through the din in the intercom, and he picked up just enough to know the elevators were probably out of commission. Outside the hospital the inspectors posted around the main entrance were exchanging shots with the four hovercars, and the Russian guards posted at the bottom of the hill were helping them.

Weinberg organized the other three men who were off duty and started down the center stairway just as the invaders abandoned the elevators and started up. Gas and flying bullets filled the stairwell. The hospital security guard posted at the bottom of the stairs tried to intervene, but a bullet from downstairs killed him instantly. Weinberg dragged a bed out of one of the rooms and jammed it across the stairs, and two of his men went to block the stairway at the other end of the hall.

The inspectors who had been walking guard in back of the hospital came inside through a back entrance and managed to pour bullets into the lobby from one more direction. The gas was being pulled out by the ventilating system, and the raiders seemed to be out of bombs. In the first minutes of the battle they had filled the lobby with three times the gas they needed.

The raiders backed out of the hospital and ran for their hovercars. They screamed down the hill with bullets cracking all around them as the Russian guards revved up their vehicles and sped after them.

In Washington everybody in the monitoring room was standing up. When an inspector pressed his alarm, the command car automatically relayed everything the local intercom system picked up. The monitor assigned to the hospital had flashed Moscow, and the night watch at the embassy was recording everything the monitoring room received.

I got to the monitoring room just as the raiders were leaving. Burnham came in looking grim and listened over my shoulder while the monitor filled me in. In the background the noise at the hospital crackled in the loud speaker.

Weinberg reported while Prieto was recovering from the gas. Three inspectors had been wounded and the inspector who had been shot in the lobby was dead. "We've found two of them dead," Weinberg said.

"We're examining them now to see if we can find anything on their bodies. Novikov's been doing everything he can to help us."

The Ambassador and the Chief of Inspection for the USSR had come in on the embassy screen. They looked as bad as we felt. The Chief of Inspection was wearing a bathrobe and the Ambassador had been pulled away from a full dress dinner.

"I think we can all see what the possibilities are," Burnham said. "Either the hard-liners tried to pull a coup or the government has something hidden there it wants very bad. Either way they'll tell us it was an anti-treaty faction. If it really was, then we've got two possibilities—either there's something hidden there, or they did it to make an incident and bust the treaty that way. I suggest we tell the Foreign Minister we want to question Rudnev and Grechko. If they'll talk, we won't have to bother any legitimate patients."

The Ambassador left the screen to call the Foreign Ministry. Weinberg got his men organized, and the Chief of Inspection and I sent ten more men to the hospital. Burnham sent an urgent message to the White House, and the President asked us to give Prieto his personal thanks.

Little by little the men in the monitoring room got themselves under control. The Foreign Ministry told the Ambassador they were mortified, and another phone call from the White House advised us Premier Kutzmanov had already apologized to the President via the hot line. Every attempt would be made to track the anti-treaty hoodlums down, Kutzmanov claimed. A battalion of crack Russian troops was already speeding toward the hospital.

Secret police roused Rudnev and Grechko and rushed them to the hospital in an official limousine, and Weinberg and Prieto questioned them while Novikov looked on. Grechko remained affable and unruffled, and Dr. Rudnev threw out every explanation for the raid he could think of. The whole thing was a trick to sabotage the treaty, Rudnev shouted. Someone was trying to make him and his hospital look bad. Some of his patients were very important and had enemies, and someone might be trying to make sure one of them stayed in the hospital. Why wouldn't anyone believe him?

Weinberg and Prieto made a good interrogation team. Weinberg was calm and reasonable, and Prieto went after the two Russians like an animal which had been let out of its cage. And in the background Novikov sat in an arm chair and listened without interrupting. Novikov was a very reserved man most of the time, and I had often wondered what he was thinking when I was dealing with him at Peking, but everyone who had ever worked with him had been convinced he wanted the treaty as much as anybody in the Arms Control and Disarmament Agency. He had reacted to the raid with a fury which had looked to Weinberg like it exceeded the limits of deceit by several magnitudes, and now he sat back and let Prieto go as far as he wanted. I don't like simple explanations of human behavior, but according to our file on him, Novikov had as much reason to hate war as anybody on Earth. He had lost both parents in World War II, and his eldest son had been killed in the Siberian border incident.

Nothing could shake Rudnev and Grechko, however. Prieto's bullying merely irritated them, and with all his knowledge of programmed environment therapy Weinberg couldn't trap them in a technical mistake which would indicate there was something wrong with the programmed environment wards.

"Do what you want," Rudnev said after an hour and a half. "Go upstairs and see for yourself. I've done everything I can. It's your responsibility."

The next step, logically, was to question the rest of the staff and see if their stories all matched. That would take time, however, so Weinberg decided to try a mechanical lie-detector test instead. He set up an eye-blink camera—the lie detector in which we had the most faith—and photographed Rudnev and Grechko while they looked over a floor plan of the hospital and answered questions. The results wouldn't be conclusive, but with a little luck an analysis of the photographs might give us the information we needed to decide if we should insist on an inspection.

In spite of the raid and all the other evidence we had been accumulating, we were still hesitating. We had to balance the weight of the evidence against the consequences of a mistake. It would be a terrible tragedy if we let saboteurs wreck the treaty before we had finished the first year of the experiment.

It would be just as tragic, however, if we let the Soviet Union develop a ninety-five plus virus in secret. At the White House the President was drafting a message which left us no room for retreat if the Soviet Union failed to comply. If we didn't find a satisfactory solution in a very short time, we were going to withdraw from the treaty.

The situation wasn't hopeless. We had the eye-blink photographs, and we were exploring several other leads which might tip the scales sooner or later. It might be several days before we found a solution, however, and we had no guarantee we were going to succeed. Like it or not, I had to sit at my desk and stare at the possibility that the treaty had been an illusion instead of a victory. I wasn't sure it was something I could live with. I was getting too old to find a new hope.

Justo Prieto had been seventeen when Fidel Castro marched into Havana on January 1, 1959. His family had started out thinking Castro was the savior of their country, according to the interview he gave the CIA agents who recruited him in Guatemala, but sometime in the next eighteen months they had decided Castro had betrayed them, and they had started working in the anti-Castro underground. Prieto's brother had died in the roundup that had followed the Bay of Pigs fiasco, and his sister had spent the last twelve years of her life in a Cuban prison. And Prieto himself had escaped from Cuba two jumps ahead of Castro's police and started working for the CIA before he was twenty. The clandestine struggle for South America was probably the bloodiest, dirtiest chapter in the entire Cold War, and Prieto had spent his entire adult life in the thick of it.

He had spent five years fighting Communist terrorists in Colombia, and after that the CIA had given him the same kind of work in half a dozen other countries. Time after time, month after month, for twenty years he had seen the people he worked with shot down and tortured by Communist agents. He had been an eye-witness when Communist infiltrators had deliberately turned a provincial revolution in Chile into a blood bath, and he had seen the bodies of hundreds of men, women and children who had been murdered by people who were supposed to be Communists. And he had never forgotten that his family had been destroyed by the followers of a man who had claimed he was a Communist, too. He had been turned down every time he had asked for an assignment in Cuba because his superiors knew he had promised he would kill the man who had betrayed his sister.

To a man like that there could only be one explanation for an arms control treaty: it was a Communist trick and the people in the United States who had engineered it were either fools or traitors. You can't argue with the lessons that kind of experience teaches. I never went to a disarmament conference in the years before the treaty without remembering that the men on the other side of the negotiating table were hated by people all over the world for very good reasons. We would have been pretty stupid if we had been surprised when we started having trouble with the people in the CIA who had that kind of background.

Weinberg had taken my orders seriously, and Prieto had been under somebody's surveillance almost every minute. Weinberg was short three men, however, and the excitement and his own fatigue had put him off guard. When they left the interrogation room to have the films developed and Prieto said he was going upstairs to rest, Weinberg nodded and let him go by himself. Prieto obviously needed sleep. He had been keeping himself awake twenty hours out of every twenty-four and he was showing the strain.

It was a bad time to be lax. The hospital was still in a state of confusion. The hospital security guards were essentially orderlies trained to handle night-watchman duties and brief emergencies, and they had been standing guard for thirty-six hours because of a crisis few of them understood. On the second floor no one had replaced the guard at the center stairway who had been killed during the fight, and on the upper floors the guards were apparently standing around the corridors exchanging rumors. Thanks to the popular sentiment in favor of the treaty, the conspirators had been afraid to tell the hospital staff the truth about Lesechko.

Prieto killed the guard at the south stairway with one shot from his silenced pistol. He shot another guard on the eighth floor, and he clubbed a guard on the tenth unconscious, but he didn't set off a general alarm until he reached a three-man barricade on the twelfth floor and shot out the lights before he opened fire on the guards. By the time Weinberg learned he was on the loose, he was in Lesechko's quarters snapping pictures with a miniaturized camera with one hand and shooting it out with Lesechko's assistants with the other.

The assistants had been standing guard, too, but they were amateurs matched against a pro, and there were only five of them. The entire setup had been crowded into three rooms—a room for Lesechko and a computer installation on the eighteenth floor, and a combination sleeping room and lab on the nineteenth—by cutting the normal number of assistants in half and getting forty hours work out of every twenty-four man-hours. Animal cages lined the walls from floor to ceiling, and the three rooms were so crowded with equipment they made a space capsule look like a good place to stretch your legs. If we had inspected formally, they could have destroyed the records and presented us with a setup which could have been exactly what they claimed it was —a programmed environment for a mentally ill biochemist. And afterwards they could have back tracked a few months and started again.

The fight probably didn't last very long. There was no room to maneuver in, and the work benches were the only things any of them could have hidden behind. Prieto apparently started shooting as soon as he entered the lab—either he didn't care or he decided it was an illegal facility as soon as he saw it looked like a lab—and two of the assistants went down right away. Another assistant ran downstairs and hid with Dr. Lesechko, but the other two assistants managed to get their guns out and trade a few shots before he put them out of action, too. They had been trained in marksmanship and hand-to-hand combat, but from what we learned later, I gather none of them had ever been in a real fight before. They were no match for an experienced man driven by emotions so strong he had apparently become a ruthless fanatic.

He grabbed an empty animal cage and started stuffing it with all the files and notebooks that looked interesting to him. Alarms were hammering all over the place, but he stopped long enough to pick up a stack at least eighteen inches high.

He ran into the hall with the cage under his arm. A psycho-gas bomb stopped the Foreign Ministry agents who were coming up the stairs, and he covered his retreat by breaking into the legitimate programmed environments and running through the rooms yelling at the top of his lungs and firing his pistol. Patients and role-players in fantastic varieties of dress and undress crowded into the hospital and ran from environment to environment. The hospital guards had to choose between a pursuit they didn't understand and the horrors of a full-fledged riot which might erupt into the rest of the hospital. The government agents pursuing Prieto suddenly found themselves shouting through locked doors at bewildered members of the hospital staff. With one crisis piled on another, and the chief administrators of the institution locked in the interrogation room, the administrative structure of the hospital collapsed.

Weinberg had already advised Washington that Prieto was on the loose. He had tried to talk to Novikov, but the Russian had waved him off. Russian agents had closed in on the command car, and our men and theirs were eyeing each other warily. The situation was escalating into an international crisis of the first magnitude. I was in the monitoring room listening to Weinberg and talking to the White House and the Moscow Embassy. Burnham was on his way.

Weinberg looked disgusted. He didn't say it, but he obviously blamed himself. He had dropped his guard for five minutes and now he had to sit in the command car and watch the whole situation go up in flames. There wasn't a thing we could do except tell the Russians we were sorry and cross our fingers.

"I can't find a thing out," Weinberg said. "The Russians won't tell us anything, and we can't get Prieto to answer the intercom. I don't know how he expects to get out. They're moving in every man they've got except the ones they've got around us. It looks like they've got a couple of men at every exit."

"How do they look?" I asked. "Do they look hostile?"

"They look more like they're puzzled."

Burnham came in and stood beside me. "What the Hell happened?" he said.

Weinberg looked embarrassed. "He slipped through before they got re-organized," I said.

The President came in on the White House screen, and Burnham and I sat down in another booth and filled him in. He was just as upset as we were, but he decided not to cancel a television debate with Senator Moro which was supposed to take place in only three hours—nine-thirty p.m. Washington time. It would be an ordeal, but he still didn't want the press to know something special was going on.

Inside the hospital Prieto was working his way down floor by floor. He had put on a robe and a mask he had stolen from a role-player in one of the programmed environment wards. He had shot his way into a maximum security ward and added to the chaos by setting free some of the more violent patients. Thirty minutes after he left Lesechko's lab, he was crouching on a balcony in the back of the hospital.

He probably could have gotten away if he had jumped, but for a person with his outlook that was impossible. If they had shot him while he was running down the hill, the Russians would still have known most of the results of Lesechko's experiments, and we wouldn't have known enough to develop an immunization. He wanted to wreck the treaty, but he didn't want to leave the world at the mercy of the Kremlin. He called Weinberg on the intercom instead and made a proposition.

Weinberg listened with a poker face. Prieto wanted him to break through the Russian guards and drive the car under the balcony. Once the car was parked he was supposed to get out and keep running until he was at least a hundred meters from the car—far enough that he couldn't get to the body before the Russian guards in case he pulled a doublecross and shot Prieto. In addition, when Prieto got in the car Senator Moro or one of Senator Moro's best known aides had to be standing by on a radio and phone hookup.

Weinberg turned around in the car so it looked like he was talking to the three men sitting with him. It was a bitter moment, but he managed to keep thinking. "All right, Justo," he murmured. "We'll have the car under the balcony as soon as we get Senator Moro. I hope you live to see the results."

"Tell it to your mother," Prieto said. "Move."

Weinberg shut off the intercom mike and called Washington. "This is a field recommendation. I don't have time to explain. Have somebody from Moro's camp stand by on this hookup. Don't tell him what it's all about, but have him ready. You've got about ten minutes to do it."

I glanced at Burnham. Weinberg was tired out and he had made a bad blunder, but he was still one of my best men. "I suggest we do what he says," I said.

Burnham studied the round face in the screen. For a moment he and Weinberg stared at each other across eight thousand kilometers and twenty years of experience. We could both guess Weinberg was making a request which could mean the end of everything we had worked for.

"Can you save the treaty?" Burnham said.

"I'm going to try," Weinberg said.

"Go ahead."

Weinberg's screen blanked. Burnham stood there with a hard look on his face, and I sat down in a vacant booth and started calling Senator Moro's headquarters.

Weinberg made sure the three men in the command cars were properly armed, and then he started whispering orders. They were to stay where they were until we had somebody from Moro's team standing by. After that, if he was still talking with the Russians, they were to give him ten more minutes. If he signalled, or if the Russians attacked him, they were supposed to break out and get to Prieto.

"If you have to shoot—shoot," Weinberg said. "Do whatever you have to to help Justo get away. If the treaty goes, we've got to have whatever he's got."

The Russians watched him walk across the snow toward their command car. A Foreign Ministry agent stepped in front of him as soon as he got close enough to hear their car radio.

"I have to have a private conference with your chief," Weinberg said. "Tell him it's urgent."

The agent relayed the message and Weinberg waited while Novikov talked to the men sitting in the car with him—two secret police and an army officer. The hospital was lit up from top to bottom, and men were running around as if the place were on fire. Two of the violent patients Prieto had set free were running loose on the lower floors.

Novikov got out of the car and stalked toward Weinberg. He gestured and the Russians standing around the car backed out of earshot.

"What do you want?" Novikov said.

Weinberg explained the situation as fast as he could. "I don't have to spell it out for you," he said. "Everybody in Washington says you worked hard to get the treaty. If we let Prieto get away from here with what he's got, the treaty is finished. If he doesn't get away with the records, on the other hand—if we let you keep whatever Lesechko has in his head—then your country will have mine at its mercy. There's only one way we can save the treaty—let us have the records, and we'll keep the violation a secret. If you'll help me get the records away from him, that's what we'll do."

Novikov looked from his men to our command car. In the Russian command car the officer and the two secret police were watching the conversation.

"How do you know it was an illegal lab?" Novikov asked. "Dr. Lesechko's program called for a mock laboratory."

"Prieto read me some of what's in the records. Even if he's wrong, the evidence is good enough that we have to assume he's right. Washington knows there may have been a lab there, and they know you may have been developing a ninety-five plus virus. I think you can imagine what will happen if they think you may start mass producing the virus soon—and we don't know enough about it to develop a cure. The arms race we just finished will look like a game of chess."

"What do you want me to do?"

"Let me get to him first. Tell your men not to interfere with me.

Tell them to keep out of shooting distance. Don't interfere with our car either."

Novikov put his hands behind his back and stared at the hospital. Weinberg waited while he thought.

"Someone in my country set up that laboratory," Novikov said. "Do you think my government did it?"

"For our purposes it doesn't matter."

"Prieto will still know about it. Can't he still reveal the information later?"

"He won't have the evidence."

"Won't some people in your country take his word?"

Weinberg swallowed. He had been hoping he wouldn't have to commit himself. He had made up his mind before he left the command car, however. If Prieto ever got in touch with anybody who worked for Senator Moro, with or without the evidence, it might be enough to swing the election.

"He's disobeying orders," Weinberg said. "If I arrest him and he tries to resist . . ."

Novikov shook his head wearily. "You're a young man. Are you sure you know what you're saying?"

Weinberg hesitated again. Only a few days before, he and Dr. Shamlian had been talking about *War and Peace* as they drove across the Russian countryside, and he had mentioned a passage which had stuck in his mind ever since he first read it. Whenever people talk about the good of humanity, Tolstoy had said, they are always getting ready to commit a crime.

"I can do what I have to do," Weinberg said. "I don't like it but it's the only choice we've got."

Novikov shook his head again. "When do you want to enter the building?"

"As soon as I talk to my men."

"Don't waste a second. I'll do my best, but I may have problems."

Weinberg returned to his car while Novikov called some of the Foreign Ministry men to him and started giving them instructions. Novikov could talk to most of his men on his intercom system, but the hospital guards had to be reached by a messenger.

Weinberg explained the situation to the inspectors in the car. They were to start forward five minutes after he entered the hospital. If all went well, he would be on the balcony by the time they got there.

When he turned around Novikov was talking with one of the secret police. The army officer and the other police agent were climbing out of the car.

He started toward the hospital. Several Foreign Ministry agents entered ahead of him and started spreading the word. When he looked back Novikov was shaking his intercom unit and arguing with the army officer and the police agents. One of the police agents jerked the intercom out of Novikov's hand, and the army officer shouted something.

Weinberg crossed the lobby at a trot. One of the American inspectors posted there fell in beside him when he yelled an order, and they ran up the stairs with their pistols in their hands. "No one in pistol range," the Foreign Ministry agents shouted. "Let the Americans through. Stay out of pistol range."

The Russians got out of their way. Behind them two inspectors took up positions at the bottom of the stairs.

They ran down the rear corridor and stopped in front of the office which opened onto the balcony on which Prieto was hiding. There were no Russians in sight. If the car broke out on schedule, they were all right.

Weinberg took a strip of explosive out of the kit he had gotten out of the car and fastened it onto the lock. The noise would tell Prieto he was coming, but he didn't have time to fool around with a pick. From what he had seen of the argument between Novikov and the other three Russians, he could probably expect visitors at any minute.

His hand started shaking, and he stopped and got himself under control. In spite of what he had told Novikov, he wasn't ready for this. He liked Prieto—he sympathized with anybody he thought he understood —and his training had taught him just how little men are responsible for their actions. He had become a doctor because he wanted to heal and an arms control inspector because he wanted to help put an end to slaughter.

He was scared, too. He had never been shot at in his life, but Prieto was a trained fighting man who had just proved he was exceptionally competent.

A Russian appeared at the end of the corridor. The other inspector brandished his weapon and the Russian disappeared.

Weinberg pulled the detonator strip off the explosive and stepped back. The explosion hammered at the walls of the corridor. The door shook on its hinges, and he dropped to one knee and jerked it open.

He was facing an outer office. In the light from the hallways he could see another door a few feet away. When he tried the handle, the second door was locked, too.

Voices shouted in the hall. An inspector yelled a warning from the stairs. Guns cracked.

He stuck a strip of explosive on the inner door and jerked the detonator off. Again he swung the gun around an empty office looking for a target. He could make out the door to the balcony on the other side of the room. The only window in the place was a narrow, vertical pane far to one side of the balcony; it obviously wasn't meant to be opened, and he could have fired at the balcony from it only if he had been able to lean out. Prieto had picked his rathole with the skill of a craftsman.

The inspector in the hall ran into the outer office and flopped behind a desk. Bullets ricocheted off the walls of the corridor. Hovercar turbines screamed.

Weinberg hopped into the inner office and slammed the door behind him. The inspector outside yelled at him to hurry.

He stood on one side of the balcony door and blew the lock off. Two bullets crashed through the wood from the other side. Prieto hissed something in Spanish.

His eyes fell on a swivel chair. He pulled it to him and heaved it out as he threw the door open. Prieto grunted and he stepped outside.

Prieto's gun flamed in his face. He fired and Prieto fired back. A bullet slammed into his chest. He heard Prieto gasp, and they both fired again. A bullet cracked above his head as he slid down the door frame.

The inspectors in the car yelled at him. He was going under, but he was conscious enough to realize Prieto was down and the cage with the records in it was sitting on the floor in front of him.

He slumped to his knees and picked the cage up. Before he blacked out he managed to push it over the edge of the balcony. The men in the car grabbed it and took off with two Russian hovercars hot on their tail.

The chase lasted half an hour at the most. Once Dr. Shamlian had scanned the records and transmitted the important data to Washington, we had the advantage. Novikov took command again, and the Russian medics rushed Weinberg to the operating room. Doctors flew in from both capitals to keep him alive. He ended up with a new lung and a daily shot to correct the brain damage, but he survived.

We negotiated in secret all through the presidential campaign. For weeks we examined the situation as exhaustively as we had originally examined the treaty. We were faced with the same old mystery. Did the Soviet government want the treaty or had the men in the Kremlin planned the violation from the start? In a world where rapid technological change was the norm, could we police an arms control agreement if our opponent was determined to violate it?

The events at the hospital proved nothing. The Soviet claim that the violation had been committed by a militarist faction fitted the facts as well as the theory that the violation had been directed by the Kremlin. Even the last minute attempt to stop Weinberg was explained as a spontaneous move by three over-zealous men who thought Novikov had exceeded his authority. The three men were given prison sentences, as were Lesechko, Rudnev and Grechko, but what did that prove? Clandestine agents have often gone into danger knowing they would be richly rewarded if they succeeded and disowned and severely punished if they failed.

Even if the violation had been planned by the Soviet government, Kutzmanov and his aides could have done it to quiet down the hardliners and the military men who were getting nervous about our political victories in Africa and South America and wanted a good weapon in reserve in case we got carried away and pushed toward their homeland. A violation, paradoxically, could be evidence that a government wanted to preserve the treaty.

The President made his decision right after Christmas. We would keep the violation a secret and stick with the treaty. We came out of the negotiations with three more unrestricted inspections per year and an increase in the number of inspectors we could post in the Soviet Union.

The official records show Prieto died by accident. Burnham asked the President to give him some kind of posthumous honor, but the President declined. He felt it would be an empty gesture, since Prieto had no living kin, and might attract attention which would endanger everything we had accomplished.

We all thought it was stupid to hate people who opposed us, however. We were working with inadequate information, and we knew it woud be years or even decades before we could be sure we had made the right decisions. Justo Prieto was a brave man. He made the choices that looked right to him, and he stuck with them to the end.

Late that March Soviet inspectors entered a prison in Illinois and discovered that the warden and a tax-exempt foundation were operating a clandestine lab and developing a new technique in psychological warfare. In the years that followed. . . .

Communications between Nations

Like individuals, countries need to communicate their positions
and feelings to others, and a wide variety of techniques have been
developed to accomplish this. One basic need is to communicate
the relative importance of a specific event to the national interest.
Another is the assuming of general positions in broad terms. For
example, the Monroe Doctrine of 1823 told the world that the
United States would continue to isolate itself from the political
and military entanglements of Europe, but warned others to keep
out of the Western Hemisphere. Similarly, the Truman Doctrine of
1947 announced America's willingness to resist what it viewed as
Communist aggression in Europe and opened the way toward
what became the NATO Alliance. Other means of communicating
include the "Hot Line" which provides for direct contact between
Washington and Moscow; the exchange of formal diplomatic
notes, usually intended to complain about a real or imagined
grievance; and secret contacts between diplomats who cannot
use normal channels of communication for one reason or another
—such as those that took place between Israel and Jordan and
the United States and the People's Republic of China (before
former President Nixon's visit).

However, some of the most important communications are
those which consist of *actions.* These actions may be positive or
negative—calling up reserve forces, arranging for the exchange
of sports teams, granting foreign aid on favorable terms, raising
tariff rates, or recalling an ambassador. These measures may be
more important than mere words because they are tangible
expressions of intent. However, they may also be misinterpreted,
with one side reading more into the action than may be really
intended.

The terms employed in communications are of the utmost

importance. Language can bring those in conflict closer together or it can further divide them. Labels like "Marxist," "Capitalist," "warmonger," "international gangster," and "terrorist" can produce reactions that make peace harder to achieve. In this story, Christopher Anvil vividly demonstrates the importance of language to the conduct of international relations.

A ROSE BY OTHER NAME . . .

by Christopher Anvil

A tall man in a tightly-belted trenchcoat carried a heavy brief case toward the Pentagon building.

A man in a black overcoat strode with a bulky suitcase toward the Kremlin.

A well-dressed man wearing a dark-blue suit stepped out of a taxi near the United Nations building, and paid the driver. As he walked away, he leaned slightly to the right, as if the attaché case under his left arm held lead instead of paper.

On the sidewalk nearby, a discarded newspaper lifted in the wind, to lie face up before the entrance to the United Nations building. Its big black headline read:

U. S. WILL FIGHT!

A set of diagrams in this newspaper showed United States and Soviet missiles, with comparisons of ranges, payloads, and explosive powers, and with the Washington Monument sketched into the background to give an idea of their size.

The well-dressed man with the attaché case strode across the newspaper to the entrance, his heels ripping the tables of missile comparisons as he passed.

Inside the building, the Soviet delegate was at this moment saying:

"The Soviet Union is the most scientifically advanced nation on Earth. The Soviet Union is the most powerful nation on Earth. It is not up to you to say to the Soviet Union, 'Yes' or 'No.' The Soviet Union has told you what it is going to do. All I can suggest for you is, you had better agree with us."

The United States delegate said, "That is the view of the Soviet government?"

"That is the view of the Soviet government."

"In that case, I will have to tell you the view of the United States government. If the Soviet Union carries out this latest piece of brutal aggression, the United States will consider it a direct attack upon its own security. I hope you know what this means."

There was an uneasy stir in the room.

The Soviet delegate said slowly, "I am sorry to hear you say that. I am authorized to state that the Soviet Union will not retreat on this issue."

The United States delegate said, "The position of the United States is already plain. If the Soviet Union carries this out, the United States will consider it as a direct attack. There is nothing more I can say."

In the momentary silence that followed, a guard with a rather stuporous look opened the door to let in a well-dressed man, who was just sliding something back into his attaché case. This man glanced thoughtfully around the room, where someone was just saying:

"*Now* what do we do?"

Someone else said hesitantly, "A conference, perhaps?"

The Soviet delegate said coolly, "A conference will not settle this. The United States must correct its provocative attitude."

The United States delegate looked off at a distant wall. "The provocation is this latest Soviet aggression. All that is needed is for the Soviet Union not to do it."

"The Soviet Union will not retreat in this issue."

The United States delegate said, "The United States will not retreat on this issue."

There was a dull silence that lasted for some time.

As the United States and Soviet delegates sat unmoving, there came an urgent plea, "Gentlemen, doesn't anyone have an idea? However implausible?"

The silence continued long enough to make it plain that now no one could see any way out.

A well-dressed man in dark-blue, carrying an attaché case, stepped forward and set the case down on a table with a solid *clunk* that riveted attention.

"Now," he said, "we are in a real mess. Very few people on Earth want to get burned alive, poisoned, or smashed to bits. We don't want a ruinous war. But from the looks of things, we're likely to get one anyway, whether we want it or not.

"The position we are in is like that of a crowd of people locked in a room. Some of us have brought along for our protection large savage dogs. Our two chief members have trained tigers. This menagerie is now straining at the leash. Once the first blow lands, no one can say where it will end.

"What we seem to need right now is someone with skills of a lion tamer. The lion tamer controls the animals by understanding, timing, and *distraction*."

The United States and Soviet delegates glanced curiously at each other. The other delegates shifted around with puzzled expressions. Several opened their mouths as if to interrupt, glanced at the United States and Soviet delegates, shut their mouths and looked at the attaché case.

"Now," the man went on, "a lion tamer's tools are a pistol, a whip, and a chair. They are used to distract. The pistol contains blank cartridges, the whip is snapped above the animal's head, and the chair is held with the points of the legs out, so that the animal's gaze is drawn first to one point, then another, as the chair is shifted. The sharp noise of gun and whip distract the animal's attention. So does the chair.

". . . And so long as the animal's attention is distracted, its terrific power isn't put into play. This is how the lion tamer keeps peace.

"The thought processes of a war machine are a little different from the thought processes of a lion or a tiger. But the principle is the same. What we need is something corresponding to the lion tamer's whip, chair, and gun."

He unsnapped the cover of the attaché case, and lifted out a dull gray slab with a handle on each end, several dials on its face, and beside the dials a red button and a blue button.

"It's generally known," he said, looking around at the scowling delegates, "that certain mental activities are associated with certain areas of the brain. Damage a given brain area, and you disrupt the corresponding mental action. Speech may be disrupted, while writing remains. A man who speaks French and German may lose his ability to speak French, but still be able to speak German. These things are well-known, but not generally used. Now, who knows if, perhaps, there is a special section of the brain which handles the vocabulary *related to military subjects?*"

He pushed in the blue button.

The Soviet delegate sat up straight. "What is that button you just pushed?"

"A demonstration button. It actuates when I release it."

The United States delegate said, "Actuates *what?*"

"I will show you, if you will be patient just a few minutes."

"What's this about brain areas? We can't open the brain of every general in the world."

"You won't have to. Of course, you have heard of resonant frequencies and related topics. Take two tuning forks that vibrate at the same rate. Set one in vibration, and the other across the room will vibrate. Soldiers marching across a bridge break step, lest they start the bridge in vibration and bring it down. The right note on a violin will shatter a glass. Who knows whether minute electrical currents in a particular area of the brain, associated with a certain characteristic mental activity, may not tend to induce a similar activity in the corresponding section of another brain? And, in that case, if it were possible to induce a sufficiently *strong* current, it might actually overload that particular—"

The United States delegate tensely measured with his eyes the distance to the gray slab on the table.

The Soviet delegate slid his hand toward his waistband.

The man who was speaking took his finger from the blue button.

The Soviet delegate jerked out a small black automatic. The United States delegate shot from his chair in a flying leap. Around the room, men sprang to their feet. There was an instant of violent activity.

Then the automatic fell to the floor. The United States delegate sprawled motionless across the table. Around the room, men crumpled to the floor in the nerveless fashion of the dead drunk.

Just one man remained on his feet, leaning forward with a faintly dazed expression as he reached for the red button. He said, "You have temporarily overloaded certain mental circuits, gentlemen. I have been protected by a . . . you might say, a jamming device. You will recover from the effects of *this* overload. The next one you experience will be a different matter. I am sorry, but there are certain conditions of mental resonance that the human race can't afford at the moment."

He pressed the red button.

The United States delegate, lying on the table, experienced a momentary surge of rage. In a flash, it was followed by an intensely clear vision of the map of Russia, the polar regions adjoining it, and the nations along its long southern border. Then the map was more than a map, as he saw the economic complexes of the Soviet Union, and the racial and national groups forcibly submerged by the central government. The strong and weak points of the Soviet Union emerged, as in a transparent anatomical model of the human body laid out for an operation.

Not far away, the Soviet delegate could see the submarines off the coasts of the United States, the missiles arcing down on the vital industrial areas, the bombers on their long one-way missions, and the unexpected land attack to settle the problem for once and for all. As he thought, he revised the plan continuously, noting an unexpected American strength here, and the possibility of a dangerous counterblow there.

In the mind of another delegate, Great Britain balanced off the United States against the Soviet Union, then by a series of carefully planned moves acquired the moral leadership of a bloc of uncommitted nations. Next, with this as a basis for maneuver—

Another delegate saw France leading a Europe small in area but immense in productive power. After first isolating Britain—

At nearly the same split fraction of an instant, all these plans became complete. Each delegate saw his nation's way to the top with a dazzling, more than human clarity.

And then there was an impression like the brief glow of an overloaded wire. There was a sensation similar to pain.

This experience repeated itself in a great number of places around the globe.

In the Kremlin, a powerfully-built marshal blinked at the members of his staff.

"Strange. For just a minute there, I seemed to see—" He shrugged, and pointed at the map. "Now, along the North German Plain here, where we intend to . . . to—" He scowled, groping for a word. "Hm-m-m. Where we want to . . . ah . . . destabilize the . . . the ridiculous NATO protective counterproposals—" He stopped, frowning.

The members of his staff straightened up and looked puzzled. A general said, "Marshal, I just had an idea. Now, one of the questions is: Will the Americans . . . ah—Will they . . . hm-m-m—" He scowled, glanced off across the room, bit his lip, and said, "Ah . . . what I'm trying to say is: Will they forcibly demolecularize Paris, Rome, and other Allied centers when we . . . ah . . . inundate them with the integrated hyperarticulated elements of our—" He cut himself off suddenly, a look of horror on his face.

The marshal said sharply, "What are you talking about—'demolecularize?' You mean, will they . . . hm-m-m . . . disconstitute the existent structural pattern by application of intense energy of nuclear fusion?" He stopped and blinked several times as this last sentence played itself back in his mind.

Another member of the staff spoke up hesitantly, "Sir, I'm not exactly sure what you have in mind, but I had a thought back there that struck me as a good workable plan to deconstitutionalize the whole American government in five years by unstructing their political organization through intrasocietal political action simultaneously on all levels. Now—"

"Ah," said another general, his eyes shining with an inward vision, "I have a better plan. Banana embargo. Listen—"

A fine beading of perspiration appeared on the marshal's brow. It had occurred to him to wonder if the Americans had somehow just landed the ultimate in foul blows. He groped around mentally to try to get his mind back on the track.

At this moment, two men in various shades of blue were sitting by a big globe in the Pentagon building staring at a third man in an olive-colored uniform. There was an air of embarrassment in the room.

At length, one of the men in blue cleared his throat. "General, I hope your plans are based on something a little clearer than that. I don't see how you can expect us to co-operate with you in recommending *that* kind of a thing to the President. But now, I just had a remarkable idea. It's a little unusual; but if I do say so, it's the kind of thing that can clarify the situation instead of sinking it in hopeless confusion. Now, what I propose is that we immediately proceed to layerize the existent trade routes in *depth*. This will counteract the Soviet potential nullification of our sea-borne surface-level communications through their underwater superiority. Now, this involves a fairly unusual concept. But what I'm driving at—"

"Wait a minute," said the general, in a faintly hurt tone. "You didn't get my point. It may be that I didn't express it quite as I intended. But what I mean is, we've got to really bat those bricks all over the lot. Otherwise, there's bound to be trouble. Look—"

The man in Air Force blue cleared his throat. "Frankly, I've always suspected there was a certain amount of confusion in both your plans. But I never expected anything like this. Fortunately, *I* have an idea—"

At the United Nations, the American and Russian delegates were staring at the British delegate, who was saying methodically, "Agriculture, art, literature, science, engineering, medicine, sociology, botany, zoology, beekeeping, tinsmithing, speleology, wa . . . w . . . milita . . . mili . . . mil . . . hm-m-m . . . sewing, needlework, navigation, law, business, barrister, batt . . . bat . . . ba— Can't say it."

"In other words," said the United States delegate, "we're mentally hamstrung. Our vocabulary is gone as regards . . . ah— That is, we can talk about practically anything, except subjects having to do with . . . er . . . strong disagreements."

The Soviet delegate scowled. "This is bad. I just had a good idea, too. Maybe—" He reached for pencil and paper.

A guard came in scowling. "Sorry, sir. There's no sign of any such person in the building now. He must have gotten away."

The Soviet delegate was looking glumly at his piece of paper.

"Well," he said, "I do not think I would care to trust the safety of my country to this method of communication."

Staring up at him from the paper were the words:

"Instructions to head man of Forty-fourth Ground-Walking Club. Seek to interpose your club along the high ground between the not-friendly-to-us fellows and the railway station. Use repeated strong practical urging procedures to obtain results desired."

The United States delegate had gotten hold of a typewriter, slid in a piece of paper, typed rapidly, and was now scowling in frustration at the result.

The Soviet delegate shook his head. "What's the word for it? We've been bugged. The section of our vocabulary dealing with . . . with . . . you know what I mean . . . that section has been burned out."

The United States delegate scowled. "Well, we can still stick pins in maps and draw pictures. Eventually we can get across what we mean."

"Yes, but that is no way to run a wa . . . wa . . . a strong disagreement. We will have to build up a whole new vocabulary to deal with the subject."

The United States delegate thought it over, and nodded. "All right," he said. "Now, look. If we're each going to have to make new vocabularies, do we want to end up with . . . say . . . sixteen different words in sixteen different languages all for the same thing? Take a . . . er . . . 'strong disagreement.' Are you going to call it 'gosnik' and we call it 'gack' and the French call it 'gouk' and the Germans call it 'Gunck'? And then we have to have twenty dozen different sets of dictionaries and hundreds of interpreters so we can merely get some idea what each other is talking about?"

"No," said the Soviet delegate grimly. "Not that. We should have an international commission to settle that. Maybe there, at least, is something we can agree on. Obviously, it is to everyone's advantage not to have innumerable new words for the same thing. Meanwhile, perhaps . . . ah . . . perhaps for now we had better postpone a final settlement of the present difficulty."

Six months later, a man wearing a tightly-belted trenchcoat approached the Pentagon building.

A man carrying a heavy suitcase strode along some distance from the Kremlin.

A taxi carrying a well-dressed man with an attaché case cruised past the United Nations building.

Inside the United Nations building, the debate was getting hot. The Soviet delegate said angrily:

"The Soviet Union is the most scientifically advanced and unquestionably the most gacknik nation on Earth. The Soviet Union will not take dictation from anybody. We have given you an extra half-year to make up your minds, and now we are going to put it to you bluntly:

"If you want to cush a gack with us over this issue, we will mongel you. We will grock you into the middle of next week. No running dog of a capitalist imperialist will get out in one piece. You may hurt us in the process, but *we* will absolutely bocket *you*. The day of decadent capitalism is *over*."

A rush of marvelous dialectic burst into life in the Soviet delegate's mind. For a split instant he could see with unnatural clarity not only why, but how, his nation's philosophy was bound to emerge triumphant—if handled properly—and even without a ruinous gack, too.

Unknown to the Soviet delegate, the United States delegate was simultaneously experiencing a clear insight into the stunning possibilities of basic American beliefs, which up to now had hardly been tapped at all.

At the same time, other delegates were sitting straight, their eyes fixed on distant visions.

The instant of dazzling certainty burnt itself out.

"Yes," said the Soviet delegate, as if in a trance. "No need to even cush a gack. Inevitably, victory must go to communi . . . commu . . . comm . . . com—" He stared in horror.

The American delegate shut his eyes and groaned. "Capitalis . . . capita . . . capi . . . cap . . . rugged individu . . . rugged indi . . . rugge . . . rug . . . rug—" He looked up. "Now we've got to have *another* conference. And then, on top of that, we've got to somehow cram our new definitions down the throats of the thirty per cent of the people they *don't* reach with their device."

The Soviet delegate felt for his chair and sat down heavily. "Dialectic materia . . . dialecti . . . dial . . . dia—" He put his head in both hands and drew in a deep shuddering breath.

The British delegate was saying, "Thin red li . . . thin re . . . thin . . . thin— This *hurts.*"

"Yes," said the United States delegate. "But if this goes on, we may end up with a complete, new, unified language. Maybe that's the idea."

The Soviet delegate drew in a deep breath and looked up gloomily. "Also, this answers one long-standing question."

"What's that?"

"One of your writers asked it long ago: 'What's in a name?'"

The delegates all nodded with sickly expressions.

"Now we know."

International Economics: Another Form of Warfare

The development of nuclear weapons and delivery systems for these weapons, and the prospect of the proliferation of these weapons to more and more countries in the years ahead have focused attention on nonmilitary ways for nations to compete with one another. So have the activities of the Organization of Petroleum Exporting Countries (OPEC) in controlling the supply and price of a commodity of the utmost importance to the world. However, countries have used economics as an instrument of foreign policy *and* warfare for a very long time. On the positive side, the foreign aid and assistance programs of the United States have benefited a great many people around the world even though they have not always benefited America in a political sense. From one point of view, altruism is never present in foreign aid (with the possible exception of disaster relief), because if it were, countries would channel their contributions through more efficient devices than is presently the case. In any event, there are other means to reward and punish in an economic sense. One can raise or lower tariff rates and barriers for friends and enemies; one can guarantee prices and the sale of certain commodities such as sugar for certain countries; one can manipulate interest rates and other terms of aid; one can grant "most favored nation" status to particular countries; and in extreme cases (as in U.S.-Cuban relations), one can prohibit the sale of anything to selected targets.

Economic warfare can get very rough—a country can blacklist individuals who do business with countries it does not like or boycott all goods from certain countries, as the Arab League nations have done for almost thirty years with Israel. In the final analysis, one country can impose a blockade on another in an attempt to prevent the arrival of any goods. But a blockade is an act of war in international law. This is the reason why the United States described its blockade (a selective blockade in this case) of Cuba during the 1962 Missile Crisis as a "quarantine."

Today, with economic needs increasing dramatically, those countries fortunate enough to possess exportable quantities of vital supplies like food, oil, and certain minerals seem to have the upper hand. The struggle between the haves and the have-nots is intensifying, and the industrialized world feels threatened as the finite resources of the planet are consumed at increasing rates. There is great danger here. Those presently in the driver's seat in regard to natural resources must manage their campaigns of controlled "extortion" with care, for if they go too far, they may drive those with military power to the point of desperation, with consequences that are difficult to predict.

"Unlimited Warfare" affords us a thought-provoking and hilarious look at economic warfare between two countries. It offers us a number of lessons, including the sometimes unpredictable consequences of this form of combat.

UNLIMITED WARFARE

by Hayford Peirce

The muted tones of Big Ben tolled mournfully through the late afternoon fog. Not far from St.-James' Barracks three men warmed themselves before an Adams fireplace.

"A scone?" inquired the Permanent Secretary.

"Waistline, you know," muttered the Minister, and served himself a cucumber sandwich. He waved the silver teapot invitingly.

"Terribly barbarian of me, really," said Colonel Christie, "but I'd much prefer a glass of that quite excellent sherry."

The Permanent Secretary raised a deprecatory eyebrow, but covertly. Colonel Christie was not a man who worked easily or effectively under direct orders. His interest must be aroused, his flair engaged, his methods thereafter unquestioned.

The Permanent Secretary sighed inaudibly. It was all very difficult. His master, the Minister, was a politician, adroit in the use of the elegant double-cross, the subtle treachery, the facile disavowal. Easy enough for him to wash his hands afterwards. But he himself was a civil servant, with a lifetime's predilection for agenda, minutes, memoranda, position papers, the Word committed to Paper. And of course, whenever Colonel Christie was involved, none of that was remotely possible. Very difficult indeed.

The Minister was staring into the flames and talking. Rather inconsequentially, it seemed. Three government officials, gentlemen all, taking their tea, making small talk.

Colonel Christie listened very closely indeed to his Minister's insubstantial chatter. It was his job to listen, and out of it would presently emerge, in carefully-guarded circumlocutions to be sure, an indication of what the current complication might be, a hint—but only a hint—in what direction the solution might lie.

They were orders, of course, all very tenuous and spectral, but orders nevertheless. And if a brick were dropped, Christie would carry the can. Misplaced zeal, a subordinate's unwarranted . . . He smiled grimly. This way, at least, the initiative was generally left to him. Afterwards, no one questioned success.

". . . after that man de Gaulle, naturally one hoped for an amelioration of the situation . . . completely shameless . . . trying to buy our way into the Common Market by subscribing to that preposterous *Concorde* project . . . utter blackmail . . . under Pompidou hardly any better . . . open subsidization of the French farmer . . . staggering inflation of our food prices . . . no unity whatsoever . . . the goal of a United Europe smashed, perhaps irreparably . . . *no house spirit* . . . they're simply *not team players*." Colonel Christie frowned. The Minister was being unwontedly lucid. He must be very troubled indeed.

". . . this new government, even more hopeless . . . pride, gentlemen, overweening pride, pure and simple . . . no proper respect and cooperation . . . during the days of the Marshall Plan . . . neither the inclination nor the means to play the international gadfly . . . a quite second-rate power basically . . . must be made to realize . . . can't expect them perhaps to come hat in hand, *but . . .*" He waved an arm vaguely, encompassing in a gesture the vast realm of the possible, then rose briskly. "You agree, Jenkins?"

"Up to a point, Sir William, up to a point."

"Splendid, splendid. I am so glad we are of one mind. Colonel Christie, good day."

In a room hardly less elegant but infinitely more comfortable Colonel Christie summoned his second-in-command.

"Sit down, Dawson, we have much to discuss. We are about to declare war."

"War, sir? May I ask against whom?"

"Certainly, this isn't the Ministry of Defense. France."

"France? There's no denying they're a shocking lot of—"

"Quite. I'm afraid I may have misled you somewhat. An entirely unofficial declaration is what I had in mind. The hostilities to be carried out by our Section."

"I see."

"Do you?" Colonel Christie laughed shortly. "I shouldn't tease you, but the ministerial manner is dreadfully catching. I must watch myself. Pour yourself a drink, Dawson, and let's consider this matter."

"Thank you."

"Now then, what exactly is our goal? It is to coerce the sovereign state of France into a situation in which it will be inevitably and inexorably compelled to recognize its actual status as a lesser power, to reintegrate itself within the Common Market, and in general to rejoin the comity of Western nations. Not at all an easy task. Especially as the means must absolutely preclude the open declaration of hostilities or the traditional methods thereof, which could only invite mutual destruction."

Dawson pondered, then said, "In other words, our purpose is to render ineffective their armed forces, or to smash the franc, or to destroy their morale, but without recourse to atomic warfare, naval blockade, armed invasion, massive propaganda, or other overtly hostile acts? As you say, not an easy task."

"Which makes it all the more enthralling, don't you think? A stern test of our native ingenuity. Come, let us begin by considering the beginning. France. What, Dawson, is France?"

"Well. Where does one start? A European power, roughly fifty million people, area something over two hundred thousand square miles, nominal allies—"

"Let's probe deeper than that. To the spirit of France, Joan of

Arc, the Revolution, Napoleon, Balzac, the Marne, de Gaulle, *la mission civilisatrice française* . . ."

"Ah. What precisely is it that makes a Frenchman a Frenchman, rather than an Englishman? To subjugate France we first identify, then subjugate, her soul . . ."

"Excellent, really excellent. Well, Dawson, what *is* the soul of France? What springs instantly to mind?"

"Sex. Brigitte Bardot. The Folies Bergere. The—"

"A two-edged weapon, I'm afraid."

"Surely the deprivation of sex in England would hardly be noticed?"

"Perhaps not, but it is difficult to see how a campaign of sexual warfare could be successfully implemented. But this is quite promising, Dawson, do carry on."

"Well. The Eiffel Tower, the Arc de Triomphe, the Riviera, châteaux on the Loire, perfume, camembert cheese. French bread, rudeness, independence, *bloodymindedness*. High fashion, funny little cars, berets, mustaches, three-star restaurants, wine—"

"Wine . . . wine, Dawson, wine! Red wine, white wine. rosé wine, champagne, Chateau-Lafite '29, *vin du table,* Bordeaux, Burgundy, Provence, Anjou. Wine. Nothing but wine. A nation of winedrinkers, a nation of wine! Splendid, Dawson, really quite splendid."

"But—"

"Dawson. The flash is blinding, it has me quite dazzled. Kindly hand me that almanac by your side, no, the French one, *Quid?* Let me see now, wine, wine, wine . . ." Colonel Christie hummed as he flipped through the pages. "Ah, yes, yes indeed. Listen to this, Dawson: 1,088,000 winegrowers, 1,453,000 vineyards, more than 4,500,000 persons living directly or indirectly from the production of wine. Average annual production, sixty-three million hectoliters, what on earth is a hectoliter? Twenty-two gallons? Good heavens, that's 1,386 million gallons per year. Eight percent is exported. Consumption: about forty gallons per person per year.

"Ah, as I thought, in 1971 France imported only 124,147,000 francs' worth of Scotch whisky, while exporting to England 494,833,000 francs' worth of wine and spirits. To England alone, mind you.

"Bearing those figures in mind, Dawson, is it any wonder that the French are an extremely unstable and disputatious race, or that England suffers a catastrophic balance of payments deficit? But here we have the means to redress the situation."

"We do?"

"Certainly we do. This inestimable almanac is kind enough to list the enemies of the vine: mildew and oidium phylloxera. Surely you have heard that in the 1880's the vineyards of France were almost totally destroyed overnight by phylloxera. Millions of vines had to be sent from the United States and replanted. Interestingly enough, after a few years in their new soil the transplanted vines produced wine of the same quality and characteristics as the original vines. It was, Dawson, the first example of American foreign aid, an early Marshall Plan. And equally forgotten.

"But I think that if a similar catastrophe were to overtake France today you would find few Americans in the mood to succor France yet again with Liberty Ships full of grapevines. After all, California is now one of the great wine-producing regions of the world; they would have no reason to help their fiercest competitor. No, Dawson, from every angle the prospect pleases. If I were a mathematician I should be tempted to call it elegant.

"Think of it. Economic and political chaos in France. Fifty million Frenchmen drinking water, with the inevitable result that they will see the world clearly for the first time in centuries. A shocking deficit in their balance of trade, total demoralization of a civilization founded on the restaurant and bistro, the collapse of their armed forces—recruits are forced to drink a liter of *gros rouge* per day—a notable boost for British exports—I foresee Red Cross vessels loaded to the scuppers with Scotch and sound British ale—and a dramatic return to the days when Britannia ruled the waves."

"But, sir. What are *we* to drink? I must confess, a nice glass of—"

"Nonsense, Dawson. Stock your cellar if you must. Or refine your palate. Personally, I find a regimen of sherry, hock, and port entirely pleasing. None of them, you will note, from France."

"But—"

"Dawson. 'Say, for what were hopyards meant/Or why was Burton built on Trent?' "

"I beg your, Pardon?"

" 'Ale, man, ale's the thing to drink/For fellows whom it hurts to think.' "

"Really, sir," said Dawson reproachfully.

"The poet, you know. Housman."

"Ah, I see, But the means . . ."

"Oh, come. Why do we support all those beastly biological warfare establishments if not for situations such as this? I hardly think the boffins will have explored the possibility of a mutated and highly-virulent oidium phylloxera fungus, but I should think that the prospect of developing a nasty bug which poisons grapevines rather than entire populations ought to appeal to whatever small spark of common humanity they may yet retain. After that, a few aerosol bombs . . ."

Colonel Christie's keen eye seemed to pierce the future's veil. He smiled.

"Sir. Retaliation."

"Retaliation? Don't spout nonsense, Dawson. How *can* they retaliate? Atomic attack? Naval blockade to interdict trade in wheat and iron? That's *war*. Psychological warfare, propaganda? Impossible. No one in France speaks English and no one in England understands French. Sabotage? What could they sabotage?

"Think, Dawson, of British life, its placid, straightforward, *sensible* course, devoid of fripperies or eccentricities. Its *character*. No, no. I assure you, Dawson. The British way of life is quite invulnerable."

". . . and totally ravished. I tell you, St.-Denis, it will mean mobilization and inevitable war. Already the President has designated a War Cabinet, and we are to meet later this evening. Ah, who would have thought it, that nation of shopkeepers, that race of hypocrites, that even they could sink so low? Not only an act of naked aggression but also an insult to the very honor of France herself. Ah, Perfidious Albion!"

Colonel St.-Denis nodded deferentially. "If I may suggest, however, *M. le Ministre,* it is less a question of Perfidious Albion than a question of rank Britannic amateurism. Ah, these English *milords,* with their love of the hunt, their cult of the gentleman, their espousal of the amateur, their scorn of the professional. Because of a long-forgotten battle won on the playing fields of Eton they have never learned that the rest of the world has never attended Eton, nor needed to. They have not learned that we—that I, Jean-Pierre François Marie Charles St.-Denis—that we are not gentlemen and that we do not fight like gentlemen. We fight like professionals and we fight to win."

"Bravely spoken. But are you saying—"

"Exactly, *M. le Ministre.* A plan. A riposte. Check and mate."

"But the vineyards, totally ruined, beyond reclamation. A nation on the verge of depression or revolution. Were it not necessary to mobilize the Army it would be necessary to confine it to barracks."

"Details. Of no importance. Do not the British still boast of their

Battle of Britain and of Their Finest Hour? So it shall be with France: Her Finest Decade." St.-Denis waved a hand scornfully: "A few epicures, a few tosspots, they may suffer. For the rest of us there is work to do, work for the Glory of France!"

". . . like a charm, sir. Complete panic and demoralization. Already there's talk of a Sixth Republic. No, Intelligence reports no indication of a counterattack. Simply a nationwide balls-up."

"Exactly. As I told our masters this morning. How can one expect a committee of Froggies to come to a decision without a bottle of wine to hand, eh, Dawson?"

"Up to a point, sir."

"Come, come, Dawson, not getting the wind up, are you? I tell you, you're far more likely to find your name on the next Honors' List."

. . . not bloody likely, with you to hog all the glory . . .

". . . and now, St.-Denis, if you would kindly tell us of what your plan consists?"

"Certainly, *M. le President.* You may recall your last visit to England, the sporting weekend with the Prime Minister at his country residence, Chequers?"

The President of France did not attempt to conceal his shudder.

"I thought so. I am certain then that after some ungodly meal of boiled mutton, brussels sprouts, and treacle pudding, you retired to your chamber for a restorative glass of cognac and a troubled sleep?"

"Really, St.-Denis, you surpass yourself."

"Thank you, *M. le President.* After a troubled sleep, then, you were most certainly roused at some ghastly hour of the morning by a discreet knock upon your door. Contrary to your expectations, perhaps, it was a manservant, a butler even, come to wake you for a strenuous day amidst the fogs and grouse. And what, *M. le President,* did this unwelcome intruder bear inexorably before him? The so-renowned breakfast *anglais?* Ah, no! I will tell you what this English devil placed before you for your ever-lasting torment."

The President shied back before an accusatory finger.

"He placed before you, *M. le President, a pot of tea!"*

"Tea?"

"Tea."

"Ah. Tea. Yes, I remember it well." He shuddered anew. "But

surely, Colonel St.-Denis, you are not proposing that we poison the English population by forcing them to consume tea? The rest of the world, yes, it would be mass genocide. But the English, they *drink* tea, they thrive on tea, it would be, how do they say, bearing charcoals to Windsor Castle."

"Not exactly, *M. le President*. I am certain that as an intellectual exercise you are prepared to admit to the fact that Englishmen drink tea. But do you comprehend it *here?*" He clutched both hands to his heart. "Here, with your soul? Or—it is almost indelicate to speak of this—have you ever grasped the sheer *quantities* of tea consumed within the British Isles? Of course not.

"Page 906 of the invaluable *Quid?* informs us that an Englishman takes at least 2,400 cups per year—six to seven per day—compared to thirty-three per year per Frenchman . . . Good heavens, are you all right?"

"I felt quite giddy for a moment. What appalling statistics."

"Only the Anglo-Saxon could contemplate them without reeling."

"One hardly knows which is worse, the English consumption or the fact that *Frenchmen* appear—"

"Let your mind be at rest. French consumption is confined entirely to immigrants from our former North-African colonies, or to herbal *infusions* quite incorrectly called tea."

"Ah, thank heavens for that. But returning to—"

"Once you have grasped the *magnitude* of the consumption, you must then grasp the social *importance* of the consumption. It is the very fabric with which English society is constructed. Before-breakfast tea. 'Elevenses.' 'Put the kettle on, dearie, and let's have a nice cuppa.' Thick black tea drunk by the mugful in the Army and Navy. Entire industries coming to a halt at a wildcat-strike called because of improperly-brewed tea. Afternoon tea with its cakes and crumpets and cucumber sandwiches and who dares guess what else?"

"I feel quite ill."

"I also. Fortunately there remains only the Ceremony of the Teapot, the single article of faith which sixty million Englishmen hold in common. First the teapot must be heated, but *only* by filling it with boiling water. Then—"

"St.-Denis. I can bear no more. You have a course of action?"

"A simple virus, *M. le President*. Can the land of Pasteur and Curie fail before such a challenge?"

The room was somberly but richly furnished. A Persian rug lay on the floor. A fire crackled in the hearth.

The Permanent Secretary nodded approvingly. It was always satisfactory when a muddle began to regularize itself.

"Kind of you to drop by like this," said Colonel Christie. "Whisky-soda? The syphon's behind you."

"Kind of you." He limned the room with a gesture. "You do well by yourself here."

The Colonel shrugged urbanely. "You wanted to see me?"

"That is, the Minister wanted me to see you. He thought you might be interested in an informal tally sheet we have drawn up regarding the results of last year's Operation . . . er . . . Bacchus."

"Very good of him indeed."

"In so very informal a minute we thought it might be profitable to list the items under the headings *Credits* and *Debits*. The Minister was a former Chartered Accountant, you know."

"I recall," said Colonel Christie as he began to read the first sheet of notepaper.

Credits:

1. Destruction of all French vineyards, with concomitant confusion and social unrest in France, as apparently planned.

2. Twenty percent increase in the exportation of Scotch whisky, for a three-week period before the blockade.

Debits:

1. Retaliation in the form of complete destruction of the world's tea supply by means of a still-uncontrollable mutated virus.

2. Tea-rationing, followed by riots. Three general elections in the space of eight months. Martial law eventually declared.

3. Tea no longer available, nor in the foreseeable future.

4. Total decomposition of the fabric of British society.

5. This peculiarly-depraved act of war is currently being litigated at Geneva and before the World Court as a Crime Against Humanity, but we have reason to believe that our suit is not being well-received.

6. Expulsion of England from the Common Market.

7. The world's opprobrium.

8. Economic embargo and naval blockade by a task force of seventy-three countries. Only the London Airlift and the United States Navy maintain England as a viable state.

9. Dwindling supplies of French wine. Blackmarket, and concomitant problems.

10. After a few months' confusion, unexpected and absolute unification of the French people in the face of adversity.

11. As the world's now-largest importer of wine, France is directly responsible for the sudden Economic Miracles in Italy and Algeria, both of which have doubled their vineyard acreage under production. Algeria has joined the Common Market and is considering becoming once again an integral part of France. German, Spanish, and Greek wine production has also benefited greatly.

12. To further promote this rapidly-rising spiral of prosperity, France and the other members of the Common Market are nearing Economic Union and hope shortly to achieve Political Union. It is felt that France will dominate and direct this nation of 250 million people.

13. To counter the cost of wine importation and the subsequent balance of payments deficit, France has already donated its armed forces (and expenses) to a United European Command.

14. Millions of acres of tea-producing land and millions of people in sixty-eight countries suddenly have become available for other forms of agricultural production. With the vast market unexpectedly open in France and other countries to the importation of wine, most of this acreage has been given over to wine production.

15. Some 4.6 million Frenchmen have spread to all corners of the world to aid the undeveloped countries in their effort to produce potable wine.

16. Due to the high professionalism of the French Secret Service, it is accepted unhesitatingly throughout the world that the American CIA was responsible for the mass destruction of the tea plant. Spurred by the efforts of 4.6 million ambassadors of goodwill, French has completely replaced English as the secondary language being taught in the world's schools. It has, of course, become once again the standard language of diplomacy. It is thought that these factors will result in the emigration of at least half-a-million teachers from France, and

a corresponding momentum will be given to the *mission civilisatrice française.*

17. The first wine-fair has opened in China. It was attended by Chairman Mao, who pronounced his unqualified approval of a *Nuits-St.-Georges* '66.

18. It is entirely foreseeable that with the accelerating rate of spread of French culture and influence, and as eventual leader of a United Europe, within a decade France will be the world's dominant power.

"Rather gripping, don't you think?" said the Permanent Secretary.

"Quite," replied Colonel Christie dryly.

"Interesting, the amenities of your . . . er . . . suite," said the Permanent Secretary as he strolled about the room in unabashed fascination. "One had no idea such comfort obtained in the Tower. One naturally thinks of dank dungeons and durance vile, that sort of thing, eh?"

"Quite," said Colonel Christie. "Oh, quite."

Conflict Resolution: Cooperation

Countries are constantly cooperating to resolve the conflicts among them. Unfortunately, however, the most serious and dangerous conflicts often are not dealt with in a cooperative fashion because the essential ingredients of trust and goodwill are not present. In these cases, cooperation can sometimes be artificially induced through the use of third parties, a practice that ranges from carrying messages back and forth between countries who will not talk to each other directly—as Gunnar Jarring did for Egypt and Israel—to the offering of proposed solutions to conflicts to the parties, as Secretary of State Henry Kissinger did for the same two countries and for Israel and Syria. On rare occasions, the decision of a third party may be binding on the disputants (this decision is obtained through a process called arbitration) with each side agreeing in advance to accept the decision of an arbitrator. However, if countries are willing to accept the dictates of a third party, it must mean that their national interests were not involved to any great degree.

One of the best ways to resolve conflict through cooperation is by joining with one's opponents to resist a foe that threatens the interests of both. This happens frequently in prewar and war situations—the Allies uniting against Hitler, with the United States joining with the Soviet Union, is but one example. We often see the threat from abroad used in domestic political situations, when a national leader wishes to divert the attention of people at home from local problems. This can be a dangerous practice, as the late President Gamal Abdel Nasser of Egypt discovered in 1967.

In theory, joining forces to meet a common foe or to solve a common problem could unite the entire globe. Here, James E. Gunn and Randall Garrett present two interesting examples of such an opportunity, one that involves an exciting drama in outer space, and one that takes place much closer to home.

THE CAVE OF NIGHT

by James E. Gunn

The phrase was first used by a poet disguised in the cynical hide of a newspaper reporter. It appeared on the first day and was widely reprinted. He wrote:

"At eight o'clock, after the Sun has set and the sky is darkening, look up! There's a man up there where no man has ever been.

"He is lost in the cave of night . . ."

The headlines demanded something short, vigorous and descriptive. That was it. It was inaccurate, but it stuck.

If anybody was in a cave, it was the rest of humanity. Painfully, triumphantly, one man had climbed out. Now he couldn't find his way back into the cave with the rest of us.

What goes up doesn't always come back down.

That was the first day. After it came twenty-nine days of agonized suspense.

The cave of night. I wish the phrase had been mine.

That was it, the tag, the symbol. It was the first thing a man saw when he glanced at the newspaper. It was the way people talked about it: "What's the latest about the cave?" It summed it all up, the drama, the anxiety, the hope.

Maybe it was the Floyd Collins influence. The papers dug up their files on that old tragedy, reminiscing, comparing; and they remembered the little girl—Kathy Fiscus, wasn't it?—who was trapped in that abandoned, California drain pipe; and a number of others.

Periodically, it happens, a sequence of events so accidentally dramatic that men lose their hatreds, their terrors, their shynesses, their inadequacies, and the human race momentarily recognizes its kinship.

The essential ingredients are these: A person must be in unusual and desperate peril. The peril must have duration. There must be proof that the person is still alive. Rescue attempts must be made. Publicity must be widespread.

One could probably be constructed artificially, but if the world ever discovered the fraud, it would never forgive.

Like many others, I have tried to analyze what makes a niggling, squabbling callous race of beings suddenly share that most human emotion of sympathy, and, like them, I have not succeeded. Suddenly a distant stranger will mean more than their own comfort. Every waking moment, they pray: Live, Floyd! Live, Kathy! Live, Rev!

We pass on the street, we who would not have nodded, and ask, "Will they get there in time?"

Optimists and pessimists alike, we hope so. We all hope so.

In a sense, this one was different. This was purposeful. Knowing the risk, accepting it because there was no other way to do what had to be done, Rev had gone into the cave of night. The accident was that he could not return.

The news came out of nowhere—literally—to an unsuspecting world. The earliest mention the historians have been able to locate was an item about a ham radio operator in Davenport, Iowa. He picked up a distress signal on a sticky-hot June evening.

The message, he said later, seemed to fade in, reach a peak, and fade out:

". . . and fuel tanks empty. —ceiver broke . . . transmitting in clear so someone can pick this up, and . . . no way to get back . . . stuck . . ."

A small enough beginning.

The next message was received by a military base radio watch near Fairbanks, Alaska. That was early in the morning. Half an hour later, a night-shift worker in Boston heard something on his short-wave set that sent him rushing to the telephone.

That morning, the whole world learned the story. It broke over them, a wave of excitement and concern. Orbiting 1,075 miles above their heads was a man, an officer of the United States Air Force, in a fuelless spaceship.

All by itself, the spaceship part would have captured the world's attention. It was achievement as monumental as anything Man has ever done and far more spectacular. It was liberation from the tyranny of

Earth, this jealous mother who had bound her children tight with the apron strings of gravity.

Man was free. It was a symbol that nothing is completely and finally impossible if Man wants it hard enough and long enough.

There are regions that humanity finds peculiarly congenial. Like all Earth's creatures, Man is a product and a victim of environment. His triumph is that the slave became the master. Unlike more specialized animals, he distributed himself across the entire surface of the Earth, from the frozen Antarctic continent to the Arctic icecap.

Man became an equatorial animal, a temperate zone animal, an arctic animal. He became a plain dweller, a valley dweller, a mountain dweller. The swamp and the desert became equally his home.

Man made his own environment.

With his inventive mind and his dexterous hands, he fashioned it, conquered cold and heat, dampness, aridness, land, sea, air. Now, with his science, he had conquered everything. He had become independent of the world that bore him.

It was a birthday cake for all mankind, celebrating its coming of age.

Brutally, the disaster was icing on the cake.

But it was more, too. When everything is considered, perhaps it was the aspect that, for a few, brief days, united humanity and made possible what we did.

It was a sign: Man is never completely independent of Earth; he carries with him his environment; he is always and forever a part of humanity. It was a conquest mellowed by a confession of mortality and error.

It was a statement: Man has within him the qualities of greatness that will never accept the restraints of circumstance, and yet he carries, too, the seeds of fallibility that we all recognize in ourselves.

Rev was one of us. His triumph was our triumph; his peril—more fully and finely—was our peril.

Reverdy L. McMillen, III, first lieutenant, U.S.A.F. Pilot. Rocket jockey. Man. Rev. He was only a thousand miles away, calling for help, but those miles were straight up. We got to know him as well as any member of our own family.

The news came as a great personal shock to me. I knew Rev. We had become good friends in college, and fortune had thrown us together in the Air Force, a writer and a pilot. I had got out as soon as possible, but Rev had stayed in. I knew, vaguely, that he had been testing rocket-powered airplanes with Chuck Yeager. But I had no idea that the rocket program was that close to space.

Nobody did. It was a better-kept secret than the Manhattan Project.

I remember staring at Rev's picture in the evening newspaper—the straight black hair, the thin, rakish mustache, the Clark Gable ears, the reckless, rueful grin—and I felt again, like a physical thing, his great joy in living. It expressed itself in a hundred ways. He loved widely, but with discrimination. He ate well, drank heartily, reveled in expert jazz and artistic inventiveness, and talked incessantly.

Now he was alone and soon all that might be extinguished. I told myself that I would help.

That was a time of wild enthusiasm. Men mobbed the Air Force Proving Grounds at Cocoa, Florida, wildly volunteering their services. But I was no engineer. I wasn't even a welder or a riveter. At best, I was only a poor word mechanic.

But words, at least, I could contribute.

I made a hasty verbal agreement with a local paper and caught the first plane to Washington, D.C. For a long time, I liked to think that what I wrote during the next few days had something to do with subsequent events, for many of my articles were picked up for reprint by other newspapers.

The Washington fiasco was the responsibility of the Senate Investigating Committee. It subpoenaed everybody in sight—which effectively removed them from the vital work they were doing. But within a day, the Committee realized that it had bitten off a bite it could neither swallow nor spit out.

General Beauregard Finch, head of the research and development program, was the tough morsel the Committee gagged on. Coldly, accurately, he described the development of the project, the scientific and technical research, the tests, the building of the ship, the training of the prospective crewmen, and the winnowing of the volunteers down to one man.

In words more eloquent because of their clipped precision, he described the takeoff of the giant three-stage ship, shoved upward on a lengthening arm of combining hydrazine and nitric acid. Within fifty-six minutes, the remaining third stage had reached its orbital height of 1,075 miles.

It had coasted there. In order to maintain that orbit, the motors had to flicker on for fifteen seconds.

At that moment, disaster laughed at Man's careful calculations.

Before Rev could override the automatics, the motors had flamed for almost half a minute. The fuel he had depended upon to slow the ship so that it would drop, reenter the atmosphere and be reclaimed by Earth was almost gone. His efforts to counteract the excess speed resulted only in an approximation of the original orbit.

The fact was this: Rev was up there. He would stay there until someone came and got him.

And there was no way to get there.

The Committee took that as an admission of guilt and incompetence; they tried to lever themselves free with it, but General Finch was not to be intimidated. A manned ship had been sent up because no mechanical or electronic computer could contain the vast possibilities for decision and action built into a human being.

The original computer was still the best all-purpose computer.

There had been only one ship built, true. But there was good reason for that, a completely practical reason—money.

Leaders are, by definition, ahead of the people. But this wasn't a field in which they could show the way and wait for the people to follow. This was no expedition in ancient ships, no light exploring party, no pilot-plant operation. Like a parachute jump, it had to be successful the first time.

This was an enterprise into new, expensive fields. It demanded money (billions of dollars), brains (the best available), and the hard, dedicated labor of men (thousands of them).

General Finch became a national hero that afternoon. He said, in bold words, "With the limited funds you gave us, we have done what we set out to do. We have demonstrated that space flight is possible, that a space platform is feasible.

"If there is any inefficiency, if there is any blame for what has happened, it lies at the door of those who lacked confidence in the courage and ability of their countrymen to fight free of Earth to the greatest glory. Senator, how did you vote on that?"

But I am not writing a history. The shelves are full of them. I will touch on the international repercussions only enough to show that the event was no more a respecter of national boundaries than was Rev's orbiting ship.

The orbit was almost perpendicular to the equator. The ship traveled as far north as Nome, as far south as Little America on the Antarctic

Continent. It completed one giant circle every two hours. Meanwhile, the Earth rotated beneath. If the ship had been equipped with adequate optical instruments, Rev could have observed every spot on Earth within twenty-four hours. He could have seen fleets and their dispositions, aircraft carriers and the planes taking off their decks, troop maneuvers.

In the General Assembly of the United Nations, the Russian ambassador protested this unwarranted and illegal violation of its national boundaries. He hinted darkly that it would not be allowed to continue. The U.S.S.R. had not been caught unprepared, he said. If the violation went on—*"every few hours!"*—drastic steps would be taken.

World opinion reared up in indignation. The U.S.S.R. immediately retreated and pretended, as only it could, that its belligerence had been an unwarranted inference and that it had never said anything of the sort, anyway.

This was not a military observer above our heads. It was a man who would soon be dead unless help reached him.

A world offered what it had. Even the U.S.S.R. announced that it was outfitting a rescue ship, since its space program was already on the verge of success. And the American public responded with more than a billion dollars within a week. Congress appropriated another billion. Thousands of men and women volunteered.

The race began.

Would the rescue party reach the ship in time? The world prayed.

And it listened daily to the voice of a man it hoped to buy back from death.

The problem shaped up like this:

The trip had been planned to last for only a few days. By careful rationing, the food and water might be stretched out for more than a month, but the oxygen, by cutting down activity to conserve it, couldn't possibly last more than thirty days. That was the absolute outside limit.

I remember reading the carefully detailed calculations in the paper and studying them for some hopeful error. There was none.

Within a few hours, the discarded first stage of the ship had been located floating in the Atlantic Ocean. It was towed back to Cocoa, Florida. Almost a week was needed to find and return to the Proving Grounds the second stage, which had landed 906 miles away.

Both sections were practically undamaged; their fall had been cushioned by ribbon parachute. They could be cleaned, repaired and used again. The trouble was the vital third stage—the nose section. A new one had to be designed and built within a month.

Space-madness became a new form of hysteria. We read statistics, we memorized insignificant details, we studied diagrams, we learned the risks and the dangers and how they would be met and conquered. It all became part of us. We watched the slow progress of the second ship and silently, tautly, urged it upward.

The schedule overhead became part of everyone's daily life. Work stopped while people rushed to windows or outside or to their television sets, hoping for a glimpse, a glint from the high, swift ship, so near, so untouchably far.

And we listened to the voice from the cave of night:

"I've been staring out the portholes. I never tire of that. Through the one on the right, I see what looks like a black velvet curtain with a strong light behind it. There are pinpoint holes in the curtain and the light shines through, not winking the way stars do, but steady. There's no air up here. That's the reason. The mind can understand and still misinterpret.

"My air is holding out better than I expected. By my figures, it should last twenty-seven days more. I shouldn't use so much of it talking all the time, but it's hard to stop. Talking, I feel as if I'm still in touch with Earth, still one of you, even if I am way up here.

"Through the left-hand window is San Francisco Bay, looking like a dark, wandering arm extended by the ocean octopus. The city itself looks like a heap of diamonds with trails scattered from it. It glitters up cheerfully, an old friend. It misses me, it says. Hurry home, it says. It's gone now, out of sight. Good-bye, Frisco!

"Do you hear me down there? Sometimes I wonder. You can't see me now. I'm in the Earth's shadow. You'll have to wait hours for the dawn. I'll have mine in a few minutes.

"You're all busy down there. I know that. If I know you, you're all worrying about me, working to get me down, forgetting everything else. You don't know what a feeling that is. I hope to Heaven you never have to, wonderful though it is.

"Too bad the receiver was broken, but if it had to be one or the other, I'm glad it was the transmitter that came through. There's only one of me. There are billions of you to talk to.

"I wish there were some way I could be sure you were hearing me. Just that one thing might keep me from going crazy."

Rev, you were one in millions. We read all about your selection, your training. You were our representative, picked with our greatest skill.

Out of a thousand who passed the initial rigid requirements for education, physical and emotional condition and age, only five could qualify for space. They couldn't be too tall, too stout, too young, too old. Medical and psychiatric tests weeded them out.

One of the training machines—Lord, how we studied this—reproduces the acceleration strains of a blasting rocket. Another trains men for maneuvering in the weightlessness of space. A third duplicates the cramped, sealed conditions of a spaceship cabin. Out of the final five, you were the only one who qualified.

No, Rev, if any of us could stay sane, it was you.

There were thousands of suggestions, almost all of them useless. Psychologists suggested self-hypnotism; cultists suggested yoga. One man sent in a detailed sketch of a giant electromagnet with which Rev's ship could be drawn back to Earth.

General Finch had the only practical idea. He outlined a plan for letting Rev know that we were listening. He picked out Kansas City and set the time. "Midnight," he said. "On the dot. Not a minute earlier or later. At that moment, he'll be right overhead."

And at midnight, every light in the city went out and came back on and went out and came back on again.

For a few awful moments, we wondered if the man up there in the cave of night had seen. Then came the voice we knew now so well that it seemed it had always been with us, a part of us, our dreams and our waking.

The voice was husky with emotion:

"Thanks . . . Thanks for listening. Thanks, Kansas City. I saw you winking at me. I'm not alone. I know that now. I'll never forget. Thanks."

And silence then as the ship fell below the horizon. We pictured it to ourselves sometimes, continually circling the Earth, its trajectory exactly matching the curvature of the globe beneath it. We wondered if it would ever stop.

Like the Moon, would it be a satellite of the Earth forever?

We went through our daily chores like automatons while we watched the third stage of the rocket take shape. We raced against a dwindling air supply, and death raced to catch a ship moving at 15,800 miles per hour.

We watched the ship grow. On our television screens, we saw the construction of the cellular fuel tanks, the rocket motors, and the fantastic multitude of pumps, valves, gauges, switches, circuits, transistors, and tubes.

The personnel space was built to carry five men instead of one man. We watched it develop, a Spartan simplicity in the middle of the great complex, and it was as if we ourselves would live there, would watch those dials and instruments, would grip those chair-arm controls for the infinitesimal sign that the automatic pilot had faltered, would feel the soft flesh and the softer internal organs being wrenched away from the unyielding bone, and would hurtle upward into the cave of night.

We watched the plating wrap itself protectively around the vitals of the nose section. The wings were attached; they would make the ship a huge, metal glider in its unpowered descent to Earth after the job was done.

We met the men who would man the ship. We grew to know them as we watched them train, saw them fighting artificial gravities, testing spacesuits in simulated vacuums, practicing maneuvers in the weightless condition of free fall.

That was what we lived for.

And we listened to the voice that came to us out of the night:

"Twenty-one days. Three weeks. Seems like more. Feel a little sluggish, but there's no room for exercise in a coffin. The concentrated foods I've been eating are fine, but not for a steady diet. Oh, what I'd give for a piece of home-baked apple pie!

"The weightlessness got me at first. Felt I was sitting on a ball that was spinning in all directions at once. Lost my breakfast a couple of times before I learned to stare at one thing. As long as you don't let your eyes roam, you're okay.

"There's Lake Michigan! My God, but it's blue today! Dazzles the eyes! There's Milwaukee, and how are the Braves doing? It must be a hot day in Chicago. It's a little muggy up here, too. The water absorbers must be overloaded.

"The air smells funny, but I'm not surprised. I must smell funny, too, after twenty-one days without a bath. Wish I could have one. There are an awful lot of things I used to take for granted and suddenly want more than—

"Forget that, will you? Don't worry about me. I'm fine. I know you're working to get me down. If you don't succeed, that's okay with me. My life wouldn't just be wasted. I've done what I've always wanted to do. I'd do it again.

"Too bad, though, that we only had the money for one ship."

And again: "An hour ago, I saw the Sun rise over Russia. It looks like any other land from here, green where it should be green, farther north a sort of mud color, and then white where the snow is still deep.

"Up here, you wonder why we're so different when the land is the same. You think: we're all children of the same mother planet. Who says we're different?

"Think I'm crazy? Maybe you're right. It doesn't matter much what I say as long as I say something. This is one time I won't be interrupted. Did any man ever have such an audience?"

No, Rev. Never.

The voice from above, historical now, preserved:

"I guess the gadgets are all right. You slide-rule mechanics! You test-tube artists! You finding what you want? Gettting the dope on cosmic rays, meteoric dust, those islands you could never map, the cloud formations, wind movements, all the weather data? Hope the telemetering gauges are working. They're more important than my voice."

I don't think so, Rev. But we got the data. We built some of it into the new ships. *Ships,* not *ship,* for we didn't stop with one. Before we were finished, we had two complete three-stages and a dozen nose sections.

The voice: "Air's bad tonight. Can't seem to get a full breath. Sticks in the lungs. Doesn't matter, though. I wish you could all see what I have seen, the vast-spreading universe around Earth, like a bride in a soft veil. You'd know, then, that we belong out here."

We know, Rev. You led us out. You showed us the way.

We listened and we watched. It seems to me now that we held our breath for thirty days.

At last we watched the fuel pumping into the ship—nitric acid and hydrazine. A month ago, we did not know their names; now we recognize them as the very substances of life itself. It flowed through the long special hoses, dangerous, cautiously grounded, over half a million dollars' worth of rocket fuel.

Statisticians estimate that more than a hundred million Americans were watching their television sets that day. Watching and praying.

Suddenly the view switched to the ship fleeing south above us. The technicians were expert now. The telescopes picked it up instantly, the focus perfect the first time, and tracked it across the sky until it dropped beyond the horizon. It looked no different now than when we had seen it first.

But the voice that came from our speakers was different. It was weak. It coughed frequently and paused for breath.

"Air very bad. Better hurry. Can't last much longer . . . Silly! . . . Of course you'll hurry.

"Don't want anyone feeling sorry for me. . . . I've been living fast . . . Thirty days? I've seen 360 sunrises, 360 sunsets . . . I've seen what no man has ever seen before . . . I was the first. That's something . . . worth dying for . . .

"I've seen the stars, clear and undiminished. They look cold, but there's warmth to them and life. They have families of planets like our own sun, some of them . . . They must. God wouldn't put them there for no purpose . . . They can be homes to our future generations. Or, if they have inhabitants, we can trade with them: goods, ideas, the love of creation . . .

"But—more than this—I have seen the Earth. I have seen it—as no man has ever seen it—turning below me like a fantastic ball, the seas like blue glass in the Sun . . . or lashed into gray storm-peaks . . . and the land green with life . . . the cities of the world in the night, sparkling . . . and the people . . .

"I have seen the Earth—there where I have lived and loved . . . I have known it better than any man and loved it better and known its children better . . . It has been good . . .

"Good-by . . . I have a better tomb than the greatest conqueror Earth ever bore . . . Do not disturb . . ."

We wept. How could we help it?

Rescue was so close and we could not hurry it. We watched impotently. The crew were hoisted far up into the nose section of the three-stage rocket. It stood as tall as a 24-story building. *Hurry!* we urged. But they could not hurry. The interception of a swiftly moving target is precision business. The takeoff was all calculated and impressed on the metal and glass and free electrons of an electronic computer.

The ship was tightened down methodically. The spectators scurried back from the base of the ship. We waited. The ship waited. Tall and slim as it was, it seemed to crouch. Someone counted off the seconds to a breathless world: ten—nine—eight . . . five, four, three . . . one—*fire!*

There was no flame, and then we saw it spurting into the air from the exhaust tunnel several hundred feet away. The ship balanced, un-moving, on a squat column of incandescence; the column stretched it-self, grew tall; the huge ship picked up speed and dwindled into a point of brightness.

The telescopic lenses found it, lost it, found it again. It arched over on its side and thrust itself seaward. At the end of 84 seconds, the rear jets faltered, and our hearts faltered with them. Then we saw that the first stage had been dropped. The rest of the ship moved off on a new fiery trail. A ring-shaped ribbon parachute blossomed out of the first stage and slowed it rapidly.

The second stage dropped away 124 seconds later. The nose section, with its human cargo, its rescue equipment, went on alone. At 63 miles altitude, the flaring exhaust cut out. The third stage would coast up the gravitational hill more than a thousand miles.

Our stomachs were knotted with dread as the rescue ship disappeared beyond the horizon of the farthest television camera. By this time, it was on the other side of the world, speeding toward a carefully planned rendezvous with its sister.

Hang on, Rev! Don't give up!

Fifty-six minutes. That was how long we had to wait. Fifty-six minutes from the takeoff until the ship was in its orbit. After that, the party would need time to match speeds, to send a space-suited crewman drifting across the emptiness between, over the vast, eerily turning sphere of the Earth beneath.

In imagination, we followed them.

Minutes would be lost while the rescuer clung to the ship, opened the airlock cautiously so that none of the precious remnants of air would be lost, and passed into the ship where one man had known utter loneliness.

We waited. We hoped.

Fifty-six minutes. They passed. An hour. Thirty minutes more. We reminded ourselves—and were reminded—that the first concern was Rev. It might be hours before we would get any real news.

The tension mounted unbearably. We waited—a nation, a world—for relief.

At eighteen minutes less than two hours—*too soon,* we told ourselves, lest we hope too much—we heard the voice of Captain Frank
Pickrell, who was later to become the first commander of the *Doughnut.*

"I have just entered the ship," he said slowly. "The airlock was
open." He paused. The implications stunned our emotions; we listened
mutely. "Lieutenant McMillen is dead. He died heroically, waiting
until all hope was gone, until every oxygen gauge stood at zero. And
then—well, the airlock was open when we arrived.

"In accordance with his own wishes, his body will be left here in its
eternal orbit. This ship will be his tomb for all men to see when they
look up toward the stars. As long as there are men on Earth, it will
circle above them, an everlasting reminder of what men have done
and what men can do.

"That was Lieutenant McMillen's hope. This he did not only as an
American, but as a man, dying for all humanity, and all humanity
can glory for it.

"From this moment, let this be his shrine, sacred to all the generations of spacemen, inviolate. And let it be a symbol that Man's dreams
can be realized, but sometimes the price is steep.

"I am going to leave now. My feet will be the last to touch this deck.
The oxygen I released is almost used up. Lieutenant McMillen is in
his control chair, staring out toward the stars. I will leave the airlock
doors open behind me. Let the airless, frigid arms of space protect
and preserve for all eternity the man they would not let go."

Good-by, Rev! Farewell! Good night!

Rev was not long alone. He was the first, but not the last to receive a
space burial and a hero's farewell.

This, as I said, is no history of the conquest of space. Every child
knows the story as well as I and can identify the make of a spaceship
more swiftly.

The story of the combined efforts that built the orbital platform
irreverently called the *Doughnut* has been told by others. We have
learned at length the political triumph that placed it under United
Nations control.

Its contribution to our daily lives has received the accolade of the
commonplace. It is an observatory, a laboratory, and a guardian.
Startling discoveries have come out of that weightless, airless, heat-

less place. It has learned how weather is made and predicted it with incredible accuracy. It has observed the stars clear of the veil of the atmosphere. And it has insured our peace . . .

It has paid its way. No one can question that. It and its smaller relay stations made possible today's worldwide television and radio network. There is no place on Earth where a free voice cannot be heard or the face of freedom be seen. Sometimes we find ourselves wondering how it could have been any other way.

And we have had adventure. We have traveled to the dead gypsum seas of the Moon with the first exploration party. This year, we will solve the mysteries of Mars. From our armchairs, we will thrill to the discoveries of our pioneers—our stand-ins, so to speak. It has given us a common heritage, a common goal, and for the first time we are united.

This I mention only for background; no one will argue that the conquest of space was not of incalculable benefit to all mankind.

The whole thing came back to me recently, an overpowering flood of memory. I was skirting Times Square, where every face is a stranger's, and suddenly I stopped, incredulous.

"Rev!" I shouted.

The man kept on walking. He passed me without a glance. I turned around and stared after him. I started to run. I grabbed him by the arm. "Rev!" I said huskily, swinging him around. "Is it really you?"

The man smiled politely. "You must have mistaken me for someone else." He unclamped my fingers easily and moved away. I realized then that there were two men with him, one on each side. I felt their eyes on my face, memorizing it.

Probably it didn't mean anything. We all have our doubles. I could have been mistaken.

But it started me remembering and thinking.

The first thing the rocket experts had to consider was expense. They didn't have the money. The second thing was weight. Even a medium-sized man is heavy when rocket payloads are reckoned, and the stores and equipment essential to his survival are many times heavier.

If Rev had escaped alive, why had they announced that he was dead? But I knew the question was all wrong.

If my speculations were right, Rev had never been up there at all. The essential payload was only a thirty-day recording and a transmitter. Even if the major feat of sending up a manned rocket was beyond their means and their techniques, they could send up that much.

Then they got the money; they got the volunteers and the techniques.

I suppose the telemetered reports from the rocket helped. But what they accomplished in thirty days was an unparalleled miracle.

The timing of the recording must have taken months of work; but the vital part of the scheme was secrecy. General Finch had to know and Captain—now Colonel—Pickrell. A few others—workmen, administrators—and Rev . . .

What could they do with him? Disguise him? Yes. And then hide him in the biggest city in the world. They would have done it that way.

It gave me a funny, sick kind of feeling, thinking about it. Like everybody else, I don't like to be taken in by a phony plea. And this was a fraud perpetrated on all humanity.

Yet it had led us to the planets. Perhaps it would lead us beyond, even to the stars. I asked myself: could they have done it any other way?

I would like to think I was mistaken. This myth has become part of us. We lived through it ourselves, helped make it. Someday, I tell myself, a spaceman whose reverence is greater than his obedience will make a pilgrimage to that swift shrine and find only an empty shell.

I shudder then.

This pulled us together. In a sense, it keeps us together. Nothing is more important than that.

I try to convince myself that I was mistaken. The straight black hair was gray at the temples now and cut much shorter. The mustache was gone. The Clark Gable ears were flat to the head; that's a simple operation, I understand.

But grins are hard to change. And anyone who lived through those thirty days will never forget that voice.

I think about Rev and the life he must have now, the things he loved and can never enjoy again, and I realize perhaps he made the greater sacrifice.

I think sometimes he must wish he were really in the cave of night, seated in that icy control chair 1,075 miles above, staring out at the stars.

FIGHTING DIVISION

by Randall Garrett

*"I would rather have one good fighting division than a full army corps
of untrained, unsure, vacillating troops, however well-meaning their
intentions might be."*

Douglas MacArthur

Braden Kane slammed the palm of his hand on Senator Nordensen's
desk with a sound like a pistol shot. It cracked out and echoed back
from the paneled walls of the room, but was quickly smothered by
the heavy, old-fashioned velvet drapes that covered the windows.

"Damn it, Senator!" His voice seemed to have the same pistol-shot
quality. "There's your evidence! Treason! Not just high misdemeanors;
not just misfeasance, malfeasance, and nonfeasance, but *treason!* He's
giving this country over to Asia just as Sol has sunspots!" Kane pulled
his hand back off the desk top. "And yet you just sit there as though
I'd told you it might rain tomorrow."

Senator Edgar Nordensen was a big, broadly-built man in his mid-
fifties, a heavy punisher of expensive, custom-made shoes. He had
folded his hands on the desk before him and looked up at Kane
through deep blue-gray eyes. He said: "You get too excited, Kane. You
have a tendency to run off at the mouth first and think about it afterwards. What do you expect me to do with this information?"

"Do with it? Why, give it to the press! Give it to the Senate! Get
him impeached before it's too late!"

"Calm down. And shut up." The senator leaned back in his chair.
"Sit down and try deep-breathing exercises; they may help you to
think. Do you know what would happen if I gave this stuff to the
press?" He indicated a big folder on his desk. "Or to the Senate? It's

not easy to impeach the President of the United States, Kane. Oh, this evidence would raise Hell, all right. Eventually, there might be an impeachment brought. But can you imagine the turmoil this country would be in, in the meantime? Do you think we can afford that at this dangerous time? We are prepared for war, Kane; all-out, total, cataclysmic war; the damndest war this planet has ever seen. We have stuff today that makes the armaments of the Cold War, back in the Sixties, look like firecrackers pretending to be hand grenades.

"If we tell the public, in the midst of all this, that the President is plotting treason, the tension will be a thousand times worse than it was a month ago. Tell them that this invasion from space is a phony, and all Hell will be out for noon."

"And if we *don't* tell 'em," Kane said sharply, "the President will have this country amalgamated with the Asian Bloc, and they will have taken over this country without a shot being fired."

"How do you know that's what he has in mind?"

"Bah! Can you think of any other reason for getting all buddy-buddy with the Asian Premier on the basis of a threat he *knows* to be false? And the Premier is here in Washington right now, just waiting for this sweetness and light to come about. You can bet your life that *he* knows this threat is phony, too."

"That's one part of it we have no proof of," the senator said. "Not one iota of proof. If we gave this thing out now, just as it is, it would do a thousand times more harm than good."

"Are you going to let it just ride, then?" There was utter astonishment in Braden Kane's voice.

"Don't be silly! Of course not! You're the best investigator I've ever had on my staff, Kane, but this has got you into a tizzy. What we're going to do is think about it. Think! Understand? Nothing's going to happen before tomorrow, so get some sleep. Tomorrow, we'll make plans on some way to use this stuff without blowing the world sky-high and ourselves with it. Meanwhile, go to bed and think about being Attorney General after the next election; that should put you in a more reasonable state of mind."

A wry smile came over Braden Kane's face, and he showed a visible effort to force himself to calmness. "I'm sorry, Senator," he said after a moment. "I realize I shouldn't let myself get worked up that way. My apologies."

"Unnecessary. Now go home. Be here at nine tomorrow morning."

Senator Edgar Nordensen himself did not take the advice he had given his aide. Instead of sleeping, he thought. And an hour later he was wearing a light topcoat, walking toward 1600 Pennsylvania Avenue, a bulky attaché case in his hand.

Once he stopped at a newsfac vendor, dropped in a coin, and waited a few seconds while the machine light-printed a copy of the Washington *Bulletin*. Then he pulled it out of the dispensing niche and read it while he walked on.

ALIEN FLEET STILL DECELERATING BEYOND SATURN ORBIT

"Still No Visual Contact," say Observatories.

Senator Nordensen skimmed through it rapidly to see if there was anything new. There wasn't. The situation was as it had been three hours previously.

He looked at the article headlined UNIFIED DEFENSE COMMAND. Nothing there, either, except that a bulletin was "momentarily expected from the White House."

After making sure that the situation, publicly at least, was unchanged, the senator folded the newsfac and slipped it into the side pocket of his topcoat. By that time, 1600 Pennsylvania Avenue was only two blocks away.

The newsmen who saw him walk up to the gate made notes, and one of them asked him a question.

The senator smiled. "I don't know anything more than you do, boys. Maybe less. No comment on anything else."

They shrugged in a friendly fashion and went on waiting. Even the arrival of the leader of the Opposition Party was of little moment at this time.

The Secret Service guard at the gate was not so easy to deal with. "I'm sorry, Senator," he said respectfully, "but I have no orders pertaining to you. The President does not wish to be disturbed."

The senator took an envelope from his inside coat pocket. It was addressed to the President of the United States and was marked PERSONAL AND URGENT. "See that he gets this immediately. I'll wait here until he's read it."

"But, Senator, it's after ten o'clock!"

The senator raised an eyebrow. "Emergencies have a habit of not paying any attention to what the clock says. Your job is to guard the

President; mine is to help run the country. I suggest you do your job without interfering with mine, son."

Ten minutes later, Senator Nordensen was being shown into the President's office.

"Good evening, Mr. President," he said formally, taking the hand the Chief Executive offered.

"Good evening, Senator. Take off your topcoat and have a seat. Would you like something to drink?"

"Not just now, thank you, Mr. President. Later perhaps." The senator settled himself into the proffered chair and the President sat down behind his desk.

"Your letter, Senator," said the President in a formal but still friendly tone, "was a little disturbing—as, of course, you intended it to be. Still, I appreciate your couching it in terms that only I would understand."

"Thank you, Mr. President."

"What is it you want, Senator? An explanation?"

"Not . . . just yet, Mr. President. Let me tell you what I know first. Perhaps there won't be any need for explanations."

The President was surprised, but only the faintest trace of it showed on his face. "Very well. Go ahead."

"I don't want to take up too much of your time, sir, but I want to show you how my own thoughts ran. I want to present not only my evidence but my reasoning. So if I repeat facts of history that every schoolboy knows, I ask your indulgence; I won't do it more than necessary."

"Senator, at a time like this, clear thinking is necessary. If you feel it worthwhile to explain to me why the Fourth of July is a national holiday, I shall listen carefully, I assure you." There was not one iota of irony in his voice or manner.

Senator Nordensen chuckled. "Thank you, Mr. President. I won't need to go back quite that far, nor be quite that explicit.

"However . . . when you started your first term in office, the world was at peace. Oh, we were still having the African Brush Wars; but that was only to be expected, the way Africa is divided into so many little squabbling states. But the threat of Armageddon hadn't hung over us for nearly fifteen years. Nuclear disarmament and free inspection by both sides. The Cold War had been over for a decade and a half. We had a happy, peaceful world, even without a World Government.

"Then came the Guadalcanal Incident. The Asians had secretly built a nuclear testing lab there. Something went wrong and the island was half destroyed and wiped clean of life. It was like Krakatoa all over again, except that the radioactivity left no doubt about the cause of the explosions, even though there was no evidence left.

"Of course, the Asians denied it, said it was *our* doing, not theirs, but I choose to believe our own reports. I know how the Asian mind works.

"That was six years ago, and things have been going steadily from bad to worse at an accelerating pace. No more inspections; nuclear buildup; spacecraft with inertiogravitic drives being fitted as launchers for space torpedoes with thermonuclear warheads. The situation had become about as touchy as dry nitrogen iodide."

The senator stopped, frowned, and looked at the President intently. "You and I are on opposite sides of the political fence, Mr. President, but we know and . . . I hope . . . respect each other."

The President nodded. "I have always respected your honesty and integrity, Senator, even when I disagreed with your viewpoint."

"Thank you. And I may say the same. Also, I've been in politics long enough, and been involved in top-level government long enough, to know what a burden the past six years has been to you."

"Does it show?" the President asked wryly.

The senator smiled. "We all get older, sir. It's just that Presidents of the United States are in a position to do it faster than the rest of us." His smile faded. "Trying to stave off Armageddon is, in the long run, a man-killing job, Mr. President."

There were several levels of meaning in that sentence, and both men recognized them.

The President nodded slowly. "Yes. Yes, it is."

"I think you may have hit upon a solution," the senator said abruptly, "but I am not yet certain how good it is. If you're found out, you'll be sunk without a trace. Things will be worse than before. And I, personally, don't see how you can escape being found out."

"Go on." The President's voice was level.

"Six weeks ago, according to reports, a spaceship of unknown manufacture, reportedly having been already spotted decelerating from just below light velocity, attacked one of our Moon bases. The torpedoes it sent were intercepted and detonated. It then attempted to attack an Asian base a thousand miles away and was destroyed by an Asian space torpedo. Since then, the radio observatories have announced that there are a dozen more ships coming in. Since the first one attacked without warning, it is assumed that the others will do the same.

"Because of this threat, all thought of international conflict has vanished. We are co-operating wholeheartedly with the Asians, and they are working with us. The Premier is here in Washington at this moment, working with you on an agreement that will practically give, *in toto,* control of the combined armed forces of the civilized world into the hands of a Unified Command. The Secretary General of the European Coalition is expected to land tomorrow and is expected to concur. A meeting of the Prime Ministers of the British Commonwealth has already agreed to let the Prime Minister of Canada act as their ambassador with plenipotentiary powers, and he will be here at about the same time as the European Secretary General.

"Unless certain information—which I have—comes to light, the treaties and agreements will be made. The Senate will almost certainly back you unanimously in validating the treaties.

"We will then have a unified world for the first time in history. Mankind, with its collective back presumably to the wall, will be ready to fight a truly alien enemy. All very fine.

"But, Mr. President—*what are you going to do when that enemy doesn't show up?*"

After a pause, the President said mildly: "What makes you think they won't show up, Senator?"

"Please, Mr. President," the senator said, a pained expression on his face. "Let's not play games. I told you I had evidence. More than evidence; it is proof. You know and I know that that attack on the Moon was rigged. That 'alien ship' was one of our own, robot controlled, and set up to make a realistic but nondamaging attack and be destroyed in the process. If the Asians hadn't got it, we would have. Do you deny that, Mr. President?"

A long moment, then, with a sigh: "No. No, Senator, I do not deny it. What you say is true. The attack was a phony."

"All right. Fine. We understand each other, then," the senator said. "I think the idea was brilliant. Practically overnight our internal differences were forgotten in the face of this threat. As I say, the idea was brilliant. But I am not so sure about the execution of that idea. Where do we go from here?"

He held up a hand. "Now, wait, Mr. President. Before you say anything more, let me assure you of one thing. I give you my word that I will never use this politically. I lost the election to you last time, but only by a small margin. I think my party will nominate me again next time, and you can't run a third time. Furthermore, I don't think there's a man in your party now who can beat me at the polls. Do you?"

"Personally," said the President cautiously, "I will concede that. Publicly, I could name half a dozen men who could carry us to glorious victory. Go ahead and make your point."

"All right. I intend to be the next President of the United States. But I give you my word of honor that I will never use the information I have as a political weapon . . . *unless—*"

"Unless?"

"Unless you bungle it yourself. That will, of necessity, force my hand. But it may also mean that Armageddon will come at last, and there will be no United States left for me to be President of. All ambition aside, Mr. President, I don't think I should care to lose the United States.

"Now, I cannot believe that you, with your brilliance, have actually put yourself into the blind alley that you seem to be in. But I like to think that my own mind is not altogether a dull one, and I can't see what your out is.

"You have rigged a phony attack. You have, on the basis of that phony attack, brought about the unification of Mankind, a project with which I am in hearty agreement.

"But it seems to me that you have overreached yourself. The incoming fleet is supposed to be approaching. People are going to wonder why it never gets here. Surely you don't intend to have a skirmish with a dozen robot-controlled spacecraft, which will be wiped out with ease?"

"No."

"Mr. President, I admit that I do not know all the facts. I should like very much to know them. I assure you of my cooperation—one hundred per cent—but I must know how I can help. I must know the facts."

"Senator," the President said firmly, "you'll get them. But first I will have to tell you something that may upset you just a little."

"Which is?"

"That the facts you have are correct, but the theory you have based on them is all wrong. I am not quite the altruist you think I am."

Senator Nordensen blinked. Was Kane right, after all? Was the President actually plotting treason? Was he plotting a short-term threat solely in order to turn control of the United States over to the Asians? Ridiculous! And yet . . .

"I engineered a war threat, all right," the President went on, "but not the one you think I did. And let me assure you that we are going to have a war on our hands, but not the one you think we will.

"Let's go back to the Guadalcanal Incident. In fact, to just a little before that.

"I am no scientist, Senator; you have had more training in that field than I. But I think I have my facts straight.

"Shortly before the Guadalcanal Incident, one of our Lunar observatories, checking interstellar gamma radiation, picked up a peculiar source of radiation coming from the direction of the constellation of Scorpio. No Earthside observatory could have detected the radiations because of the blanketing effect of the atmosphere. After a little time, the scientists deduced what was causing the radiation.

"Imagine a body traveling at a velocity very close to that of light. The hull of the ship—and God only knows what those hulls are made of!—strikes the hydrogen atoms that are found everywhere, even in interstellar space. The result, at those velocities, is the same as proton bombardment in a synchrotron or other such particle accelerator. You get gamma radiation.

"The change in wave length indicated that the source was decelerating, and, furthermore, that the deceleration would bring the object to a stop relative to the Solar System. That information was reported directly to me, of course. I asked that it be kept under wraps for a while, until the Lunar Naval observatory could be more certain of its facts. Shortly thereafter, the object ceased to radiate. Its velocity had dropped low enough so that it no longer struck the hydrogen atoms with sufficient force to cause nuclear reactions.

"What added to the confusion at the time was a fainter source of radiation from the same area. The scientists were uncertain of their previous analysis.

"Then the scout ship landed."

"Scout ship?" The senator's mind was still trying to adjust.

"That's what it was. A scout ship in advance of the main fleet. Not six weeks in advance, but six *years* in advance.

"The alien ship managed to foul up our radar somehow. It was nearly twenty hours before we got word of what was happening on Guadalcanal, where they landed.

"Senator, we don't know yet what they used, but they killed every living thing on that island with the exception of themselves. Every man, woman, and child. Every bird, every beast, every insect, every plant. All died.

"The Asian Premier got me on the Hot Line, and we gave joint orders to certain selected units.

"We hit Guadalcanal with seven thermonuclear bombs.

"That, Senator, was the Guadalcanal Incident."

"My . . . *God!* But, then we were at war with the aliens six years ago! Why didn't you announce it? Why all this—" He stopped himself abruptly and his eyes changed. "Oh. I see."

"Certainly," said the President. "What would have happened? We were not prepared for war. We had exactly three more bombs between us. Peace, it's wonderful, but it wasn't worth a damn to us just then."

"Just what did you do, Mr. President?"

Instead of answering, the President of the United States looked over at a door that led into an adjoining room. "Would you please come in, Mr. Premier?"

The door opened, and the Premier of Asia came into the President's office. Almost automatically, Senator Nordensen rose to his feet.

He smiled a little as he took the Premier's outstretched hand. "I'm pleased to meet you, Mr. Premier. So you gentlemen had the room bugged, eh?"

"Your President and I have worked together for six years, Senator," the Premier said with a heavy Russian accent. "We each need to know what other is doing. Is necessary for efficiency."

"That's the way we've *had* to work," the President said as the other two seated themselves.

"What would have happened if we had announced an impending invasion from interstellar space at that moment?" the President went on. "What proof did we have? We had blasted the scout into radioactive plasma. We had only one indication, and that was a funny gamma source in Scorpio. What would that mean to the average man? Oh, we could have gotten something started, but would anyone have really had their heart in it?"

"Was exactly same with my people in Asia," said the Premier. "Is impossible to work up to fighting pitch against enemy which remains theoretical."

"So you agreed to disagree?" the senator said.

"Exactly," said the President. "Neatly put. It was the Cold War all over again, only more so. I called the Premier a dirty Communist . . ."

"And I retaliated by calling President dirty Capitalist," the Premier said with a grin. "Is very effective. Is kind of war people can understand instead of unbelievable space opera."

"And we had it under control," the President explained. "We both knew that no matter how close to boiling our new Cold War got, it could not boil over because we were holding the lid down." He smiled at Senator Nordensen. "The election three years ago gave us a tough time, I'll admit. If you'd won, as you very nearly did, it would have been you, not me, who would have been helping the Premier sit on that lid. Fortunately, I was sure you would be able to handle it. If Fenner had won your party's nomination, though . . ."

The senator winced. "Ugh. Let's not think about it."

"*He* was calling me dirty names *before* Guadalcanal Incident," the Premier said with a reminiscent smile. "Not *kulturny,* that one."

"Anyhow," the President said, "we managed. What's your opinion now, Senator?"

"I'm still frightened," Nordensen said. "More than ever before. But not of the same thing.

"I think you did right. Both of you. How else could we have jacked the taxes up so high to take care of these enormous expenditures? A few gamma rays from the stars couldn't have made Congress vote those taxes and those hellishly high budgets. To say nothing of reenacting the draft law."

"If I had tried taxing Asia so greatly," the Premier said, "Grand Presidium would have found nice home in Ukraine for me to retire to. And Vladisensky? Is almost as bad as Fenner." His slightly Oriental eyes narrowed at the thought.

" 'United we fall, divided we stand,' " the senator misquoted.

"Precisely," agreed the President. "As it is, we are armed to the teeth with every weapon we know how to build. We still may not win, but we'll give them a Hell of a good show for their money."

"Only one thing," the senator said. "Braden Kane knows about the phony attack on Luna. I agree that it was necessary in order to give us some preparation. The people are eager to believe in it now, since it is a relief from the threat of global war. But Kane is convinced you're a traitor—and I don't think Kane would understand the truth. He isn't capable of it."

"Can you hold him back for three days?"

"Yes. Why three days?"

"You have mentioned Armageddon before, Senator. In three days, Armageddon will begin. After that, it won't matter what Kane says."

The senator closed his eyes. Then he made another misquotation.

"As Tiny Tim says, 'God help us, each and every one.' "

International Organizations: The Functional Approach to Peace

At this writing, it appears that the United Nations Organization is in danger of going the way of its predecessor, the League of Nations. The political disputes and alignments of large and small countries seem to have been transferred wholesale into the forums of the U.N., with voting patterns closely following the apparent dictates of a number of blocs—poor countries, nonwhite countries, Afro-Asian countries, Free World countries, and so on. The depressing knee-jerk reactions of all groups to the complicated and dangerous problems facing them allows precious little room for hope. Structural limitations such as those imposed by the veto in the Security Council only add to the difficulties, and the organization that was to bring light unto the nations of the world has so far produced only heat.

One ray of hope filters through this otherwise dark universe. The U.N. has done much laudable work in the areas of health, education, agriculture, and the fight against illiteracy. Specialized agencies of the United Nations have brought the vision and (in some cases) the reality of a better life to a considerable number of human beings. There are some who argue that this cooperation in the humanitarian field can be extended to the political; that once nations cooperate through international agencies they will come to understand and appreciate—even cherish—the things they have in common rather than the ideas that divide them. This general concept is known as *functionalism.*

Indeed, there already exists considerable cooperation between countries in a wide variety of areas. For example, many countries work together (including some countries in conflict over other matters) to control the illegal traffic of drugs. Police forces the world over exchange information on suspected terrorist groups and individuals. The World Health Organization receives cooperation in its fight against the spread of disease—a task that requires monitoring all over the globe. Unfortunately, it has proved very difficult to transfer this cooperation to the political sphere. The inability of the United Nations to agree in practice on an acceptable definition of the term "aggression" is but one example.

Among the many problems facing the world at the present time is the real prospect of famine. Already, tens of millions of people go to bed hungry each night and the situation seems sure to deteriorate further. The possibility of "food wars," or more broadly, "resource wars," is being openly discussed. In "Triage," we witness an international organization of the future attempting to deal with this problem at a time when real power has been transferred to it. It is a grim picture, one that is difficult to imagine but which is not farfetched. As you read the story, think of countries like Bangladesh and the current concern over predicted changes in the world's climate. If you are a religious person, a short prayer may be in order.

TRIAGE

by William Walling

(Tre-áhzh) [Fr. "sorting"]. Classification of casualties of war, or other disaster, to determine priority of treatment: Class 1—those who will die regardless of treatment; Class 2—those who will live regardless of treatment; Class 3—those who can be saved only by prompt treatment.

We have met the enemy, and he is us. From Walt Kelly's cartoon strip, *Pogo.*

The man waited with outward patience, standing stiff-backed, knees together, opposite the desk where a nervous male secretary feigned work under his punishing scrutiny. Seemingly quite at ease, the man was tall, forceful in appearance, with a proud aquiline nose, sleek dirty-blond hair, and chill hazel eyes. The wraparound collar of his pearl-gray jacket was buttoned even though a power brownout had once again paralyzed Greater New York during the night and early morning hours, leaving the anteroom overwarm and stuffy.

The secretary darted occasional furtive looks toward the tall man. At last, their glances crossed. The secretary squirmed. "Sorry . . . for the delay, Mr. Rook. I can't imagine what's keeping her."

"Madame Duiño is busy, Harold." The man folded his arms. "Don't trouble yourself; pretend that I'm not here."

"Yes, sir." The secretary plunged back into his paperwork. When the intercom buzzed, moments later, he said hastily, "You can go right in now, sir." The inner door eased shut; the secretary looked immensely relieved.

The office of Dr. Victoria Maria-Luisa Ortega de Duiño, Chairperson of the Triage Committee, UN Department of Environment and Population, was as severe and desiccated as the woman herself. A blue-and-white United Nations ensign hung behind her desk on the left; on the right, atop a travertine pedestal, the diorite bas-relief presented to her by Emilio Quintana, Mexico's preeminent sculptor, depicted a stylized version of UNDEP's logo: the globe of Earth, with a set of balanced scales and the motto TERRA STABILITA superimposed across it. A pair of guest chairs hand-crafted of clear Honduras mahogany were adrift upon a sea of wall-to-wall shag the color of oatmeal. Save for an old-fashioned French pendulum clock, and the floor-to-ceiling video panels—now dark—Sra. Duiño's sanctum was enclosed by barren, oyster-white walls. Lined damask draperies shrouded a picture window overlooking the East River ninety floors below.

Rook did not take a seat. He chose a spot just inside the door, studying the old woman with an indolent expression.

If aware of the man's presence, Dr. Duiño gave no sign, occupying herself with the sheaf of papers before her on the desktop. Her hair, as short and brittle as her temper, was roached stiffly backward to form a platinum aura; her features were wrinkled, sagging, though her eyes retained the dark and shining luster of youth. Around her frail neck, pendant against the lace *mantilla* thrown over her shoulders, was a large silver crucifix. In six months and eleven days, Victoria Duiño would celebrate her eighty-eighth birthday. She was the most reviled and detested human on Earth.

"My apologies, Bennett." The old woman looked up at last. "Please sit down. I had not intended to keep you away from your desk so long."

"Quite all right, Victoria." The tall man made it a point to remain standing. "I take it the matter is pressing?"

"No. Not really." She touched a button; a hologram condensed in the largest video tank across the office, allowing them to eavesdrop on a courtroom scene. Now in its penultimate stages, the trial was taking place half a continent away. "I merely wished to assure myself that we were obtaining full PR value from the Sennich Trial," she said. "Have you been following it?"

Bennett Rook turned with leisurely grace. He listened briefly to the defense attorney's final plea. "Alas, no," he said. "Actually, I've been too busy. Is it the gluttony action you mentioned in your memo?"

The old woman made no rejoinder. Her interest in the trial was exclusively political. In her mind, the guilty verdict soon to be handed down was a foregone conclusion. One Nathan Sennich, and a pair of miserable codefendants, had resurrected the ancient sin of gluttony, which reflected but one symptom of an ailing society in her opinion. But, for UNDEP, the trial carried important propaganda overtones; widespread public indignation, fanned by tabloid journalism, had begun to create a welcome avalanche of letters and calls. If UNDEP press releases were to add fuel to the fire, were to milk the sordid affair for all it was worth . . .

"The gall of those swine!" she said. "In a starving world, they dared slaughter and gorge themselves on the roasted flesh of a fawn stolen from Denver's zoo."

Rook's lip curled. His voice was resonant, unruffled. "Grotesque, Victoria. But I can't imagine what's in it for us. In forty-eight hours, or less, the remains of our mischievous gourmands will be fertilizing crops in Denver's greenbelts; or perhaps those of the Denver Zoo itself. Poetic justice, eh?"

"Don't make light of it." A throaty burr crept into Sra. Duiño's voice. "I asked you to get PR cracking on this action. You have ignored my request. We stand to reap a certain amount of public sympathy if trial coverage is properly handled, Bennett."

"We?" The man's brows lifted. "Triage Committee? Nothing could improve our image, Victoria. Day before yesterday, *L'Osservatore Romano* once again referred to you as the 'Matriarch of Death'. PR abandoned all attempts to 'sell' the committee years ago."

"You know perfectly well what I meant," said the old woman tautly.

"Bennett, must we always fence? Can't you ever sit down and converse with me sociably?"

Rook smiled an arctic smile. He rocked on his heels, returning her stare with steadfast calm. "There are several matters we shall never see in the same light, Victoria. Nothing personal, you understand; if you want the truth, I rather like you. If I did not, I would tell you so. I am no hypocrite."

"No," she agreed, "you are not a hypocrite. Blunt, perhaps; but not a hypocrite."

He made a slight gesture, turning over the flats of his hands. "Blunt, then, if you will."

Dr. Duiño watched him with unwinking concentration. "I want your cooperation," she said, "not your enmity."

Rook sighed. "I'd rather not discuss it."

"Why not? Are you afraid?"

Rook tensed the least bit. "I'm afraid of nothing. Pardon me; of almost nothing."

"Your use of a qualifier makes me curious."

"My only fear," he said slowly, "is for the continuation of our species."

"And mine, Bennett. But that is what we are laboring so earnestly to ensure."

"To little avail," he said.

"That is not a fair and reasonable statement."

"Oh?" Rook stood firm under her withering gaze, his eyes aglow with patriotic fervor. "You are familiar with this week's global delta, of course."

Victoria Duiño hesitated. "I am. It is most encouraging—less than one-quarter of one percent."

"Bravo!" Rook clapped his hands in genteel emphasis. "Despite our sanctions, proscriptions, lawful executions and extensive triage judgments; despite floods, earthquakes, plagues and the further encroachment of desertlands upon our remaining arable soil, there are now some twenty-five thousands *more* human beings on Earth than the nine and three-quarter billions we could not feed last week. And you tell me all's right with the world."

Sra. Duiño looked taken aback. After a moment, she said quietly, "Zero population growth will be a reality in one and one-half to three years."

"Too damned little, Victoria—too damned *late*. With sterner measures, we would be on the downslope instead of approaching the crest."

"I am familiar with your views," said the woman. " 'Sterner measures', as you call them, would have made us less than human. I refuse to subscribe to inhumanity as a cure-all for the world's ills."

"Humane philosophy is a luxury we cannot afford."

"Bennett, Bennett! You are intelligent, industrious, thoroughly dedicated; that is why I selected you from the crowd these many years past. But have you no compassion, no slight twinge of conscience for the dreadful judgments we must pass day after day, month after month, year after year?"

"None," said Rook. "It's an interesting facet of human nature: mortal danger to a single individual—the victim of a mine disaster, or someone trapped in a fire—never fails to stimulate a tidal wave of public sympathy, while similar disasters affecting gross numbers are mere statistics, hardly worth a shrug. We do what must be done. We do it analytically, dispassionately, dutifully. Were it otherwise, there would be no sane committee members."

"I . . . see. And you think me a senile, idealistic old fool who should step aside and allow a younger individual, such as yourself, to chair the committee?"

Bennett Rook stood perfectly still. "Senile? Hardly. Your mind is clear and sharp as ever; you are one of very few who can best me in debate. Idealism I will not answer; I am not qualified. But you are less of a fool than anyone I have ever met. I admire you vastly, respect you enormously, even love you in my own manner, perhaps. Yet, given the opportunity, I would replace you tomorrow."

"Because I am too soft?"

"Because you are too soft," he said.

"Thank you for stopping by, Bennett. May I remind you once again to prod PR on the Sennich Trial coverage?"

"I'll take care of it immediately." Rook tipped his head; there was nothing sarcastic about his deference. "Good day, Victoria." His eyes were veiled as he left the office.

In silent reflection, Victoria Duiño gazed at the closed door for quite some time before resuming her labors.

And the Egyptians will I give over into the hand of a cruel lord; and a fierce king shall rule over them, saith the Lord, the Lord of hosts.

And the waters shall fail from the sea, and the river shall be wasted and dried up. (Isaiah 19:4,5)

In midafternoon, the intercom's buzz interrupted Victoria Duiño's train of thought. "Yes, Harold?"

"Cardinal Freneaux is in the anteroom, madame. And your granddaughter is calling—channel sixteen."

She glanced at the clock. "If I am not mistaken, His Eminence made an appointment for three. It is now but two fifty-eight. Surely he will allow me two minutes to indulge my only grandchild."

"Surely he will, madame. I will tell him."

"Thank you, Harold." Keeping one eye and a portion of her attention on a flashing digital readout, Dr. Duiño switched on the vidicom. "Monique, I can't talk very long just now. I trust that you and Stewart are well?"

"Hello, Grandma." The image that formed in the small tube was of a petite, attractive young woman whose dark hair was in disarray. Her eyes were red-rimmed, desperate.

Victoria Duiño straightened in her chair. "What is it, child? What has happened?"

"I've got . . . big troubles, Grandma."

"What sort of troubles? Can I help?"

"Oh, God, I hope so! I . . . doubt it. I just got back from the doctor. I'm . . . in the family way, if you know what I mean."

"Monique!" Sra. Duiño clutched the arms of her chair. "How did it happen? Were you careless?"

"No. I don't know. I . . . took my pills. I never missed. I just don't know, Grandma. Fate, I guess—or bad luck."

After the first flush of emotion had washed through her, Victoria relaxed and began to think. She seized a yellow legal pad and a stylus. "I want to know where you buy your birth-control tablets."

"What? But, Grandma, what does that have to do with—?"

"Never mind, child. Just tell me. I assume you buy them regularly in one specific place?"

"Uh, yes. At Gilbert's Pharmacy here in the arcology complex. But I—"

"Have you any left?"

"A few," said the younger woman. "I think. Yes; a few."

"Send them to me. Mail them this afternoon—special delivery, and insure the package. Address it to Harold Strabough, United Nations

Tower, and beneath the address write the initials V.M.L. That will assure prompt attention. I should receive it tomorrow."

"I . . . all right, Grandma. I will. Oh, Stew's so broken up; we would have been approved for parenthood within the year. What can we do?"

"Leave that to me."

"Can you . . . ? Do you think you can do something?"

"I think so, Monique. I want you to be as calm as you can about this. Follow the doctor's instructions verbatim, and let me know at once if any complications arise."

"Grandma, wh . . . what will they do to me—to my baby?"

"Nothing, for the time being," said Dr. Duiño with assurance. "Unauthorized birth is a crime; unauthorized pregnancy is not. We have many months to effect a solution. Don't be afraid."

"Stew's talking kind of wild," said her granddaughter. "He's been raving about running off to Brazil."

"Hum-m-mph! To live in the jungle with the other outcasts, I suppose. Think about that, Monique. Would the Amazon Basin be a fit place for Stewart and yourself to raise an infant? It is a jungle, just now, in more ways than one. You wouldn't last long enough to give birth, let alone build anything more than an animal existence for yourselves."

"Are you sure, Grandma?"

"Absolutely certain," said the old woman. "I am in a position to know. Do exactly as I have advised. I'll call you later in the week when we have more time to chat. Above all, don't despair, my dear. Until later, then."

"God bless you, Grandma. And . . . thank you. I love you."

Seething inside, Victoria switched off the vidicom. She permitted herself the use of an expletive not in keeping with the dignity of her high office, then seized her bamboo cane and rose stiffly to stand upright, her mind whirling. Monique's call had come at a most inopportune moment; she had only seconds to contemplate its ramifications before receiving the Cardinal.

Diminutive and birdlike, she hunched beside the desk, squinting down at the carpet. It was an attack, of course. But from what quarter? She had been the victim of numberless attacks, both political and physical, during her long career. She had survived eleven attempts on her life, attempts ranging from clumsy bunglings like the home-made bomb thrown by that theology student in Buenos Aires which had permanently impaired the hearing in her right ear, to the ingenious poisoned croissants, four years ago, which had resulted in the death of a loved and trusted friend.

The old woman heaved a sigh, feeling something wither and die inside her. Damn them! There was no time to think about it now. No time. She closed her eyes tightly, washing the residue of Monique's call from her mind, and pressed the intercom button. She hobbled to mid-office, leaning on her cane.

His Eminence, Louis Cardinal Freneaux stood framed in the doorway, a wasted figure whose rich robe hung loosely about him. Victoria knew that he made it a point of honor to limit his caloric intake to something commensurate with that of the most deprived member of his vast flock. She respected him for it, and considered him one of the more intelligent churchmen in her acquaintance. Beneath the red skullcap, the Cardinal's eyes were lackluster and sad.

"You are looking very well, my dear," he said.

"Thank you, Louis. At my age, I can't imagine a nicer compliment." She bent stiffly as if to kiss the prelate's ring.

"That . . . is not necessary," he said, withdrawing. "My visit is official, I'm afraid."

Sra. Duiño straightened slowly. "Is it to be like that?"

"Please don't be offended, Victoria."

"I take it the Holy Father is even more displeased with me than usual," she said. "I am truly sorry to have caused him further pain. What is it this time?"

"Egypt."

The old woman nodded once. She turned slowly and stumped toward her desk, motioning the Cardinal to a chair. "Four million inhabitants of the Nile Delta, formerly Class Three, were declared Class One last week. I fear there was little choice; the vote was unanimous."

"Deplorable!" said the Cardinal.

"No one deplored its necessity more than I. Damanhûr, El Mansûra and Tanta, Zagazig, El Faiyûm and El Minya share the fate of numberless villages scattered along the dry gulch that was once a mighty river."

"There are many Coptic Christians in Egypt," said Cardinal Freneaux. "They have petitioned the Holy See for redress."

"Oh?" Victoria's dark eyes flashed. "And why, pray, have they not petitioned the Father and Teacher in Moscow who refused to allow them to help themselves? More than a decade ago, UNDEP warned of what the Aswan Dam was doing to the Nile. The weight of Lake Nasser upon the land, swollen by spring floods in East Africa, helped create a severe seismic disturbance; the upper Rift Valley developed a subsidiary fracture, and the river found a new path through Nubia to the Red Sea. Today, Cairo is a dusty ruin, as dead and forgotten as the pyramids to the west."

"Rationalization is useless, Victoria." The Cardinal frowned. "We must be practical."

"*Practical,* is it? In modern Egypt, more than three thousand *fellahin* crowd every remaining square mile of arable land. *Something* had to give, Louis."

The Cardinal coughed apologetically. "Four million . . . somethings," he said in a low voice.

Victoria Duiño reacted as if the Cardinal had slapped her. "That was unkind of you. They are four million helpless human beings; they work and love and have aspirations and laugh together on rare occasions, even as you or I. Unfortunately, they also have appetites. Do you—does the Holy Father—suppose that we *enjoy* our work?"

"Of course not, Victoria."

"Then why does he refrain from exercising whatever influence he has over Eastern Orthodox churchmen inside the Soviet Union? Why can't they aid in making the Kremlin realize that its insensate drive for world domination is literally starving millions? With Soviet help instead of hindrance our triage activities would dwindle significantly."

Cardinal Freneaux made a small sound of disgruntlement. "You know how little public opinion is worth in Russia."

Sra. Duiño silently recited a Hail Mary, allowing her temper to subside. She tapped a stylus on the desktop. "Louis, the impoverished portion of the Third World sprawling across Africa, Asia Minor and the Arabian Peninsula is a Russian creation; it is perpetuated solely as a political weapon. Soviet-controlled military forces outnumber UN forces two to one; we are powerless to inflict our wills upon the Third World, save for the Indian subcontinent and South America, except as Russia allows. The Great Northern Bear graciously condescends to permit triage judgments rendered wherever and whenever we choose, then points a long propaganda finger and calls us 'murderers of millions'.

"But let us suggest something *beneficial,* such as the Qattara Project, and the Bear immediately exercises his veto. The measure dies without question of recourse."

Cardinal Freneaux looked uncomfortable. "I am not familiar with the project," he dissimulated, hoping against hope to divert the old woman's waxing anger.

"Really?" Victoria's eye radiated pale fire. She spun a tickler file, then touched a series of buttons on the video controller. A full-color map of the Middle East formed in the large tank. "Just southwest of Alexandria, is El Alamein, a town of some historical significance. Near there, Britain's armored forces turned back those of Nazi Germany in one of the climactic land battles of the Second World War.

"Which is neither here, nor there, except that Britain chose that particular site to make her winner-take-all stand for an excellent reason. To the uninitiated, it would have seemed easy for Rommel's *Panzers* to swing out into the open desert, avoiding Montgomery's trap on his drive toward Alexandria and the Suez. Such was not the case; on a larger scale, the area is a corridor much like Thermopylae, and British strategy much like that of the Greeks who stood off the Persian hordes in classical times. You see, Rommel had neither the petrol, nor supplies, to skirt a huge natural obstacle.

"Let your eye drift southward from El Alamein, Louis. See the long crescent marked Qattara Depression? It is a vast sink rather like Death Valley, which lies between the Libyan Plateau and the Western Desert, and is more than four hundred feet below the level of the Mediterranean in most places.

"UNDEP's ecosystems engineers proposed a fifty kilometer-long canal, excavated by use of 'clean' mini-fusion devices from a point east of El Alamein to the depression. A hydroelectric power station was to have been built on the brink; seventy years would have been required for a large, fan-shaped inland sea to form, stretching from Siwa Oasis near the Libyan border to the foundations of the pyramids at El Giza, with a long neck reaching southward along the Ghard Abu Muharik almost to El Kharga. The Qattara Sea would have altered the climate of the Western Desert, bringing rainfall to the parched, rich soil; in ancient times, much of the region was a garden. Egypt could have reclaimed millions of hectares of arable land, helping to alleviate her perpetual famine.

"The Father and Teacher in Moscow vetoed the proposal out-of-hand." With an abrupt gesture, Victoria switched off the video map. "Pardon me; I did not mean to lecture."

Cardinal Freneaux shifted disquietly in his chair. "You make it sound so brave and simple. The situation is much more complex. Visionary schemes, such as this Qattara Project—"

"There is nothing 'visionary' about it," she said in an icy tone. "I could name a dozen similar UNDEP proposals vetoed by the USSR."

The Cardinal ran his tongue around his upper lip. He rose and began pacing the office, hands clasped behind his back. "The Church is not blind," he said. "Russia's geopolitical game is far from subtle. Yet the Bear is not to be provoked, Victoria. His Holiness dreads war. Have you any concept of the carnage thermonuclear weapons would wreak among the vast populations of Asia, Africa, Europe and the Americas?"

"I have indeed; a global holocaust would either extinguish our species, or reduce our numbers to something the Earth could once again tolerate. Triage on a grand scale, Louis."

The Cardinal was aghast. "How can you even *think* such a thing?"

The old woman shrugged. "There are wars, and then there are wars. We are engaged in a global war right this instant, and one of the major battles is taking place in Egypt. If His Holiness refuses to recognize this fact, I am hard-put to explain it."

"I've never heard you speak like this before, Victoria."

Victoria sighed. "I suppose my optimism and diplomacy have begun to wear out, like the rest of me." She searched the Cardinal with her eyes. "No, that isn't true. Louis, we are not winning the war just yet. But, we will—must! There are, after all, only three alternatives left: triage, Armageddon, or a sniveling decline that is certain to end in a whimper."

Cardinal Freneaux remained silent for a time. "Our conversation has wandered far afield," he said. "Victoria, do you consider yourself a good daughter of the Church?"

"You know that I do."

The churchman pondered something invisible which had obtruded between himself and the old woman. He cleared his throat. "His Holiness was unusually stern when he dispatched me on this mission. He instructed me to plead immediate reclassification of the four million inhabitants of the Nile Delta. He urged me strongly not to take 'no' for an answer."

Victoria Duiño looked solemn. "Then the stern Father must discover that he has an equally stern daughter," she said. "My answer must be . . . no. Battles are never without casualties; grain shipments to Egypt have already halted."

"I warn you; he has spoken of excommunication."

The old woman grew very pale, very calm. "And do you expect me to be intimidated by such a threat?"

"I do not. I have known you too long."

"I am literally amazed that the Holy Father would stoop to attack me personally, would choose to threaten damnation of my immortal soul in order to destroy me professionally. Were he to carry out this awful threat, it would mean absolutely nothing to the Triage Committee or its works. Doesn't he realize that?"

"I'm not . . . sure."

Victoria fingered her crucifix. "Louis, what have we come to? The Church, our Church, has grown quite permissive on the question of homosexuality, now countenances therapeutic abortion, even condones euthanasia when the pain of life becomes too great for her sons and daughters to bear, yet obstinately faces away from the fact that without triage judgments our planet will *never again* be a fit environment for the human species."

"Discussion is painful to me. I must ask you for a definite answer, Victoria."

"You have had it. Tell His Holiness that the Matriarch of Death considers eternal fire a small price to pay for the work she does, and must continue to do."

The Cardinal's eyes were misted. He bowed. "Then I will bid you good-bye, my dear Victoria. I sincerely hope that our next meeting will be more pleasant."

"I hope so."

The causal chain of the deterioration is easily followed to its source. Too many cars, too many factories, too much detergent, too much pesticide, multiplying contrails, inadequate sewage treatment plants, too little water, too much CO_2—all can be traced easily to too many people. Dr. Paul Ehrlich, *The Population Bomb*

Monique's package arrived in late forenoon the following day. Dr. Duiño sent two of the suspect birth-control tablets to the UN lab for analysis, receiving a report in less than one hour. Properly stamped with the infertility symbol, the placebos lacked the chop of any pharmaceutical house, and were therefore quite illegal. If found, the seller would be liable to harsh prosecution.

After an evening snack of thin vegetable soup and soya toast, Sra. Duiño retired to her quarters high on the two-hundredth floor, feeling roughly battered by life. She had been attacked from the left and the right, from above and below.

She pondered Monique's problem all evening, sitting alone in the cramped two-room suite. She rarely left the UN Tower nowadays; there would be little purpose in it. Almost everything that remained in her life was here: her meager creature comforts, the small chapel on the twelfth floor where she heard mass and went to confession—more and more infrequently of late—and her work.

Sudden nostalgia spun her mind back to the early days in Argentina when Vicky Ortega, a serious-minded medical student newly risen from the tumbled shacks and endemic poverty of a Buenos Aires *barrio,* had visited the clinic and been lovestruck at first sight of a young doctor named Enrique Duiño. Love had come in the blink of an eye, in the macrocosmic slice of eternity it had taken for the handsome doctor to look at her infected throat and prescribe three million units of penicillin and bedrest.

Oh, she had pursued him; no mistake about that—two months of thoroughly premeditated "accidental" encounters, while her studies went neglected and she lived in terror of losing him.

But she remembered the miraculous day when she had led Enrique up a crooked, debris-strewn alley to the ramshackle lean-to her parents and brothers and sisters called home, the day Enrique had turned his hat brim slowly, nervously in his deft surgeon's hands while he asked her father's permission to make her his bride. Later, mentioning the five children she'd prayed God would allow them to have, Vicky had received the lecture which was to change her life.

In those days, Enrique had been a walking encyclopedia, stuffed with demographic statistics, facts and figures on family planning, on the fantastic rate at which the world's population was doubling, on the coming extinction of fossil fuels, and on and on. They, he had insisted, would have *one* child—two at most. At first, Vicky had been horrified, then resentful, then fascinated.

Their first decade together had been an exciting hodgepodge: the missionary hospital in Bolivia; their studies together in Madrid, and at the Sorbonne, and later in Mexico; finally, the years in America and, somewhat late in life, the birth of young Hector Duiño. That had been the richest, most tranquil period, Victoria reflected. Enrique and she had practiced in San Francisco, and in New York; the boy had grown to manhood almost overnight, so it seemed. And when Enrique's crusading articles won him selection as a delegate to the third International Population Control Convention in New Delhi, she had been so proud, even though her practice had kept her home in New York.

Curiously enough, Enrique had always tended to neglect his own health. When the cholera epidemic erupted, he had refused to be flown home with the majority of other delegates, staying on in India to lend what help he could. The first prognosis from the hospital where they had taken him had been favorable. But Victoria had had an ugly premonition. All her prayers had gone unanswered; her beloved had come home in a plain wooden casket.

The ensuing years of loneliness melted into a blur—long years of struggle and disappointment. She had carried on Enrique's great work, making a nuisance of herself by shouting his message into deaf political ears. But at last—not too late, perhaps; but *very* late—after the Mideast conflagration which all but destroyed Israel and placed the whole of Islam under Russia's thrall, she and the other criers-in-the-wilderness had at last been heard. After much panicking and pointing of fingers, the UN peace-keeping troops had been bolstered and united into a true international armed force. Then—could it be nearly twenty-five years ago?—UNDEP's Triage Committee had been formed. Dr. Duiño had been its first and only chairperson.

The old woman raised withered hands. There were times when she imagined she could see light streaming through the mottled parchment stretched over her bones. Where was pretty little Vicky Ortega now? Submerged in this twist of exhausted flesh, she supposed.

She rose with the aid of her bamboo cane and shuffled to the window. It was after midnight, and fairly clear. She looked up at the few visible stars for a time, then stood gazing far out over the inky wash of the Atlantic into the depths of night.

Two days later, a preliminary report arrived from the UN Intelligence Agents who were investigating the bogus birth-control tablets. The assistant manager of Gilbert's Pharmacy, thirty-third layer, twelfth sector, northwest quadrant of the gargantuan arcology complex where Monique and her husband lived, had recently applied for parenthood. Pressure was brought to bear—and a hint of amnesty if full cooperation were forthcoming. During the ensuing week, the trail led from the pharmacy to a disreputable retired chemist in Cleveland, to a thrice arrested though never convicted Philadelphia dealer in black market pharmaceuticals, to a drug wholesaler with shady connections in Trenton, and finally to the legman for a prominent Congressman. A second week passed before the UN Intelligence Director called Sra. Duiño and mentioned a name.

"Are you certain?" she asked, stiffening.

"No, madame. There's no way short of a trial to be certain, and I doubt whether the DA would indict upon the sort of evidence we've managed to gather."

"Are you yourself certain?"

"I . . . yes, madame. I myself am quite certain."

"Thank you for all your efforts," she said. "Please make sure your findings remain confidential."

Dr. Duiño snapped off the vidicom and sought her cane. She stumped from the office, startling Harold and three VIP's who were waiting to see her. She rode upward in the private lift, failed to acknowledge everyone who greeted her in the corridor, and spent the remaining afternoon hours closeted with her fellow Triage Committee members behind closed doors.

Late the following day, Victoria entered Bennett Rook's anteroom, breezing past his receptionist unannounced.

The inner office was crowded; Rook was at the chalkboard, running over some statistics with a group of underlings. He telescoped the collapsible pointer he had been using. "Dr. Duiño. To what do we owe this honor?"

"I must speak to you at once in private." She shooed them out with her cane, causing a concerted fumbling for notebooks and other papers. The UNDEP employees filed out, studiously avoiding one anothers' eyes.

When the door closed behind the last straggler, she said, "Is this room safe?"

"Quite safe, Victoria."

The old woman inspected Rook analytically. "Well, is it to be 'wroth in death, and envy after'? Or will you bargain?"

"Pardon me?"

"Come, come, Rook; bluffing was never your forte. If for some reason I should choose to step down," she said, speaking slowly, distinctly, "will you allow my granddaughter to bear her child in peace?"

"Why, certainly, Victoria. As I once told you, I'm not a hypocrite."

"No," she said, "merely a . . . !" She choked off the gutter term that came to her lips. "May I ask what I have done to you to deserve *this?*"

"Personalities aren't involved," he said. "It's the job—the job you are *failing* to accomplish. You left me no choice."

The old woman swayed, leaning heavily on her cane. Rook moved as if to help her, but she fended him off, saying sharply, "Please keep your hands to yourself."

Settling herself in a chair, Victoria Duiño looked up at the man, her eyes bright. With measured intonation, she enumerated certain facts concerning an assistant pharmacy manager, a Cleveland chemist, a Philadelphia dealer in pharmaceuticals, a drug wholesaler, and a Congressman's stooge.

Rook was nonplused. "Thorough," he said smoothly. "You've been very thorough, as I anticipated. You realize, of course, that such 'evidence' would never hold up in court."

"No district attorney, judge, or jury will ever hear it."

"Then, how—?"

"Tomorrow morning," directed the old woman sternly, "you will personally arrange official parenthood sanction for my granddaughter and her husband. Spare me the seamy details of how the deed is to be accomplished."

"And . . . if I refuse?"

Victoria's smile was thin, totally lacking in humor—the smile of a canary who has successfully evaded the cat. "I visited with the other seven members of our committee yesterday, Rook. They all seemed quite eager to see things *my* way. Persist in your endeavor, and you will find yourself out on the street, looking in. Discovering another meal ticket might become a serious problem."

Bennett Rook took a moment to digest this information. "Then I suppose you have won," he said at last.

"Yes, I suppose so. As such things are reckoned."

"Do you blame me?" Rook sounded the injured party. "I'm not really an ogre, Victoria. You've lived long, worked hard; you've seen the world change into something ill and decrepit. Was it so despicable to try and force you to lay down your burden and rest?"

"It was," she said, "though I don't expect you to understand why. You are not a flesh and blood creature, Rook; no juices of life flow within you. You are cold and rational—both a superb asset, and a potentially terrible liability to triage activities."

"I'll make the necessary arrangements tomorrow," he said.

Victoria Duiño nodded. "Good. Now that we understand one another, I have a bombshell for you: the Matriarch of Death has at last decided to abdicate. Not, however, because of your foolish blackmail scheme.

"You were correct, Rook: I am indeed old, feeble and used up. And tired—very tired. You strike at me through my grandchild; His Holiness attacks me through my faith; my name is anathema from Antarctica to Greenland, and all around the world."

"You've managed to amaze me, Victoria."

"Furthermore," she went on, disregarding his incredulous stare, "had you refrained from this silly coup, you might well have been elected Chairperson of the Triage Committee next week. As it is, while eminently qualified, you have proved yourself utterly unworthy."

"Bitter gall." Rook grimaced. "That does sting, Victoria. But don't count me out just yet. I—"

"Hear me, Bennett!" She twisted the cane savagely in her hands. "This will be our final encounter, and I intend to have the last word. I want to clarify something, now and forever; something you *must* comprehend.

"You have repeatedly condemned my triage philosophy as being too lenient, too soft. It is not. Triage is, and has always been, a concession to the inevitable, not premeditated mass-murder. Twenty-five years ago, in the white heat of a new crusade, we set a rather idealistic goal: semi-immediate reversal of runaway overpopulation. We were dismayed to find it not that simple. How can an illiterate Third Worlder, whose single recreation in an otherwise drab existence is sex, be persuaded to remain chaste during his wife's fertile period?

"But now, whether you care to acknowledge it or not, a dim glow brightens the far end of the tunnel. We faced cold facts, long ago, asking ourselves whether it would be wiser to disrupt every socio-economic system on Earth by seeking a quick solution, or to wage a strategically paced, long-range war. The latter policy is saner, more practical, and far more humanitarian; the ultimate solution may lie farther in the future, but victory is also much more assured.

"I will not live to see even a partial victory; nor, in all likelihood will you, Rook. But my great-grandchild-to-be, whose strange godfather you are, might do so—*if* you and the others make the best possible use of the varied technological weapons we will someday have at our disposal: new bio-compatible pesticides, new hybridized grains, reclamation of desertlands, perhaps interplanetary migration.

"As in any war, we will face mini-triumphs and small setbacks, major victories and hideous defeats; we must bear up equally under good fortune and adversity alike. We must take what we have to take, and give what we have to give to re-create a world where my great-grandchild-to-be can enjoy a noble, cheerful life, a world where a gallon of potable water is not a unit of international exchange, where reusable containers are not an article of law, where food is abundant and air is fit to . . ."

Victoria broke off, shaking her head sadly. "I can see that I am wasting breath. Very well; if you choose to have your lesson the hard way, so be it. I wish you luck; you will need all you can get."

The old woman labored to rise. Though he dared not help her, Bennett Rook came forward half a step despite himself. She did not deign to look at him again, making her way slowly to the door, dignity pulled tightly about her like a cloak.

Her mind at peace, Victoria went to her quarters and phoned St. Patrick's Cathedral. She spent two minutes persuading the young priest who buffered all incoming calls that she was indeed who she said she was. Finally, he allowed her to speak to Cardinal Freneaux.

"Oh, Louis, I'm so glad; I was afraid you had already left the city. I called to invite you to have dinner with me."

"Delighted, my dear Victoria." He sounded pleased and surprised. "I had made other plans, but they can be changed."

"This is an occasion," she said. "A UNDEP news bulletin of some importance will be released tomorrow morning. I want you to be the first to know. May I come by for you in an hour, Louis?"

"Fine! That will be fine. I'll look forward to seeing you."

She dressed without haste—the black gown reserved for formal affairs—and slipped on a diamond bracelet Enrique had given her many years before. She had difficulty fastening the clasp of an emerald brooch at her neck.

When she was ready, she took up a large satin handbag, the fancy black cane with the ivory tip, and called down to the garage. The electric limousine and its driver, accompanied by omnipresent UN Security Agents, were waiting for her outside the tower's staff entrance.

They rode in silence, with the windows rolled up despite the muggy summer evening. With keen interest, Victoria watched the defeated multitudes overspilling the sidewalks; four hours, and more, remained until the midnight curfew. They crawled west through dense traffic on East 48th Street, turning right at Fifth Avenue.

When the limousine nosed its way into an enormous queue of hungry supplicants gathered outside St. Patrick's Cathedral, Dr. Victoria Maria-Luisa Ortega de Duiño crossed herself.

Conflict Resolution: War

Armed conflict has characterized the age of the nation-state. In fact, periods of peace are so rare that it often seems that war is "normal." However, the nature of war has changed drastically since the introduction of nuclear weapons in 1945. Before that momentous year, countries usually had considerable time to prepare for war. It was possible to be surprised, as the United States was at Pearl Harbor in 1941, although this was somewhat unusual. A country could afford to absorb the first blow because it knew it had time to recover, mobilize its forces, declare war, and convert from a peacetime to a wartime economy.

This "luxury" no longer exists. The devastation of a nuclear attack means that sufficient forces-in-being must be present to deter others from attacking. It also means that the power *potential* of states is not as important as it used to be, since there will be no opportunity to convert this potential into power. Needless to say, the decision to use war as an instrument of national policy is more important than before, since the existence of the entire nation (not to mention the planet) may very well be at stake.

Because of the existence of nuclear weapons, attention to warfare has shifted to its nonnuclear varients, because the atomic and hydrogen bombs have not prevented countries from fighting each other. For one thing, not all countries possess nuclear weapons, and even those who do have them feel constrained in using them. For example, many countries, including the United States, have engaged in *limited* wars like the Korean and Vietnamese. There were conflicts in which one or more sides refrained from using all its available strength. In addition, there have been numerous civil wars and guerrilla insurgencies since the end of World War II, and an entire mythology surrounding the latter form has grown up. From one point of view, the world is a much more violent place than it used to be because the major nuclear powers have been unable or unwilling to "police" the medium and smaller powers as they used to. The end of the age of "gunboat diplomacy" has many virtues, but it also has its disadvantages.

In "Men of Good Will," we are witness to an armed conflict on the moon between the United States and the Soviet Union. It is a limited war, but one that is limited only by the nature of the terrain.

MEN OF GOOD WILL

by Ben Bova & Myron R. Lewis

"I had no idea," said the UN representative as they stepped through the airlock hatch, "that the United States' lunar base was so big, and so thoroughly well equipped."

"It's a big operation, all right," Colonel Patton answered, grinning slightly. His professional satisfaction showed even behind the faceplate of his pressure suit.

The pressure in the airlock equalibrated, and they squirmed out of their aluminized protective suits. Patton was big, scraping the maximum limit for space-vehicle passengers. Torgeson, the UN man, was slight, thin-haired, bespectacled, and somehow bland-looking.

They stepped out of the airlock, into the corridor that ran the length of the huge plastic dome that housed Headquarters, U. S. Moonbase.

"What's behind all the doors?" Torgeson asked. His English had a slight Scandinavian twang to it. Patton found it a little irritating.

"On the right," the colonel answered, businesslike, "are officers' quarters, galley, officers' mess, various laboratories, and the headquarters staff offices. On the left are the computers."

Torgeson blinked. "You mean that half this building is taken up by computers? But why in the world . . . that is, why do you need so many? Isn't it frightfully expensive to boost them up here? I know it cost thousands of dollars for my own flight to the Moon. The computers must be—"

"Frightfully expensive," Patton agreed, with feeling. "But we need them. Believe me we need them."

They walked the rest of the way down the long corridor in silence. Patton's office was at the very end of it. The colonel opened the door and ushered in the UN representative.

"A sizable office," Torgeson said. "And a window!"

"One of the privileges of rank," Patton answered, smiling tightly. "That white antenna mast off on the horizon belongs to the Russian base."

"Ah, yes. Of course. I shall be visiting them tomorrow."

Colonel Patton nodded and gestured Torgeson to a chair as he walked behind his metal desk and sat down.

"Now then," said the colonel. "You are the first man allowed to set foot in this Moonbase who is not a security-cleared, triple-checked, native-born, Government-employed American. God knows how you got the Pentagon to okay your trip. But—now that you're here, what do you want?"

Torgeson took off his rimless glasses and fiddled with them. "I suppose the simplest answer would be the best. The United Nations must —absolutely must—find out how and why you and the Russians have been able to live peacefully here on the Moon."

Patton's mouth opened, but no words came out. He closed it with a click.

"Americans and Russians," the UN man went on, "have fired at each other from orbiting satellite vehicles. They have exchanged shots at both the North and South Poles. Career diplomats have scuffled like prizefighters in the halls of the United Nations building. . . ."

"I didn't know that."

"Oh, yes. We have kept it quiet, of course. But the tensions are becoming unbearable. Everywhere on Earth the two sides are armed to the teeth and on the verge of disaster. Even in space they fight. And yet, here on the Moon, you and the Russians live side by side in peace. We must know how you do it!"

Patton grinned. "You came on a very appropriate day, in that case. Well, let's see now . . . how to present the picture. You know that the environment here is extremely hostile: airless, low gravity. . . ."

"The environment here on the Moon," Torgeson objected, "is no more hostile than that of orbiting satellites. In fact, you have some gravity, solid ground, large buildings—many advantages that artificial satellites lack. Yet there has been fighting aboard the satellites—and not on the Moon. Please don't waste my time with platitudes. This trip is costing the UN too much money. Tell me the truth."

Patton nodded. "I was going to. I've checked the information sent up by Earthbase: you've been cleared by the White House, the AEC, NASA, and even the Pentagon."

"So?"

"Okay. The plain truth of the matter is—" A soft chime from a small clock on Patton's desk interrupted him. "Oh. Excuse me."

Torgeson sat back and watched as Patton carefully began clearing off all the articles on his desk: the clock, calendar, phone, IN/OUT baskets, tobacco can and pipe rack, assorted papers and reports—all neatly and quickly placed in the desk drawers. Patton then stood up, walked to the filing cabinet, and closed the metal drawers firmly.

He stood in the middle of the room, scanned the scene with apparent satisfaction, and then glanced at his wristwatch.

"Okay," he said to Torgeson. "Get down on your stomach."

"What?"

"Like this," the colonel said, and prostrated himself on the rubberized floor.

Torgeson stared at him.

"Come on! There's only a few seconds."

Patton reached up and grasped the UN man by the wrist. Unbelievingly, Torgeson got out of the chair, dropped to his hands and kness, and finally flattened himself on the floor, next to the colonel.

For a second or two they stared at each other, saying nothing.

"Colonel, this is embar—" The room exploded into a shattering volley of sounds.

Something—many somethings—ripped through the walls. The air hissed and whined above the heads of the two prostrate men. The metal desk and file cabinet rang eerily.

Torgeson squeezed his eyes shut and tried to worm into the floor. It was just like being shot at!

Abruptly it was over.

The room was quiet once again, except for a faint hissing sound. Torgeson opened his eyes and saw the colonel getting up. The door was flung open. Three sergeants rushed in, armed with patching disks and tubes of cement. They dashed around the office sealing up the several hundred holes in the walls.

Only gradually, as the sergeants carried on their fevered, wordless task, did Torgeson realize that the walls were actually a quiltwork of patches. The room must have been riddled repeatedly!

He climbed slowly to his feet. "Meteors?" he asked, with a slight squeak in his voice.

Colonel Patton grunted negatively and resumed his seat behind the desk. It was pockmarked, Torgeson noticed now. So was the file cabinet.

"The window, in case you're wondering, is bulletproof."

Torgeson nodded and sat down.

"You see," the colonel said, "life is not as peaceful here as you think. Oh, we get along fine with the Russians—now. We've learned to live in peace. We had to."

"What were those . . . things?"

"Bullets."

"Bullets? But how—"

The sergeants finished their frenzied work, lined up at the door, and saluted. Colonel Patton returned the salute and they turned as one man and left the office, closing the door quietly behind them.

"Colonel, I'm frankly bewildered."

"It's simple enough to understand. But don't feel too badly about being surprised. Only the top level of the Pentagon knows about this. And the President, of course. They had to let him in on it."

"What happened?"

Colonel Patton took his pipe rack and tobacco can out of a desk drawer and began filling one of the pipes. "You see," he began, "the Russians and us, we weren't always so peaceful here on the Moon. We've had our incidents and scuffles, just as you have on Earth."

"Go on."

"Well—" he struck a match and puffed the pipe alight—"shortly after we set up this dome for Moonbase HQ, and the Reds set up theirs, we got into some real arguments." He waved the match out and tossed it into the open drawer.

"We're situated on the *Oceanus Procellarum,* you know. Exactly on the lunar equator. One of the biggest open spaces on this hunk of airless rock. Well, the Russians claimed they owned the whole damned *Oceanus,* since they were here first. We maintained the legal ownership was not established, since according to the UN Charter and the subsequent covenants—"

"Spare the legal details! Please, what happened?"

Patton looked slightly hurt. "Well . . . we started shooting at each other. One of their guards fired at one of our guards. They claim it was the other way around, of course. Anyway, within twenty minutes we were fighting a regular pitched battle, right out there between our base and theirs." He gestured toward the window.

"Can you fire guns in airless space?"

"Oh, sure. No problem at all. However, something unexpected came up."

"Oh?"

"Only a few men got hit in the battle, none of them seriously. As in all battles, most of the rounds fired were clean misses."

"So?"

Patton smiled grimly. "So one of our civilian mathematicians started doodling. We had several thousand very-high-velocity bullets fired off. In airless space. No friction, you see. And under low-gravity conditions. They went right along past their targets—"

Recognition dawned on Torgeson's face. "Oh, no!"

"That's right. They whizzed right along, skimmed over the mountain tops, thanks to the curvature of this damned short lunar horizon, and established themselves in rather eccentric satellite orbits. Every hour or so they return to perigee . . . or, rather, periluna. And every twenty-seven days, periluna is right here, where the bullets originated. The Moon rotates on its axis every twenty-seven days, you see. At any rate, when they come back this way, they shoot the living hell out of our base—and the Russian base, too, of course."

"But can't you . . ."

"Do what? Can't move the base. Authorization is tied up in the Joint Chiefs of Staff, and they can't agree on where to move it to. Can't bring up any special shielding material, because that's not authorized either. The best thing we can do is to requisition all the computers we can and try to keep track of all the bullets. Their orbits keep changing, you know, every time they go through the bases. Air friction, puncturing walls, ricochets off the furniture . . . all that keeps changing their orbits enough to keep our computers busy full time."

"My God!"

"In the meantime, we don't dare fire off any more rounds. It would overburden the computers and we'd lose track of all of 'em. Then we'd have to spend every twenty-seventh day flat on our faces for hours."

Torgeson sat in numbed silence.

"But don't worry," Patton concluded with an optimistic, professional grin. "I've got a small detail of men secretly at work on the far side of the base—where the Reds can't see—building a stone wall. That'll stop the bullets. Then we'll fix those warmongers once and for all!"

Torgeson's face went slack. The chime sounded, muffled, from inside Patton's desk.

"Better get set to flatten out again. Here comes the second volley."

Psychological Warfare

The goal of psychological warfare is to change the behavior of countries and their populations. Normally, the intent is to weaken the loyalty and confidence that people have in their leaders and their leaders' policies. Although psychological warfare is used during actual wars (Tokyo Rose being a prime example) it is also common during times of "peace." Indeed, one measure of the relationships between countries is the degree to which they engage in this kind of activity. During the Cold War, for example, the United States, through Radio Free Europe and the Voice of America, broadcast programs in many languages into the Soviet Union, Eastern Europe, Mainland China, and numerous other countries in an attempt to influence the attitudes of the people living there. Likewise, Radio Moscow, Radio Peking, Radio Cairo, and the BBC attempted to use the airwaves as an instrument of psychological warfare on selected target populations. At the present time, this activity has been deemphasized (although it has not ended), but there is still a feeling that "the truth will make you free," depending, of course, on what your definition of "the truth" is.

More broadly, ideological buzz words like capitalist, Marxist, and Red, are still used to deflate the claims made by all sides in the international arena, and the deliberate selective use of facts is still a common occurrence. However, as listening populations have become more sophisticated, a definite cynicism has developed, and many people have become resistant to the grosser forms of psychological warfare. The emphasis now seems to be on propaganda based on real or fabricated achievements—space exploration, technological breakthroughs of various types, Olympic medals, and the like—equating achievement with supposed ideological "superiority."

In its most extreme form, psychological warfare means brainwashing, with the target population so convinced by the other side's propaganda that it becomes easy to control and manipulate. In "I Tell You, It's True," Poul Anderson provides us with a stimulating fictional example.

I TELL YOU, IT'S TRUE

by Poul Anderson

The mansion stood on the edge of Ban Pua town, hard by the Nan River. Through a door open to its shady-side verandah, you saw slow brown waters and intensely green trees beyond that flickered in furnace sunlight. Somewhere monkeys chattered. A couple of men in shabby uniforms stoically kept watch. Their rifles looked too big for them. George Rainsdon wondered if they had personally been in combat against his countrymen.

He brought his attention back to the interior. *Now,* he thought. The sweat that plastered his shirt to him felt suddenly cold. Yet this room, stripped of the luxuries that the landlord owner had kept, was almost serene in its austerity. The four Thais across the table were much more at ease than the five Americans.

Rainsdon knew what implacability underlay those slight, polite smiles. Behind Chukkri hung portraits of Lenin and Ho Chi Minh.

Attendants brought tea and small cakes.

Rainsdon made a sitting bow. "Again I thank Your Excellency for agreeing to receive our delegation," he said with the fluency that years as a diplomat in Bangkok had given him. "Believe me, sir, the last thing my government wishes is a repetition of the Vietnam tragedy. We desire no involvement in the conflict here except to act as peacemakers." He laid on the table the box he was carrying. "In token, we beg that you accept this emblem of friendship."

"I thank you," the leader of the Sacred Liberation Movement answered. "The solution of your difficulty is quite simple. You need merely withdraw your military personnel. But let us see the gift you graciously bring."

He opened the package and took forth a handsome bronze statuette in an abstract native-derived style. Its plaque held soft words. One of his generals frowned. Chukkri flashed him a sardonic glance that might as well have said aloud, *Not even the Americans are stupid enough to imagine that assassinating us will halt the advance of our heroic troops.* "Please thank your President on my behalf," he uttered.

The warmth of his touch completed the activation of a circuit.

Rainsdon leaned forward. *Go for broke!* His slight giddiness passed into a feeling that resembled his emotions when he had led infantry charges in Korea in his long passed youth. The rehearsed but wholly sincere words torrented from him:

"Your Excellency. Gentlemen. Let me deliver, at this private and informal conference, the plain words of the United States Government. The United States has no aggressive intentions toward the people of Thailand or any other country. Our sole desire is to help Thailand end the civil war on terms satisfactory to everyone. The first and most essential prerequisite for peace is that your organization accept a cease-fire and negotiate in good faith with the legitimate government to arrange a plebiscite. Your ideology is alien to the Thai people and must not be forced on them. However, you will be free to advocate it, to persuade by precept and example, to offer candidates for office. If defeated, they must accept with grace; if victorious, they must work within the existing system. But we do not want you to renounce your principles publicly. If nothing else, you can be valuable intermediaries between us and capitals like Hanoi and Peking. Thereby you will truly serve the cause of peace and the liberation of the people."

They sat still, the short, neat Asian men, for a time that grew and grew. Rainsdon's back ached from tension. Would it work? Could it? *How* could it? He had said nothing they hadn't heard a thousand times before and scorned as mendacious where it was not meaningless. They had fought, they had lost friends dear to them, they were ready to be slain themselves or to fight on for a weary lifetime; their cause was as holy to them as that of Godfrey of Bouillon had been to him—though it was no mere Jerusalem they would rescue from the infidel, it was mankind.

Finally, frowning, a fist clenched beside his untasted cup of tea, Chukkri said, very low and slow: "I had not considered the matter in just those terms before. Would you explain in more detail?"

Rainsdon heard a gasp from his aides. They had not expected their journey would prove anything except a barren gesture. Glory mounted in him. *It does work! By God, it works!*

He got busy. The circuitry in the statuette would fuse itself into slag after three hours. That ought to be ample time. The CIA had planned this operation with ultimate care.

The laboratories stood on the peninsula south of San Francisco, commanding a magnificent view of ocean if it were possible to overlook the freeway, the motels, and the human clutter on the beach. The sanctum where Edward Sigerist and Manuel Duarte had brought their guests made it easy to ignore such encroachments. The room, though big, was windowless; the single noise was a murmur of ventilators blowing air which carried a faint tinge of ozone; fluorescent panels threw cold light on the clutter of gadgetry burying the workbenches around the walls, and on the solitary table in the center where six men sat and regarded a thing.

Fenner from MIT spoke: "Pretty big for that level of output, isn't it?" His tone was awed; he was merely breaking a lengthy silence.

"Breadboard circuit," Sigerist answered, equally unnecessarily considering what a jumble of wires and electronic components the thing was. "Any engineer could miniaturize it to the size of your thumb, for short-range work, in a few months. Or scale it up for power, till three of them in synchronous satellites could blanket the Earth. If he couldn't do that, from the cookbook, he'd better go back to chipping flints." He was a large, shaggy, rumpled man. His voice was calm but his eyes were haunted.

"Of course, he'd need the specs," said his collaborator, lean, intense, dark-complexioned Duarte. His glance ranged over the visitors. Fenner, physicist, sharp-featured beneath a cupola of forehead; Mottice, biochemist from London, plump and placid except for the sweat that now glistened on his cheeks; tiny Yuang of the Harvard psychology department; and Ginsberg of Cal Tech, who resembled any grocer or bookkeeper till you remembered his Nobel Prizes for quantum field theory and molecular biology. "That's why we brought you gentlemen here."

"Why the secrecy?" Yuang asked. "Our work has all been reported in the open literature. Others can build on it, as you have done. Others doubtless will."

"N-n-not inevitably," Sigerist replied. "Kind of a fluke, our success.

This isn't a big outfit, you know. Mostly we contract to do R and D on biomedical instrumentation. I'm alone in having a completely free hand, which is how come I get away with studying dowsing. I was carrying on Rocard's investigations, which were published back in the mid-'60's and never got the attention they deserved."

Receiving blank stares: "Essentially, he gave good theoretical and experimental grounds for supposing that dowsing results from the nervous system's response to variations in terrestrial magnetism. I was using your data too, Dr. Mottice, Dr. Ginsberg. Then at the Triple-A-S meeting three years ago, I happened to meet Manuel at an after-hours beer party. He was with General Electric . . . He called to my notice the papers by Dr. Yuang and Dr. Fenner. We both took fire; I arranged for him to transfer here; we worked together. Kept our mouths shut, at first because we weren't sure where we were going, later because we made a breakthrough and suddenly realized what it meant to the world." He shrugged. "An unlikely set of coincidences, no?"

"Well," Ginsberg inquired, "what effects do you anticipate?"

"For openers," Duarte told him, "we can stop the war in Thailand. Soon after, we can stop all war everywhere."

The room was long, mirrored, ornate in the red plush fashion of Franz Josef's day. The handful of men who sat there were drab by contrast, like beetles.

Not a bad comparison, thought the President of the United States. *For Party Secretary Tupilov, at least. Premier Grigorovitch seems a bit more human.*

He made the slight, prearranged hand signal. His interpreter responded by nervously tugging his necktie. It energized a circuit in what appeared to be a cigarette case.

"First," said the President, "I want to express my appreciation of your cooperativeness. I hope the considerable concessions made by the United States, especially with regard to the Southeast Asia question, seemed more than a bribe to win your presence here. I hope they indicated that my government genuinely desires a permanent settlement of the conflicts that rack the world—a settlement such that armed strife can never occur again."

While his interpreter put it into Russian, he watched the two over-lords. His heart thumped when Grigorovitch beamed and nodded. Tupilov's dourness faded to puzzlement; he shook his big bald head as if to clear away an interior haze.

His political years had taught the President how to assume stern-ness at will, however more common geniality was. "I shall be blunt," he continued. "I shall tell you certain home truths in unvarnished lan-guage. We can have no peace until every nation is secure. This re-quires general nuclear disarmament, enforced by adequate inspection. It requires that the great powers join to guarantee every country safety, not against overt invasion alone, but also against subversion and in-surrection. Undeniably, every nation that we Americans label 'free' is not. Many of their governments are tyrannical and corrupt. But liberation is not to be accomplished through violent revolution on the part of fanatics who, if successful, would upset the world balance of power and so bring us to the verge of the final war.

"Instead, peace requires that the leading nations cooperate to make available to the people of every country the means for orderly replace-ment of their governments through genuinely free elections. This pre-supposes that they be granted freedom of speech, assembly, petition, travel, and worship, in fact as well as in name.

"Gentlemen, we have talked too long and done too little about democracy. We must begin by putting our own houses in order. You will not resent my stating that your house is in the most urgent need of this."

For the only time on record, Igor Tupilov wept.

"I find it hard to believe," Mottice whispered. "That fundamental a change . . . from a few radio quanta?"

"We found it hard to believe, too," Sigerist admitted, grimly rather than excitedly. "However, your work on synergistics had suggested that the right combination of impulses might trigger autocatalytic transfor-mations in the synapses. It doesn't take a lot, you see. These events happen on the molecular level. What's needed is not quantity but quality: the exact frequencies, amplitudes, phases, and sequences."

"Our initial evidence came from rats," Duarte said. "When we could alter their training at will, we proceeded to monkeys, finally man. The human pattern turned out to be a good deal more complex, as you'd expect. Finding it was largely a matter of cut-and-try . . . and, again, sheer luck."

Yuang scowled. "You still don't know precisely what the chemistry and neurology are?"

"How could we, two of us in this short a time? Our inducer ought to make quite a research tool!"

"I am wondering about possible harm to the subject."

"We haven't found any," Sigerist stated, "and we didn't just use volunteers for experimentation, we took part ourselves. Nothing happens except that the subject believes absolutely what he's told or what he reads while he's in the inducer field. There doesn't seem to be decay of the new patterns afterward. Why should there be? What we have is nothing but an instant re-educator."

"Instant brainwasher," Ginsberg muttered.

"Well, it's subject to abuse, like all tools," Fenner said. They could see enthusiasm rising in him. "Imagine, though, the potentialities for good. A scalpel can kill a man or save his life. Maybe the inducer can save his soul."

The agent of the Human Relations Board smiled across his desk. "I think our meeting has a symbolic value beyond even what we hope to accomplish," he said.

Hatred smoldered back at him from dark eyes under a bush of hair. One brown fist thumped a chair arm. The bearded lips spat: "Get with it, mother! I promised you an hour o' my time for your donation to the Black Squadron, and sixty minutes by that clock is what you're gonna get, mother."

The local head of Citizens for Law and Order turned mushroom pallid. His dull-blue eyes popped behind their rimless glasses. "What?" he exclaimed. "You . . . gave government funds . . . to that gang of . . . of nihilists—?"

"You will recall, sir," the Human Relations agent replied, mildly, "that you agreed to come after I promised that the investigation of the assault on Reverend Washington would be dropped."

He pressed a button on his desk. "Ringing for coffee," he said, repeating his smile. "I suspect we'll be here longer than an hour."

He leaned forward. As he spoke, passion transfigured his homely features. "Sirs," he declared, "you are both men whose influence goes well beyond this community. Your power for good is potentially still greater than your power for evil. A moderate solution to the problems which called forth your respective organizations must be found . . . before the country we share is torn apart. It can be found! If not perfect satisfaction, then equal and endurable dissatisfaction. If not utopia, then human decency. The white man must lay aside his superiority complex, his greed, his indifference to the suffering around him. The black man must lay aside his hatred, his impatience, his unrealistic separatism. We must work and sacrifice together. We must individually strive to give more than we get, in order that our children may inherit what is rightfully theirs: freedom, equality, and well-being under the law. For we are in fact all equals, all Americans, all brothers in our common humanity."

He spoke on, and his visitors looked from him to each other with a widening gaze, and at last, slowly, their hands reached forth to clasp.

"And if a mistake is made," Duarte answered Fenner in a sarcastic tone, "why, you give the patient a jolt of inducer and straighten him out again." He grinned. "Sig and I actually got to playing with that. He made me a Baptist. I retaliated by making him a vegetarian."

"How'd it feel?" Yuang inquired, sharp-voiced.

"M-m-m . . . hard to describe." Sigerist rubbed his chin and leaned back in his chair till he looked at the ceiling. "We knew what was going on, you see, which our test subjects didn't. Nevertheless, vegetarianism seemed utterly right. No, let me rephrase that: it *was* right. I'd think of what I've read about slaughterhouses and— We foresaw this, naturally. We stuck by our promises to return next day and be, uh, disillusioned, told we'd been forced into a channel, that our prior beliefs and preferences were normal for us. I thought I could make the comparison later, having then experienced both attitudes, and decide objectively which was better. But right away, when Manuel spoke to me, after the slight initial fogginess of mind had cleared, right away I decided what the hell, I do like steak."

Duarte sobered. "For my part," he said, "frankly, I miss God. I've considered going back to religion. Might have done so by now, except I realize certain faiths are . . . well, easier to hold, and I'd be sensible to investigate first."

Penny twisted a strand of blonde hair nervously between her fingers. Her bare foot kicked an old copy of the *Tribe* against a catbox ammoniacally overdue for changing, with a dry rustle and a small puff of flug. Sunlight straggled through the window grime to glisten off bacon grease on the dishes which filled the sink in one corner of her pad.

"Like, talk," she invited. "Do your thing."

"I hope you don't consider me a busybody," said the social worker in the enormous hat. She sighed. "You probably do. But with your unemployment compensation expiring—"

Penny sat down on the mattress which served for a bed, lit a cigarette, and wished it were a joint. "I'll get along."

The social worker raised a plump arm to point at Billy, playing contentedly with himself in his playpen. At eighteen months, his face had acquired enough individuality that Penny had felt sure Big Dick was the father. She often wondered where Big Dick had gone.

"I'm concerned about him," the social worker proceeded. "Don't you realize you're creating a misfit?"

"This is a world he ought to fit into?" Penny drawled. "Come off it." The smoke was pleasantly acrid in her nostrils.

"Do listen, darling." The social worker gripped her big purse, almost convulsively, squeezing together the brass knobs on its clasp. "You're throwing away his life as well as your own."

For a moment the peace emblem drawn on the wall wobbled. *Damn tobacco,* Penny thought. *Cancer.* She stubbed out the cigarette on the floor. It occurred to her that she really must unplug the bathtub drain, or anyway wash her feet in the sink . . . Oddly hard to concentrate. The woman in the enormous hat droned on:

"—you'll move in with yet another man, or he'll move in with you. Don't you realize that a kiss can transmit syphilis? You could infect your little boy."

Oh no! Horror struck. *I never thought about that!*

"—You say you are protesting the evil and corruption of society. What evil? What corruption? Look around you. Look at the Thailand Peace, the Vienna Détente, the Treaty of Peking. What about the steady decline of interracial violence, the steady growth of interracial cooperation? What about the new penological program, hundreds of prisoners let out of jail every day, going straight and staying straight?"

"Well," Penny stammered, "well, uh, yeah, I guess that's true, like I seen it in the papers, I guess, only can you trust the kept press?"

"Of course you can! Not that the press is kept. This is a free country. You have your own newspapers of dissent, don't you?"

"Well, we got a lot to dissent about," Penny said. The way the visitor talked and acted, she had to be a person who'd understand. "I don't work on one myself, though. Like, that's not my bag. I'm not the kind that wants to kill pigs or throw rocks, either. I mean, a pig's human too, you know? Only when my friends keep getting busted or clubbed, like that, I can't blame they get mad. See what I mean? If we could all love each other, the problems would go away. Only most people are so uptight they can't love, they don't know how, and the problems get worse and worse." Penny shook her head, trying to clear out the haze. *But things* are *getting better like she said!* "Maybe they've finally begun to learn how in the establishment?"

"They have always known, my dear," the social worker answered. "What they have found at last is practical ways to cure troubles. We have a wonderful future before us. And violence, dropping out, unfair criticism is not what's bringing it. What we need is cooperation within the system.

"You're not with it, Penny. I'll tell you where it's at. Law is where it's at; the police aren't your enemies, they're your friends, your protectors. Cleanliness is where it's at, health, leaving dope alone, regular habits, regular work; that's how you contribute your share to the commune. And marriage. You simply don't know what love is till you're making it with one cat, the two of you sharing your whole lives, raising fine clean bright children in a country you are proud of—"

I . . . I never saw . . . never understood. . . .

Finally Penny cried on the large bosom, in the comforting circle of the plump arms. The social worker soothed her, murmured to her, breathed in her ear, "You don't have to give up your friends, you know. On the contrary. Help them. Help me call them together for a rally where we can tell them—"

"What happens to the person who operates the inducer, hands out the propaganda?" Fenner wondered.

"Oh, the impulses can be screened off," Sigerist replied. "You can easily imagine how. We used a grounded metal-mesh booth. Manuel's since designed a screen in the form of a net over the head, which could be disguised by a wig or a hat. For weak short-range projections, anyhow. Powerful ones, meant to cover a large area, would doubtless continue to require a special room for the speaker." He hesitated. "We haven't established whether psychoinduction occurs with more than one type of radio input. If it does, perhaps a shield against a given type can be bypassed by another."

"I tried to lie, experimentally, while under the field myself," Duarte said. "And I couldn't. I'd try to convince a volunteer that, oh, that two and two equals five. Right off, I'd get appalled and think, 'You can't do that to him! It isn't a fact!' Of course, fiction or poetry or something like that was okay to read aloud, except I got some odd looks from our subjects when I kept explaining at length that what they were hearing was untrue."

"So we'd either speak our lies from the booth," Sigerist put in, "or we'd tell them things we knew . . . believed . . . were real. That's another funny experience. Reinforcement in the brain, I suppose. At any rate, you grow quite vehement, about everything from Maxwell's equations on up. We confined ourselves to that sort of thing with the volunteers, understand. First, we'd no right to tamper with their minds. Second, we didn't want to give the game away. They were always told this was a study of how the tracings on a new kind of three-dimensional EEG correlate with verbal stimuli. Our falsehoods were neutral items. 'Have you heard Doc Malanowicz is trying to use the Hilsch tube in respiratory function measurements?' Next day we'd disabuse them, always in such a fashion that they didn't suspect. We hope. The spectacular lies we saved for each other." His chuckle was not too happy a sound. "I'm a Republican and Manuel's a Democrat. When we were experimenting, both of us under the inducer field—the temptation to make a convert grew almighty strong."

"Ladies and gentlemen, the President of the United States."

"My fellow Americans. Tonight I wish to discuss with you the state of the nation and of the world. Our problems are many and grave. You know them both by name and by experience—international turmoil; cruel ideologies; subversion; outright treason; lawlessness; domestic discord, worsened by the unfair criticism of certain so-called intellectuals—a small minority, I hasten to add, since by and large the intellectual community is firmly loyal to the American ideal.

"What is that ideal? Let me tell you the eternal truths on which this country is founded, for which it stands. We believe in God. We believe in country; we stand ready to fight and die if need be, in the conviction that America's cause is always just. We believe in the democratic process, and therefore in the leaders which that process has given us—"

Ginsberg whistled. "If this gadget fell into the wrong hands—Help!"

"Would it necessarily?" Fenner asked. His glance flickered around the table. "I know what you're thinking," he said in a hurried voice. " 'The H-bomb's not in a class with this.' Right? Well, let me remind you that thermonuclear fusion is on the point of giving us unlimited power . . . clean power, that doesn't poison air or soil. Let me remind you of lives saved and knowledge gained through abundant radionuclides. And the big birds haven't flown yet, have they?" He drew breath. "If this, uh, inducer is as advertised, and I see no reason to doubt that, why, can't you see what it'll mean? Research. Therapy. Yes, and securing the world. I don't mind admitting I'd turn it on some of those characters who're destroying the ecology that keeps us all alive. Why not? Why can't the inducer be used judiciously?"

"One problem is, when you have the specs, this is an easy thing to build, at least on a small scale," Sigerist replied. "Now when in history was perfect security achieved? You can't reach the entire human race, you know. You may broadcast 'Love thy neighbor' while flooding the planet with inducer waves. But what of the guy who doesn't tune you in? Suppose he happens to be reading *Mein Kampf* instead? Or is down in a mine or driving through a tunnel? Or simply asleep?

"Is everyone who's to be given any knowledge of the inducer's existence . . . will everybody be dragooned first into a mental Janissary corps? I don't see how that can be practical. Their very presence and behavior would tip off shrewd men. And then there are ways . . . burglary, assassination, duplication of research. . . . And once the fact is loose—"

Pidge had to stand a minute and fight his nerves after he stepped out of the car. What if something went wrong?

The suburban street (trees, hedges, lawns, flowers, big well-built houses, under afternoon sunlight that brought forth an odor of growth and a chorus of birdsong) pressed him with its alienness. He was from the inner city, tenements, dark little stores, bars and poolhalls that smelled of urine, smog and blowing trash and thundering trucks and gray crowds. This place was too goddamn quiet. Nobody around except a couple of kids playing in a yard, a starchy nurse pushing a stroller down the sidewalk, a dog or two.

Pidge squared his narrow shoulders. *Don't crawfish now! After the casing you've done, the money you've laid out—* He rallied resentment. *You're not doing a thing except claiming your share. The rich bitches have pushed you around too goddamn long.*

And he wasn't drawing any attention here. He was sure he wasn't. White, and small, not like those bastards who'd shoved him out of their way through his whole life, oh, he'd show them how brains counted. . . . Shave, haircut, good suit, conservative tie, shined shoes, Homburg hat (the wires and transistors beneath his wig enclosed his scalp like claws), briefcase from the Goodwill and car borrowed but you couldn't tell that by looking. And he'd spent many hours in the neighborhood, watched, eased into conversation with servants; everything was known, everything planned, he'd only to go through with his program.

And They wouldn't appreciate his backing out. He'd had a tough time as was, wheedling till They let him in on the operation—the set of operations—he'd gotten wind of. Buying in had cost him all he could scrape together and a third of the haul when he was finished. And it had demanded he do his own legwork and prove he had a good plan.

Well, sure, they'd had plenty of trouble, expense, and risk beforehand, to make these jobs possible. Finding out what was being done in the jails that turned so many guys into squares, hell, into stoolies; finding guards who could be bought; arranging for an apparatus to be smuggled out and stuff to be left behind so the fuzz would think it'd simply been busted; getting those scientific guys to copy the apparatus. And of course it couldn't be used more than for maybe a week, on the scale that they intended. Though people were awful stodgy, unalert, these days—those that watched the speeches on TV or read the papers; don't ever do that, Pidge—the cops wouldn't be too dumb to understand what had happened. Then the apparatus wouldn't be good for anything but hit-and-run stuff.

If Pidge screwed up now, They would be mad. Probably They'd make an example of him.

He shivered. His shoes clacked on the sidewalk.

The doorbell of his target sounded faintly in his ears. He tried to wet his lips, but his tongue was too dry. The door swung noiselessly open. A maid said, "Yes, can I help you?"

Pidge pressed the clasp of his briefcase, the way he'd been taught. "I have an appointment with Mr. Ames," he said.

For an instant she hesitated. His heart stumbled. He knew the reason for her surprise; he'd studied this layout plenty close. The industrialist always spent Wednesdays at home, seeing no one except people he liked. He could afford to.

The maid's brow cleared. "Please come in, sir."

After that, it was a piece of cake. Ames got on the phone and managed to arrange the withdrawal of almost two million in bills, certified checks, and bearer bonds without causing suspicion. He thought Pidge was giving him a chance to make a killing. His wife and staff made no fuss about waiting in an offside room, when Pidge whispered to them that national security was involved.

Naturally, the Brink's truck took a couple of hours to arrive. Pidge had himself a bonus meanwhile. Ames' daughter came back from high school, and she was a looker. Not expert in bed, you couldn't expect that of a virgin, but he sure made her anxious to please him. Pidge had never had a looker before. He was tempted to bring her along. But no, too risky. With his kind of money he'd be able to have whatever he wanted. He would.

After the armored truck was gone and the haul had been transferred in suitcases to Pidge's car, he told the people of the house that life was worthless and an hour from now they should let Ames shoot them. Then the man should do himself in. Pidge drove off to his rendezvous with Their representative, who held his ticket and passport.

"Oh, you can raise assorted horrors," Fenner argued, "but to be alive is to take chances, and I don't see any risks here that can't be handled. I mean, the United States Government isn't a bloc, it's composed of people, mostly intelligent and well-meaning. Their viewpoints vary. They're quite able to anticipate a possible monolith and take precautions."

"Tell me, what is a monolith?" Sigerist retorted. "Where does rehabilitation leave off and brainwashing begin? What are the constitutional rights of Birchers and militants? Of criminals, for that matter?"

"You're right," Mottice said. The sweat was running heavily down his face; they caught the reek of it. "This must never be used on humans without their prior consent and full understanding."

"Not even on those who're killing American boys and Thai peasants?" Sigerist asked. "Not even to head off nuclear war? Given such an opportunity to help, can you do nothing and live with yourself afterward? And once you've started, where do you stop?"

"You can't keep the secret forever," Duarte said. "Believe me, we've tried to think of ways. Every plausible consequence of the inducer's existence that we've talked about involves the destruction of democracy. And none of the safety measures can work for the rest of eternity. The world has more governments, more societies than ours. Maybe you can convert their present leaders. But the fact of conversion will be noticed, the leaders will have successors, the successors could take precautions of their own and quietly instigate research."

In his last years George Rainsdon always had a headache. He was old when the mesh was planted beneath his scalp, and the technique was new. The results were therefore none too good in his case; and the doctors said that doing the job over would likely cause further nerve damage. As a rule the pain was no worse than a background, never completely outside his awareness. Today it was bad, and he knew it would increase till he lay blind and vomiting.

"I'm going home early," he told his secretary, and rose from the desk.

Penelope Gorman's impeccable façade opened to reveal sympathy. "Another sick spell?" she murmured.

Rainsdon nodded, and wished he hadn't when the pain sloshed around his skull. "I'll recover. The pills really do help." He attempted to smile. "The cause is good, remember."

Her lips tightened. "Good? Only in a way, sir. Only because of the Asians, the radicals, the criminals. Without them, we wouldn't need protection."

"Certainly not," Rainsdon agreed. The indoctrination lecture, required of every citizen before implantation was performed, had made that clear. (A beautiful ceremony had evolved, too, for the younger generation: the eighteen-year-old candidates solemn in their new clothes, families and friends present, wreaths of flowers on the inducer, religious and patriotic exhortations that stirred the soul.) To be sure, crime and political deviancy were virtually extinct. Yet they could rise again. Without preventive measures, they would, and this time the inducer would let them wreck America. Eternal vigilance is the price of liberty.

Tragic, that indoctrination of the whole world had not been possible. But in the chaos that followed the Treaty of Peking, the breakup of the Communist empires after Communism was renounced . . . a Turkoman adventurer somehow welding together a kingdom in Central Asia, somehow obtaining the inducer, probably from a criminal . . . the United States too preoccupied with Latin America, with inculcating those necessary bourgeois virtues that the pseudointellectuals used to sneer at . . . and suddenly the Asians had produced nuclear weapons, insulating the helmets for everybody, their domain expanded with nightmare speed, soon they too were in space and could cover the Western Hemisphere with inducer signals, turning all men into robots unless defenses were erected, civilian as well as military—Rainsdon forced his mind out of that channel. Truth was truth; still, people did tend to get obsessed with their righteous indignation.

"You knock off too, Mrs. Gorman," he said. "I've no chores for you

till I recover." The small advisory service—international investments—
that he had founded after leaving a diplomatic corps that no longer
needed many personnel used public data and computer lines. His
office was thus essentially a one-man show.

"Thank you, sir. I appreciate your kindness. I'm snowed under by
work in the Edcorps."

"The what?" he asked, having scarcely heard through a fresh
surge of migraine.

"Educational Corps. You know. Volunteers, helping poor children.
The regular schools teach them to honor their country and obey the
law, of course. But schooling can't overcome the harm from generations of neglect, can't teach them skills to make them useful and productive citizens, without extra coaching." Mrs. Gorman rattled her
speech off so fast that it must be one she often gave. Repetition didn't
seem to lessen her earnestness. *Sexual sublimation?* Rainsdon wondered. He'd had occasion to visit her apartment. Aside from photographs of her late husband, it might almost have been a cell in a
convent.

They left together. She matched her pace to his shuffle. The elevator took them down and they emerged on Fifth Avenue. Sunlight
spilled through the crisp autumn air that could blow nowhere but in
New York. Pedestrians strode briskly along the sidewalks. How wise
the government had been to phase out private automobiles! How wise
the government was!

"Shall I see you home, Mr. Rainsdon? You look quite ill."

"No, thank you, Mrs. Gorman. I'll catch a bus here and—"

The words thundered forth.

PEOPLE OF AMERICA! CLAIM YOUR FREEDOM! YOUR
DIABOLICAL RULERS HAVE ENSLAVED YOU WITH LIES
AND SHUT YOU AWAY FROM THE TRUTH BY WIRES IN
YOUR VERY BODIES. EVERYTHING YOU HAVE BEEN
FORCED TO BELIEVE IS FALSE. BUT THE HOUR OF YOUR
DELIVERANCE IS AT HAND. THE SCIENTISTS OF THE
ASIAN UNION HAVE FOUND THE MEANS TO BREAK OPEN
YOUR MENTAL PRISON. NOW HEAR THE TRUTH, AND
THE TRUTH SHALL MAKE YOU FREE! HELP YOUR
FRIENDS, YOUR LIBERATORS, THE FREE PEOPLE OF THE
ASIAN UNION, TO DESTROY YOUR OPPRESSORS AND EX-
PLOITERS! RISE AGAINST THE AMERICAN DICTATOR-
SHIP. DESTROY ITS FACTORIES, OFFICES, MILITARY FA-

CILITIES, DESTROY THE BASIS OF ITS POWER. KILL THOSE WHO RESIST. DIE IF YOU MUST, THAT YOUR CHILDREN MAY BE FREE!

Down and down the skyscraper walls, from building after building, from end to end of the megalopolis, the voices roared. Rainsdon knew an instant when there flashed through him, *Megaphone-taper units, radio triggered, my God, they must've planted them over the whole country, a million in New York alone, but they're small and cheap, and somewhere beyond that bright blue sky a spacecraft is beaming—* Then he knew how he had been betrayed, chained, vampirized by monsters of cynicism whose single concern was to grind down forever the aspirations of mankind, until the Great Khan had been forced to draw his flaming sword of justice.

Penny ripped apart her careful hairdo. Graying blonde tresses spilled, Medusa locks, over her breasts while she discarded gown, shoes, stockings, corset, the stifling convict uniform put on her by a gaoler civilization. Her shriek cut through the howl of the crowd in the only words of protest she knew, remembered from distant childhood. *"Fuck the establishment! Freedom now!"*

Rainsdon grabbed her arm. "Follow me," he said into her ear. His headache was nearly gone in a glandular rush of excitement, his thoughts leaped, it was like being young again and leading a charge in Korea, save that today his cause was holy. "Come on." He dragged her back inside.

She struggled. "What you at, man? Lemme go! I got pigs to kill."

"Listen." He gestured at the human mass which seethed and bawled outside. "You'd be trampled. That's no army, that's a mob. Think. If the Asians can develop an inducer pattern that gets past our mesh, be sure the kept American technicians have imagined the possibility. Maybe they've developed a shield against it. They'd have sat on that, hoping to keep secret— Anyway, they'll have made preparations against our learning the truth. They'll send in police, the Guard, tanks, helicopters, the works. And these buildings, they probably screen out radiation, they must be full of persons who haven't had the slave conditioning broken. Penelope, our best service is to find that voice machine and guard it with our lives. Give more people a chance to come out where the truth can reach them."

They located the device in an office and waited, deafened, tormented, stunned by its magnitude of sound. Hand in hand, they stood their prideful watch.

But no one disturbed them for the hour or two that remained, and they never felt the blast that killed them.

The Asians knew that American missile sites were insulated against any radio impulses that might be directed at the controllers. They counted on those missiles staying put. For what would be the point of an American launch, when Washington could no longer govern its own subjects? At the agreed-upon moment, their special envoy was offering the President the help of the Great Khan in restoring order; at a price to be sure.

The Great Khan's advisors were wily men. However, being themselves conditioned, they did not realize they were fanatics; and being fanatics, they did not have the empathy to see that their opponents would necessarily resemble them.

In strike and counterstrike, the big birds flew.

"Well, that's certainly a hairy bunch of scenarios," Fenner admitted after a long discussion. "Are you sure things would turn out so bad?"

"The point is," Sigerist replied, "do we dare assume they wouldn't?"

"What do you propose, then?" Mottice asked.

"That's what we've invited you here to help decide," Duarte said.

Ginsberg shifted his bulky body. "I suspect you mean you want us to ratify a decision you've already made," he said, "and its nature is obvious."

"Suppression— No, damn it!" Fenner protested. "I admit we need to exercise caution, but suppressing data—"

"Worse than that," Sigerist said most softly. "As the recognized authorities in your different fields, you'll have to steer your colleagues away from this area altogether."

"How will we do that?" Yuang demanded. "Suppose I cook an experiment. Somebody is bound to repeat it."

"We're big game, you know," Mottice put in. "A new-made Ph.D. who found us out would make a name for himself. Which would reinforce him in pursuing that line of work."

"The ways needn't be crude," Sigerist said. "If you simply, without any fuss, drop various projects as 'unpromising,' well, you're able men who'll get results elsewhere; you're leaders, who set the fashion. If you scoff a bit at the concept of neuroinduction, raise an eyebrow when Rocard is mentioned . . . it can be done."

He paused. Drawing a breath, rising to his feet, he said, "It must be done."

Ginsberg realized what was intended and scrabbled frantically across the table at the device. Sigerist pinioned his arms. Duarte pulled an automatic from his pocket. "Stand back!" the younger man shouted. "I'm a good target shooter. Back!"

They stumbled into a corner. Ginsberg panted, Fenner cursed; Mottice glared; Yuang, after a moment, nodded. Duarte held the gun steady. Sigerist began crying. "This was our work too, you know," he said through the tears. He pressed a button. A vacuum tube glowed and words come out of a tape recorder.

Five years afterward, Sigerist and his family tuned in a program. Most educated persons did, around the world. The Premier of the Chinese People's Republic had announced a major speech on policy, using and celebrating the three synchronous relay satellites which his country had lately put into orbit. Simultaneous translation into many languages would be provided.

Considering the belligerence of previous statements, Sigerist joined the rest of the human race in worrying about what would be said. He, his wife, the children who were the purpose of their lives, gathered in a solemn little group before the screen. The hour in Peking was well before dawn, which assured that India was the sole major foreign country where live listening would be inconvenient. Well, the eastern Soviet Union too, not to mention China itself; but there would be rebroadcasts, printed texts, commentaries for weeks to come.

When the talk was over, Sigerist's wife sought his arms and gasped with relief. He held her close and grinned shakily across her shoulder at the kids. The Premier's words had been so reasonable, so unarguably right. They had opened his eyes to any number of things which had not occurred to him before. For a moment during those revelations he'd wondered, been afraid . . . and then, actually quite early in the speech, the Premier had smiled with his unmatched kindliness and said: "The enemies of progress have accused us of brainwashing, including by electronic methods. I tell you, and you will believe me, nothing of the sort has ever happened."

Intervention in International Politics

Intervention is a term used to describe practices that are as old as the nation-state. The agents of one country have been sticking their individual and collective noses into the affairs of others since at least biblical times. Two major goals are involved when intervention occurs—(1) the acquiring of information, and (2) the weakening of the enemy. The difficulties associated with simply defining "intervention" are truly formidable, and what constitutes intervention has largely been a matter of taste. We say largely, because there is *some* agreement on this matter. If, for example, the United States government armed, supported, and paid for the attempted assassination of Fidel Castro, this would clearly be intervention in the internal affairs of Cuba. But what about granting political asylum to those who dissent from the Soviet system? Is this intervention? Military aid to Chile may well be considered intervention by those who wish to overthrow the present Chilean government. The old cliché about "one person's food is another person's poison" certainly applies to this subject.

Obviously, activities engaged in by one country at the invitation or with the consent of another is probably not intervention in the classical sense. However, the activity may be considered to be intervention by those out of power who had no voice in the invitation in the first place—thus, the legitimacy (and justice) of those in power must be taken into consideration. It should also be pointed out that intervention is manifestly legitimate when undertaken in a good cause such as (in the minds of most people) the rescue of Israeli hostages at Entebbe Airport in Uganda. In addition, intervention is ideologically appropriate (in fact, can become an obligation) for certain nations professing particular philosophical positions. For example, the at least verbal Soviet and Chinese commitments to the support of "wars of national liberation" provide justifications for both countries to intervene in the affairs of others. If the object of intervention is viewed as illegitimate, as Israel is by some of her Arab neighbors, then no justification is given at all.

The author of the present story, Mack Reynolds, is one of the few science fiction writers who has concentrated on political and social themes in his work and who has treated topics like international politics. He is also one of the few writers to place some of his fiction in the "developing" world. Here he shows us intervention in one of its most extreme forms—the decision of one government to take the life of the leader of its enemy.

PSI ASSASSIN

by Mack Reynolds

Supervisor Lee Chang Chu said, "But Sid, are you sure? I have never approved of personal assassination."

Sidney Jakes, of Section G, Bureau of Investigation, Department of Justice, Commissariat of Interplanetary Affairs, of United Planets, was less than his exuberant self. His face was as unhappy as his colleague's. "There's no alternative, Lee Chang. This is the third troupe we've had swallowed up in the maw of El Primero's goonies. He's built a police state unknown since Adolf the Aryan's under Himmler. We've got to get rid of him."

She was less than convinced. "Why the immediacy? Suppose it came out? The reputation of Section G is already so high that if something like this . . ."

Sid Jakes was making negative motions with a forefinger to interrupt her. "That's the point. This Michael Ortega, El Primero of the planet Doria, has our number and is using it in an attempt to club us over the head. Commissioner Metaxa made a big mistake when he revealed to so many chiefs of state the true nature of United Planets. That the basic *raison d'être* of our organization is to push scientific, industrial, and socioeconomic progress, no matter what institutions might stand in the way. Too many were allowed into the secret. Some, evidently, leaked it."

The diminutive Chinese woman—more a girl, in physical appearance—shifted her slight, *cheongsam* clad figure in her chair. "But what is he doing?"

Sid Jakes grunted disgust. "Seemingly not much. He invokes Article One of the United Planets. *The United Planets organization shall take no steps to interfere with the internal political, socioeconomic or religious institutions of its member planets.* And he threatens, if we persist in opposing his policies, to pull out of UP, and, further, to reveal to the total membership of the confederation the fact that Section G, in particular, has been subverting the institutions of the more backward worlds."

"I'm not up on Doria. What are the particular institutions stymieing progress there?"

"A personal dictatorship interested in maintaining the status quo at any price."

Lee Chang said, in protest, "We have many tyrannies in UP. Religious hierarchies, industrial feudalism, matriarchies, patriarchies and so on . . ."

Sid Jakes was waggling his finger at her again. "Not like this. He's comparable to Russia's Stalin, to the Dominican Republic's Trujillo, back in the twentieth century."

A frown on Lee Chang's face was a gentle thing. She said, "I've heard of Stalin, of course."

"Trujillo. Rafael Trujillo," Sid Jakes said impatiently. "Trained by the U.S. Marines in the days when at the drop of a sombrero, the marines landed in any Latin American country that didn't toe the United States mark. Back in the 1920s when the marines were making the world safe for those who had them." He snorted amusement, the usual Sid Jakes showing face for a moment. "With American backing, he seized power in 1930 and held onto it until he was shot in 1961. During those thirty years he ruled absolutely for himself, his family, and a small circle of associates. He milked his little country dry. Finally, even the American elements that had originally supported him, got fed up. But he lasted more than a generation, Lee Chang. We can't afford to have Ortega do the same."

Lee Chang Chu looked unhappily and unseeingly about the Octagon office in which they sat. She said, at last, "But assassination. My experience has been that it seldom accomplishes the desired. Take the

Grand Duke Ferdinand. The South Slavonian patriots who shot him, there on the streets of Sarajevo, hardly expected his death to precipitate the First World War. Take Philip of Macedon, an extremely capable organizer, cut down in his capital. The result? Alexander, his son, evidently a god in physical appearance but no great brain, rampaged through the civilized world with Philip's army, butchering millions in building his empire. And what happened to it on his drunken death? It fell apart, and for generations his generals and their sons, and their sons, fought it out, destroying Greece and the Near East to the point that the stolid Romans were able to take over."

"Two examples," Sid Jakes grimaced.

Lee Chang said softly, "The most famous lynching of all time didn't accomplish that which was desired. That is the silencing of the teachings of the Rebel."

Sid Jakes looked at her in speculation. His own voice was impatient. "Are you so sure? I assume you refer to the troubles in Jerusalem. True enough, His name went on, but did His teachings? Assuming He had original teachings, which has been debated."

Lee Chang frowned. "The Sermon on the Mount went on, even though He died."

"There is nothing original in that sermon. It is all to be found in the writings of the latter prophets in the Old Testament. I was referring to original teachings. If He had any, they were soon forgotten, or"—he twisted his mouth cynically—"deliberately suppressed by those who called themselves followers, but who had their own axes to grind."

"But . . . the Golden Rule."

"Ye Gods, you babe in the woods," Jake snorted. "The Golden Rule hardly originated with Joshua of Nazareth. There hasn't been a religion, a holy man or even a philosopher, who hasn't stated that bit of truth, down through the ages." He turned grimly serious. "There's no use arguing, Lee Chang. El Primero must go. We can't allow him to hang on for a generation or two. Doria is crucial in the economic development of United Planets. We can't have this ruling hierarchy, headed by Ortega, continue to drag their heels. We need an assassin. You say we have one in this Special Talents group of yours?"

"Yes, we have one," Lee Chang Chu said slowly. She came to her feet, preparatory to leaving.

Sid said, "Send him in. We've lost too many good operatives on Doria. El Primero has got to go."

She hesitated before turning to leave. "Any word from Ronald?"

Again his face was empty. "No. We can't raise him. Ronny Bronston, nor any of his troupe. We can only assume the secret police got to him, Lee Chang."

Her words were so low as hardly to be heard. "I see. I'll send Sam in, Citizen Jakes."

"Sam?"

"The assassin you wanted."

At the knock on his partly ajar door, Sid Jakes called, "Come in, come in! It's open. It's always open!" he looked up expectantly.

And frowned.

The little man said, hesitantly, "Citizen Jakes?"

Sid Jakes said: "Ah, come in. Take a chair. Excuse me for a minute."

While the colorless newcomer found himself a seat and settled down, hands in lap, Sid Jakes flicked on his orderbox.

"Irene," he complained. "Didn't I tell you I was expecting a top priority . . ."

The box squawked and Sid Jakes flinched. He grinned. "All right, all right, I love you, too. But the thing is, I'm sure this"—he looked over at the newcomer—"ah, gentleman, has something very important. If he got past *you*, it must be something important. However, I'm momentarily expecting one of Lee Chang's new Special Talents agents and . . ."

The orderbox squawked.

Sid Jakes did a double take.

He switched off the interoffice communicator and said accusingly, "You're Sam?"

The other flushed embarrassment and nodded.

Sid Jakes closed his eyes for a long moment. His face worked slightly. He shook his head. Finally, it was as though something new had occurred to him. He opened his eyes again, hopefully.

He said, "Cosmetics and Wardrobe have certainly done a fine job on you, ah Citizen . . ."

"Goodboy," the other squeaked. He cleared his throat apologetically.

"I beg your pardon?" Sid Jakes said.

"Goodboy," the other said. "Samuel Goodboy."

"Oh," Sid Jakes said, forcing heartiness into his voice. "Well, they certainly did do a good job on you. You'll snake past the Dorian immigration and police like . . ."

"Who?" the little man said.

Jakes looked at him. "Who what?"

"Who did a good job on me?"

"The Wardrobe and Plastic Surgery people over in the Department of Dirty Tricks."

Sam Goodboy looked at him blankly.

Sid Jakes said, "Oh, no."

It was the newcomer's turn to say, "I beg your pardon?"

"Never mind," Jakes said painfully. "Lee Chang is our most astute recruiter. She's never pulled a bad fling yet." He took in the other again and repeated his last word. "Yet."

"Yes, sir," Goodboy said apologetically.

Jakes looked at him for a long time, an element of bafflement there. Finally, he took a deep breath and said, "All right, here's the assignment." Something came to him and he said, "This is your first?"

"Yes."

"You've never even been on a minor assignment, along with a troupe of operatives? Something to, well, kind of blood you?"

"No, sir." The little man swallowed. "Supervisor Chu just signed me up last week."

"Last *week!* What kind of training've you been through?"

"Training?"

Sid Jakes counted down for a moment. Then, "Look, ah, Goodboy. In the old days, it would take up to five years to turn out a Section G agent. A couple of years to locate a potential with the required mental and physical elements and especially the dedication."

"Oh," the other said in a wistful sort of way. "I've got the dream. The United Planets dream."

The Section G higher-up ignored him. "Then another three years of training and apprentice level work. Most didn't make it. It took a lot to become a full fledged agent, complete with silver badge."

"Oh, I've got a badge," the other said proudly. His hand fumbled over his pockets. He frowned apologetically. "I'm sure I had it right here, somewhere."

Sid Jakes closed his eyes again. When he opened them the little fellow was displaying a bronze badge, lettered simply *Samuel Goodboy, Section G, Bureau of Investigation, United Planets.* It seemed to glow in the small, inoffensive man's hand.

"Who gave you that!"

"Why, Supervisor Chu."

"Oh, she did. After recruiting you only last week?"

The other nodded.

"Well, you can tell Supervisor . . ." Sid Jakes broke it off. "No, sir," he said. "I won't do it. She's sucked me in on others in this Special Talents gang of hers. If Lee Chang says you're an assassin, I'll ride along with her until she takes a Brody. She's issued you a communicator and a Model H gun?"

"No, I'm afraid of guns."

There was another lengthy silence. Sid Jakes said, after a while, "I get the feeling that I came into this conversation half an hour too late."

Sam Goodboy said, "She didn't think I ought to take a Section G communicator with me. Or anything else they might detect. There's only one spaceport on Doria and the police are ever so sharp about detecting anything like a weapon, or a cloak and dagger device such as a Section G communicator."

Sid grunted. "She's right." His built-in optimism fought its way to the surface. "Undoubtedly, that's where your special talent comes in. You've got a better way of assassinating El Primero than with a gun. But we'll get to that later. First, let me give you a rundown on the assignment."

He settled back in his chair. "Down through the ages, we've always had assassins. In the past, no man in power could adequately defend himself against a really dedicated assassin. The very term comes from an organization which, high on Indian hemp, pulled off some of the most notable political killings on record." Jakes was warming to his tale. "The story is told that Richard the Lion Heart was first inclined to give Hasan Ben Sabbah, the Old Man of the Mountain, and head of the assassin sect, a hard time. But when he awoke one morning, there was a knife on the pillow next to him. He doubled his guard, but the next morning, there was another knife. In a rage, he again doubled his security. And the next morning, another knife. Richard made his peace with Hasan Ben Sabbah."

"Yes, sir," the other said, as though encouragingly.

"Then there were the Nihilists of Russia; at least, some of them, one wing of the organization. They were convinced they could scare the aristocracy into granting reforms. They were wrong, for various reasons, but they tried. They thought that individuals were at the root of Russia's evils. They pulled off some noteworthy assassinations, sometimes blowing up whole trains to get a Czar or a Grand Duke."

Sid Jakes shook his head. "No. In the past, a political figure had no chance against a determined, organized group which wished to assassinate him. Even individuals could pull it off, given determination, since a political figure could not avoid the public. To maintain himself, he had to show. Take the American presidents, for example. Lincoln, at a theatre, killed by a single man—Booth. McKinley, again in public, shaking hands with a long line of people. The anarchist, Czolgosz, approached with his hand supposedly in a bandage, actually concealing a gun. The first Kennedy, driving in a procession; once again, killed by an individual."

Sam Goodboy said, "Yes, sir. You make your point." He cleared his throat. "Ah, what is your point?"

Sid Jakes scowled at him. How in the name of Holy Jumping Zen could Lee Chang have ever turned up this yokel in the name of recruiting Section G operatives?

However, he went on. "The point is that almost invariably, before, the ruler, the victim of assassination, was got to by the assassin while appearing in public, a thing he could not avoid." He paused. "Today, it is no longer necessary. Since the advent of radio and especially television, centuries ago, and now Tri-Di, the public figure no longer need appear *in person* to the people. And politicians, and those in power in general, soon found it out. Until, today, such potential victims of the assassin as El Primero, never, but never, leave the security of their quarters."

Sam Goodboy nodded, and tried to project earnest intelligence, failing miserably.

Sid Jakes said, "El Primero's defense is as strong as any the human race has ever seen. If our information is correct, he has a method, utilizing brain surgery and psychedelic drugs, of insuring the faithfulness of his bodyguard and those connected with his security. They are incapable of being seduced by his enemies, incapable of betraying him. The first troupe we sent to undermine his regime, made that mistake."

Sam swallowed. "He had them shot?"

"No. He had them treated. After spilling everything they knew about Section G and the workings of United Planets, they became members of his bodyguard and hold that position now."

"Oh."

"So we sent in another troupe. This one with orders to bring El Primero down, whatever. They decided to get him from a distance and set up some special weapons from the Department of Dirty Tricks."

"And?"

"The first troupe, now faithful members of Michael Ortega's bodyguard, knew all about such special weapons. The second group was captured by the first and became part of his bodyguard, too."

Sam winced. "You said that three troupes preceded me."

"Yes. We finally went the whole hog and sent three of our top men, headed by Ronny Bronston, our best field man. We lost communication with them last week."

"And?"

"And assume they're either dead or now part of El Primero's bodyguard, completely devoted to him." Sid Jakes let a flash of his characteristic humor, albeit a bit on the sour side, come through. "So now, after the expenditure of ten of our veteran agents, we have you, Sam. With one week of seniority to your credit."

"Yes, sir," Sam said, cooperatively.

"And now, would you mind telling me just what this neat trick of yours is? Why it was that Lee Chang made you an agent after only one week of, uh, training?"

"Yes, sir. My special talent is I can kill people." He cleared his throat. "People, or anything else."

"How?" Sid Jakes blurted.

"I think them to death."

Lee Chang Chu, her small feet twinkling in the ages old shuffle of the Chinese woman, burst into the office of Irene Kasansky, secretary extraordinary of Ross Metaxa, Commissioner of Section G.

Irene looked up from her banks of orderboxes, her switches and buttons. The dourness faded from her harried face. Supervisor Chu was one of the very few in the department who was immune from the acid of Irene Kasansky. She began a greeting but Lee Chang, her face pale, snapped, "I've got to see the Commissioner."

The other had never heard that particular tone of voice from the Chinese operative before. She said into one of her orderboxes, "Shut up, I'll call you back." She looked up at Lee Chang again. "The Commissioner is in conference but . . ."

The feminine supervisor was sweeping past. "With Jakes?"

"Yes, but . . ." Irene's voice rose. "You can't go in there now. I had definite orders that . . ."

But Lee Chang was past her and through the door to the sanctum sanctorum. Irene Kasansky stared after her. She caught herself, flicked a switch and bit out, "Commissioner, I told you. You've put too much on poor Lee Chang. She's obviously gone drivel-happy and . . ."

Ross Metaxa looked up, taken aback as his only female supervisor darted in the door, unannounced. He was a middle-aged man, sloppy of dress, weary of expression—but he was a disciplinarian.

Across from him, Sid Jakes lounged, hands in trouser pockets. His eyebrows went up as well. He grinned. "That's what I like about this department," he chortled. "Informality."

"Shut up, you laughing hyena," Metaxa growled. He glowered at Lee Chang. "What'd you think this is, the ladies' room? What's the idea of bursting in . . ."

She ignored him, snapped at Sid Jakes, "Where's Sam?"

"Easy, easy," Sid said soothingly. "I took your word for it. Well, not exactly. I made him demonstrate. You know, he killed that fern I had in my office at twenty paces." He grinned and looked over at his superior. "Just by concentrating on it. How's that for a secret weapon? Neat trick, eh?"

Ross Metaxa looked from one of them to the other. "What are you two yokes blithering about?"

Lee Chang still ignored the Commissioner of Section G. She said, her voice in agony, to Sid Jakes, "Where's Sam Goodboy?"

Sid Jakes didn't understand as yet. "I tested him still further, with a chimp from the zoo. A chimpanzee at half a mile distance. One minute he was as chipper as . . ."

"Where's Sam Goodboy!"

Jakes broke it off. Both he and Ross Metaxa stared at the diminutive Section G supervisor.

Sid said, "Why, he's on his assignment to Doria. He's on his way. I had him shuttle over to Nuevo Albuquerque yesterday. By now, he's on his way."

"Get in contact, immediately! Order him back!"

"Order him back?" Jakes said plaintively. "You're the one recommended him. He's gone to crisp old El Primero. Couldn't happen to a nicer cloddy. I can't get in touch with him. He has no communicator. If he had one, the secret police'd detect it. He's on his own."

Metaxa roared, "What is going on here?"

Lee Chang sank into a chair, thin shoulders slumped. She said, "Ronny Bronston broke silence."

"Broke silence," Metaxa said. "We haven't heard from him for at least . . ."

She looked up wearily, "Don't you see what must have happened? The agents who were captured and treated by Ortega's police—they had communicators. Doria's scientists aren't cloddies. They've obviously been able to analyze the subspace band utilized. In other words, tune in on our communications. Ronny must have found out and discontinued calling us."

Sid Jakes said, "He could have used code."

"Any code is breakable, especially by the stutes on police state worlds. They devote any given amount of time to such items."

Ross Metaxa was scowling again. He reached into a desk drawer and brought forth a squat brown bottle and a glass. He didn't offer any of the clear liquid the bottle contained to his subordinates, knowing better. He knocked a jolt back over his palate, then growled, "Then why'd he break silence now?"

There was an embarrassed element in Lee Chang's voice. She said, "We . . . that is, in our, uh, personal relationship. Well, for amusement, I taught him a few words of Mandarin."

"Mandarin?" Sid Jakes queried.

She looked at him. "Chinese. It's a dead language everywhere except on Han, the planet of my birth."

"Oh," Sid said. Then the meaning came home to him. He laughed. "Chinese. Their cryptograph people would have their work cut out deciphering that. What'd Ronny say?"

"He only has a few words. A very few." She looked down at a note she held in a small hand. "He said . . ." for a moment her voice broke. She took a deep breath and started again. "He said, 'Me take Number One . . . Me change face . . . Me Number One.' "

They bug-eyed her, speechlessly.

Her eyes went from one to the other, in desperation. "Don't you see? Somehow, somehow, Ronny has pulled off the biggest romp of his career. He's kidnapped Michael Ortega. Somehow, somehow. He's evidently undergone plastic surgery. Somehow, somehow, he's taken El Primero's place."

Metaxa said hoarsely, "Did he say anything else?"

"Yes. The rest of the message was, 'Me make big talk . . . No more Number One.'"

Sid Jakes who had been sitting erect in unwonted fashion, said excitedly, "He's going to address the whole planet. All of Doria. Make some sort of announcement. Free elections or something."

"Impossible," Metaxa rumbled. "Fantastic." He glared at Lee Chang. "How do you know it was really Ronny?"

"Who else on Doria would know Mandarin, or, even if they did, know enough to beam a message to Section G in that tongue?"

"Kidnap El Primero?" Sid Jakes said in second thought. "What kind of curd is that? We all know he's the most security conscious dictator in United Planets. How could you ever kidnap the funker, not to speak of substituting someone else in his place?"

Lee Chang looked at him strangely. "I can think of only one possibility. According to our dossier on Michael Ortega, he has one Achilles' heel. Remember Svetlana Alliluyeva? Or, better, Svetlana Stalin?"

Sid Jakes bothered to shake his head. Metaxa poured himself another drink of Denebian tequila and waited for her to go on.

"The only person Joseph Stalin evidently ever really cared for," Lee Chang said. "His daughter and one of the very few relatives, friends and associates that long survived him. Well, from what I hear, Michael Ortega has the equivalent in Concha Ortega."

Metaxa growled, "What's this got to do with Bronston and his taking over the position of El Primero?"

Lee Chang made a feminine move. "It wouldn't be the first time our quiet, unassuming Ronald has made his mark with the ladies. Remember Amazonia?"

Sid laughed suddenly. "So one of our teams tried to bribe El Primero's guards. The second troupe tried to blow him up from a distance. But Ronny turns on the Bronston charm and . . ." Sid Jakes ground to a halt. "Holy jumping Zen," he yelped. "Sam Goodboy. He's zeroing-in on Ronny!"

Ross Metaxa spun in his chair and blurted into his orderbox, "Irene! Sam Goodboy, a new agent. On assignment to Doria. What's his cover?"

Lee Chang and Sid Jakes failed to make out the answer.

Metaxa snapped, "Find out, soonest. A mistake has been made. He's on assignment to kill Ronny Bronston."

"And . . . he . . . never . . . fails . . ." Lee Chang added lowly.

"And he never fails," Metaxa repeated into the interoffice communicator.

For a moment, Irene Kasansky held silence, then she said, the rasp gone from her voice, "I didn't handle Goodboy's cover. I'll check immediately."

Metaxa looked back at his two top supervisors.

Sid Jakes chortled, "Get that sudden change in voice. Irene's sugar on our Ronny."

Metaxa glared at him, but then turned his eyes to Lee Chang. "What'd you mean he never fails?" he demanded sourly. "Anybody can fail, no matter how proficient. Certainly, professional killers can."

Lee Chang was shaking her head. "Ross . . . this one doesn't use weapons. He's one of my Special Talent recruits."

Her superior looked at her blankly. "You mean judo or one of those other old . . ."

She was still shaking her head. "He doesn't know how he does it." She added, as though that explained everything, "He comes from the planet Rubata."

"Rubata!" Jakes snorted. "Those crackpots."

She turned to him, frowning again. "If you will." She went back to Metaxa. "You'll recall the planet originally colonized by would-be witches, spiritualists, psi adepts, or would-be adepts, so forth and so on?"

"Vaguely," Metaxa growled. "As Sid says, crackpots."

Lee Chang shrugged prettily. "I would have said the same, until I began my search for special talents to recruit for Section G. Quite a few of them have come from Rubata. I don't pretend to explain; however, few would deny that down through the ages the human race has thrown some, well, out of the ordinary persons. Do you deny, for instance, that occasionally a human turns up with total recall? That others have the ability to do mathematical problems in their heads that put computers to shame? I am not mentioning such oft recorded phenomena as telepathy, clairvoyance and even precognition."

"All right," Metaxa growled. "So from time to time offbeat talents have shown. I'll accept that, in a limited way. What's it got to do with this Sam Goodboy?"

"The original colonists of Rubata numbered but a few thousands," Lee Chang pursued. "However, they bred—with each other." She shrugged again. "Not only did the posterity continue and strengthen the as-you-say, offbeat talents, but evolved some new ones. Among the original colonists were witch doctors and libans, sorcerers and wizards, hex doctors and shamanists, practitioners of black magic, of voodoo, of the left hand path. Admittedly, as Sid has put it, largely crackpots. But you can't explain away, with that term alone, all the evidence that has come down to us through the ages of such items as bantu witchmen, voodoo priests and hex doctors killing persons through their . . . special talents. At any rate, Sam's own belief is that he numbers at least several of these among his ancestors, not to speak of telepaths, clairvoyants and so forth. The thing is, this talent of his *works*."

The orderbox spoke up. Irene said, "Commissioner, I've tracked down Goodboy's cover. He's going in as a tourist. Doria makes a play for tourism, it's supposed to be very scenic."

"All right, all right. How's he getting there? We'll have to contact him on his ship."

"He's on the Space Passenger Freighter *Mola*." She hesitated, then added, "Commissioner, it's a Dorian spacecraft."

"That doesn't make any difference. We'll contact him in our own code."

Lee Chang said emptily, "He isn't checked out on Section G code, Commissioner. Even if he was, Dorian security is familiar with our codes. Remember, they number two of our former troupes in their secret police."

Sid Jakes was on his feet. He bent over the orderbox. "Irene," he snapped. "Get a move on. Arrangements for Supervisor Chu and me to depart soonest for Doria. If necessary, requisition a Space Forces four-manner."

Ross Metaxa scowled at him. "We can't risk your neck on a drivel-happy romp like this."

Jakes looked at him bleakly. "Ronny Bronston is my best field man, Ross. On top of that, Doria is the biggest sore thumb in United Planets right now. If that planet spills all it knows about the inner workings of Section G, then the member planets will drop out of UP like dandruff."

Lee Chang was standing as well. "I'll get ready," she said.

The trip was an agony.

They were lobbed over to Nuevo Albuquerque to the spaceport. And jittered while waiting for the small Space Forces craft which had to be recalled from Calisto.

"Isn't there any way this could be speeded up?" Lee Chang murmured, knowing as well as her colleague that there wasn't.

Sid Jakes looked at her in understanding. "There is no speed in underspace, Lee Chang. Before entering it, yes; after leaving it, yes. But in underspace, there is no speed. The most sluggish freighter gets there as fast as the nattiest Space Forces one-man scout."

"Sam'll be on Doria two days before we arrive, then."

He didn't bother to answer that.

They spent most of their time on the *Gremlin* in the tiny mess. They tried to play battle chess to kill the time, but couldn't concentrate. They sought out the ship's small library and played tapes, but only the lightest fictional things would come through. And even then they were hard put to follow the story line.

They must have been halfway when Lee Chang blurted, *"Why?* Why is it that after all these centuries of supposed civilization we wind up with such worlds as Doria? Why should there be a need for a Section G, to try and contain such planets? How did they ever evolve? How can man be so stupid?"

Sid Jakes grinned sourly. "You know the answer as well as I. Weren't you born in a commune, on the planet Han, settled by disgruntled followers of . . . what was his name?"

"Mao," Lee Chang murmured unhappily.

Sid Jakes grunted amusement. "The pioneers in space travel must never have dreamed of the method by which the suitable worlds eventually would be colonized. Once the basic breakthroughs were made, we took to space like an eruption of lemmings. Every religious sect, every socioeconomic system group, every race that thought it wasn't getting a fair shake on Mother Earth, took off seeking its own version of Utopia." He chortled. "It was bad enough when outfits such as the anarchists settled their own planet, but you know one that I ran into the other day?"

She looked at him. Anything to divert her mind.

He laughed ruefully. "A couple of thousand colonists with I.Q.'s of less than one hundred. They figured they were a minority, had to take too much jetsam. So they've found their own world. Refuse to join United Planets, by the way."

Lee Chang's face mirrored the nearest thing to a scowl of which it was capable. "But, Sid, what will happen to them?"

He shrugged. "Who knows? Perhaps they'll go back to the Neanderthal. Or, who knows? Perhaps the ruggedness of existence will be such that they'll breed up their I.Q.'s. The fit will survive, the too stupid go under. It's the way the race started."

She returned to her point. "But what I meant was, now that humanity is faced with a common danger, the intelligent alien life form that we've finally come in contact with. Why don't we meet it together?"

Sid chuckled ruefully, and gave up trying to look at the historical fiction Tri-Di show they'd been projecting. "Lee Chang, Lee Chang, you dreamer. Man stops being a thinking animal when you deal with his institutions, his subconscious beliefs, his religion. The Christians were willing to die in the arena before giving up their creed. The Aztecs fought it out, almost to the last man, although Cortez daily offered them surprisingly good terms, in view of the fact they didn't have a chance. Hitler tried to the very last to bring down the whole Third Reich in flames, rather than surrender. Earlier in that same war, the Russian communists slugged it out, long, long after the world thought that the Wehrmacht had defeated them.

"No, it's a fallacy to think man will give up his beliefs to meet a danger. When the H-Bomb first threatened universal destruction, did man patch up his politico-economic difficulties? *Better dead than red,* was one slogan, and the other side had just as strong ones. When the population explosion threatened to lead to complete chaos, did the old religions, the old institutions, in such lands as Europe and India change? Not by a long shot. Man is at his most stubborn when his religious, political or socioeconomic beliefs need change."

She sighed deeply and her eyes went back to the Tri-Di stage.

They were met at the Doria spaceport by what would have been described as an honor guard of twenty men. They hardly had any illusions. Before landing, the ensign who skippered the four-man crew of the little *Gremlin* had been required to state the purpose of the set down, and to enumerate the passengers who expected to disembark. They had made no effort to disguise their identities, if for no other reason than that there had been no time to improvise a cover, had that been possible, considering the craft in which they had arrived.

The guard snapped to attention, presented arms, as Lee Chang Chu and Sid Jakes emerged from the United Planets Space Forces ship.

A nattily uniformed officer approached and came to the salute. "Supervisor Jakes, Supervisor Chu," he clipped out. "Welcome to Doria."

*

Sid Jakes grinned at him, ruefully. "Hi, Desmond." He held out a hand.

The other hesitated, then shook. "It's been a long time, Sid."

Sid Jakes turned to Lee Chang. "You know each other?"

Desmond bowed over her hand. "We operated in different sections, but I have heard a great deal of Supervisor Chu."

Lee Chang said demurely, "Thank you."

Sid Jakes chuckled. "We hardly expected quite this reception, Desmond. How are the rest of the boys?"

The other was a man in his mid-thirties. Healthy; at least on the surface, adjusted and at ease. His eyes were as clear as those of his former superior. He smiled, a faint mocking quality in the background. "Like myself. For the first time in life, really happy and at peace with themselves. Doria is a great planet, Sid."

The smile on Sid Jakes's face faded. He said, his voice slightly tight. "Nothing like being coked up to make the world rosy."

But the now Dorian security officer only laughed. "If you don't understand it, Sid, don't knock it. Somebody wrote once that censors were mostly illiterates. Suffice to say, that we former Section G agents, now serving El Primero, are considerably happier than we were taking orders from Ross Metaxa and trying to live up to the way *he* thought things ought to be."

Sid said snappishly, "And does El Primero needle himself with the same happy dust he gives you?"

There was the most distant of glints in the other's eyes, but he said, still pleasantly, "Sid, you remind me of those fat old ladies I saw depicted on a historical fiction Tri-Di show not so long ago. They belonged to an outfit called the WCTU, an anti-alcohol organization. They'd beat the drums against drinking guzzle and then after the meeting serve refreshments of cakes, cookies, pies, candy and well sweetened lemonade or tea. I imagine nobody ever got around to telling them that alcohol and sugar do much the same thing in the human body. After the meeting, they'd go home and lie around, eating chocolates and fouling up their health by going to lard."

Lee Chang said mildly, "There are some small differences between guzzle and candy."

Desmond looked at her. If he had lost any of his composure, he had regained it now. He said, "Either, taken moderately, won't hurt you. Either taken in excess can jetsam up your health, irreparably."

He switched the subject. "May I ask that you accompany me to Interrogation? Formality, upon landing on Doria."

They followed. A noncommissioned officer bit out a command and the guard very briskly wheeled and fell in behind.

At the edge of the field, they entered an attractive administration building and, now followed only by the noncom and two of his men, proceeded down a short hall to a door lettered, in small, simple gold type, *Interrogation*.

The room beyond was most comfortably furnished. A desk, several comfortable chairs, a small bar in a corner.

The ex-Section G agent went through the formalities, held a chair for Lee Chang, offered them both a drink, which they refused in view of the morning hour. He finally took his place behind the desk. The two soldiers had remained outside the door. The noncom had entered behind them and stood to one side, his face expressionless; however, his side arm was in a quick-draw holster.

Sid Jakes said testily, "You had the last word on that WCTU thing, that, 'if you don't comprehend it, don't knock it,' routine. Would you mind elaborating?"

"Not at all," Desmond smiled. "You've got the United Planets dream, Jakes. I've got the Dorian dream. It's an easier dream. All we want on Doria is to be left alone, and leave others alone, including any bogeyman alien life forms. You're patriotic—the old term. You come from Earth, the mother planet. You bleed for Earth and want to impose on all the rest of the humanity settled planets, the things that Earth stands for. To accomplish this, you beat the drums about the need to unite against an alien foe. It's a new takeoff on the old Roman adage, if you have trouble at home, stir up war abroad."

"You think patriotism is stupid?"

Desmond smiled still once again. "It's according to what epoch you're living in. In early society, it was a necessity if the tribe—or later the city-state—was to survive. But in late society, if indulged in, it meant suicide for the whole race."

Lee Chang said hesitantly, "I don't believe I follow that."

The Dorian security officer looked at her and nodded. "In the old days, before man left his home world, you had a multitude of nations. A man would say, 'I'm proud to be an Englishman. God save the king. I'm patriotic. I'd die for England.' And he often did. Why was he proud to be an Englishman? He hadn't done anything to achieve that status. By an accident of fate, he had parents who were living in England at the time of his birth. Had he been born in India, he could then have been proud of being an Indian, and willing to kill other nationalities—including English—in the name of patriotism. It particularly became nonsense, after the advent of nuclear fission."

He waved a hand negatively. "Patriotism belongs to the childhood of the species. But let us get to the point. The purpose of your landing on Doria. In view of your office . . ."

Sid Jakes said, "I'll be glad to tell you all about it."

Desmond nodded. "Do you mind if I put a truth beam on you?"

Sid Jakes hesitated only momentarily. "Of course not."

A light, centered on the desk, lit up, white.

Desmond said, "In the way of test: Are you opposed to the government of El Primero?"

"Yes," Sid said.

The light burned green.

"Do you think Supervisor Lee Chang Chu an ugly woman?"

Sid grinned. "Yes," he said. "Very ugly."

The light burned red. Both Desmond and Lee Chang smiled.

Desmond said, "Have you stopped beating your mother?"

Sid chuckled. "Well, yes and no," he said.

The light remained white.

Desmond said, his voice sharper now, "What is the purpose of your visit to Doria?"

"To apprehend a killer and return with him to Earth."

The Dorian security officer's eyes widened infinitesimally, and he darted a glance at the light which turned green.

"Where did the killer come from?"

"Earth." The light was green.

"Did he come here to kill someone?"

"Yes." The light was green.

"Who?"

Sid Jakes said, very slowly, "El Primero. Michael Ortega."

The other was suddenly on his feet, his face chalk, his voice shrill. "That is impossible!"

Sid Jakes shook his head. "Do you think that I, assistant to Commissioner Metaxa, would be here on a mission less important?"

The other, his eyes bugging, leaned over the desk, his fists supporting him. "Section G has been trying to destroy El Primero and his government. Do you contend that now you are trying to prevent him from being assassinated?"

Sid Jakes answered evenly. "Supervisor Chu and I have come from Earth to save the life of the present El Primero."

The light burned green.

The other stared at it, momentarily, then brought his eyes back to the Section G second-in-command. "It is impossible to assassinate El Primero. His security is impregnable. Even now he is preparing to address the entire population on a matter of the utmost importance, but he will never leave the palace grounds."

Lee Chang spoke softly. "Do you think we are not familiar with all this, Citizen? But no security can thwart this killer."

The light burned green, acknowledging the truth of her statement.

The other slumped back in his chair, his mouth working, a trickle of saliva at its side.

"Sir!" the noncom said anxiously.

"Shut up!" his superior rasped. Then to Jakes, "Who?"

Sid Jakes shook his head. "I must have assurance that if and when we apprehend him, we will be allowed to return with him to Earth."

"No! We of the Dorian police will see to him!"

Sid Jakes shook his head again. "This is not an ordinary assassin, Desmond. You have not the time to put pressure to bear on us. He may strike momentarily. Your guarantee, sent in a subspace cable to the Octagon, on Earth, that he will be put in our custody, or we do not reveal his identity. Otherwise, *I* guarantee the present El Primero will die shortly."

The light burned green, and the security officer once again stared unbelievingly at it.

Psycho-altered he might be, but his reflexes were still the same as those required, years before, when his application as a Section G trainee had been accepted. He flicked on an orderbox.

"Crash priority! Clear channels to Generalissimo Chavez!"

At the door of the room in the tourist hotel, Sid Jakes turned to the three security officers who were escorting him and Lee Chang.

He said, "I suggest you remain here, until we have dealt with him. This is the most dangerous man in all United Planets."

Desmond said, "Our orders are to cooperate with you to the utmost."

Sid Jakes knocked and, without waiting for an answer, flung open the door. Lee Chang entered first. They didn't want to startle the other, and were aware that Sam Goodboy knew her the best.

The drab little man was in the process of seating himself before the room's Tri-Di stage. He looked up in surprise. "Why, Supervisor Chu!" he said. He blinked and his eyes went in turn to Sid Jakes. Sid closed the door behind him, blocking the view of the security men beyond.

Lee Chang blurted, "Sam! Everything has been changed! You mustn't kill El Primero."

He looked at her blankly, and then at Sid Jakes. He was aghast. "But . . . but I have already killed him."

Lee Chang collapsed into a chair. "Oh, no."

For the briefest of moments, Sid Jakes closed his eyes in pain. But then he brought himself back to the immediate reality. He snapped, "The fat's in the fire now. We've got to rescue what we can. We've got to get out of here, someway; and back to the *Gremlin*. Ronny's gone, and there's nothing we can do about it."

Sam Goodboy was looking back and forth between them, his face in dismay, ineffectual appearing as never before. "I . . . I don't understand. I . . . I followed orders exactly. I've never done this sort of thing before. On my home planet, I used to work occasionally for the police. Some escaped killer, or something like that."

Sid's eyes had been darting about the room, looking for another exit. There was none. He went to the window and stared down. Four stories of smooth wall.

"You killed the wrong man," he bit out.

"But . . . I never kill the wrong man."

"One of our agents, Ronny Bronston, somehow infiltrated the palace and took Ortega's place."

"Oh, *that*," Sam Goodboy said, in relief.

"Oh *that*," Lee Chang echoed. "You're talking about . . ."

"Oh, I didn't kill *Ronny*," Sam explained seriously. "My orders were to kill El Primero, not somebody disguised as him. And just in time, too. He had managed to escape from where Ronny had him locked up and was about to reorganize his men to recapture the palace. Oh, he's very dead."

The Tri-Di stage lit up, and there, standing simply alone, garbed in a Dorian enlisted man's uniform, without decoration, stood a strong faced, domineering personality.

The three-dimension figure, lifelike, save in size, stared out at them for a moment, then spoke. "Citizens of Doria!" he began. "I have a most important message."

"There's Ronny now," Sam Goodboy said in satisfaction.

Sid Jakes and Lee Chang stared at him, turned and stared at the Tri-Di figure, now fully launched into its epic speech.

"How did you know!" Sid demanded.

The little man squirmed. "I don't know," he said in apology. "It all just kind of comes to me. But I never make mistakes. I never kill the wrong person. That would be awful."

The Art of Diplomacy

International relations is characterized by discussions and bargaining over issues between countries conducted by individuals called *diplomats.* These *negotiations* assume that the parties to a dispute will retreat from their publicly stated maximum positions. If they will not, then you are not negotiating—you are either watching a surrender, a pointless exercise, or the prelude to war. For negotiations to be completely successful, each side must feel that it has received more than it has given, or at least that it has received as much.

Historically, negotiations were very involved processes in which the minute details of time, place, shape of the table, who entered a room first, and other matters of protocol received great attention. This is still the case on occasion (witness the Paris Peace Conference on Vietnam), especially when one or both of the parties are not serious or represent very different cultures. Although almost never admitted, negotiations on important issues may involve lying, blackmail, and other forms of behavior which we would consider reprehensible if they occurred between individuals. Countries may also fight and talk peace at the same time, with conditions on the battlefield dictating the course of negotiations. On other occasions, the purpose of the negotiations may be simply to "keep talking" in order to prevent the outbreak of hostilities.

Diplomats themselves are men (and increasingly, women) who represent national decision-makers when dealing with other countries. However, they are severely circumscribed by the boundaries dictated by their superiors in the policy-making hierarchy. Of course, if the negotiations are being conducted by very high ranking persons such as presidents, prime ministers, secretaries of state, or foreign ministers, then shifts in position can occur relatively quickly.

The author of "The Negotiators," Keith Laumer, was once a member of the United States Foreign Service. He therefore brings a unique expertise to the many tales he has written featuring "Retief," an intergalactic diplomat and troubleshooter who is one of the favorite series characters in science fiction. Here Retief encounters some of the strangest negotiations ever faced by a diplomat; including dealing with creatures who, if they need a hand, can grow one. *what they hold as value*

THE NEGOTIATORS

by Keith Laumer

The basic purpose of negotiation is to get the other guy to agree to a deal that's grossly favorable to you.

"Oh, Retief!" the reedy voice of First Secretary Magnan called anxiously. Retief turned to see the slight figure of the senior officer hurrying toward him across the slanting expanse of gray-tan rock where the little group of newly-arrived Terran diplomats waited to be greeted by the appropriate officials of the local government.

"The Ambassador is most eager to have a word with you," Magnan panted, arriving at Retief's side. "Gracious, I've searched all over for you. I shouldn't wonder if this were a crucial point for you, career-development-wise, Retief. His Excellency and I were chatting at lunch about possible new modes of approach to the problem. In that connection, I was able to bring up your name, quite casually, of course. I had no wish to seem to be thrusting you forward over the heads of senior officers, naturally."

"I'm three questions behind," Retief commented. "You've searched all over what? All there is is this three-quarters of an acre of exposed rock, surrounded by a few million square miles of unexplored ocean."

"To be sure," Magnan replied crisply. "It was this selfsame three-quarter acre of rock which I searched in quest of you."

"I've been luxuriating right here on the site of the future officers' lounge for the last couple of hours," Retief pointed out.

"Oh, indeed?" Magnan looked around with an expression of severity. "It's not like you, Retief, to idle away the working day in a bar, even an imaginary one."

"That comment has a rather cynical ring to it, Mr. Magnan—how can you term our luxurious facilities imaginary, when you've seen the actual programming documents which call for construction to begin within six months of funding of the project, which will no doubt take place within a year or two of the submission of the CDT construction program, which I'm sure will rank high on Ambassador Fullthrottle's agenda—as soon as he achieves full Embassy status for the Mission here on Sogood."

"Doubtless; Retief, please overlook the lapse. By the way, what have you been doing, here in the imaginary luxury of the hypothetical future clubroom?"

"Drinking imaginary booze and watching theoretical bar girls, what else?"

"What else, indeed?" Magnan gazed around with an expression of disapproval at the bleak expanse of sea-worn rock and the two dozen forlorn bureaucrats who wandered aimlessly or crouched tensely beside suitcases and crated forms, under the remote blue sun of Sogood. Sofar, the water-world's sister planet, hung in the sky, a pale gray disk pitted with craters which formed a pattern resembling the leering visage of a plump sexual deviate.

"You said you'd mentioned my name to the Ambassador," Retief prompted. "In connection with new modes of approach, I believe you said. That has an ominous ring."

"Why, *au contraire*, Retief," Magnan twittered. "It's just that having been dispatched here as Terrestrial emissaries on the basis of exhaustive interstellar dialogues between the Department and the Soggies, with assurances that the latter enjoy a high level of technological competence, it was somewhat unsettling to his Excellency—as to us all —to arrive and find nothing but a bald knob of unadorned rock projecting above the surface of this unending ocean! In the absence of opposition negotiators, normal diplomatic gambitry is rendered nugatory in advance of the initial overture. Why, after thirty-six hours of residence, we've not so much as met a representative of the people, to say nothing of members of the government to which we're accredited. It's unheard of, Retief. Something must be done! I suggest you hurry along before the Ambassador has cause to consider you dilatory."

"Sure. Where is he?"

"Why, in the Chancery, of course. The proposed Chancery, that is. But don't make mention of the illusory nature of his Excellency's present accommodations. He's a diplomat of great sensitivity in matters of protocol and RHIP, you know, though a natural democrat at heart. I sense that an effective performance now could well be the making of you, Retief. And in my assessment of his Excellency's present mood, you must recognize I bring to bear an encyclopedic familiarity with his highly complex character. I fancy I enjoy an unusual special relationship with his Excellency, Retief; indeed, I think I may say that I enjoy the role of special confidant."

"Don't worry, I won't shatter his illusions." Retief went across toward the spot where a cluster of advancement-conscious functionaries surrounded the tall, lean figure of the Terrestrial Ambassador Extraordinary and Minister Plenipotentiary.

"What do you think, Retief? A hoax staged by the Groaci to make monkeys out of us Terries?" inquired a small, dapper Military Attache, as Retief paused.

"Aha, got an angle working, eh, boy?" the Press Attache said, falling in step beside Retief. "Let us in on it, huh? Don't hoard the news. What is it, a secret invasion scheme, dumping us here on this crummy little island to distract 'em, while the Peace Enforcers hit 'em six ways from the ace on the mainland?" *use of language*

"What mainland?" Retief asked. "This was the only patch of land visible on the screens as we came in."

"Oh, playing 'em close to the gravy stains, eh? OK, be like that." The fat newsman dropped back, muttering.

"Ah there, my boy," Ambassador Fullthrottle cried as he noticed Retief. He made shooing motions with his long knobby hands, scattering the other aspirants for ambassadorial attention. "Come right in." He rose from the Hip-U-Matic power swivel chair which had been uncrated for his use, and leaned on the nine-foot iridium desk (Field), Chief of Mission, for the exclusive use of.

"Now, that infernal little favor-currier, Magnan, was pestering me this morning, as usual," the great man said. "And he hinted that you, Retief, might well be the member of my staff most highly qualified to offer a useful proposal for placing this Mission on a somewhat less farcical footing. Ah, have a chair, my boy."

"There isn't one. OK if I have this rock instead?" Retief seated himself on a low, smoothly eroded boulder.

"Of course, my boy. Smoke if you got 'em." The Ambassador beamed at Retief. "Now, in essence," he said, "our initial challenge appears to consist in the circumstance that I, we, that is, have been dispatched here, in good faith, to establish diplomatic relations with the local inhabitants—a consummation somewhat impeded by the apparent absence of local inhabitants—a circumstance which, unless nullified, will render impossible the conclusion of advantageous agreements between Terra and Sogood."

"If you mean we can't sell iceboxes to nonexistent Eskimos, I agree with you, Mr. Ambassador," Retief said.

"Just so," Fullthrottle said, placing his fingertips together and assuming a judicious expression. "It would appear to be essential to my career—to protection of Terran interests, that is to say—to turn up some sort of local authorities without further delay."

"What about that bunch of Soggies down on the beach?" Retief inquired, nodding toward a group of perhaps two dozen bulky, shiny-black creatures vaguely resembling flipperless seals slumped at the water's edge a hundred feet distant.

"Nothing doing there," Fullthrottle said, shaking his head. "I dispatched Colonel Betterpart to open a dialogue with the creatures, and he reported that they seem unable to grasp the most elementary concepts of communication. Even friendly shouting didn't help."

"I wondered what the yelling was all about."

"Yes. So there they sprawl: some twenty gross and torpid creatures innocent of clothing, equipment or adornment, obviously bearing no conceivable relationship to the highly sophisticated biped beings with whom we've been in contact via screen for some months. So—what to do? I for one don't fancy sitting here in my office, waiting, while the initiative slips from my hands. Our handling of this initial contact will doubtless establish the pattern of Terry-Soggy relations for centuries to come. Ergo—*do* something, Retief! I have no wish to report to the Department utter failure on the part of my staff in meeting this emergency." The Ambassador leaned back, causing his Hip-U-Matic chair to groan in protest as he braced a foot against the effort of the power swivel attachment to rotate him to one side.

"I quite agree that we can't open peaceful relations with Sogood unless we can find someone to be peaceful with," Retief said. "It seems that bunch down on the beach is the only lead we have, so I'd better give it another try."

"As you will, my boy. If you succeed, I'll be the first to congratulate you. If you fail, I'm sure you won't be so naive as to seek to imply that I authorized you to approach them. It's my personal conviction that these are a group of outcasts from whatever society may exist here—wherever it may be found in this wilderness of seawater."

Retief rose, inquired the way to the theoretical door, and walked down across the slope of rock toward a lone Soggy sprawled somewhat apart from his fellows.

"Heavens, Retief! Let me save you from a horrid blunder, discipline-wise," Magnan cried, hurrying to intercept Retief. "I had assumed you were conversant with the Ambassador's fiat anent fraternization with these casteless rejects. His Excellency has decided these chaps"—Magnan indicated the herd of Soggies at the water's edge—"are defectives or criminals culled from Soggy society and exiled here far from civilization, to die alone. Doubtless, any contact with them would contaminate the contactor with the same social stigma attaching to these unfortunates. A sad-looking lot, eh? Their degeneracy is apparent at a glance, now that Ambassador Fullthrottle has so perceptively pointed it out. Look at that fellow—" Magnan indicated the nearest Soggy, who sprawled some yards apart from the group. "He's apparently in the last stages of a loathsome disease. Note the lesions on his body. Great pustulent buboes at the point of bursting. Faugh!"

Retief glanced at the bulky form slumped on the rock like a mound of inert, shiny-black-skinned jelly. A number of prominent swellings marred the otherwise unadorned expanse of glossy hide. The only other visible surface feature of the creature was a ridiculously small tail into which the smooth curve of the bag-like body tapered at one end. Magnan prodded the Soggy with a fastidious toe. "Go on, shoo, you obscene thing," he muttered. "Crawl into the water to die, can't you?"

" 'Fraid not, chum," a moist voice came from somewhere. "And let's watch that footwork. Don't you dried-out foreigners have any respect for youth and beauty, if not for rank and dignity?"

Magnan recoiled, hopping on one foot as if to disassociate himself from the offending member. "Dear me," he choked, "for a moment, Retief, I almost imagined this formless bulk of protoplasm was speaking to us—to you, that is—in a tone of ill-natured reprimand."

"I thought it was *you* that kicked him," Retief said mildly.

"Hardly a kick, Retief! A mere good-natured prod, if that!"

"I heard Colonel Betterpart reported no luck in communicating with them," Retief said.

"So he did. Apparently he jumped to an erroneous conclusion."

"If you boys are talking about that little fancy-pants in the hat who tried to pump me about Soggy defenses and armament," the wet voice came again from the general direction of the creature before them, "naturally I clammed up. I'm not spilling Soggy military secrets to the first clown that comes nosing around—and besides, I don't know what armaments and defense are, such concepts being alien to the peace-loving and inoffensive nature of us Soggies."

"I see," Magnan sniffed. "Well, you could have at least answered the colonel when spoken to. Most rude of you to simply ignore him, thereby giving him an erroneous impression of your capabilities."

"It's legitimate technique to lead potential adversaries astray, according to time-honored Soggy lore," the watery voice countered, "or it would be if us guileless natives had any history."

"See here, sir," Magnan said, "just how is it you're able to speak Terran, since I see no evidence of vocal apparatus apparent on your person."

"Let's lay off the personal-type remarks, bud," the Soggy retorted. "You managed to get here from wherever you came from, but I don't see any rockets on you, now that you mention it."

"You would seem to imply, by parallel, that you employ technology to supplement your natural communicative endowments, if any!" Magnan stated with asperity. "However, this still ignores the question as to your knowledge of Terran."

"Easy, Jack. We've been in telecommunication with you Terries for months. If we hadn't doped out your language, that would have been kind of a waste of time, hey?"

"The fellow is insolent," Magnan adjudicated, and turning, strode away toward a gaggle of wide-eyed diplomats observing from a safe distance.

"You'll have to excuse Mr. Magnan," Retief said. "His career hasn't developed quite along the lines he dreamed of back in Peoria. It's made him a trifle bitter."

"What's his flavor got to do with it? Is he edible?"

"Only in an emergency."

"It looks like he's in a hurry to report the latest developments."

Retief turned; Magnan was engaged in an arm-waving conversation with half a dozen of his companions, pausing occasionally to point toward Retief and the alien.

"I'll give you odds he's up to no good," the Soggy stated in a voice like an underwater pipe organ. "Oh-oh, here he comes, with fire in his eye."

Magnan was striding briskly back toward Retief wearing an expression of Patience Outraged (721-b).

"See here, Retief!" the First Secretary barked as he came up. "On behalf of his Excellency, and in consideration of his strict instructions, and in light of my own exalted position as Chief of the Political Section, I really must protest your hobnobbing with this loathsomely diseased outcast! The least you could do, if you insist on defying policy, is to strike up an acquaintance with those rather more clean-cut-appearing locals yonder."

"By the way, what's your name, chum?" the alien inquired in his gurgling voice. "I'm known as Sloonge to those privileged to address me by name."

"I'm Retief. This is Mr. Magnan."

"Never mind him; I got a feeling him and me will never be close."

"Not if I can avoid it," Magnan snapped, leaping back and flicking imaginary slime from his sleeve. "Very well, Retief, you have been cautioned." Magnan marched away yanking the overlapping lapels of his early mid-morning hemi-semi-informal cutaway into line.

"That one is a pain in the third somite," Sloonge commented. "Look, Retief, I got to nip down to the pad to check on a couple of items. Want to come along?"

"Where's your pad located?" Retief asked, gazing out over the restless surface of the sea.

"About a quarter-mile east and six hundred feet down."

"I'd like to go," Retief said, "if you'll give me a couple of minutes to make preparation."

"Yeah, sure. I guess your kind of metabolism don't work so hot once you get a few feet under water. Tough, chum, but I guess we all got our, like, drawbacks. No offense." With a rippling of his huge bulk, Sloonge flopped over. For the first time, Retief noted that at the end of the six-foot ovoid body of the alien opposite the undersized tail, there were two small protuberances which might have been eyes, plus a pair of small nostril-like perforations and a mouth as lipless as a saber wound. This, he deduced, represented the alien's face, which was otherwise undifferentiated from the rest of his rubbery bulk.

With further ripplings, the ungainly creature slithered down the slope of rock and entered the water. Retief walked past the still-gossiping group standing nearby and made his way to a heap of baggage resting near the center of the island where the landing shuttle had dumped it a day and a half earlier. He lifted aside a large pigskin suitcase and extracted a metal-clad steamer trunk which he hoisted to his shoulder. Carrying the trunk, he went across to an unoccupied spot, lowered the trunk to the ground and opened it. From the items packed in the upper tray, he selected a pair of goggles and a heavy cylinder the size and shape of a beer bottle.

"Jerry, give me a hand, will you, please?" he said to a slack-jawed youth passing by.

"Oh, going to break out the Poon gear, huh, Mr. Retief?"

"That's right, Jerry. Looks like everything's here," he added, examining the array of equipment laid out in the trunk.

"Sure, Mr. Retief, I'll help you get the stuff buckled on. Pretty smart bringing it out here, I guess. You going for a swim now, huh?"

"It looks that way. I was kind of hoping I wouldn't have to use this gear, but it seemed like a good idea to bring it, when I heard that the total visible land mass of Sogood was three-quarters of an acre, on a world bigger than Terra." Retief stripped off his late midmorning utterly informal coverall, and began donning the gear.

"Lessee," Jerry mumbled, counting on his fingers: "propulsion, communication, lights, breathers, emergency gear. Want me to help you with the water foils, Mr. Retief?"

"Thanks." Retief closed the trunk and sat on the lid, and the lad fitted large swim fins to his feet. Then he rose while Jerry rummaged in the trunk and brought out a portable apparatus with a tank, compressor, and hose with a wide nozzle.

"OK, get set and I'll start squirting," Jerry said. He started up the compressor, twiddled the knobs, then directed a heavy spray of viscous gray fluid on Retief's chest, working it in a pattern that covered him to the knees, front and back; then he shut it down and set about changing hoses and tanks.

"How about a special job, my own design, Mr. Retief? I call it a Hungry Jack."

"Better just give me a straight Big Mouth outfit, Jerry. I'm not sure what kind of appetites I might run into down there, and I'd just as soon look as noncompetitive as possible."

"Right, Mr. Retief." Jerry continued spraying, this time with a garish yellow mixture with which he covered Retief's upper half, topping him off with a peaked crest. The thick, soft layer hardened quickly on his skin, forming a tough, seamless protective covering, with only the clear face-mask exposed.

Jerry rummaged again, produced a light, short-barreled rifle from the muzzle of which a razor-edged spear-head protruded.

"I hope I don't need it," Retief said, "but I'll take it."

Furtive-eyed diplomats moved aside uneasily as Retief, in his baroque costume, made his way through them and down to the water's edge. He slung the rifle on his back, waded out knee-deep, and dived forward into the clear water. A bulbous black shape rose up before him, executed a turn, and darted away toward the depths, propelled by rapid flagellations of its undersized tail. It was Sloonge; Retief recognized the outcast by the four painful-looking swellings marring the contour of his bag-like body. In spite of his unwieldy bulk, the alien swam smoothly, propelled by undulations of his body and his inadequate-looking tail. Retief fell in behind him, followed as they descended into increasingly green and opaque depths. Ahead, a sunken mountain peak loomed through the murk; simultaneously, Retief became aware of a dozen or so bulky, dark shapes rising from the depths to form a rough circle around him and his guide. More of the dark shapes appeared, emerging, Retief saw, from openings in the mountainous obstacle ahead. Sloonge quickened his pace, darting swiftly toward a dark spot in the side of the peak directly ahead, which, Retief saw as they approached, was a large orifice beyond which he could vaguely discern a grotto inside the rocky mass. The encircling forms drew close; Retief saw that they resembled the Soggies he had seen on the beach, except that each possessed four muscular limbs, two of which were arms, terminating in hands, which gripped efficient-looking guns. There was a sudden burst of bubbles from the weapon of the nearest of the ambushers. A two-foot spear with a barbed head emerged from the bubble cloud, lancing toward Sloonge. Retief put on a burst of speed, snatched the missile from mid-water, and spun, bringing his gun to bear on the alien who had fired. The latter checked, wriggling frantically, and swam hastily away, paddling with all four limbs. Another alien appeared, holding his gun aimed at Retief, who, without hesitation, shifted aim and fired. The harpoon buried itself in the bulky body; an ochre stain leaked into the water from the wound. The stricken creature sank slowly away out of sight, and the others scattered. Retief resumed his previous path, followed Sloonge in through the opening into a spacious colorfully-walled chamber.

"Nice shooting, Retief," Sloonge burbled. "That will save the state the cost of tracking the miscreant down and executing him. By the way, how do you like the pad?"

Swimming close to the wall, Retief saw that the interior of the spacious chamber was entirely covered by skillfully executed mosaic murals, done in crystals of sparkling colored minerals. Sloonge moved past Retief to bump against a small white panel set in the wall. At once, soft light sprang up, emanating from the walls. Each point of color was now glowing with an internal illumination. There were a number of door-sized openings in the walls, each opening on an adjoining room; Retief glanced into a couple of them; each was decorated with glowing wall murals; one room was furnished with what appeared to be a gigantic gold-colored bathtub, ornamented with grape-sized green pearls set in intricate patterns.

"Pretty fancy," Retief said.

"Sure, why not?" Sloonge replied cheerfully. "After all, it's the imperial palace."

"Maybe we'd better get out of here before the emperor gets back," Retief suggested.

"Oh, didn't I mention? I'm the emperor," Sloonge said. "Or I will be, as soon as a couple of minor details are cleared up, like that bunch of anarchists we ran into outside."

"Don't tell me I've stuck my nose into the middle of a revolution?" Retief said.

"Not really. Those guys are just troublemakers," Sloonge said. "Nobody can deny I'm the rightful heir, even if I am a little slow getting in shape."

"I take it you're referring to whatever ailment you have, that's causing those swellings."

"Yeah, right. You're pretty perceptive for a foreigner," Sloonge said, and swam past Retief into the room with the golden bathtub into which he settled himself with every appearance of luxurious ease.

"The condition looks highly uncomfortable," Retief said. "Can't anything be done to help it?"

"Just takes time," Sloonge said carelessly. Retief approached, studied the swellings nearest him; the glossy skin was bulged up to a height of several inches over an oval area of almost a square foot, and stretched to translucence.

"I'm no doctor," Retief said. "But I think that ought to be opened. It's been my experience that any time there's a swelling like that, Mother Nature is trying to push something out."

"Maybe you're right," Sloonge said indifferently. "But what can I do about it?"

"If you'll hold still a minute, I'll try something," Retief said.

"Sure, go ahead."

Retief took the knife from its sheath at his hip, checked the edge with his thumb, then delicately stroked the keen blade across the bulge of the immense swelling, which instantly burst, releasing pale yellow fluid which quickly dissipated in the surrounding water. Inside the wound thus made lay a complicated dark shape, which twitched, unfolded and thrust out: it was a perfectly formed, muscular, knobby-kneed leg, terminating in a wide webbed foot.

"Say, that's a lot better!" Sloonge exclaimed, stretching the member one full length, and admiring the toes. "Pretty neat trick," he added. "The itch has been driving me balmy, to say nothing about cramps. If I could just get one more unlimbered, I'd be ready to take on that crowd outside, and show 'em who's head Soggy around here."

"Turn over," Retief said.

Ten minutes later, he and Sloonge, the latter now swimming briskly with four limbs, emerged into the deep-green gloom and headed for the surface.

"Well, those malcontents won't try anything now," Sloonge remarked. "Too bad my particular branch of the imperial dynasty is always a little slow in breaking through. I'll bet those deadbeats up on the beach are still lying around like the no-good bums they are, without a limb to show among 'em. Thought they were going to pull something fancy, I'll bet. Will they be surprised when they see me come ankling up the beach."

"Who are they?" Retief asked. "More rebels?"

"Not exactly," Sloonge said. "They're a bunch of relatives of mine, cousins and brothers and such—nobody but the royal family is allowed on Imperial Rock, you know—at least, they weren't until you Terries came along and turned it into a hobo jungle. When I said I was coming up to catch a little air and sunshine, they came along on the pretext of attending to my wants while I waited to break through; but in the six weeks I was there, they never offered me so much as a drink of water. They're going to be a down-hearted crowd of would-be usurpers. I guess they were playing the odds that one of them would break through ahead of me and ace me out of the imperial tub."

In shallow water, Retief rose to his feet and walked toward the shore. With a great deal of splashing and gasping, Sloonge tottered to his new-found limbs, and after staggering for a few steps, found his stride and walked along steadily at Retief's side, his bulky body balanced rather precariously on his long but skinny legs. At sight of them, the torpid Soggies heaped on the beach became agitated; the gurgling of their excited voices was audible from a hundred yards.

"That was pretty neat how you helped me along," Sloonge commented. "You put an end to the political crisis in a hurry."

"Nothing to it," Retief said casually. "Why didn't you arrange to have it done weeks ago, instead of just waiting around for nature to take its course?"

"On account of the, like, concept of the cutting edge is unknown among us Soggies. But if you'll leave me have that knife, I'll have it consecrated by Bishop Drooze and from now on, it'll be kept guarded, along with the imperial crown and other treasures, to be used only for helping a new emperor to break through."

"Ah, there, Retief," Magnan said, falling in step beside him. "I really must caution you against fraternization with the local undesirable element. If you must hobnob with locals, why not pick one of those more clean-cut Soggies yonder?"

"Hey, Retief," Sloonge said, "tell this bird to shove off before he gets my ire working."

"By the way, sir, I meant to ask you," Magnan addressed the local: "You folks don't mind our calling you Soggies, I hope? No offense was intended, of course; it was just a convenient nickname—short for Sogooders—since we don't know your own word for yourselves."

"Heck, no, sport. Matter of fact, I think it's got a nice ring to it: it sounds sort of soft and juicy, you know; but you can call us by our native designation, if you like: *Vermin*."

"On the whole, I think 'Soggies' has less unfortunate connotations," Magnan said.

As they came up to the group of Soggies lying on the beach, the aliens flopped about, arranging themselves in orderly rows aimed toward Sloonge. Most of them, Retief saw, exhibited the same sort of swellings which Sloonge had had, in varying degrees of development.

Retief drew Magnan aside. "I'd better tip you off," he said. "Sloonge is the emperor of this entire planet."

"Really? Not that I hadn't suspected something of the sort, of course," Magnan replied. "As you know, my knack for instant recognition of natural nobility is one of my most outstanding traits. Sloonge is as different from this crowd of idlers, for example, as I am from a herd of swine."

"They're all members of the imperial family," Retief pointed out.

"Really?" Magnan gasped.

"Yeah, but not a leg in the bunch!" Sloonge commented. "Ha! I wonder how they figured on knocking me off."

"You imply these fellows would have killed you?" Magnan said in a shocked tone.

"Sure. They were banking on breaking through ahead of me and then finishing me off. Of course they'd probably have gotten to squabbling among themselves about who had priority, and maybe only a couple of 'em would have lived to report my unfortunate demise by accident."

"Do you want me to operate on them?" Retief asked, drawing his knife.

"Cut their throats if you want to; I'll have to have 'em all executed anyway. In a way, it's kind of a shame; my big brother Glorb isn't a bad sort of fellow, and he plays a mean game of boof. I'm going to miss him."

"Then why not let him live?" Retief said in a reasonable tone.

"Nope. Glorb is an ambitious cuss; he'd never stop itching to slip into the imperial tub. He'd be a focal point for malcontents."

"You could turn his ambition to good account," Retief said. "By putting him in charge of your police force, with the job of nipping off revolution in the bud."

"Kind of a wild idea, Retief," Sloonge said. "The ruling emperor having a living relative. It's never been done; maybe I'll give it a try at that. Hey, Glorb? How does 'Field Marshal Prince Glorb' sound to you? I'm thinking about putting you in charge of the imperial security forces, with the job of stamping out treason in the realm."

One of the limbless Soggies, indistinguishable from his fellows, rippled his bulk and flopped forward a yard or two.

"As an alternative to being strangled to death with chuzz-weed, it might be OK," he gurgled. "My first official act will be to order half a ton of chuzz-weed to take care of this bunch of traitors." He nodded toward his former associates.

"Take it easy, Field Marshal," Sloonge said. "You might be able to find spots for some of 'em in your organization."

"I'll find spots for 'em all right: I'll cement 'em into abandoned gimp holes at about two thousand fathoms."

"Ah, there you are, Retief!" the hearty voice of Ambassador Fullthrottle sounded from behind him. "For a moment I almost didn't recognize you in that outlandish Pupoony get-up. Any progress to report on the matter I mentioned to you earlier?"

Retief turned. "I have one or two items of interest," he said.

"Shhh! Not in front of this local." Fullthrottle stared distastefully at Sloonge.

"It looks like a Soggy," he said in a stage whisper, "but where'd he get those limbs?"

"I grew 'em, sport," Sloonge called cheerfully. "Same as you, I guess, except maybe a little suddener. If you boys don't mind my asking, I'm kind of curious about you Terries. Except for Retief here, you aliens don't hardly look like you're equipped to survive in a normal environment. No gills, no tails, and you look sort of dried out and scratchy, and I haven't seen any of you even stick a toe in the water. Aren't you getting a little dehydrated? If so, you're welcome to jump in my ocean."

"Actually," Fullthrottle said, "on our native world, the majority of higher life forms live their entire lives on dry land."

"Sounds like a weird kind of place," Sloonge said. "Maybe your strange habits are on account of your whole planet is rock, without any ocean such as we Soggies are lucky enough to have covering approximately 99.44 percent of the planet, according to a quick mental calculation I just made."

"Why, no," chirped Magnan, who had come up beside the Ambassador, "as a matter of fact three-quarters of Terra—" he broke off abruptly as Retief trod on his foot.

"Say," Sloonge mused. "Now that you Terries have familiarized me with the concepts of space travel and alien worlds, and all, the thought comes to me: maybe us Soggies could do with a little more marine real estate to help out our overpopulation problem. You don't know of a nice planet with plenty of ocean where we could maybe hatch out a few zillion tons of fertilized ova, do you?"

"Ugh!" Magnan cried. "Imagine the Atlantic teeming with giant polywogs!"

"See here, Magnan," Fullthrottle said testily, "it's hardly in consonance with the dignity of a Terran Ambassador, or even of you lesser ranks, to stand out in the wind nattering with a low-caste local."

"The wind, sir?" Magnan objected. "Why, we're right here in the handsomely appointed Embassy lounge, as designated by your Excellency only yesterday."

"To be sure," the Ambassador conceded. "But that's hardly the point. The impudence of this untouchable in addressing me is the issue."

"Oh, didn't I tell you, Mr. Ambassador?" Magnan inquired. "This is His Imperial Highness, the Emperor Sloonge, hereditary sole and absolute ruler of Sogood."

"You jape at such a solemn moment as this, Magnan?" Fullthrottle responded indignantly. "My ability to instantly recognize true aristocracy is well-nigh a legend in the Corps. This fellow is quite obviously a reject of such primitive society as exists here on this benighted planet."

"Heck, I hate to appear to like contradict your Excellency or anything, but I have it from a usually reliable source . . ." Magnan eyed Retief bleakly. ". . . that Sloonge is, indeed, the emperor."

"What about that, fellow?" Fullthrottle demanded, turning to eye Sloonge dubiously. "Do you have the temerity to put forth such a claim?"

"Them are the facts, sport," Sloonge said airily, waving a hand to indicate the knob of rock on which they stood. "The whole thing's my realm."

"Well, Your Imperial Majesty," Fullthrottle said in a somewhat choked voice, glancing furtively around at what, to the uninitiated, would have appeared to be three-fourths of an acre of bare rock, "I'm sure that an individual of Your Majesty's sophistication won't take amiss my lighthearted remarks just now." He shot his cuffs and extended his right hand to be shaken.

Sloonge yawned, exposing the intimidating array of shark-like teeth lining his wide mouth.

"No, thanks," he said. "I never snack between meals. By the way, maybe you better present some credentials about now, just to keep matters on a correct footing."

"But of course, Your Majesty; I was about to propose a suitable ceremony as soon as possible."

"Yeah, hand 'em over," Sloonge said. "But don't bother unless you're ready to agree to my modest proposal for using your unused ocean worlds."

"I fear the matter will require study," Fullthrottle hedged.

"You got Terra," Sloonge cried happily. "Why not let us have the Atlantic?"

"We need it! And the Pacific too, to say nothing of the Indian and Arctic Oceans," Magnan sputtered. "We *don't* need annual plagues of seven-foot meat-eating Vermin croaking on the shores."

"Let's deal, Retief," Sloonge cried. "Sounds like you got four whole ocean worlds you ain't even using! But I guess you're holding out for an equal swap. How about it. Let's work out a trade: I'll swap you the entire land area of Verm, or Sogood, as you call it, namely Imperial Rock, a very high-class neighborhood, for your oceans. That's a square deal for you Terries and us Vermin, too!"

"I'm afraid we can't get together on that, Sloonge, but how about an alternate proposal? We've been having a little difficulty developing our marine resources, and perhaps instead of just hatchlings, you could supply us with a few thousand skilled craftsmen to build underwater structures, like that palace of yours; very fine workmanship!"

"Sure, I can supply all you need; but a few hundred thousand couldn't hardly build you a first-class privy. How about a couple hundred million to start with?"

"Would these be, er, spawn, or fully developed adults?" Magnan interposed.

"Trained workers, every one," Sloonge reassured him. "All they need is about a hundred pounds of fresh meat a day apiece."

"Heavens," Magnan cried. "I'm not sure we have enough fish in our seas to supply such a demand."

"No sweat, Mr. Magnan," Sloonge said easily. "They'll catch their own eats—even if they have to forage ashore—just so you got plenty of game on hand."

"Our only surviving land animal is man," Magnan said stiffly.

"OK, we ain't particular—leastways a bunch of hungry hard-hats ain't," Sloonge said agreeably.

"Well, let me see," Magnan muttered. "Two hundred million, ah, Vermin—times one hundred pounds, times 365, for the annual requirement . . . Hm-m-m, I think perhaps we're on the verge of a solution to our overpopulation problem."

"Ah, Your Imperial Majesty will excuse Magnan for carelessly referring to your people as 'Vermin', I trust," Fullthrottle put in quickly. "I'll personally see to it that he is appropriately dealt with at Departmental level." He turned to Magnan with a glacial expression. "I must say I'm surprised to hear a diplomat of your experience openly refer to these obnoxious creatures as Vermin," he whispered behind the symbolic privacy of a hand.

"Their own local name for themselves—or so I'm told," Magnan alibied, giving Retief an accusatory look.

"Don't waste a 729-t on me, Mr. Magnan," Retief said. "Emperor Sloonge told us so himself, if you recall."

"Ah," Fullthrottle said dubiously to Magnan. "I fear I can never bring myself to call these creatures 'Vermin' to their faces, if any."

"Hey—what's wrong with our name?" Sloonage demanded. "I hope you Terries ain't figuring to like meddle in Soggy internal affairs and all!"

"Well—as to that," Fullthrottle gasped, "faced with a choice between referring to your people as, ah, 'Soggies' or—alternatively, as 'Vermin', I'm not quite sure what CDT regs stipulate."

"What's wrong with 'Vermin'?"

"Ah, by a curious coincidence, the term has unfortunate connotations in Terran. It implies a certain lack of fastidiousness as well as various other disgusting traits."

"It figures," Sloonge commented thoughtfully. "Fits most Soggies like a glove. If you knew these nogoods like I do, you wouldn't be quibbling."

"Quite the contrary," the Ambassador objected, facing the Emperor squarely. "It's a time-honored truism of diplomacy that the most resented epithet is the one most accurately depicting the deficiencies of the recipient. Those who refuse to work, for example, dislike being called 'loafers', while the industrious would be merely amused by the appellation."

"I get the idea; but I was talking about the lower classes, natch. Vermin they are, by anybody's definition."

"Your proposal for relocation of Soggies on Terra occasions certain grave difficulties, Your Majesty," Fullthrottle commented. "For example, provision for wives and families would constitute a problem. And then the details of vacations, recreational facilities, and pocket money—to say nothing of repatriation at the end of the term of the contract."

"Don't sweat it, chum. Do like I do: work 'em till they drop, and if they start bitchin', I'll supply you with plenty of chuzz-weed. And if they *don't* bitch, give 'em the works anyway. And don't worry about returning 'em. I got plenty more; just let the sharks have 'em, if shark's innards can handle Soggy-meat."

"How unfeeling!" Fullthrottle exclaimed. "Though this practical approach does simplify matters considerably. Still," he added, giving Magnan a glum look, "I trust none of my personnel will be so naive as to suggest at any inquiry which might develop in future, that *I* in any way gave approval to any such scheme!" He walked away without further comment.

"I assume we may safely take that as authorization to go ahead," Magnan said briskly.

"You boys just fix up a title to all Terran oceans, and I'll see to it the work force is on hand for pickup in a week—*plus* a deed to Imperial Rock, here," Emperor Sloonge said, and headed for the surf.

"Just a minute," Retief demurred. "Before we give away three-fourths of a planet for three-quarters of an acre I think we ought to hold out for more consideration accruing to Terra."

"Why," Magnan gasped, "we mustn't appear greedy, Retief."

"Why not? Better greedy than suckers," Retief replied.

"Speaking of suckers, Retief," Sloonge said in a glutinous undertone, pausing beside Retief. "Let's you and me retire to the palace for a couple of quick ones and ditch all these nobodies, Terry and Soggy alike. We can work out a deal that includes some goodies for number one—and you, too."

"I take it that's an imperial command," Retief said, "that a mere bureaucrat has no option on."

"Right. Let's go—before Glorb gets into the act. He's a boy that's always got a hand out, even if he has to grow one special. And from the looks of him, this Mr. Ambassador of yours is the same type. They're both probably figuring an angle to ace you and me out of some legitimate graft—and after we earned it, too! I'll be expecting you, Retief."

Sloonge waved and waded into the breakers.

"Ah, excuse my interruption, Retief," Fullthrottle butted in, having re-approached from downwind. "I appreciate the potential benefits to accrue from your establishing a cordial relationship with His Imperial

Majesty, by nattering informally of this and that. But, ah . . ." he sidled closer, "candidly, I was wondering if perhaps you and I might not, ah, draw aside and look more deeply into all aspects of the Terran posture *vis-à-vis* Sogood at this juncture . . . with a view to the possibility of so influencing the development of affairs as to enhance the professional profiles of those most instrumental in bringing about a Terran-Sogoodian accord. Between ourselves," he added, with a glance at the royal Soggies heaped nearby, "that chap Field Marshal Prince Glorb strikes me as being on the make, to employ the vernacular."

"Emperor Sloonge had the same idea, Mr. Ambassador," Retief said.

A few moments later, Magnan tugged at his sleeve. "Er, Retief," he muttered, "if you can spare a moment . . . I've been wondering why you and I should do all the work, as usual, only to have the brass grab all the credit. Accordingly, I suggest we approach Glorb—he seems a reasonable chap—and see if a rapprochement can't be worked out more favorable to the interests of hard-working diplomats of intermediate rank than could be expected if finalization of the treaty and protocols are left to his Excellency and his Majesty."

"Seems like a popular idea," Retief said. "Just a moment, Mr. Magnan. Let's see what the Field Marshal has in mind." He nodded toward the Soggy inching his way toward the Terrans, wriggling awkwardly on his limbless torso.

"Look here, you Terries, I got pretty keen hearing—couldn't help overhearing some of your conversation. How about it, Retief?" Glorb said. "Let's get together on the practical end of this deal, what say? I always kind of hankered to get into the construction game; now's the chance to get both feet dry—you Terries will need a knowledgeable contractor to handle your imported labor. I've got the boys that will shape those loafers up in a hurry."

"Sounds reasonable, Your Imperial Highness," Magnan conceded. "How many extra personnel will your supervisory staff consist of?"

"Forget it, chum; just consider 'em as included in the original hundred zillion figure."

"But—I thought we'd agreed on a hundred *million*," Magnan protested. "We mustn't exceed available transport capacity."

"A million, or a zillion, who cares?" Glorb said carelessly. "Let's get to the meat of the matter. Frankly, where I get well is supplying materials. Masonry specialties, plumbing fixtures—all that."

"Really, I must draw the line!" Magnan declared. "It's apparent, I fear, that Your Imperial Highness has no grasp of interstellar freight rates. Shipping concrete and lead pipes, indeed! Out of the question!" He retired to a distance of ten feet, turning his back, and radiated outrage. "I might have suspected a kick-back arrangement," he mused. "Such gall!

"Retief, come along," he went on in a colorless tone. "Ambassador Fullthrottle will be getting restless unless we reassure him that no irretrievable indiscretions have been committed."

"First, I have to pay a duty call on the Emperor," Retief demurred.

"Look, Retief," Glorb said in the confidential tone employed by men of the world when discussing matters not understood by non-men of the world. "Your chum don't seem to realize our boys are pretty sensitive artistic types. They got to work in the familiar materials they know and love; gold, emeralds, diamonds, rubies, granite and stuff like that. You Terries need to supply the right stuff, or they go into a premature decline. And I can fix you up with everything you need to keep 'em happy, OK?"

"What kind of payment do you have in mind?" Retief asked.

"Why, Magnan let slip a mention of a minor sea-world called Mediterranean," Glorb said. "How's about just deeding it to me as a modest personal estate . . ."

"OK on gold, diamonds, emeralds and rubies," Retief said. "Hold the granite."

"Say, that's big of you, Retief, accepting the stuff we got a surplus of, and foregoing the rare and expensive granite. I may make a small profit on this deal after all."

"Building materials!" Ambassador Fullthrottle exclaimed, eyeing Retief with an expression of incredulous indignation, a variation on the 291-x developed by the Ambassador himself in his youth, when a delegate to a Special Tribunal on Unsound Prehistoric Events, a group which had been on the verge of a unanimous endorsement of a resolution introduced by young Fullthrottle condemning every mass migration in human prehistory as imperialistic proto-fascism, when some busybody had mentioned the invasion of the European continent from Africa by *Homo erectus* some 15,000 years BC. An unfortunate piece of water-muddying which had nipped in the bud what might have been a valuable entry in the Fullthrottle dossier. In spite of this frustration of early hopes, Fullthrottle still looked back with a benign nostalgia on the days of STUPE, his first entry into the large arena of affairs, though he felt a pang of regret as he reflected that but for an unkind quirk of fate, his 291-y would today be officially listed in the CDT Career Officer's Guide, with himself credited as originator, his name ranged alongside such giants of interstellar diplomacy as Crodfoller, Largspoon, Bayshingle and Prutty.

But, he recalled himself, back to the immediate problem:

"Is it possible, Retief," the great man continued, "that you are unaware of the costs of interstellar transport? I assure you there are better uses for Corps bottoms than hauling bricks and lead piping."

"Yes, sir," Retief replied. "But as Field Marshal Prince Glorb pointed out, his craftsmen would work much more skillfully in their accustomed medium."

"Ah, yes, a significant point, no doubt, my boy. Giving consideration to the personal preferences of these, er, Vermin, will of course, look good in the 'Empathy and Involvement' column of your next ER, if I should happen to recall the matter when preparing it, which, I may as well point out, is unlikely in view of the sensation your proposal for massive waste of Corps funds will create in the Bureau of the Budget. So resign yourself to the realization that our Soggy labor corps will of necessity learn to lay Terry bricks and install native pipes and fittings, including bathtubs, which, I noted on your proposed schedule of cargoes, were specified most explicitly—as if the place of manufacture of a porcelain bathtub were a matter of vast concern in the conduct of interplanetary affairs!"

"I'm afraid I've committed myself on the tubs," Retief said. "Prince Glorb insisted on it."

"Hm-m-m," Fullthrottle mused. "I wonder just who is finessing whom in this negotiation. It was a most adroit gambit on my, ah, *our* part, I suppose I should say, to escalate Sloonge's request for breeding grounds into a solution to our marine development problem. But his arrogance in levying demands, bathtub-wise, gives me pause. Perhaps there were nuances which I, that is, you and Magnan, missed. Still, I suppose it's too late now to abrogate the treaty of eternal chumship now that the Council has approved it, and made the appropriate notations in my 201 file."

"Too late, or too soon," Retief said. "The first shipload of bathtubs is in parking orbit now."

"So . . . well, matters have ripened somewhat precipitously, Retief. I fear you place me in a delicate position. CDT regs are quite explicit as to the proper handling of the matter, however. Inasmuch as you exceeded your approval authority in okaying these freight charges, I have no choice but to issue a Statement of Charges, permitting you the opportunity to salvage your career by merely paying these charges personally. I daresay they'll be paid off in a few years."

"I understand, Mr. Ambassador. What about the two ships following, loaded to the gunwales with masonry specialties? No granite, I told Glorb he'd have to make do with Terry granite."

"Quite right!" Fullthrottle said firmly. "By the way, in accordance with Paragraph 97, Subsection B of the Manual, you'll of course be obligated to take personal title to these unauthorized cargoes. I suggest you make immediate arrangements for disposal to cut down on your demurrage."

"Oh, there you are," Magnan said brightly, peeking in the door at Retief. "Why, hi there, Mr. Ambassador. I just wanted to tip you off, sir; there's a fantastic rumor afoot to the effect that you've stuck poor Retief here with the bill for hauling bricks and so on all the way from Sogood. I suggest you scotch it, sir, before it goes any further. Just confidentially, sir," Magnan added furtively, "the Corps' image has already had its luster dimmed a trifle just by the terms of the treaty—you know how difficult it is for the public to distinguish between a diplomatic victory and a disaster—socking it to one of our own will make very bad copy from a PR standpoint—nothing personal, of course—I quite understand that Retief is legally responsible."

"It's quite all right," Retief said. "I'll take my medicine without griping—just let me have it in writing."

perspective of one guy, look good to btb
side

Select Bibliography

Allison, Graham T. *Essence of Decision: Explaining the Cuban Missile Crisis.* Boston: Little, Brown, 1972.

Aron, Raymond. *Peace and War: A Theory of International Relations.* Garden City, N.Y.: Doubleday, 1966.

Axline, W. Andrew, and Stegenga, James A. *The Global Community: A Brief Introduction to International Relations.* New York: Dodd, Mead, 1972.

Barnet, Vincent. *The Representation of the United States Abroad.* New York: Praeger, 1965.

Barringer, Richard E. *War: Patterns of Conflict.* Cambridge: MIT Press, 1972.

Beard, Charles A. *The Idea of National Interest.* New York: Macmillan, 1934.

Black, Cyril, and Falk, Richard, eds. *The Future of the International Legal Order.* Princeton: Princeton University Press, 1969.

Bloomfield, Lincoln P., and Leiss, Amelia C. *Controlling Small Wars.* New York: Knopf, 1970.

Cantori, Louis J., and Spiegel, Steven L. *The International Politics of Regions: A Comparative Approach.* Englewood Cliffs, N.J.: Prentice-Hall, 1970.

Cardozo, Michael H. *Diplomats in International Cooperation.* Ithaca, N.Y.: Cornell University Press, 1962.

Chittick, William O. *State Department, Press and Pressure Groups: A Role Analysis.* New York: Wiley-Interscience, 1970.

Claude, Inis L., Jr. *Swords Into Plowshares: The Problems and Perspectives of International Organization.* 4th ed. New York: Random House, 1971.

Coplin, William D. *Introduction to International Politics: A Theoretical Overview.* 2d ed. Chicago: Rand McNally, 1974.

Cox, Robert, and Jacobsen, Harold, eds. *Anatomy of Influence: De-*

cision-Making in International Organizations. New Haven: Yale University Press, 1972.

Davis, David Howard. *How the Bureaucracy Makes Foreign Policy: An Exchange Analysis.* New Brunswick, N.J.: Rutgers University Press, 1972.

de Rivera, Joseph. *The Psychological Dimensions of Foreign Policy.* Columbus, Ohio: Charles E. Merrill, 1968.

Deutsch, Karl W. *The Analysis of International Relations.* Englewood Cliffs, N.J.: Prentice-Hall, 1968.

Dougherty, James E., and Pfaltzgraff, R. L. *Contending Theories of International Relations.* Philadelphia: Lippincott, 1971.

Edwards, David. *Arms Control in International Relations.* New York: Holt, Rinehart and Winston, 1968.

Eubank, Keith. *The Summit Conferences, 1919–1960.* Norman: University of Oklahoma Press, 1966.

Finlay, David J., and Hovet, Thomas Jr. *7304: International Relations on the Planet Earth.* New York: Harper & Row, 1975.

Fisher, Roger. *International Conflict For Beginners.* New York: Harper and Row, 1970.

Frankel, Joseph. *The Making of Foreign Policy.* New York: Oxford University Press, 1963.

Gareau, Frederick H. *The Balance of Power and Nuclear Deterrence.* Boston: Houghton Mifflin, 1962.

Greenberg, Martin H., and Warrick, Patricia. *Political Science Fiction.* Englewood Cliffs, N.J.: Prentice-Hall, 1974.

Grieves, Forest L. *Supranationalism and International Adjudication.* Urbana: University of Illinois Press, 1969.

Haas, Ernst B. *Beyond the Nation State: Functionalism and International Organization.* Stanford, Calif.: Stanford University Press, 1964.

Hanrieder, Wolfram F. *Comparative Foreign Policy: Theoretical Essays.* New York: David McKay, 1971.

Henkin, Louis. *How Nations Behave: Law and Foreign Policy.* New York: Praeger, 1968.

Herz, John H. *International Politics in the Atomic Age.* New York: Columbia University Press, 1959.

Hoffman, Stanley H. *Contemporary Theory in International Relations.* Englewood Cliffs, N.J.: Prentice-Hall, 1960.

Holsti, K. J. *International Politics: A Framework for Analysis.* 2d ed. Englewood Cliffs, N.J.: Prentice-Hall, 1972.

Hopkins, Raymond F., and Mansbach, Richard W. *Structure and Process in International Politics.* New York: Harper and Row, 1973.

Janis, Irving L. *Victims of Group Think: A Psychological Study of Foreign Policy Decisions and Fiascoes.* Boston: Houghton Mifflin, 1972.

Jervis, Robert. *The Logic of Images in International Relations.* Princeton, N.J.: Princeton University Press, 1970.

Johnson, Richard A. *The Administration of U.S. Foreign Policy.* Austin: University of Texas Press, 1971.

Kahn, Herman. *On Thermonuclear War.* Princeton, N.J.: Princeton University Press, 1961.

Kahn, Herman, and Wiener, Anthony J. *The Year 2000.* New York: Macmillan, 1967.

Kaplan, Morton A. *System and Process in International Politics.* New York: Wiley, 1957.

Klineberg, Otto. *The Human Dimension in International Relations.* New York: Holt, Rinehart and Winston, 1964.

Knorr, Klaus, and Rosenau, James N. (ed.) *Contending Approaches to International Politics.* Princeton, N.J.: Princeton University Press, 1969.

Lieber, Robert J. *Theory and World Politics.* Cambridge, Mass.: Winthrop Publishers, 1972.

Macridis, Roy C. *Foreign Policy in World Politics.* Englewood Cliffs, N.J.: Prentice-Hall, 1967.

Mennis, Bernard. *American Foreign Policy Officials.* Columbus: Ohio State University Press, 1971.

Merritt, Richard L. *Communication in International Politics.* Urbana: University of Illinois Press, 1972.

Modelski, George. *Principles of World Politics.* New York: Free Press, 1972.

Morgenthau, Hans J. *Politics Among Nations.* 5th ed. New York: Knopf, 1973.

Nye, Joseph Jr. *Peace in Parts.* Boston: Little, Brown, 1971.

O'Leary, Michael K. *Politics of American Foreign Aid.* New York: Atherton, 1967.

Paige, Glenn D. *The Korean Decision: June 24–30, 1950.* New York: Free Press, 1968.

Pruitt, Dean G., and Snyder, Richard C. *Theory and Research on the Causes of War.* Englewood Cliffs, N.J.: Prentice-Hall, 1969.

Puchala, Donald J. *International Politics Today*. New York: Dodd, Mead, 1971.

Rapoport, Anatol. *Fights, Games, and Debates*. Ann Arbor: University of Michigan Press, 1960.

Ridgeway, James. *The Last Play: The Struggle to Monopolize the World's Energy Resources*. New York: E. P. Dutton, 1973.

Riker, William H. *The Theory of Political Coalitions*. New Haven: Yale University Press, 1962.

Rosecrance, Richard N. *International Relations: Peace or War?* New York: McGraw-Hill, 1973.

——. *The Scientific Study of Foreign Policy*. New York: Free Press, 1972.

Rourke, Francis E. *Bureaucracy and Foreign Policy*. Baltimore: Johns Hopkins University Press, 1972.

Russett, Bruce M. *Economic Theories of International Relations*. Chicago: Markham Publishing, 1970.

Seabury, Paul, ed. *Balance of Power*. San Francisco: Chandler, 1965.

Sheehan, Neil, ed. *The Pentagon Papers*. New York: Bantam Books, 1971.

Singer, Marshall R. *Weak States in a World of Powers: The Dynamics of International Relationships*. New York: Free Press, 1972.

Spiro, Herbert J. *World Politics: The Global System*. Homewood, Ill.: Dorsey, 1966.

Sprout, Harold, and Sprout, Margaret. *Toward a Politics of the Planet Earth*. New York: Van Nostrand Rheinhold, 1971.

Stagner, Ross. *Dimensions of Human Conflict*. Detroit: Wayne State University Press, 1967.

Sullivan, David S., and Sattler, Martin J. *Change and the Future International System*. New York: Columbia University Press, 1972.

Thayer, Charles W. *Diplomat*. New York: Harper and Row, 1959.

Thayer, George. *The War Business: The International Trade in Armaments*. New York: Clarion Books, 1970.

Triska, Jan F., and Finley, David D. *Soviet Foreign Policy*. New York: Macmillan, 1968.

Waltz, Kenneth N. *Foreign Policy and Democratic Politics*. Boston: Little, Brown, 1967.

Ward, Barbara. *The Rich Nations and the Poor Nations*. New York: W. W. Norton, 1962.

Wohlstetter, Roberta. *Pearl Harbor: Warning and Decision.* Stanford, Calif.: Stanford University Press, 1962.

Wright, Quincy. *The Study of International Relations.* New York: Appleton-Century-Crofts, 1955.

Young, Oran R. *The Intermediaries: Third Parties in International Crises.* Princeton, N.J.: Princeton University Press, 1967.

About the Editors

Martin Harry Greenberg is Professor of Modernization Processes and Director of the Office of Graduate Studies at the University of Wisconsin, Green Bay. Joseph D. Olander is Special Assistant to the Florida Commissioner of Education. They are coeditors of a number of science fiction anthologies, including *Run to Starlight: Sports Through Science Fiction,* which in 1975 was selected by *The New York Times* as an "Outstanding Book of the Year," and *Criminal Justice Through Science Fiction,* published in 1977 by New Viewpoints.